WHERE ARE THE WOMEN

MARY KAY REMICK

ISBN: 0966712862
ISBN 13: 9780966712865
PEN OAK PRESS
Published in the United States of America, May, 2014

PEN OAK PRESS
First Edition

Cover art and design by Liz Morgan
Author photograph by Jack Remich

CHAPTER 1

Despite the chilly March air, Marcie opened the car window. Instantly rewarded by the heavenly scents of a newborn Alabama spring, she drew the sweet air deep into her lungs. Bradford pear trees whipped by gusts of wind sent snowflake-like petals whirling in the air. Purple phlox, creeping verbena spilled over rock walls and onto cracked sidewalks. Tiny yellow flowers covered the arms of forsythia and delicate pink blossoms streamed from weeping cherry trees.

After the blooms faded away and the hot and hazy days of summer began, Marcie's two teenaged children would plant their feet on Alabama soil once more. If her son didn't talk his sister into postponing their return yet again.

Thoughts of her kids had to put on hold this morning. In less than fifteen minutes, she would be sitting for the second most important job interview in her life. She would still be working for her mentor and one of Huntsville's foremost clinical psychologists, George Rutledge, had the state not cut funding for their substance abuse treatment program. Since then she had tried and failed at two jobs out of her field of expertise. Today she must pay rapt attention to every word Mrs. Sarah Fleming-Thornton uttered. She must also remain fully aware of her own words and actions.

Now, having arrived too early for the interview, she sat in the Dairy Queen parking lot directly across the street from Port Victor, the halfway house for recovering alcoholic women where Marcie hoped to work.

The time on her trusty Timex showed nine minutes until nine. Nine minutes to kill. Nine minutes to work herself into a frenzy of anxiety over meeting Mrs. Sarah Fleming-Thornton, the lady who would offer her a job— or not.

She had been a nervous wreck ever since George informed her that Mrs. Thornton needed a director to establish a treatment program for the women and he had nominated her. Supposedly, George told Mrs. Thornton that she, Marcie Parker, was the perfect candidate for the job. Marcie had sat in stunned silence. That she could be the director of anything defied belief. She couldn't even direct her own children.

George had told her not to worry, that the interview was a mere formality, that the job was hers. But what if Mrs. Sarah Fleming-Thornton didn't like her?

Starting to feel sorry for herself, she sat up straight and squared her shoulders as though to prove to herself and the world that she, Marcie Matthews-Parker, was about to be offered a job.

What had prompted her to use her maiden name, Matthews, as part of her identity? She had forsaken the Matthews name when her parents forsook her.

Turning her attention to the house across the street, Marcie wondered whose idea it was to build such a grand place between the family's brickyard and building supply company. Here, in the midst of the business district, the white brick, two- story Colonial, with its four scrolled columns, circular drive, manicured lawn, gazebo, and greenhouse, looked as out of place as a tar paper shack on New York's Fifth Avenue. Not that Marcie had ever been to Fifth Avenue, but she had enough sense to know that a shack did not belong there.

If the exterior was any indication, the interior would be regal as well, and in — she checked her watch — three more minutes, she would walk through the front door and into the parlor or wherever Sarah Fleming-Thornton chose to conduct the interview. The very idea of sitting amid such finery with a woman of such stature made her stomach lurch.

At two minutes till nine she started the engine, backed out of her slot and pulled around to the exit. As soon as traffic permitted, she crossed the street and started up the driveway. Some kind of shells— probably mussels from the nearby Tennessee River— crunched under her wheels.

In an effort to hide her battered Ford station wagon, Marcie pulled around to the side where the garage was located. She took a moment to compose herself. Climbing out of the car, she adjusted her clothing, and casually strolled toward the first column as if she didn't have a care in the world.

Standing ramrod straight she reached for the doorbell, but before her hand could touch it the door swung open.

"Ah," said an imposing white-haired lady dressed in powder blue, "you must be Marcie Parker, and right on time. Come in, dear, come in." She stepped aside so Marcie could enter.

"Actually, I was too early," Marcie said, "so I parked across the street. I do that a lot. Arrive early, I mean. I can't tell you how many times I have sat and waited for a bank or a store to open. I'm always first in line for a movie or a play. I've been that way all my life. When I was little, my father said I'd be early for my own funeral. It was a terrible thing to say to a child, and for years I worried about dying..."

Marcie knew she was babbling but she couldn't seem to stop. "My mother said I was afraid I might miss something. That my Grandpa Harry was the same way. But I don't know ... these past two years in particular I have to wonder, what is there to miss?"

Mrs. Thornton didn't seem put off by her drawn-out explanation. She spoke in a cultured voice with a hint of a Southern accent. "You should have come straight to the house. Being early is an admirable trait. I expect it of all my employees. The ones who come dragging in late one too many times are handed a pink slip. Which reminds me, the boys at the brickyard will dawdle if I'm gone too long. Follow me." Her black patent heels clicked across the marble-floored foyer until muted by the plush rose-colored carpet in the hallway.

Following in Sarah's lilac-scented wake, Marcie admired the way the lady carried herself— to the manor born came to mind. Instead of the short, tightly curled hair favored by a lot older women, Sarah wore her thick white mane in a brushed back do with a flip on one side. It looked as youthful and smart as her tailored linen suit. A blend of pearls and diamonds decorated her neck, ears, and fingers.

Marcie felt dowdy in comparison. Her rubber-soled loafers didn't make a sound and her new shirtwaist dress, topped with a navy-blue blazer, seemed to hang on her thin frame like a gunny- sack. She wore no jewelry, only a light coat of makeup, and wispy strands of her strawberry blonde hair tickled her jaw. But she was not to the manor born.

Midway down the hall a loud burst of raucous laughter came from behind a closed door on her right. Startled, Marcie jumped. Another burst sounded, this one followed by cheers and applause. Even though she recognized the sound of a TV, she felt a chill.

"That's Bitsy's suite," Sarah said when Marcie caught up with her. "She watches entirely too much TV."

"Is she one of the residents?" Marcie asked.

"Heavens, no" Sarah said without elaborating.

She turned toward an open doorway on her left and made a sweeping gesture with her hand. "This will be the director's office. Make yourself comfortable." Sarah went to the large leather chair behind a gleaming mahogany desk.

Marcie stepped inside. The walnut-paneled walls; floor-to- ceiling bookcases, partially filled with thick leather bound tomes; a pipe smoker's table between two green velvet club chairs; an oak file cabinet; a freestanding medicine chest; a hat rack, and a spittoon had obviously been designed with a man in mind.

The room must have suited George well. Ever since Port Victor became a reality last October, he had been coming down from Huntsville two or three times a week to counsel the women, but as his practice grew and his time became limited, he convinced Sarah to hire a full-time director.

"Do sit down, Marcie."

"Sorry" Marcie said. She followed the brilliant beams of sunlight streaming through the sheer curtains to the club chair nearest the windows. Instead of flopping onto the chair as she usually did at home, she lowered and arranged herself carefully. The warmth of the sun eased the chill she had felt in the hall.

Sarah tilted the swivel chair forward and clasped her hands atop the desk. "Now, Marcie" she said, "George has spoken very highly of your work at New Start. That your training qualifies you to take over the direction of Port Victor is not in question. I trust George's judgment implicitly." She paused. "However, when I consider hiring someone their job skills are secondary to that of their moral character. That is particularly true in this case. The girls who reside here are what we used to call loose women. They have lost their moral bearings. What they need is a role model. Someone they can look up to and try to emulate. Do you think you qualify in that respect?"

Marcie replied automatically. "Yes, ma'am."

Sarah sat back and laced her fingers over her midriff. "Now then, tell me all about yourself. Where you come from, who your people are ... that sort of thing."

Your people. Meaning her long-ago parents, the very *people* Marcie did not want to think about, much less talk about. The very *people* who kept intruding on this very important day. What did her *people* have to do with the job? Who they were and where Marcie came from was none of Sarah's business. What had George said? That the interview was a mere formality, that the job was hers? So why the questions about her *people*? She had expected to discuss her work methodology. And what exactly did Sarah mean about her moral character? Marcie certainly never thought of herself as a loose woman. She'd had only one man in her life, her ex-husband. And she had only been drunk once, on her thirtieth birthday when a friend bought her a martini and then kept refilling her glass. As for her *people*, for more than twenty years, starting the day she went to live with her aunt and uncle, she had kept the events of her eleventh year and the aftermath to herself and she was not about to reveal them now.

"Marcie," Sarah said with a pinched look on her face. "I asked about your background. We rarely have newcomers in town. Except for what George had to say about your work, I know nothing about you."

Marcie tensed. Like it or not, she had to tell Sarah something. It wasn't up to her to question the woman's motives. She crossed her legs, looked Sarah in the eye and started talking. About how she'd been born in a small town in North Carolina, where her father owned the local print shop and her mother did volunteer work, mostly for the Methodist Church. Except for wanting siblings, her childhood had been a happy one. She even told Sarah about her very first clock, the Mickey Mouse windup. She did not tell her it was the last gift she ever received from either parent. All that and more was true.

Then came the lie.

"My parents were killed in an automobile accident when I was eleven. They were on the way home from choir practice and a truck ran a red light and smashed into them. After the funerals, my aunt and uncle took me to their home in Petersburg, Virginia. They were wonderful people who did their best to care for me." That they were eking out a living on a small farm and had three children of their own was beside the point.

Next came a summary of her struggle to get through college on scholarships and working part-time. How after graduation she married First Lieutenant David Parker. How many moves they had made around the country because of his Army career. She talked about the births of their children, Julie and David Junior. Lastly, she spoke about her work at New Start, a three-week treatment program for male alcoholics. How devastated she was when the state cut off their funding.

"And that's about it," Marcie said.

Sarah frowned and said, "I have never understood why people can't stay put. They flit from place to place like a pack of gypsies. Why, I have lived in this town all my life and that's the way it should be. How else are you going to put down roots?"

Marcie found it hard to believe that out of all the information she'd divulged Sarah focused on her rootlessness. If only the woman knew that Marcie's roots were cut out from under her with a scythe when her mother went crazy and her father disappeared.

She cleared her throat and said, "When I married David I knew we'd be moving around a lot, but since I'd never been anywhere it sounded exciting. After years of having to start over again in the cramped quarters of Army housing, where none of the furniture or curtains fit, where storage space was limited, and where the front and back yards consisted mainly of dirt and weeds it became tiresome. When David was assigned to Redstone Arsenal in Huntsville, he was told to plan on staying for the duration of his service. We were so thrilled we bought a house. No more Army quarters for us. We would live happily in our own home." Unexpected tears welled in her eyes. Shifting her gaze from Sarah to the world outside the windows, she tried to blink them away. Still, she could stop her chin from quivering when she added, "Or so we thought."

"If you had a home in Huntsville why did you move to Fleming's Hill?"

Marcie's eyes burned from unshed tears, her lower back ached from holding herself so stiffly and a tension headache had started at the base of her skull.

If only she could stand up and stretch. If only Sarah would offer her a cold drink. If only this interrogation would end.

She said, "I had every intention of staying in Huntsville, but after the divorce and David's transfer—"

Sarah cut her off. "Am I to understand that you and David are no longer married?"

"That is correct. Our marriage ended two years ago." Had George forgotten to tell Sarah about the divorce when he recommended her? As if mental telepathy was in play, she could hear him say: *It's perfectly useless information.* Useless to him but from the look on Sarah's face, certainly not useless to Sarah Fleming-Thornton.

"Well now," Sarah said. "That puts a new light on matters."

Neither woman spoke for several seconds. Then Sarah said, "Did your husband remarry after the— the...?" She left the word hanging in the stale air as if she couldn't bear to utter it.

"The divorce?" Marcie said. "No, he prefers the single life."

"Any chance the two of you might get back together?"

"None whatsoever," Marcie replied. "I tried everything to save our marriage, but once David makes up his mind about something it's all but done."

"But what about the children? Did he not consider what would happen to them?"

More tears threatened and the headache had moved upwards. It pounded with every beat of her heart. "You would have to ask him. All I know is that David can be very selfish."

"I see," Sarah said. After a pause, she went on. "I may be getting too personal but I have to know. Are you seeing anyone special? Someone who might play a role in your future?"

Marcie stifled a mirthless laugh. The woman had already gotten too personal and now she wanted to know about her love life. "No, I'm not involved with anyone. It's been so long since I've dated I wouldn't know how to act."

"What a shame," Sarah said. "I was hoping maybe you and George... quite frankly I don't like the idea of hiring a divorced woman. The very word hints of scandal."

Marcie's body sagged with sorrowful relief. Sorrow because it all came down to the divorce. All of the sacrifices she'd made to earn her degree, all of the years of training, all of the desperate people she'd tried to help... yet in Sarah's eyes it was all for naught. Her moral character had been corrupted, which meant she couldn't possibly serve as a role model. She was unfit, unqualified, and as her mother once told her, "doomed to the fiery pits of hell."

Despite all that, she was relieved to know where she stood. She could go home to her dog Charley and her family of clocks and wait for her children to come home. Yes, the bill collectors would come after her but Charley could chase them away.

She rose from her chair with as much dignity as possible, looked at Sarah and said, "It was a pleasure to meet you, Mrs. Thornton. I wish you the best of luck in finding the right person for the job." She made a move for the door.

Sarah's next words stopped her. "I've already found her. You are the right person for the job, although we still have a few issues to settle before I can make a final decision."

"What other issues could there possibly be? You obviously don't approve of me so the way I see it you're not going to hire me."

"On the contrary, my dear," Sarah said, unruffled by Marcie's candor. "I don't disapprove of you. I believe you tried to save your marriage. Of course, I would prefer to hire a happily married woman, but we can't always have what we want. My daughter was proof of that. George must have told you about Grace.

The mention of George brought one of his favorite sayings to mind: *It's not what happens to you, it's how you react.* She had no idea how to react to this situation. She tried and failed to gather her thoughts. The headache pounded away, making it difficult to concentrate, and the pain in her back had reached the burning stage. She put a fist to the hot spot and rubbed up and down, her elbow jutting out awkwardly. Her mind and body had betrayed her. She felt under attack from all sides. Was she coming down with something? It wasn't like her to fall apart like this.

Sarah eyed her keenly. "Marcie, you looked flushed. Are you all right?"

"No, Mrs. Thornton, I'm not all right. I can't think straight because my head is throbbing, I'm having painful back spasms, and my throat is so dry I can hardly swallow."

"Good heavens," Sarah said, springing up from her chair with surprised agility. She went to the medicine chest, removed something from a shelf and came around to where Marcie stood. Handing her two packets of Goody's headache powder, she said, "These should fix you right up. Drinking cups are in the lavatory up the hall. A glass of iced tea will be waiting for you."

"Iced tea would be lovely," Marcie said with the packets clutched in her hand. She hurried from the room and up the hall. The TV was still blaring from the room on the left but it didn't affect her. Too many other things occupied her mind.

Once she had taken the pain remedy and quenched her thirst with tap water, she had an important decision to make. Should she continue up the hall and out the front door? Or should she fight for the opportunity to help the women of Port Victor At this point, she was ready to flip a coin.

CHAPTER 2

Marcie spied a tall glass of iced tea sitting on the pipe smokers' table. Seated, she picked it up and took a long drink. The tea had a sweet and tangy taste that refreshed the senses. She looked at Sarah and said, "Thank you. It is delicious."

"Thank Pearl," Sara said. "You can usually find her in the kitchen at this time of day."

"Does she live here, or does she come in the cook?" Marcie asked.

"Pearl is our oldest resident", Sarah said. "Both in age and in the length of time she's been here. We are fortunate to have her." Having said that, Sarah rolled her chair back from the desk and crossed her legs.

"Marcie", she said, "did George tell you about my daughter?"

"No", Marcie said in all honesty. "His primary focus centered on the job."

"Ah yes, the job", Sarah said. "While I know that this interview has been difficult, I have my reasons for wanting to know as much about you as possible. However, there's no point in going on unless you still wish to be considered for the position."

"I must be frank. I couldn't work for someone who didn't trust my judgment. The way I see it, the women of Port Victor are not that different from the men of New Start, and in order to help them recover from their past addictions and set goals for the future, they need a stable and stress free environment. That wouldn't be possible if you and I showed signs of conflict."

While Marcie waited for Sarah's response, she took time to congratulate herself. George would be proud. When she had first gone to work for him, she had been afraid to stand up for herself. When she thought she had been wronged, she simmered in silence. Until some insignificant slight occurred and then she would lash out in anger. George labeled her as a passive-aggressive type. Then he taught her how to be assertive. One's basic instincts fight change and she still had a tendency to revert to her original type. This time she'd stood fast.

With an abruptness that signaled she had made up her mind about something, Sarah glanced at the schoolhouse clock on the wall, looked at Marcie and said, "Excuse me, I must check in with Roger." She rolled her chair forward and reached for the phone. Seconds later, she spoke into the mouthpiece. "I'm still at Port Victor", she said, foregoing a standard greeting. "Are we on schedule?" The sound of Roger's voice filled the room. Deep and purely masculine, the man spoke in the same clipped tones as his boss. When he finished, Sarah made another query. "Did the Sampson order go out?" Roger answered in the affirmative. "Don't forget Collins", Sarah said. "He's expecting delivery by noon. I should be back in fifteen minutes or so. If you need me, I'll be here. Oh, and keep an eye on Henry. I think he's been sneaking into the kiln room, and I want to know why." Without saying goodbye, she placed the receiving back in it niche.

"I didn't realize I had the speaker turned on", Sarah said. "Roger is the manager of the brickyard." Marcie nodded. Sarah continued. "You must think I'm a nosey old biddy, but I have my reasons for being cautious about whom I hire. It is my sincere hope that you'll understand after I tell you about Grace." She paused before going on. "The story isn't pleasant and I'd rather nOt tell it, but considering the circumstances I think it's necessary." Marcie empathized. She had unpleasant stories of her own. Nevertheless, she was not about to tell hers.

"Bear with me", Sarah said. She drew in a long breath, as if storing up extra oxygen to tell her story. "I had three miscarriages during the first twelve years Victor and I were married. Most men want sons but from the very beginning Victor wanted daughters. When I finally carried a baby to term he didn't stop at handing out cigars, he closed all our businesses and told the employees to go home and celebrate Grace. That's what he named her, Grace. Goodness knows it didn't suit her."

"Family members were being kind when they called her a troublesome child. She screamed over nothing, threw violent tantrums, bit, pinched, and kicked. None of the other children would go near her. Even the teachers were afraid of her. Instead of using discipline when she did something wrong, they would call us to come and get her."

Although she didn't dare to interject, Marcie wanted to tell her that she too had a troublesome child— her son. Maybe not as troubled as Grace. Davy did listen to his father, and his sister wielded a great deal of influence over him. Julie talked him into staying in school when he wanted to drop out. Julie calmed him when he threw one of his fits. Probably Julie finally gave in when he'd thrown one of his tantrums at the thought of returning to Alabama from his father's condominium in Washington, D.C.

"She'd been skipping classes for years", Sarah said, "but they kept passing her to the next level. No one told us. They didn't want to disturb us. We found out when Grace dropped out of school in tenth grade." Sarah smiled a wry smile. "I'm certain the staff at Fleming's Hill High celebrated in one fashion or another." The smile dissolved.

"The day we enrolled her in a private school in Huntsville, she ran off with a solder. I must admit I was relieved. We hadn't had one minute's worth of peace since the day Grace was born. Victor didn't see it that way. He hired a detective, had her followed, offered her money to come back home. Oh, she came for the money, but as soon as she laid her hands on it, she was gone. This became a pattern. Every time she left she took another piece of Victor's heart." Sarah gave a slight shake of her head. "Poor deluded Victor."

No wonder Sarah had focused on hers and David's moves around the country, Marcie thought. The fact that David was a soldier had undoubtedly raised issues that reminded her of Grace.

"To put it plainly, Grace was what we used to call a camp follower, an alcoholic camp follower, at that. I knew it, the whole town knew it, but Victor refused to admit it."

"He told folks that Grace was taking time to see the world before settling down. Then he started to build this house. It was a home for Grace, he said. She planned to fill it with children and wanted them close to their Grandpa's office at the brickyard. He planned to use this room as a second office so he would be closer still. For a year and a half, he spent every waking moment overseeing the construction of this house. If I hadn't taken over the businesses, we would have lost everything." She sighed deeply and briefly closed her eyes. "I know I'm talking too much and taking too long, but a lot of people still gossip."

At that, Marcie said, "Gossip can be terribly destructive. It can destroy entire families. They say children can be cruel, but children have short-term memories. Parents can be downright vicious, and they never forget."

Sarah said nothing, but her eyes turned thoughtful as they studied Marcie's face. It was as though Sarah had discovered a new facet to Marcie's nature. The moment passed and Sarah went on. "A little over two years ago, Grace came home for the last time. We heard someone pounding on the door in the middle of the night. It wasn't unusual for Grace to arrive at odd hours so naturally we thought it was she. We were wrong. It was the police chief and the fire marshal, two men we had known all our lives. They had to come to tell us Grace was dead."

Marcie's hand went to her heart. "I am so sorry."

Sarah gave no indication of having heard her. "They found her body in a Goodwill Depository. One of those little yellow houses where people take things they don't want."

"The investigation gave a clear picture of what happened. For reasons known only to Grace, she jimmied the lock on the door and made herself at home. Except for a ragged chenille bedspread, she tossed the rest of the discards into a pile next to the open door. It was still smoldering when the firefighters arrived on the scene. An empty bottle of gin lay next to her body. The investigators concluded she had been drinking and smoking and had accidently flicked a live cigarette onto the pile before falling asleep. Passing out was more likely. Contrary to what some of the newspapers reported, she did not burn to death. She died of smoke inhalation."

At Sarah's mention of the date, a chill of recognition shot up Marcie's spine. She remembered the glaring headline in bold print: **Female Found Dead in Dumpster.** The accompanying story went on to describe the scene, the location on Huntsville's South Memorial Parkway, and a detailed account of the woman's family. Marcie knew exactly where the Depository was, had driven past it hundreds of times. A mere two streets down from the site was the turn-off to hers and David's house. Caught up in the throes of divorce at the time, it had made Marcie sick to her stomach to learn that the poor woman, alone and obviously destitute, had been dying a horrible death while she, Marcie Parker, paced the floor in anguish over the end of her marriage. And now, as surreal as it seemed, she was sitting here in the dead woman's house with the dead woman's mother, whose main objection to hiring her was the divorce she had been grieving over on the night Grace died.

Sarah said, "The bible says the Lord does not give you a burden you can-not bear, but He gave one to Victor. Because of all the notoriety surrounding Grace's death, we had a private graveside service. When it was over and every-one had left, Victor remained standing at the head of the grave. Tears streamed down his cheeks and onto his lapels. I took his hand in mine and tried to coax him to the car. He held back. Then he… he fell to the ground. The doctor said he died from a massive heart attack. I know he died of a broken heart."

Sarah leaned forward, her eyes burning feverishly. "Port Victor is dedi-cated to the man I cherished. It bears his name, a good and decent name, despite his daughter's efforts to tarnish it. It must never be a source of scan-dal again." She leaned back, her face drawn, shoulders slumped, eyes growing dimmer by degrees.

It was all Marcie could do to remain seated. She wanted to go to her. Gently pat her back. Murmur soothing words of comfort. In a soft voice, she said, "Mrs. Thornton?" Sarah looked up. "If you'll give me a chance I'll do my best to make you and the town proud of Port Victor and all it stands for.

Sarah's answer seemed a long time coming.

CHAPTER 3

While Sarah spoke to Roger again, Marcie busied herself with picking imaginary lint off the sleeve of her blazer. Now that she had become an official employee of Thornton Enterprises, she appeared outwardly calm, but her insides were leaping with joy. That she was hired on a conditional basis didn't concern her. She would worry about the conditions of her employment later— a six-month trial during which time she'd have to be on her best behavior and attempt to keep the house filled with contented residents. Keeping a group of females contented would not be easy. Substance abusers were notorious manipulators, women in particular. But not only did she have a job in her field, it paid one and a half times the salary she'd made at New Start. What's more, after the six-month trial period, she would receive full medical and dental benefits along with contributions to a savings plan. The package exceeded her wildest dream. She could hardly wait to tell the kids. Even her son might be impressed.

"What about Henry?" Sarah asked Roger.

The speaker no longer activated, Marcie found herself missing the sound of Roger's strong and confident voice. She wondered what he looked like. Saved from wondering any further, Marcie's attention shifted to Sarah's angry tone.

"Fire the scoundrel," she said, "and make sure you tell everyone why. Henry broke not one, not two, but three cardinal rules. He went into the kiln room, which, as everyone knows, is off limits. He drank on the job, and he snuck around when he should have been working." Marcie made a silent vow never to enter the kiln room, whatever that was, never drink on the job, which she wouldn't think of doing in the first place, and never sneak around during working hours.

"Oh, and by the way," Sarah said, "I've hired someone to direct operations here at Port Victor. Her name is Marcie Parker. I expect you'll see her coming and going, and I wanted you to know she's a legitimate employee."

An employee, Marcie repeated to herself. Simple but beautiful words.

"Now then, Marcie," Sarah said, having completed her call, "You'll want to add your personal touches to your new office. It's perfectly all right if you want to display family photos and such as that."

"Speaking of your family, I've neglected to ask about your children. How have they adjusted to their new way of life?"

Marcie thought all the hard questions were over. In an effort to prevent further probing, she said, "They seem to be getting along all right."

"That's good," Sarah said. "I would have thought they'd miss having their father at home."

"Yes, well… " Marcie shrugged as if that was to be expected. Before Sarah could go on, she said, "How many residents can we accommodate?"

"Eight, but we only have four: Pearl, Missy, Sheila and Tiffany. Bitsy has a suite to herself — you passed it in the hall — but she doesn't count in the census because she's Port Victor's housemother."

"Ah," Marcie said for want of anything better. What had Sarah said? That Bitsy watched entirely too much TV?

"Bitsy doesn't do any actual housekeeping," Sarah said. "She monitors the girls' activities. Makes certain no hanky— panky goes on. If anyone breaks a rule, she metes out the proper punishment. You'll find copies of the rules in the file cabinet. All the other forms are there as well."

Before Marcie could ask if a housekeeper came in to clean, Sarah's tone turned confidential. "I've been very concerned about our vacancy rate. We have been losing entirely too many girls. George told me not to worry, that the ones who leave without warning weren't serious about staying in the first place. I'm not so sure about that. The girls seem so grateful when they first arrive."

"Perhaps Bitsy could cut back on her hours in front of the TV," Marcie said. "Frequent interaction between her and the residents, especially after I leave for the day, would help maintain the peace and harmony necessary for recovery."

A look of dismay crossed Sarah's face. She shifted ever so slightly in her chair. "That certainly sounds like a reasonable request. I'll speak to her about it." She paused and then added, "But I must warn you, Bitsy is very set in her ways."

Marcie nodded. "Most of us are. With Bitsy's help, I'm confident we can fill this house and keep it full. In order to motivate the women to stay with the program and work on their goals, they need an established routine. Left to themselves they grow restless and bored, especially the younger women."

Sarah said, "I have asked myself countless time what would have happened if Grace had had a place like this to go to."

A rap on the door interrupted Marcie's reply. It was a light tap, barely audible.

"Come in, Bitsy," Sarah called. "Come meet your new boss." As an aside to Marcie, she said, "She's always late. I told her to be here at nine–thirty." She glanced at the schoolhouse clock, pursed her lips and added, "And here it's past ten."

For someone who always made a supreme effort to arrive early, Marcie added another minus point to her growing list of negatives concerning the housemother. When the door remained closed, Sarah slapped her palms on the desk and pushed up from her chair. "That girl will be the death of me yet," she said to the room at large, then went to the door and opened it, only to face a blank wall.

"Bitsy! I know you're there," she said, her tone threatening. "And I'm warning you, I don't have time for your foolishness. Now, be a good girl and come here."

They waited. Nothing happened.

"All right, *Deb-o-rah!*" Sarah called, her voice echoing up the hall and bouncing back down. "Please come here!" Leaving the door ajar, Sarah marched back to her chair. Once seated, she shook herself as though trying to shed an extra layer of skin.

Who was Deborah, Marcie wondered?

"Sorry for the disruption," Sarah said, back to her businesslike self. "Bitsy can be a handful. After putting up with her all these years, I still forget she will not answer to anything but her given name, Deborah. You'd best keep that in mind when dealing with her." She looked at the clock again and said, "Heavens, look at the time."

"Yes," Marcie said, her feet itching to start walking. "It's a shame to spend such a glorious day inside." The interview, if it could be called that, had to set a record for being the longest and strangest in history.

Sarah aimed a smile her way. "Now I know why George spoke so highly of you," she said. "You're so easy to talk to. Why, I have never gone on like this … it's so unlike me. You have a gift, Marcie Parker. A gift for listening."

A red–hot flush of guilt raced through Marcie's veins. Such high praise and kind words were the last thing she'd expected to hear. Fortunately, Sarah had not been privy to her thoughts. "I suppose that's why I went into social work," she said. "Perfect strangers have come up to me and poured their hearts out. I just hope the women of Port Victor do the same."

"They had better," Sarah said. "Now, I really must get back to the office." She started to push up from her chair, but stopped when the door swung open.

There, there on the threshold, stood the most beautiful child Marcie had ever seen. She was so … so perfect … so precious… so delicate, she hardly seemed real.

The child said nothing. She just stood there with her silvery blonde hair flowing down her back, looking directly at Sarah as though waiting to hear what the lady had to say.

"Ah," said Sarah to the child, "so you finally found your manners."

"For your information," the child said in an adult's peevish tone, "I had to water Uncle Victor's flowers."

"How many times do I have to tell you to turn the TV off when you leave your room?" Sarah said.

"I have no idea," the child said in a grownup's uppity voice. "How many?"

Marcie swallowed a laugh, and then realization came crushing down on her. This… this was no child … no seven–or– eight–year–old… this perfectly formed creature was an adult. Whether she qualified as a dwarf, Marcie did not know, and it really didn't matter, for the person standing near the desk was the housemother. The one who "watches entirely too much TV," the one who could "be a handful," the one who would be "the death of me yet," the one who "was always late." Questions that had rubbed her nerves raw when Sarah asked them of her whirled around in Marcie's head like an overwrought spinning wheel. Where had this little person come from? Who were her people? Nothing registered.

"This is Marcie Parker," Sarah said to the little one. "She's the new Executive Director of Port Victor. She also happens to be your new boss."

Instead of rising, as she would normally do when preparing to meet someone, Marcie remained in her seat to be at eye level with the little one. When Deborah turned her long–lashed, azure–blue eyes on her for the first time, they glinted with obvious distaste. Marcie blanched at the look. She glanced at the door, at the clock … Oh, to be out of there.

Although she continued to focus on Marcie, the girl spoke to Sarah. "I'm pleased to meet *your* Mrs. Parker, Aunt Sarah, but you can tell her to leave now. I've had enough bosses, thank you very much."

All Marcie heard was "Aunt Sarah." The girl said she had to water "Uncle Victor's flowers." That explained the relationship. Deborah must be Sarah's niece.

"You may as well get used to the idea of having another boss," Sarah said. "We've lost entirely too many girls because someone has been neglecting her job. Marcie will not only bring order to this house, she'll provide incentives for the women to stay."

Deborah put one perfect little hand on one perfect little hip and said, "She can boss the women all she wants, but I do not need, nor do I want, a boss."

"Don't pay any attention to her, Marcie," Sarah said.

"Yes, do," said the little one.

Both women seemed to be waiting for Marcie to say something. She could feel the corners of her lips twitch when she spoke. "I'm very happy to meet you, Bitsy, ah, I mean, Deborah. You're so beautiful… perfect, really, but, un, what I, ah, wanted to tell you, honey, was that I'm not here to boss you, honest I'm not. I'm here to run a treatment program and I'm counting on your help." She extended a hand for shaking. "Between the two of us—" The rest of her sentence, along with her hand, dangled in midair when Deborah put her hands behind her back and stood there with her pert little chin jutting out.

Still keeping her eyes on Marcie, Deborah told Sarah, "You brought her here, so it's up to you to tell her the rules."

Sarah explained that the little one was afraid of catching germs; therefore, she did not like to be touched. She also suffered from numerous allergies.

Marcie looked from Deborah to Sarah and back to Deborah. "Honey, I am so sorry. And, un, I don't blame you one bit. What with all these viruses and things, well, you … un, can't be too careful."

Again, Deborah looked at Marcie while addressing Sarah. "Please inform the lady that I do not wish to be called 'honey'."

Marcie flinched. Couldn't she do anything right?

"Now, now," Sarah said, "Marcie didn't mean any harm. She was only trying to be friendly." Sarah rubbed her hands together as though rolling a piece of dough. "I just know the two of you are going to be the best of friends."

Deborah took a studied interest in her Mary Jane shoes. The gastric juices in Marcie's stomach began to churn. Best of friends? How? She already felt intimidated by Deborah's size, not to mention her beauty. Her tongue tied itself in knots when trying to speak to the little one, and where on earth did the endearment "honey" come from? She never used such terms with people she did not know.

Deborah shifted her steely eyes from Marcie to Sarah. "Ginger's out of cookies."

Sarah looked at Marcie. "You'll have to remember to keep a supply of cookies on hand. Pearl used to bake several batches a day, but Ginger got too greedy, so I told Pearl to stop wasting her time. Now we stock packaged cookies."

"Who's Ginger?" Marcie croaked. If Deborah had a twin with the same temperament, Marcie would flee the premises, go straight to George's office and punch him in the nose.

"She's Bitsy's little dog," Sarah said. "A Pomeranian."

Thank goodness, Marcie thought. Never had she been so unsure of herself when dealing with a disagreeable person, much less a disagreeable little person. This was a whole new world.

Sarah went on. "I keep telling Bitsy that feeding Ginger so much sugar will make her sick and she'll die, but Bitsy never listens to a word I say."

"That's because you must be talking to someone with the detestable name *Bitsy*. My name is *Deborah*."

Sarah's eyes narrowed to slits. "Well, you'd better hear this, *Deborah*. If I ever see one flea in this house, Ginger will go straight to the pound and be put to sleep."

"I've wasted enough of my time," the little one said. Without further ado, she hurried out the door.

Sarah called after her. "Marcie will be here Monday morning at eight o'clock sharp. I want you to help her get settled in."

After a moment of silence, Marcie said, "I don't think she heard you."

"Oh, she heard me all right."

Sarah kept watch over the doorway as though waiting for Deborah to clear the area. Marcie wasn't about to make a move until Sarah did. The wait seemed interminable, but when Sarah finally sprang into action, she hustled Marcie out of the office, up the hall, and out the front door as if their lives depended on it.

Emerging into the outside world, Marcie shaded her eyes with a hand while drawing deep breaths of fresh air. It was such a pleasant day; she could almost forget the unnerving events that had taken place inside.

Then Sarah turned to her and brought it all back. "You must do everything in your power to get along with Bitsy. Make it your top priority. No matter what she does or says, just humor her. Do you understand?"

"Yes, ma'am," Marcie lied. She thought she'd been hired to create a program for the women of Port Victor, not to coddle the housemother. "But I must say Deborah wasn't very welcoming."

Sarah dismissed the comment with a wave of her hand. "Oh, she'll come around."

"I hope so," Marcie said.

Sarah looked at her. "You'd better do more than hope so. I work long hours and I'm tired when I get home. I don't have the patience or the energy to put up with Bitsy's sass. I am warning you, Marcie Parker, I will hold you personally responsible if she comes knocking on my door. Is that clear?"

"Perfectly clear. Deborah is here to stay and my job is to keep her happy."

"Precisely."

Marcie swallowed hard. "And if I don't keep her happy, I'll be out of a job?"

Sarah drew herself up and looked down her nose. "My dear girl, if you can't handle Bitsy, you certainly can't handle the women of Port Victor." With that, the mistress of the manor set off across the lawn towards the brickyard, the heels of her pumps digging into the sod.

From over her shoulder, she looked back and said, "Call me Sarah."

CHAPTER 4

At last, Marcie turned onto her narrow, tree-lined road. She'd been questioning her sanity ever since she left Port Victor. She must be certifiably crazy to have taken the job. Of course she'd pleaded her case before Deborah entered the picture. Things might have turned out differently if she had met her sooner. If only she'd had some kind of warning, known what to expect. But no, George had let her walk into a firestorm of regrets, resentments, and long-held grudges.

Her frown melted into a smile at the sight of her faithful companion at the end of the driveway. It could be hailing, flooding, or freezing, and Charley would be waiting for her to come home. No matter how bad her own day might have been, she figured his might have been worse.

After climbing out of the car, she bent over and clasped both sides of his head. "How are you doing, pal? Did you chase the bad guys away?" The German shepherd grinned up at her, his entire body in frenzied motion. "I knew our clocks would be safe with you around."

As she straightened up a catch in her back sent a sharp pain ripping through her lumbar region. She put a balled fist to the spot and rubbed hard. The effectiveness of the Goody's powder had worn off and the ride over her pot-holed road hadn't helped. She mentally cursed every piece of furniture and every heavy box she'd lifted and set down in another Army dwelling. But the damage was done, two herniated discs, and she just had to live with it. That and the fact that her ex, the man she would have followed to the ends of the earth, had a penchant for younger women.

Once the pain eased enough for her to move about, she gave Charley the news. "I got the job. But my boss expects miracles and my assistant is an angry dwarf who doesn't want anything to do with me." Charley pricked his ears and barked. "Yeah, who does she think she is?" She headed for the side door with the dog fast on her heels. Met with the usual cacophony of clock sounds, she called, "Hello, darlings! I missed you, too!" Clocks dangled from walls, crowded the hearth, sat on windowsills, clustered on tabletops, chests, shelves, the floors. Like half-hidden Easter eggs, they stood in odd spots, waiting to be discovered by a surprised eye. A half dozen miniatures clung to the front of the refrigerator, their magnets threatening to give way each time the door was opened or closed. Somehow they'd managed to hang on, like Marcie herself.

At last count, her family of clocks numbered thirty–two. Each one deserved a showcase of its own, but because space was limited, she'd had to make do. The clocks built into the appliances didn't count because she'd had no choice in the matter. Where the chosen clocks were mostly whimsical in nature, the built–ins wore dull faces and didn't make a sound, hardly worth a glance.

That they were boring was a crying shame. Why couldn't appliance makers give the public something fresh and new, something with a little pizzazz? How fun it would be if a stove wore a clock that made us smile, and instead of a timer that screeched its alarm, we'd hear music, a big band sound, jazz, or rock 'n' roll. Homemakers would dance to the dinner table, their pot roasts held high, and everyone would laugh and cheer. But no, appliances weren't meant to be fun. Never mind. Marcie had made her own fun.

At all hours of the day and night a variety of chimes, bells, gongs, bird calls, whistles, music, and animal sounds reverberated off the cabin's knotty pine ceilings. Not only did they play off–key symphonies, most of them came to life. Elvis strummed his guitar and swung his hips; Marilyn Monroe winked and puckered her lips; James Dean gave a sexy come-hither look; W.C. Fields leered at Mae West, who leered right back at him, and the British foursome known as the Beatles sang the first bar of *Hey Jude*.

Animal clocks mooed, whinnied, barked, oinked, clucked, and quacked. Felix, the black Kit-Cat, shifted his bulging eyes and wagged his tail. The Genie, a most unusual timepiece, had clocks for eyes. Constantly rolling, the left eye told the hour and the right eye told the minutes. Potbelly, the Pink Pig's curled tail unwound and then snapped back into a tight ball, and the wee birds popped out of their wee cottages and sang the coo-coo song. The discordant sounds and the intimacy of movements gave Marcie a great sense of comfort in an otherwise silent house.

Some people, namely her ex-husband and their two teenaged children, thought her collection odd, and that was back when her clocks only numbered eleven. What was odd about it, she'd wanted to know? People collected all sorts of things: Thimbles, angel figurines, hatpins, souvenir spoons, hand-painted dishes, butterflies, china cups, stamps, hand bells ... why not clocks.

If Davy and Julie could see her current collection, they would haul her off to the funny farm. Well, she had gone a little berserk. What did they expect? That she would put on a red dress and high heels and go dancing in the street? Hardly. Any mother who loved her children was entitled to go off the deep end if they, on a month-long summer visit to their father in Washington, D.C., chose to extend their stay indefinitely.

"Please don't take it personally, Mom," said sixteen-year-old Julie over the phone last summer. Marcie could picture her son, monitoring every word his sister said, but too cowardly to get on the extension. He'd always made Julie the bearer of bad news. Julie went on. "It's not that we don't love you and miss you, Mom, but D.C. has so much to offer. We're learning a thousand times more than we could at Fleming's Hill High. Not just about history and government and stuff, but how to get around a big city on our own. Dad goes off to the Pentagon every morning and Davy and I hop on a train. We go somewhere new every day, and so far, we haven't gotten lost, not once. Please understand, Mom. We love you very much. But we really need to do this."

Oh, Marcie understood all right. She understood that her son wanted to stay as far away from her as possible, and he had undoubtedly pitched ten fits before Julie agreed to stay with him at their father's condominium. It had always been that way. Marcie couldn't begin to count the number of times Julie gave up doing something with her friends in order to placate her brother.

So, instead of putting on a red dress and high heels, Marcie had adopted more clocks, picking them up at yard sales, flea markets, and junk shops for next to nothing. Synchronizing thirty–two clocks was difficult to say the least, but she tried.

She pulled the heating pad from a shelf in the linen closet and set it on the bed. After fluffing her feather pillows and placing them against the headboard, she climbed onto the bed and settled with the heat at her back. Hunger pangs told her it was nearing lunchtime but food would have to wait. She needed an extra edge when confronting George. If she filled her tummy, she'd be no match for him. That he'd recommended her for the job was beside the point. What mattered was the information he had withheld, vital knowledge that would have prepared her for what was to come. Yet he had the nerve to preach that open and honest communication was the key to successful relationships. What a joke!

She reached for the phone on the bedside table, plucked the receiver from its base and dialed the number to his office on the chance he would be between patients.

"Dr. Rutledge's office," his secretary said.

"Hi, Diane. Marcie here. Is he busy?"

"He's always busy, Mrs. Parker," Diane replied. "Would you like to leave a message?"

Instantly annoyed at Diane's tone and the use of her married name, she mimicked Sarah's business voice. "Yes, Miss Grimes, I would like to leave a message. Please tell him to call me, Miss Grimes. It's very important, Miss Grimes. Thank you and goodbye, Miss Grimes."

She hung up the phone and settled back on the heating pad, hoping her sarcasm had worked but seriously doubting it. No matter how many times she'd asked Diane to call her by her given name the woman persisted in using her formal name. While some divorcees might want to retain the title of Mrs., she was not one of them. She was Marcie Parker, period.

No telling how long she'd have to wait until George called her back. She folded her hands over her empty stomach. Maybe she should call Diane and apologize for being so snippy. She would tell her she'd had a long and difficult job interview and it had worn her out. Diane might ask if she got the job and Marcie could tell her yes, in fact she did. She would report to work on Monday as the Executive Director of Port Victor. Then Diane might— the jangle of the telephone jarred her, giving rise to a painful spasm in her back. She snatched the receiver off the hook and grumbled a hello.

"Rutledge here," George said.

"Parker here," she snapped.

"Don't tell me you blew the interview," he said.

Using an exaggerated Southern drawl, Marcie said, "Pray tell, Doctor Rutledge, what am I supposed to do about that little charmer named Deborah?"

"You got the job," he said, sounding relieved.

"And that's another thing," she said in her normal voice. "You said the interview was a mere formality. That the job was mine unless I screwed up. Well, let me tell you, that was no interview, it was a very nosy and intense interrogation. Why didn't you tell Sarah I was a not-so-gay divorcée?"

"Because she would have crossed your name off her list. No interview, no job."

"Oh," said Marcie. He had her best interests at heart, after all. Still, he could have warned her. "Okay, I'll give you that one, but you can't possibly have an excuse for keeping Deborah a secret."

"I may omit information, but I never make excuses. I figured if you knew how difficult Deborah was you would've told me to go to hell."

"Maybe so," she said, "but you could have mentioned her size. I thought she was a child. It came as a complete shock to learn that she's not only an adult, but Port Victor's housemother. Is she always so hostile?"

"She's been mad at the world ever since Victor died. It didn't help matters when Sarah shuffled her out of the big house and into Port Victor."

"Swell," said Marcie.

"The only thing she's grateful for is having that greenhouse to escape to. Victor gave her the deed to the building, the lot it sits on, and a hefty trust fund. He said she could turn the greenhouse into an apartment if living with Sarah became intolerable."

"That's interesting," Marcie said. "According to Sarah, Deborah's the one who's intolerable."

"Sarah resented having to look after her," George said.

"Don't make me ask why."

"Deborah was left in her grandmother's care when she was five days old, which meant Granny had to take the baby to work with her. She kept house for Sarah's parents. When Granny died, Deborah became the Fleming's ward. When they died, Sarah had no choice but to take over Deborah's care. She could have put her in a home, but by then she had married Victor and he wouldn't hear of it. He treated Deborah like one of his hothouse flowers. He'd set her on a shelf amid the orchids and other exotics and then pretend to water her so she'd grow. She grew older but not much taller. On old Doc Roger's say-so, Victor prevented her from associating with anyone outside the family for fear she'd get hurt."

"Where were her parents all this time?"

"Her mother Lila was not the type to stay in touch. Neither getting pregnant nor being a mom was on her agenda. If Lila knew who Deborah's father was, she never told anyone. Essentially, Deborah was an orphan at the mercy of her keepers."

"Good grief. No wonder she's so angry."

"I tried to talk to her but she shut me out. Victor was her only ally. She adored him."

"How old is she?"

"She must be in her late thirties."

"And in all that time she's never been anywhere? Never had any friends her own age? Never met any other dwarves?"

"As far I know she's unaware of their existence."

"I'm sorry to hear that, but how am I supposed to work with her? The second I laid eyes on her, I was entranced. Not only because of her size, but she's the most perfectly beautiful female I've ever seen. It was as if I turned into some other person. I couldn't think straight, I couldn't talk straight. Here, she's this little person yet she lorded it all over me. I'll bet she's the reason Port Victor has had such a high vacancy rate. She probably runs the women off over every little infraction"

"Hold on, Marcie," George said. "You're getting yourself worked up over nothing. I have the—"

"Nothing? I'd like to see you try to keep Deborah happy. That's my main job, you know. That and keeping the house filled with women who wouldn't dream of taking off if they got an itch. As if that isn't bad enough, if one of the local gossips even hints of a scandal at Port Victor, Sarah will have Roger hang me from the highest tree."

"Roger's too nice a guy," George said. "He'd fashion a slipknot on a low limb."

"Dammit, George, I'm serious." Then, in a softer tone, she said, "You like Roger, huh?"

"Yes. Why?"

"Nothing," she said.

George said, "Are you calm enough to listen to my plan?"

"If it'll help me deal with Deborah, yes."

"You're going to groom Pearl for the housemother's job."

"Pearl? The one who does the cooking?"

"None other. She's been the unofficial housemother since the day she checked in, and just so you know, she's an uneducated country woman with a world of common sense. She's honest, trustworthy, a hard worker, and the women respect her. She's also—"

"Wait a minute," Marcie said. "If the women respect her so much why did so many of them leave?"

"Because they didn't have you to counsel them against leaving."

"Right or wrong, you've got an answer for everything."

"That's my job," he said, and she could picture the smirk on his face.

"Oh, hush," she said. Then, "Now, more than ever, I regret not having had the chance to meet Pearl. Sarah rushed me out of the house so fast I didn't have time to blink. I could've given Pearl my phone number. Told her to call me if any of the women got that certain gleam in the eye — you know the one that says I got a man waiting to take me to heaven."

George went on where he left off. "As I started to say, Pearl is the only person who has the ability to communicate with Deborah. In fact, she's the only one allowed to enter Deborah's suite. So, kiddo, I'd advise you to keep your eyes and ears open. Who knows, you just might learn something. Now be a good girl and let me get back to work."

"I'll hang up after you promise me two things. That you'll come for dinner next Friday night. I'm having your favorites. Pork chops, au gratin potatoes, green beans, pickled beets, and a batch of your precious cornbread."

"What's for dessert?"

"I suppose you want pie."

"How did you guess? I've had a craving for cherries lately."

"Oh, all right," she said begrudgingly. She'd never gotten the hang of making a decent pie crust, but Mrs. Smith would be delighted to be a guest at the table.

"Okay, you talked me into it," he said.

"The second promise is to take my calls if I say it's an emergency, and be sure to tell Miss Grimes to put me through."

"Miss Grimes?" George said. "What's that all about?"

"Ask her," Marcie replied. "Bye now." She replaced the receiver, feeling better about things in general. No doubt about it, she could count on George for the right answers. If she'd listened to him when he advised her not to sell the house in Huntsville, the kids would still be living at home instead of at their dad's place.

Well, maybe they would. And maybe they wouldn't.

Lying on the heating pad, she wondered what to do first. Pack some of her books and mementos to take to her new office? Eat lunch and then go out and mow the lawn? Search her closet in hopes of finding a sensible wardrobe, one that would make her look inches shorter?

The heating pad never felt so good. She pressed her back into it as hard as she could and shimmied her hips. Then she became still. With Charlie snoozing on the floor below and her clocks unusually quiet, she could plainly hear the mockingbird singing his heart out. She loved that bird; she hoped he lived in the hackberry tree outside her bedroom window forever.

The bird sang on, its repertoire never-ending. Ah, it was so peaceful lying there, listening to the bird and the rustle of leaves. Her eyelids felt heavy...her limbs went loose... she was drifting... drifting away on a fat pink cloud.

Marcie woke with a smile on her face. Her brain must have worked overtime while she slept, because plans for the coming week were laid out in her mind like a brand new rug.

First thing Monday morning she would gather the four residents together and introduce herself. Next, she would give them a brief resume of her qualifications and experience. After that, she would ask the women to take her on a tour of the house. The normal chatter that took place at such times would give insights into each woman's personality. It was better to take it slow, to build rapport before starting therapy.

Deborah wasn't the only one who would have to make certain adjustments. When dealing with her earlier that day, Marcie could not have been more inept. But she'd never even seen a little person, and never had she thought she'd be kowtowing to one to keep the peace and her job. Life could be so complicated. No matter, she must carry on. Deborah couldn't be *that* bad.

CHAPTER 5

On her first day as Executive Director of Port Victor, Marcie sat whiling away the minutes in the Dairy Queen's parking lot. As usual, she arrived early, and not wanting to barge in on the women and disrupt their routine, she'd chosen to park in the same spot as before simply because it offered the best view of Port Victor.

Interestingly enough, she made several observations that had escaped her the day of the interview. Though highly unsuitable for a single-family dwelling, the commercial site on which Victor Thornton had built the impressive two-story Colonial made an ideal location for a halfway house. No fussy neighbors to contend with, no threat of being closed down because those same fussy neighbors didn't want a recovery center in their midst, and no neighborhood children to snoop about and shout taunts learned from their elders. Marcie knew all about taunts. She'd been the brunt of them during the summer of her eleventh year.

On the minus side, the privacy offered by the lack of neighbors, the closed businesses, and the thick stand of Southern pines beyond the hedge in back of the house made it easy for a resident to sneak in and out late at night. They could cut across the brickyard with the stacks of bricks for cover, or go the other way through the piles of lumber outside the building supply company. No doubt the girls who'd left the program started out that way — tasting freedom for an hour or two and then, unable to resist the desires welling up within them, taking off for good, either hitching a ride with a stranger or someone they already knew.

According to Sarah, Deborah was supposed to keep an eye on things, make sure no "hanky-panky" went on. In all fairness, the housemother couldn't be expected to sit up all night and monitor everyone's activities. That meant it would be up to her to build a bridge of trust so the women would come to her if they so much as entertained the thought of leaving.

The time had come to say farewell to the Dairy Queen parking lot. From now on, she would go directly to the house no matter how early it was. After all, she was the boss. Even Sarah Fleming–Thornton had agreed to abide by her decisions. The thought scared and excited her at the same time. She reached for the ignition key and switched it on.

The dark clouds that had been building on the horizon all morning were moving closer. Marcie glanced in her rearview mirror at the cardboard cartons stacked in the back of the wagon. She'd spent hours choosing just the right things to bring to her new office. Should she try to get them inside before the thunderstorm struck or should she wait till it passed? The sky was the color of coal and getting darker.

In order to get as close to her office as possible, Marcie parked directly in line with the front door. She would pull the car around to the side as soon as she finished carrying the cartons inside. If she hurried, she could beat the storm, especially if one or more of the women offered to help. With that in mind, she skipped up the steps, pushed the doorbell and then ran back to the car to get the first carton.

On the porch, with her purse perched on top of the box, she stood before the massive oak door expecting it to open any second. Several moments passed and still no one came to the door. Maybe no one heard the bell. Straining to hoist the box higher, she managed to extend an index finger far enough to press it again. Though muffled, she could hear chimes playing the first few notes of Beethoven's Fifth.

She waited, feeling the weight of the boxed books in her back and arms. Why didn't someone come to the door? Surely they were up and about by now. Surely Sarah had told them what time she would arrive. Marcie knew better than to expect Deborah to lay out the welcome mat. The little princess was probably watching TV or out in the greenhouse. In either case, it was unlikely she would hear the bell. That didn't excuse Pearl, Missy, Sheila, or Tiffany. At least one of them must have heard the chimes.

A rumble of thunder in the distance warned of the approaching storm. At the same time, it began to sprinkle. Flash flood warnings were forecast earlier that morning, typical weather for the end of March. Marcie could feel the soft curl in her hair turning to frizz. Determined to rouse someone, she balanced the box against her hip and raised a hand to the heavy brass knocker. The pounding action caused the box to start a downward slide. She grabbed it and her purse just in time, but the effort cost her. The crook of her left arm now hurt worse than her back. If someone didn't come in the next couple of seconds, she would go back to the car and pull it around to the side of the house, which, if she'd had an ounce of sense, she should have done in the first place. So she'd have to wait for the storm to pass. Better that than being struck by lightning.

Feeling like a complete fool, she imagined Sarah watching from her office window. Sarah's shoulders would be twitching with irritation. Not only at the sight of Marcie standing at the front door for seemingly no good reason, but also at the battered station wagon parked in front of the house. Casting an anxious glance that way, she was greatly relieved to see nothing but stacks of bricks. If she couldn't see the building that contained Sarah's office, Sarah couldn't see her.

Both the raindrops and the box of books seemed to be increasing in size and weight. A sudden flash of lightning made Marcie jump. She didn't dare wait any longer. Just as she started to turn away, a thought occurred to her. Maybe the door was unlocked. Maybe she was supposed to let herself in. Once again, she shifted the carton onto her right hip, grasped the doorknob with her left hand and gave it a turn.

The door swung wide. Still gripping the knob, she tried to hang on, but the heavy oak door went one way and the box of books went the other. Thrown off balance, she stumbled over the threshold, her empty hands grasping for purchase. Finding nothing but air, she pitched forward onto her knees and the heels of her hands. The box thudded to the floor on its side and slid about a foot away. Her purse flew into the wall on her left and fell to the marbled floor.

Gritting her teeth against the burning pain that radiated from her hands and knees, she stayed in place for several seconds and then flipped over onto her butt. Because the heels of her hands burned even worse now that the shock of the fall had worn off, she kept them at an angle while her fingers probed her knees. No protruding bones, no blood, not even a tear in her panty hose.

Once she determined that her body was intact, she pushed up from the floor and stood in place until a dizzy spell passed. Outside, the storm came closer. How could she let herself get into this mess? Because she had expected someone to open the damn door.

Now, having made her grand entrance, she still hadn't attracted anyone's attention. Where were the women? What were they doing? Had they gone back to bed and pulled the covers over their heads to block out the sound of the storm? Had they all packed up and left? The house, with its disquieting stillness and weather–darkened rooms, spooked her. An image of George popped into her head. She could hear him now. *It's the weather that has you spooked, not the house. A bright, sunny day would put a whole new perspective on the environment."*

As usual, George was right. Instead of letting negative thoughts take hold, she had to think positive. The most likely explanation for why no one came to the door was that the women had gone elsewhere. Did Port Victor have a van? If so, who drove it? Unless it was equipped with hand controls, certainly not Deborah.

Had Sarah conducted a normal interview, Marcie would know the residents' daily routine. Keeping packaged cookies on hand for Ginger, and how many residents they could accommodate was all she knew. When it came time for Marcie to ask questions, she had been too rattled to think of any. She could think of plenty to ask now.

Thunder roared ever closer. She lifted the box off the floor and, anxious to bring in the rest of them in before the full force of the storm hit, she hurried across the foyer and down the long hall. Thank goodness the door to her office was open. She dumped the box on the desk and retraced her steps. Her purse went unnoticed as she raced in and out.

The heavy oak door swung shut none too soon. A crack of lightning illuminated the foyer and a loud clap of thunder boomed directly overhead. Marcie snatched her purse off the floor and scurried back to the office where wind–driven rain pelted the windowpanes.

The room was nighttime–dark. Marcie flipped on the overhead light and a banker's desk lamp. She removed her rain–splattered jacket and draped it over the back of a club chair. Chilled to the bone, she rubbed her arms to restore warmth and circulation. Her hands, knees, and back burned with pain and her bladder needed emptying. She crossed to the medicine chest, extracted two packages of Goody's powder, stuck them in her purse and headed for the bathroom up the hall.

Clutching her handbag to her chest, she paused a couple of feet from the door to Deborah's suite. Something about this section of the hall nagged at her. She had a sense of being watched. In the old horror movies, the eyes in portrait paintings followed the characters' every move. She looked up and down the hall for a pair of protruding eyeballs. Finding nothing but white paint on the ceiling and a sea green color on the walls, she moved forward, and then paused again.

Not a sound came from Deborah's room. No wildly cheering program on TV, not even a commercial. Most curious of all Ginger hadn't barked, whined, or growled when Marcie was dashing up and down the hall. Deborah must have gone to the greenhouse and taken Ginger with her. Relieved because she wanted to make herself presentable before facing the perfection of Deborah, she moved on.

Just as she reached the spot directly across from Deborah's door, it opened. Immaculate in a teal–blue velvet dressing gown and matching slippers, she looked like a perfect angel. Like a fairy tale creature who, upon seeing that Marcie had been caught in the storm, would say: "Oh you poor dear. Here let me fetch you a towel." But in the blink of an eye that fairy tale creature turned into a wicked witch. Seeming ten feet tall, the witch said, "Am I to expect to be rudely awakened every morning by crashing and banging and footsteps thundering up and down the hall?"

Conscious of her disheveled appearance, Marcie ran a hand through her frizzy hair and tried her best to speak coherently. "No, un, ah," she stammered. "I, ah, was trying—"

"For heaven sakes," Deborah said, "how do you expect to counsel the women when you can't even talk straight? If hiring you was Aunt Sarah's idea of a joke, I'm not laughing."

36

"Neither, un, am I."

"Let me explain something to you, Miss Parker. We don't cotton to noise around here. Do you understand? No noise." That said she disappeared behind her door.

A sudden burst of anger made Marcie shout, "Why didn't you open the front door? I rang the bell twice and knocked once!" With her heart pounding in her throat, she waited for an answer.

Deborah's door jerked open. She stood there for a moment, a smile of condescension playing across her face. "Well, well," she said, "the counselor can talk straight, after all. However, her powers of observation flunk the grade. My reason for not opening the front door is quite simple. The knob is too big and the door is too heavy."

Mortified, Marcie sucked in her breath. Could she have made a worse faux pas? She'd so hoped to make peace with Deborah on this her first day.

She made another attempt. "Where's Ginger? I'd like to meet her."

"If you must know, Ginger's out in the greenhouse trying to catch cave crickets."

"Cave crickets?"

"Yes. They are large, ugly things. Like some people I know." With that, she slammed her door.

Marcie made a fast retreat to the powder room. Standing before the mirror above the basin, she looked at her stupid, messy, wet self and burst out crying.

She had a quiet cry — God forbid that she should make any noise. Tears streamed down her face, her nose ran, her shoulders shook. She made it to the commode, pulled down her panty hose and panties and sank onto the seat. Letting her bladder rule, she peeled off a long sheet of toilet paper and used it to dry her eyes and blow her nose. She choked back one last sob and then took care of business.

Standing before the mirror again, she gave herself a lecture. Just because Deborah was Sarah's ward, she had no right to treat Marcie like one of the cave crickets, an insect not worth stepping on.

"Oh yes she did," a tiny voice whispered in Marcie's ear. Sarah had ordered her to keep Deborah happy, no matter what. If she failed, she'd have to go back to replenishing snack machines at old-time gas stations and mom and pop grocery stores, all of them located way out in the county, none showing a blip on a map. She must've asked for directions a hundred times and the answers always seemed the same.

"Yep," said the farmer in Bib overalls and a straw hat with a hole in its brim, "I know just where that's at. All you gotta do is turn left at the old oak stump, go past Humphrey's mailbox, take a right at the end of Willa's fence row, go straight till you see the American flag. That there's the post office. Go on in and ask Eula what to do next."

She finally learned her way around despite the U-turns and missed stop signs hidden behind tangled brush, but the pay barely covered her bills and her old wagon couldn't take many more trips down dirt roads.

After swallowing the Goody's powder, she ran a brush through her hair and crimped the ends with her fingers. Every time she looked in a mirror she couldn't believe the image looking back at her, the one with the strawberry blonde hair. Hair she'd colored the day before the interview to impress Sarah Fleming-Thornton. She looked like a different person. If only she could act like one, a woman who wouldn't fall apart at the mere sight of a dwarf.

The back of her skirt felt damp to the touch but it would have to air-dry. At least the jacket had kept her blouse dry. She looked decent, but nothing like the fresh, put-together person who'd left home forty minutes ago. So much for making a good first impression.

On her way back to the office, Marcie looked straight ahead as she passed Deborah's door. As far as she was concerned, the confrontation between them never happened.

Setting her purse on the desk, she looked around. Her eyes lit on the phone. She should call Sarah to let her know she'd arrived, and inquire about the residents' routine. A bright flash of lightning outside the twin windows convinced her to postpone the call till after the storm.

The stack of boxes waited to be unpacked and the file cabinet waited to be explored, but a cup of hot, black coffee sounded good. If a pot hadn't been made, she would make it herself.

This time on her way up the hall, she noticed the most magnificent grandfather clock she'd ever seen. Standing tall and proud at the entry to the foyer, he beckoned her to come closer. She ran a hand over his burnished wood body, pausing to finger his intricate carvings. Gazing up at his gorgeous face, she whispered, "Hello, you handsome devil. You want to go home with me? Join my little family of clocks?" His pendulum hung perfectly still and his delicate hands pointed in wayward directions. "Oh, so you're the strong, silent type. Well, not to worry. I'll bring you back to life after my coffee break."

Marcie's next stop came at the bottom of the staircase. The raging storm made it impossible to hear signs of life from above, but the lack of vibrations reinforced the idea that everyone had left the house before she arrived. But who had taken them and where did they go?

She stepped from the marble-floored foyer onto the rose-colored carpet that stretched from wall to wall in the formal living room and, separated by an archway, into the dining room. The musty odor of rooms seldom, if ever, aired came at her in waves, turning her stomach with each undulation.

Taking shallow breaths, she walked to the nearest side table and turned the switch on the lamp. Nothing happened. She reached under the shade to tighten the bulb and found an empty socket. She moved to the next lamp. The glow of a dim bulb flickered on and off and then stayed on. She wished it hadn't.

True, the living room contained rich carved woods, velvets, brocades, oil paintings and tapestries, but see-through plastic covers shrouded each upholstered piece. Was Sarah or a decorator afraid one of the residents might actually wet herself while sitting on the divan? It was not only insulting it added a rancid odor to the musty smell.

Jagged bolts of lightning outside the tall front windows created a strobe-light effect inside the dimly lit room. Marcie shuddered as ghostly shadows darted about the furniture. She half expected one of the women to pop up from behind a chair and shout, "Boo!" She hurried on, anxious to distance herself from the ghosts.

Although the dining room was large enough to serve a banquet, only eight chairs sat at a dark mahogany table. A matching sideboard and a breakfront held nothing of interest, and squares of plastic covered the upholstered chair seats.

None of the furnishings made any sense. On the one hand, they were obviously expensive; on the other; they gave the impression of being bought at a going–out–of– business sale that never went out of business. Marcie could only imagine the crinkling sound when someone sat down on the plastic, if anyone ever did.

Her sagging spirits lifted when she inhaled the aroma of brewed coffee. Following the scent, she crossed from the dining room into the large country kitchen. The room was empty but a coffee maker bearing a full pot indicated that someone was up and about. If she had to guess who, she'd name Pearl.

After flipping on the ceiling light, she plucked a mug from a treelike rack and helped herself. The coffee was strong and laced with chicory, just the way she liked it. She turned to stand with her back to the counter. Once the storm passed and the sun came out, the kitchen, with its white and yellow colors would be brighter and cheerier than it was now. A large bay window in the breakfast nook would normally offer a view of the back lawn. Today, rain pelted the sod, making for zero visibility. Still, this was one case, Marcie thought, where the household would rather eat in the kitchen than the formal but dull dining room.

She sipped her coffee. A typical kitchen clock with an apple design on its face ticked the minutes away. If she stood there long enough, Marcie reasoned, someone was bound to show up.

With a start, she realized that what she'd been staring at so intently was a shaft of light coming from beneath one of the doors at the opposite end of the room. Four closed doors led off a short hall, but only one shed any light. Praying it would lead her to the women, she headed that way.

Fearing what she might or might not find, she stood before the door debating whether to open it or not. She could not bring herself to ignore it.

The instant she pulled on the doorknob the unmistakable odor of fresh cigarette smoke drifted up to meet her. She leaned out over the void above the staircase and called, "Hello! Anybody there?"

A gravelly voice called back. "Yessum!"

"Is that you, Pearl?"

"Yessum!"

"Do you mind if I come down?"

"No'um."

Happy to know that Pearl was still there, she wanted to race down the stairs and hug the woman's neck. Instead, she made her way cautiously, gripping the banister and placing one foot at a time on the narrow, wooden steps. Halfway down, her senses were assaulted by a heavy cloud of a pine–scented deodorizer. By the time she reached the bottom step her eyes were watering.

"It's okay, it's okay," she gasped to the woman behind the cloud. Fanning the air with both hands, she added, "I don't mind if you smoke."

"Yessum," said Pearl as she set the can of spray on a shelf above a washing machine that was vibrating its way through a spin cycle. Turning back to the task of sorting through the pile of laundry that had fallen down a chute and into a holding bin, Pearl went on to say, "Miss Sarah, she don't like us to smoke. Says it ain't good for us and it ain't ladylike."

Marcie said, "According to the experts, nothing but fruit and vegetables are good for us, and then only those organically grown." She noticed Pearl giving her a quizzical look. "By the way, my name is Marcie Parker. And you are Pearl?"

"Yessum."

Marcie made a mental note to be more precise. "What is your last name?"

"Hobbs," she answered.

Marcie felt a twinge of sorrow as she looked at a bone–weary woman with gnarled, arthritic hands and stooped shoulders who was probably twenty years younger than she looked. Whether because of the ravaging effects of alcohol abuse or a hardscrabble life filled with bitter disappointments, she didn't know. Probably both.

She gave a warm smile and said, "I'm very glad to meet you, Pearl Hobbs. I was worried about you and the other women. Afraid you'd all moved out because I was coming to work here."

Pearl crooked an eyebrow and squinted up at her through rheumy eyes. "You gonna work here? What kinda job you gonna do?"

That solved one riddle. Neither Deborah nor Sarah had bothered to let the women know to expect her. "I'm going to do the same job Dr. Rutledge did, only I'm going to come every day."

The furrows in Pearl's brow deepened. "Dr. George, he ain't coming here no more?"

"Oh, he'll come to visit, just not as often."

"Yessum," she said and went back to her task, clearly unhappy with the news.

Thinking it best to gather information slowly, Marcie cleared her throat and, with a casual note, said, "Pearl, I was wondering, did you hear the doorbell or the knocker?"

"No'um. I got started on the wash right after I done the breakfast dishes."

"What about the others? I can't understand why no one heard me pounding on the door or crashing to the floor. I made enough noise to raise the dead."

Pearl gave a slight shrug. "Missy, I reckon she's up in her room readin' some book or listenin' to her music. That's mostly what she does, reads and listens."

"I didn't hear any music so she must be reading," Marcie said. "Missy, she don't play her music so folks can hear it. Missy, she's got them ear muffs."

"Ah," said Marcie, crossing that riddle off her list. "Well, I'm glad to hear that Missy's a reader. I brought a bunch of books from home. What about the other girls? Sheila and Tiffany?"

"Sheila and Tiffany, they's gone."

Marcie's heart skipped a beat. "Gone where?"

"Don't rightly know. Sheila and Tiffany, they was gone before daylight yesterday."

"Yesterday?" Marcie exclaimed.

"Yessum."

"Did you see them leave?"

"No'um, but Missy, she done told me. 'Twas after lights out when she heared 'em gigglin' on the fire escape. Said she thought they was having a smoke, but they never come back in."

42

A litany of "if only" filled Marcie's head. If only Sarah had introduced them on Friday. If only the two girls had waited. If only they had given her a chance. "I'm very sorry to hear that," she said.

Pearl looked up from her task. "We had us a AA meeting Saturday evening. I seen these two boys actin' the fool over the girls. You reckon them girls went off with them?"

"It's a strong possibility," Marcie said, grateful for the information yet sadder still to know she'd missed getting to know the girls before the AA meeting.

Pearl continued sorting, dropping white linens in one basket, colored clothing in another, and underwear in yet another. The odor of pine spray had finally dissipated, leaving that of bleach and laundry detergent, a homey combination that Marcie welcomed.

"Here, let me give you a hand." She stepped up to the holding bin.

"Don't need no help," Pearl said, waving her off.

A buzzer signaled the end of a drying cycle. Pearl responded instantly, going to the dryer and removing one article at a time, shaking and smoothing it out, then carefully placing it in a square plastic laundry basket.

A single bulb hung down from the ceiling, giving just enough light to illuminate the immediate area. Marcie imagined the rest of the basement looked like most others, a maze of dank, dark rooms where the ogres of her childhood lurked.

"When does Missy usually come downstairs?"

"Missy, she never misses her dinner."

"What time do you serve dinner?"

"Dinner's at twelve o'clock noon. Missy, she calls it lunch, but me, I call it dinner."

The washing machine thudded to a stop. Again, Pearl responded right away. Rather than removing the load and putting it in the empty dryer, she started the cycle all over again.

Marcie said, "Do you always run the laundry through twice?"

"No'um. Miss Deb, she's got to have her sheets and towels washed three times. Says that's the onliest way to get 'em clean."

"Good heavens," Marcie said, "I've never heard of such a thing. Why doesn't she do her own laundry?"

"Miss Deb, she's so scared of this cellar she won't even open the door up yonder. That's how come we can smoke down here. 'Sides, Miss Deb, she can't reach the knobs."

Darn, Marcie thought. Why did she keep forgetting? Because she'd never been around a little person before. "Is she any help to you at all?"

"No'um. Miss Deb, she's no bigger'n a yardstick. Onliest thing she can do is water Mr. Victor's flowers."

"Huh," said Marcie, wondering why, if Deborah had allergies, she wasn't allergic to flowers. And weren't the shelves in greenhouses fairly high? "So, you do all the work and all the cooking."

"Pret'near."

"Pardon me for asking, but do you get paid?"

"Don't need no pay. Got my room an' all the food I can eat. That's more'nough."

"But what about your cigarettes and toiletries and things?"

"The Social Security takes care of that."

"Oh," Marcie said. If she expressed her outrage over Pearl laboring without compensation, it wouldn't do any good.

"Well," she said, "it seems to me that instead of reading and listening to music, Missy could give you a hand. I'll talk to her about it over lunch— I mean, dinner."

"Missy, she'll come down to eat, but it ain't likely she'll stay down. Soon's she knows you come to take Dr. George's place, Missy, she'll hi-tail it back upstairs."

Taken aback, Marcie said, "Why would she do that? She doesn't know anything about me."

"Missy, she ain't one for talkin'. Mostly keeps to herself. She'll be a-scared you'll ask her a bunch of questions she don't wanna answer."

"But all I want is for us to get to know each other. Will you please tell her that for me?"

"Won't do no good. Missy, she liked Doctor George alright, she just didn't like talkin' to him."

Marcie knew it was futile to ask, but she asked anyway. "Then why is she here?"

"Don't rightly know," Pearl said. "A taxi cab dropped her off one day. Missy, she never did say where she come from or what she were doing here. Like I said, she ain't one for talkin'."

"But she talks to you."

"Yessum. Missy, she talks but she don't say much."

Swell, Marcie thought. She had a furious dwarf in one room, a resident doing exactly as she pleased in another and two girls who had run away before she could lay eyes on them. So much for establishing rapport.

"Where do you keep your cigarettes and ashtray?" Marcie asked.

Pearl's head jerked up, squinty eyes brightening. "You reckon it's alright if I smoke?"

Marcie laughed. "Sure. I'm the new boss, aren't I?"

The look on Pearl's face expressed her doubts.

CHAPTER 6

"I come here on the fourth day of October last," Pearl said in answer to Marcie's question. They were sitting across from each other in a section of the basement where the residents could smoke.

The so-called recreation room smelled like a blend of stale cigarettes, mold, Pearl's pine spray, and cheap furnishings. It looked as though someone had cruised the streets in search of furniture people had set out for the dump truck. An odd chair here and there, a stained couch, two tarnished brass lamps with dented shades, an old console TV, two end tables with chipped veneers, a coffee table pock-marked with cigarette burns, and a wobbly card table with four metal folding chairs, two of which were currently occupied because neither woman wanted to sit on the couch. Despite all that, if a resident so desired, she could smoke and watch TV.

Pearl went on. "I remember the day 'cause I'd turned sixty-six an' was durn lucky to be alive. Shoulda died in that there hospital. No thanks to Junior." She pulled a tissue from her apron pocket, held it to her mouth and spat.

"Is Junior your son?"

"Junior, I done give birth to him, but he was his Pa's boy. Both of 'em meaner'n crooked snakes." She spat again.

"Do they live around here?"

"Sam, he done passed 'bout a year ago. I reckon Junior's still out to the house. If he ain't burnt it down yet."

"You said you were in the hospital and almost died. What were you being treated for?"

"Don't rightly know. Doc, he said my organs was real sick. Said my lungs was the sickest. They put me on this breathing machine. Had tubes running every which away. Somebody always waking me up of a night to take this or do that. T'was all on account of Junior."

As a mother in conflict with her son, Marcie wondered what Junior had done to put his mother in the hospital. Back when her son, Davy, lived at home she'd had visions of being carted off in a straightjacket.

Pearl butted her half-finished cigarette and stuck it back in a pack of generic smokes. She began her story in that familiar wheezy voice that suggested emphysema. "Sam, he had to have his whiskey. Made him mean not to have it an' made him meaner when he did. Me? I never touched a drop in all my born days. Preacher, he said it was the blood of Satan an' I believe it. Couldn't abide the stink. Got sick as a dog every time Sam come near me." She fished another tissue out of her pocket and blew her nose as if to rid it of the lingering odor.

"It kilt Sam, the whiskey did. An' the night of the burial I learnt what it's like. Oh it's treacherous alright. Me an' Junior, we come back to the house from the graveyard. Right off he fixes hisself a glass of whiskey. I asked him would he bring me a Coca Cola an' he does. I thought it tasted right peculiar but I don't say nothin'. It don't do to rile Junior. "I drunk up all my Coke and he brung me another. Pret'soon I got to feeling all warm and tingly inside. Junior, he starts to hootin' an' slappin' his knee an' I fell into laughin' with him. Preacher woulda croaked. Downright blasphemous is what it was. But the durndest thing happened. That night I slept like a bear in winter. Soundest night I ever did have."

"I take it Junior doctored your Coke with whiskey."

"That's what he did alright. Junior, he did it again and again. Preacher, he come to call one day. I was down sick in the bed an' couldn't get up. He carried me to the hospital. I thought I was a goner. Preacher, he kept prayin' over me an' pret'soon I got to feeling better. Doctor George, he come to the hospital to see me. He told me 'bout this place. Said I shouldn't go home to Junior. Said sure's the world is round; I'd end up back in the hospital or dead. Fore I knowed what was happening he'd done brung me down here."

47

Marcie reached across the table and laid a hand on Pearl's forearm. "I'm awfully sorry about what happened to you, Pearl, but I'm very glad you're here."

Pearl dipped her head down, her chin quivering. When she looked up, her eyes were moist. "I 'spect we best get some meat on your bones," she said. "I'm fixin' to make a pot of chicken an' dumplin's. I 'spect you to eat seconds at dinner time an' I'll give you some to take home."

"I'd love to," said Marcie, getting to her feet. "Well, I'd better get to work before Sarah catches me down here."

"Yessum. I gotta finish this here laundry and get my stew meat to brownin'."

Marcie looked at her. "Stew meat? I thought you were fixing chicken and dumplings."

"Miss Deb, she don't like dumplin's. Says they're fattenin'. I'm fixin' her a plate of stew."

"Well, I'd say Miss Deb is mighty picky." And demanding and lazy and ornery. Marcie thanked Pearl for sharing her story and they parted ways. Pearl back to her laundry, Marcie heading for the stairs.

No sooner had she reached the bottom step than a sense of unease settled over her. It was the same kind of apprehension she'd felt earlier when she first stood in the foyer listening to the eerie silence. Just as she'd known something was wrong then, she knew it now, but then as now she couldn't pinpoint exactly what.

Something about the stairs had brought it on. She stood pondering. Instinct told her to look under the open staircase. She found a spot that, with the aid of a flashlight, would show the entire area, but she didn't happen to have a flashlight, and the single bulb hanging over the laundry room didn't throw enough light to reach this far. Bending at the waist, she set her hands on her knees and peered into the stairwell. As far as she could tell, the space appeared to be empty. She crept forward, her eyes adjusting to the darkness as she went. Stacked up against the back of the stairs close to the far wall she could plainly see an assortment of luggage.

Backing out of the stairwell and straightening up, she called to Pearl, "Can you come here for a minute?"

"Yessum," Pearl said, shuffling over in a pair of pink-flowered scuffs that almost matched her apron. Marcie gestured toward the luggage. "Do you know anything about this?"

"Yessum. Drug 'em down here myself. It's a durn shame. One'a these days this cellar's gonna come a flood an' all them pretty clothes'll be ruint."

"Then why are they here? Where did they come from?"

"The ones that run off."

"What did you say?"

"They come from—"

Marcie interrupted. "Sorry, Pearl. I heard you. It's just such a shock. How many women are we talking about?"

Pearl scratched a spot behind one ear. "Lemme see." She started a count on her fingers. "Jenny, Louise, Darlene, Carol, Margaret, an' Tiffany and Sheila. How many's that?"

"Seven," Marcie said, her voice registering disbelief. "Seven women left this house without permission?"

"Yessum."

Marcie shook her head. "I can't believe that many women would just up and leave their belongings behind."

"Jenny, Louise and Carol, they took their things, but the others didn't."

"That leaves four women who took off without their luggage. It doesn't make any sense. Why wouldn't they take their things?"

"I done studied on that," Pearl said. "Maybe they wasn't fixin' to stay gone an' changed their minds."

Marcie mulled it over. "That's possible, I guess." She tried to imagine why four women would leave their possessions behind. "Have any of them come back to claim her things?"

Pearl flung a scrawny arm towards the baggage. "Nothin's missin'."

Marcie wondered what would happen if one of the women did come back for her things. Would Deborah forbid her to enter? Marcie wouldn't put it past her.

"Did you unlock the door this morning?"

"Yessum. I always unlock it when I come down of a morning in case I'm out of pocket."

"Do you answer the phone?" She'd noticed a wall-phone in the kitchen.

"No'um. Miss Deb, she's got a telephone in her room. Said for me not to pay no mind if the phone was a ringing."

"So you really don't know if any of the women called or came by?"

"No'um."

"Can you tell me anything about them? Why they left? Where they were going?"

"No'um. I don't mess in people's business. 'Sides, I got too much work to do. Come nighttime, I'm dead to the world. If a freight train was a'comin' it'd run right over me."

"But you'd know if, like Sheila and Tiffany, any of the other women left together."

The furrows in Pearl's brow deepened. "Louise and Carol, they went off together. Them two was mighty close. Always gigglin' and talkin'. Beat all I ever seen." Her voice turned plaintive. "Can I go back to work now?"

"Just one more thing," Marcie said. "When you packed the women's things, did you find any personal papers? Like diaries? Journals? Letters? Address books? Anything that might give us a clue as to where they might have gone?"

"Miss Deb, she's the onliest one knows about that. She done the packin'. I just hauled them bags down here like she told me to."

"Huh," said Marcie, biting her tongue. Deborah certainly didn't have any trouble pawing through the women's things, yet she ordered Pearl, as overworked, weary, and stooped as she was, to lug them down two flights of stairs when one of the younger residents, like Missy, could do the job. Maybe Deborah feared Missy would ask questions, where Pearl would not. That suggested Deborah had something to hide.

Even though she knew Pearl wanted nothing more than to get back to her laundry, Marcie said, "Besides the women who ran away, how many other residents have we had?"

"Nary a one."

No wonder Sarah had been worried about the vacancy rate. "Well, I'll find out more when I look at the women's charts." She paused, then added, "Sorry I took so much of your time, Pearl. Thanks a lot for your help."

"Yessum," Pearl said, turning back to her tasks. "Dinner'll be ready at noon."

Marcie started climbing the stairs. "I'm looking forward to it," she said.

Emerging as if from a dark tunnel into the well-lit kitchen, Marcie looked out the bay window. Though pasty gray clouds still choked the skies, the worst of the storm seemed to have passed. Thank goodness the low-lying areas would be spared a flood of muddy water, mostly her area. Charley would have a barking fit if water started to invade his territory and she wasn't there to do something about it, as if she could.

Marcie took a better look at the maple table and eight matching chairs that sat in front of the window. The set looked sturdy and comfortable. The chairs, sans plastic covers, wore thick padded seats with ties to keep them in place. If all went well, it wouldn't be long before the chairs would be filled to capacity.

She poured coffee gone cold out of her mug and refilled it with hot. Though curious about where the remaining hall doorways led an exploration would have to wait. Uppermost in her mind were the women's charts. That seven women left the program was bad enough, but that four of them had left their belongings behind … well, it scared her to think what might have happened to them.

Careful not to spill her coffee, Marcie hurried through the dining and living room. Now that the dark clouds had lifted and she could see where she was going, the plastic looked even tackier. The odor remained the same. Nothing would change until she tore off the plastic covers and raised the Palladian windows. Too bad if Deborah didn't like it. She could either stay in her room or out in the greenhouse.

Pausing at the grandfather clock, Marcie set her coffee mug on the floor, opened his door, and ever-so-gently lifted his weights. Finally, she gave his pendulum a nudge. When it swayed back and forth in perfect rhythm, she relied on her watch to set his hands to the correct hour. Already tired, she couldn't believe it was only nine- oh-five, but just hearing the steady beat of

Grandpa's heart perked her up. She closed his doors, gave a satisfied smile, and said, "Now you can show your stuff." Retrieving her mug, she continued down the hall, passing Deborah's room without pausing. The less Marcie saw of her the better. So she'd had a lousy childhood, so she was too short to function like a full-grown person, and so she had allergies. That was no excuse for treating Pearl like her personal servant.

As eager as Marcie was to get to the files, it was time to check in with Sarah. It took looking in the phone book to find the number for the brickyard. That was another question she'd forgotten to ask.

Unlike George's receptionist, a pleasant female voice came over the line. Marcie introduced herself and asked to speak to Mrs. Thornton. The woman said, "Hi, Marcie. You may not remember me, but I met you when we were protesting the school's book ban. I'm Rebecca Hudson. I was the fat one."

Though Marcie didn't recall the name, she was delighted to have a fellow protester working next door. "And I was the skinny one," she said. "Pearl says she's going to put some meat on my bones."

"That sounds like Pearl. We are so lucky to have her over there. And lucky to have you, too."

"Thanks, Rebecca, I needed that. Have you joined any protests lately?"

"Oh, I'm always protesting something. Here, it's against the hours I work. I hate to tell you this, Marcie, but Mrs. T. is a slave driver. You don't know how fortunate you are to be over there and out of sight. Speaking of out, Mrs. T's making her usual rounds, but I'll see that she calls you. Don't expect it to be anytime soon. She's apt to get tied up somewhere."

"That's okay. I've got plenty to do."

"I suppose it's too soon to ask how things are going," Rebecca said.

Marcie laughed and said, "Ask me again next week."

"I'll do that. All I can say for now is good luck."

"Thanks. I'll talk to you later."

They said their goodbyes and Marcie hung up, comforted by hearing a friendly voice. Now it was time to get down to business. She crossed to the five-drawer file cabinet and started at the top. The forms that made up the charts were neatly stacked in alphabetical order, but blank forms wouldn't tell her what she needed to know. The second drawer revealed a series of familiar green folders with attached name tabs, the kind that should have held the women's charts, but both the folders and the name tabs were empty. She opened the third drawer. It contained catalogs offering office equipment and other paraphernalia. The two bottom drawers held reams of computer paper and stacks of yellow legal pads. Thinking she must have missed something, she opened the top drawer and started over. Again, she came up empty handed. She leaned against the cabinet and tried to think. Record keeping at New Start was of primary importance. Every form had to be filled out and daily progress notes had to be charted at the end of each shift. If all was in order, any counselor could pick up any chart and know what needed to be known about that particular client. The same as a doctor knows about his patient. To make certain none of the staff got sloppy, officials from the Department of Mental Health in Montgomery paid surprise visits to check the records. If so much as one chart wasn't up to date, the clinic would get a black mark on its evaluation, which could result in a loss of funding. As it turned out, the funds weren't cut off because of New Start's record-keeping, but because of a change in political parties and ideology. Even though Sarah didn't rely on federal or state funding, George was a stickler for keeping meticulous records. Yet none of the file drawers showed any signs of ever being used for that purpose. Which meant he must have stored the charts elsewhere. Why, she couldn't imagine. Unless ... unless they were kept under lock and key to prevent Deborah from snooping through them. She crossed to the closet and opened the door, expecting to find a safe and a few articles of clothing that George forgot to take with him. Except for empty hangers, she found nothing. No safe and not so much as a jacket, a sports cap, or an umbrella. Strange, she thought. George had a habit of leaving things behind. Keys, reading glasses, sweaters ... Maybe he'd collected his things the last time he was here. Surely he hadn't taken the charts with him. Had he? She went back to the desk and picked up the phone. Whether he was busy or not, George had promised to take her call in case of an emergency. He may not think this qualified but she did.

His receptionist answered before the end of the first ring.

"Hi, Diane, it's Marcie. Did George tell you to put me through in case of an emergency?"

"As a matter of fact he did, Mrs. Parker."

Here we go again. Why couldn't Diane be half as friendly as Rebecca? "Well, I'm having one now, so please ring him for me."

"What is the nature of the emergency, Mrs. Parker?"

Whose idea was this? Diane's or George's? "It concerns the residents of Port Victor, which means it's confidential. Now, please let me speak to him. It's very important."

"I'm sorry, Mrs. Parker, but there's a big difference between an emergency and matters of importance."

Marcie heaved a sigh. "What is your problem, Diane? What did I ever do to you? I would really like to know."

The line remained silent for a long moment. Then, in a frosty tone, Diane said, "I don't know what you're talking about, Mrs. Parker. I'm just doing my job."

"Do it then. Get him on the phone."

"I can't. Dr. Rutledge is attending a symposium in Tuscaloosa."

"Why didn't you tell me that in the first place?" Marcie said. "Never mind, you were just doing your job. So I'll let you get back to it." With that, she hung up, mentally cursing both Diane and George.

Her anger dissolved when a glorious sound reached her ears, that of the grandfather clock playing the Westminster chimes. She hurried into the hall, the music flowing over her. The acoustics were perfect.

The echo resounded like the brass section of a full orchestra. She could imagine it carrying up and down both sets of stairs, and from there, all the way to the heart of town. She pictured awestruck citizens stopping in their tracks and turning their heads this way and that to see where the sound was coming from. All too soon, the symphony ended.

Without thinking, Marcie applauded Grandpa's performance and shouted, "Bravo!" The word flew up and down the hall, finally landing outside Deborah's door. Expecting the woman to come charging into the hall. Marcie tried to brace herself. If his chimes had disturbed her, Deborah would find a way to silence him, for good. Much to Marcie's surprise, the door remained closed and no shouts or threats came from within. Maybe Deborah had gone to the greenhouse. Or maybe she had actually enjoyed the chimes. Unable to reach the clock's hands, maybe Deborah had been waiting for someone else to do it. Marcie returned to the office to take up where she'd left off, searching every nook and cranny for the charts.

———

The only thing worse than killing time was wasting time. Instead of carrying the emptied cartons back to the car, Marcie stacked them on the floor of the closet. Who knew? The way things were going she may be packing up and heading home before the week was over. Moving to stand behind the desk, she surveyed her handiwork. When she'd been trying to beat the storm while bringing in the boxes, she could've kicked herself for packing so much stuff, stuff that was bound to overflow the room, but now that she'd placed the framed photographs, special mementos, books and certificates, they hardly made a dent in the available space. The potted plants, a sweet-smelling hyacinth with two purple blossoms and a Calla with pink flowers, were too large for the windowsill and too lost on the floor, so she set them on top of the file cabinet.

If only she had found the charts. As she'd arranged and rearranged the items on the book shelves, she knocked on the backboards, listening for the hollow sounds of a secret compartment. She came up with nothing. Frustrated, she spoke out loud. "What did you do with the charts, George?"

She jumped inside her skin when a rap sounded on the doorjamb. Expecting to see Sarah or an angry Deborah, it surprised her when a pair of wary eyes slowly came into view.

"Ma'am?" Pearl said. "I heared you talkin' to somebody but ain't nobody here."

"Oh, I talk to myself all the time. At home, I talk to my dog and the clocks. But here ..." She made a helpless gesture with her hands. "I've looked everywhere for the women's charts. They're not in the file cabinet, they're not in the closet, and they're not in the desk drawers."

Pearl stepped just inside the room. "Far as I recollect, Doctor George, he kept 'em in that there cabinet." She nodded towards the file cabinet. "You reckon he took 'em home with him?"

"It's unlikely, but possible. It's also possible he gave them to Sarah." She glanced at the phone. "I left a message for her to call me. If she doesn't have them, we'll just have to wait till George gets back." Not knowing what else to say, she lapsed into silence.

"What I come for," Pearl said, "Do you like sweet milk, buttermilk, or iced tea with your dinner?"

"Unsweetened iced tea, please." She glanced up at the schoolhouse clock and then at her watch. "Did you hear the chimes?"

"Yessum They sound right nice. Don't know how Miss Deb'll take to 'em. Miss Deb, she don't like a lot of ruckus." She paused, then said, "And I see you done fixed up the room." Her eyes roamed over the bookshelves, the plants, and the desk, then back to the plants. "Looks mighty nice. Them's pretty flowers, I never seen such as them."

"Thanks. If I'd had more room in my car, I would've brought two more."

"Miss Deb, she'll pitch a sneezing fit when she sees 'em."

"But she waters her uncle's flowers every day," Marcie said. "Besides, this is my office and she has no business being in here. I'll lock the door when I leave."

Pearl's voice turned whiny. "Then how we gonna give 'em medicine when they need it?"

Marcie sat down in the leather chair. She held her head in her hands, closed her eyes and slowly shook her head from side to side. Was there no end to the complications caused by Deborah?

Pearl stood kneading the hem of her apron with gnarled hands. "Miss Deb, she don't never come to my room. I got two windows an' I'd be proud to keep your plants up there."

Marcie released her head and looked up. Pearl's body language showed how much she wanted the plants. What with Sam and Junior getting mean drunk all the time, she probably never had the simple luxury of growing flowers. She pushed up from her chair. "What a wonderful idea. I would be honored to have you keep the plants. I've got plenty more where they came from."

She moved to the closet and brought out one of the empty cardboard cartons. "We can take them up right now."

"No'um. I'll take 'em up when I go." She turned to leave. Sensing that Pearl did not want the sanctity of her room invaded, as was often the case in residential facilities, Marcie didn't insist. "Fine, but if you need any help, just holler."

"I gotta go stir the stew."

"Will Deborah be eating with us?" Marcie asked.

Pearl paused at the threshold. "No'um. Miss Deb, she likes to eat in her room so's she can watch the TV." She took a step and then looked back. "You wanna see Missy, you best get there a few minutes early. One look at you, Missy, she's likely to turn tail and run."

"Not if I can help it," Marcie said. She'd confronted enough brick walls for one day.

CHAPTER 7

Grandpas' chimes sounded in all their glory. Marcie glanced at her watch. Eleven–thirty on the dot. Perfect timing, she thought. After spending what seemed like hours on the phone contacting every referral agency in the state, she was more than ready for a change of scenery.

Standing, she shoved the chair out of the way with the backs of her knees, then raised her arms high above her head and stretched as far up as she could go. Holding that position, she leaned to the left, to the right, then started the routine all over again. She could hear her muscles and tendons creaking and popping. Even her ears popped. Closing the office door behind her, she headed to the kitchen. It was still quiet in Deborah's room. Maybe she'd gone out to the greenhouse to catch cave crickets with Ginger.

Because the sun had finally shown its face, the kitchen was awash with golden light. It streamed across the yellow and white checkered tablecloth, the yellow and white linoleum floor, and even found its way to the spot where Pearl was standing at the stove.

"Hi," she said to Pearl, who was stirring something in a large pot. A twin pot sat on another burner. No telling how long Pearl had been stirring one or the other so they wouldn't scorch.

Pearl dropped her long wooden spoon, clutched her chest, and gasped. "Lawd'a'mercy, child, you near'bout scared me to death."

"I'm so sorry," Marcie said, reaching out to her. "Next time I'll knock, okay?"

"You best do that," Pearl said and retrieved her spoon.

"Yum," Marcie said. The commingling of beef, chicken, and gravies made her mouth water. "I'm glad we're having chicken and dumplings."

"You'll eat stew come Thursday," Pearl said, continuing to stir. "Miss Deb, she eats like a sparrow. What's left'll go into the freezer. I'm us'ta cookin' for men what eats one meal a day and drinks the other two."

"I do the same thing," Marcie said. "I make enough spaghetti sauce for four, eat one portion, then divide and freeze the rest."

Pearl set her spoon in a dish and squinted at her. "You live alone?"

Marcie forced a smile. "Well, I have my dog and my clocks."

"Lady as nice and pretty as you?"

"Thanks, Pearl. But yes, I live alone. I was married for nineteen years and then my husband decided he wasn't cut out to be a family man."

"If that don't beat all," Pearl said, "They's no accountin' for menfolks. Ask me, they's all crazier'n a coot." She went back to her stirring.

Yes, Marcie said to herself. It did beat all, and every time she thought about it she checked her body for bruises. The trick was not to think about it.

She looked at the three doors she had yet to explore. Her trusty Timex showed enough time for her to have a quick look. She felt like a contestant on a game show as she decided which door to open first. Choosing the one at the end of the hall, her eyes widened in surprise and delight as she gazed about a large sunroom. Bright and airy, it had the atmosphere of a garden with its jalousie windows, hanging ferns, and potted palm trees. Even though the plants were made of silk, they looked like the real thing. Natural rattan chairs covered in bright shades of green, yellow, and red were arranged in a central horseshoe for meetings. Other pieces were clustered around glass–topped tables. Double French doors led to the dreary living room. What a contrast! Whom could she thank for this wonderful room? It was the perfect place to hold group therapy sessions. Aside from that, the women could use it to play cards or board games. They couldn't smoke up here, but it beat sitting in the dank cellar.

Door number one had been a pleasant surprise. She peeked behind door number two and found a small bathroom. Handy, she thought. Door number three led to a storage room large enough to hold two upright freezers, a second refrigerator, four tall metal shelves with paper products and canned goods, and a broom closet. Yet another door inside the room led to the garage, which housed a new silver van. The question remained: Who drove it? She entered the kitchen. Although it was still a few minutes before noon, Missy was sitting at the table drinking from a glass of milk.

"Hello," Marcie said, her voice as cheerful as she felt.

Startled, the girl spit out a mouthful of milk and immediately began coughing. Hunched over the table, milk dribbling down her chin, she gasped for breath. Harsh gasping sounds came from deep in her chest. She wasn't coughing, she was choking.

Marcie rushed to her side and started patting her on the back. The girl tried to catch enough air to fill her lungs. Just then Grandpa started playing his warm-up before striking his gong twelve times. She looked at Pearl, who stood rooted to her spot, a distressed look on her face. "Can you bring us some paper towels?"

"Yessum," Pearl said. She left her stove unattended and moved towards the sink. Grandpa's music resounded through the house.

The wheezing decreased in severity, but Missy still fought for every breath. To relax her, Marcie began a gentle massage of the girl's shoulders. She could feel the tension easing as she used her fingers on the tight spots.

A fluttering movement to her right caused her to look that way.

Deborah, eyes flashing fire, stood in the doorway. Stabbing a tiny finger at Marcie, she shouted, "YOU! I told you we like peace and quiet around here!"

Continuing to probe Missy's knots, Marcie said, "I think we've been exceptionally quiet considering we have a serious situation here. Missy's had a bad choking spell."

"I don't give a fig about your situation!" Deborah yelled. "I want you to stop that infernal clock!"

"Why?" Marcie asked.

Deborah set her hands on her hips. "Because it's hammering away right outside my door. I can't even hear the noon news."

Marcie shrugged, "Ah, well, most of it is bad news anyhow. Besides, the chimes are almost ready to stop."

Missy's coughing fit seemed to have subsided. Not that the housemother gave a damn. Marcie leaned down and asked the girl if she was okay. Missy gave a quick nod and tried to blot up the spilt milk with a paper napkin.

"Pearl? Are you coming?" Marcie asked.

"Yessum." Pearl had a handful of cleaning rags, but she didn't move a muscle. Marcie figured she was afraid to be caught in the crossfire. Who could blame her?

The chimes struck their last note, leaving an echo floating on air. Marcie looked at Deborah. "See? I told you they'd stop."

Deborah set her little hands on her little hips and said, "If you don't stop that clock, I will." She whirled around and disappeared into the gloom.

"Mercy," said Pearl, "I done told you Miss Deb, she don't take to noise."

"Miss Deb," Marcie muttered, "she don't take to much of anything." No plants, no open windows, no touching, no chimes, no noise. Marcie was more convinced than ever that Deborah had run the women off. She'd not only run them off, she'd denied them the right to claim their things. Thus, the luggage in the basement. Which made Marcie more determined than ever to find the women's charts.

Lord, what a morning. Her emotions had seesawed from fear to frustration and from happy to sad. How could she and the women exist in a tomb? By going from the office to the kitchen and from there to the sunroom. And, despite how shabby it was, the so–called recreation room. She wondered what their bedrooms looked like. That exploration could come later.

By the time she deposited the milky rags in the sink; Missy had stood up and was making for the door.

"Aw, come on, Missy," she said. The girl hesitated. "I've been cussed out twice already and I don't need you going on a hunger strike just because you don't want to eat with me. Especially when Pearl made chicken and dumplings just for you."

Missy gave her a sideways look.

"Please sit down. We can talk about the weather or not talk at all."

"Y'all ready to eat?" Pearl asked.

"Yes, we are," said Marcie with her eyes on Missy.

After Pearl served the meal, which included a basket of corn bread, she went back to her stove and started stirring again.

"Aren't you going to join us?" Marcie asked?

"No'um, I done eat. Miss Deb, she'll be wantin' her tray."

Marcie said nothing. Pearl seemed to be set in her ways and no amount of coaxing was going to change her. She took up a mouthful of chicken and dumplings. Except for her aunt's, Pearl's was the best. "My compliments to the cook," she said over her shoulder to Pearl.

Busy with fixing Deborah's tray, Pearl didn't appear to hear her.

Without saying a word, Missy took her seat. She kept her lips together and her eyes averted.

For the first time, Marcie got a good look at her. She had thick, shoulder-length auburn hair, small brown eyes, pug nose, and thin lips. Acne scars marred her olive complexion. A bit on the chubby side, she was about five-four. Dressed in a denim jumper over a white blouse with a Peter Pan collar she looked like your average girl next door. Marcie's job was to find out why she didn't want to talk about herself. That could prove difficult at best.

A strained silence hovered over the table as the two females ate their meal. After sopping up the last of the stock with a piece of cornbread, Marcie was about to burst, both because she had eaten too much and not talked enough.

She looked across the table and said, "I'm sorry I frightened you. I did the same thing to Pearl. It'll take time, but hopefully you'll get used to having me around."

Without so much as a nod, Missy scooted her chair back and stood up. This time she made it all the way through the door.

What was it Pearl said? "Missy, she don't talk much." As far as Marcie was concerned, Missy, she don't talk at all.

On her way back to the office, she silenced the clock by holding his pendulum still. Gently closing his door, she looked up at his handsome face. "I'm sorry, Big Boy," she said. "You sounded great while it lasted." She gave his side a pat, turned and headed down the hall.

Literally twiddling her thumbs, Marcie sat at her desk waiting for something to happen. Just then the phone rang. Snatching it up, she expected to hear Sarah's voice. She gave what was to become her standard greeting: "Port Victor, Marcie speaking."

"Rutledge, here."

She sank back in her chair. "Oh, it's you. Did Diane give you my message?"

"She did, and I have less than a minute before the next meeting."

"I can't believe she actually gave you my message."

"Marcie," George said in a crisp tone. "Get on with it."

"*It* is about the women's charts. Where did you keep them?"

"In the file cabinet. Top drawer."

"They're not there. They're not anywhere. Not in the cabinet, the desk, the medicine chest, the closet, nowhere."

"Hmm," he said. "That is not good. Have you asked Sarah?"

"I'm waiting for a call–back. Oh, and I have more bad news. Sheila and Tiffany took off Saturday night."

"That's too bad," he said.

"I hate that I never got to meet them. If only they'd waited. By the way, what's your take on the luggage in the basement?"

"What luggage?"

She started to explain, but he cut her off.

"There goes the warning bell," he said. "Gotta go." She heard a click on the line, then silence. She felt like going out in the hall and screaming her lungs out. Instead, she decided to go outside and take a look around.

She found Pearl in the storage room. Rapping on the doorjamb, she said, "It's me, Pearl."

"Yessum," Pearl turned to face her.

"Still working, I see. When are you going to take a break?"

"I'm fixin' to take them flowers up to my room."

"Good," Marcie said. "I'm going outside to get a breath of fresh air."

"Yessum," Pearl said. "I done fixed you a plate to take home for supper."

"Thank you, Pearl. I really appreciate it." She left Pearl to fetch the plants while she went out the back door located in the dining room, a wall away from the kitchen. She inhaled the kind of clean air that comes after a storm. Puffy white clouds drifted lazily through a robin's egg blue sky. The tension she's felt in the house gradually melted away.

Because the grass was still wet from the storm, she picked her way to the foot of the fire escape, the very wrought iron stairway that the women had probably used to sneak out of the house. The question was if they had tried to sneak back in, who stopped them?

In an effort to shake the images of women turned away with only the clothes they were wearing, she continued across the lawn, pausing at the side of the house where Deborah's suite was located. Instead of a window, a sliding glass door allowed Deborah to come and go without notice. A heavy drape covered half the door; the other half had tinted glass. No one could see inside but Deborah could see out. Marcie turned next to the greenhouse. She'd love to go inside and take a look around but was afraid Deborah would lash out at her again. How a dwarf could wield such power boggled the mind.

Passing the greenhouse, she moved to the edge of the lot that bordered the brickyard. From her vantage point, she could see a rather large red brick building that faced the road. Guessing it contained the showroom and offices, she was tempted to go say hello to Rebecca, the receptionist and fellow pro-tester, but thought better of it when she remembered Sarah had fired Henry for, among other things, fooling around on the job.

Larger buildings made of metal looked like airplane hangars. She watched a man in a yellow hardhat walk from one of the hangers to the brick building. He stood out in front, as if waiting for someone. Seconds later, a car pulled up. The man went around to the driver's side and opened the door. A woman got out. The man shut the car door and accompanied the woman inside. The scene made Marcie think that the man was Roger and the woman Sarah.

Rather than return to the house and wait for Sarah's call, Marcie decided to talk to her in person.

Sidestepping around the puddles left from the rain, she didn't notice the man standing outside the brick building until she almost bumped into him.

"Oops," she said, drawing herself up short when her eyes lit on a pair of men's work boots. She looked up at a tall, good–looking man about her age. He wore a yellow hardhat and carried a clipboard.

"Hello," he said in the voice she'd heard over the speaker phone. "Can I help you?"

Flustered, Marcie said, "Un, yes… I'm looking for Mrs. Thornton's office."

The man gestured behind him. "It's the first door on your right."

She started to pass, then stopped. "Do you know if she's busy? I meant to wait for her to call me but it's turned out to be such a pleasant day I thought, oh heck, I'll just walk on over. Doesn't the air smell wonderful?" She knew she was talking too much, but the man made her nervous. Worse, she sensed he knew it, for he was grinning with obvious amusement.

"Sarah's always busy," he said. "The woman's a slave driver. And yeah, now that you mention it, the air does smell good."

"Rebecca said the same thing. About Sarah being a slave driver."

His brow went up. "You know Rebecca?"

"Yes," she said. "She's such a sweet person."

"That she is. Hey, I saw you walking over from next door. You must be the new hire Sarah was talking about."

"I'm Marcie Parker, and this is my first day on the job. You probably know George. George Rutledge? He was Port Victor's director on a part–time basis. To make a long story short, he couldn't get down here often enough so Mrs. Thornton hired me. I could never take George's place but I'm going to do my best." She should have said yes and let it go at that.

"I'm sure you will," the man said. He proffered a hand for shaking.

"Glad to meet you, Marcie Parker. I'm Roger McCandliss, Sarah's yard manager."

His eyes matched the color of his work shirt and the hair that peeped out from under the hardhat was a rich chestnut brown. He didn't wear a wedding band, but then a lot of men didn't— her ex for one. And why did it matter whether Roger was married or not. Having a man in her life would push her right over the edge.

"Hi, Roger," she said. After he released her hand, it still tingled. "Is it okay if I go on in?"

"You'd better knock first."

"No, I meant is it okay if I go inside the building? I would never walk in on Mrs. Thornton, or anyone else for that matter." More nervous than ever, she made a move to pass him. She'd talked too much and lingered too long. If Sarah found her chatting ...well, she had enough trouble as it was.

"Ever been to a brickyard?" Roger asked, cocking his head to one side.

Did he flirt like this with every woman he met? Marcie wondered. She just had to be careful not to flirt back. "No, I can't say that I have."

"If you like, I'd be glad to show you around. It'd be worth your while. This is a fascinating place."

Fascinating? A brickyard? "I'm sure it is, but I really need to speak to Mrs. Thornton."

"Of course this is a small brickyard compared to some," he said. "We only keep an inventory of seven million. If Victor hadn't built that house next door, we could've expanded. Can't complain, though. We're still the only yard around."

"Well," she said, "I'm always happy to meet a man who likes his job, but I really need—"

"To speak to Sarah," he said, his clear blue eyes crinkling at the corners. "Just remember, anytime you want a tour I'll fix you up with a hardhat and off we'll go."

"Thanks. It sounds ... interesting."

He opened the door for her and stepped aside. "Oh, it is," he said, with that amused grin. "I guarantee it."

Marcie caught a whiff of workman's sweat as she passed him. It wasn't rank, more like a mixture of sweet and sour, a not altogether unpleasant odor.

The first door on the right was open. Sarah was talking on the phone. Her desk held piles of paper, legal pads, ledgers, folders. Marcie regretted not waiting for her call. Not knowing what else to do and still flustered by her encounter with Roger McCandliss, she stood in the doorway until Sarah noticed her, waved her in and motioned for her to sit down.

The room was so cluttered it was hard to tell what was what. One of the two visitors' chairs held a pile of miniature bricks, the other a stack of catalogs. Marcie set the catalogs on the floor and sat, certain that dust would cling to the back of her skirt. The windows along the wall looked as though they'd been painted shut, and the air in the room smelled as stale and musty as that of Port Victor's formal rooms. Marcie would go mad if she had to work under such conditions.

Sarah finally hung up, jotted a note on a memo pad, and dropped her pen on the desk. When she looked up, Marcie could see the weariness etched in her face. "Hello, dear," Sarah said. "How are you getting along?"

"Fine, thank you," Marcie said, a lie if ever there was one. "I just have a few questions. Things we didn't cover last Friday."

Sarah's brow knitted together in a frown. "I hope you haven't come calling with a problem."

It took a moment for Marcie to sort through her list: The women's charts, the luggage in the basement, the disappearance of Sheila and Tiffany, the residents' routine ... She decided to ask an easy question first. "I noticed a van in the garage. Do you mind if I drive the residents to Vocational Rehabilitation or wherever they have to go?"

"Not at all. That's what it's for." She opened a desk drawer, rummaged around, and came up with a key ring with four keys attached. She held them out one at a time and described their function. "The garage door opener is in the van's glove compartment. You may also use the van for running errands and shopping trips."

Marcie accepted the keys and sat back down. "Oh, but I'd really rather drive my car. A van is—"

"Nonsense," Sarah said. "Pardon me for saying so, but that car of yours looks like it's ready to fall apart."

Marcie had hoped she didn't notice. True, it had numerous dents in the frame and patches of rust here and there, but it was all she could afford. "I plan on getting a newer car as soon as I'm able."

"Fine," Sarah said. "I'll tell Herman to be on the lookout. He's been in the car business for years. He'll know exactly what you need."

"Oh, but I'm not quite ready. I'll have to save for it first."

"As long as you work for me," Sarah said, "you've got excellent credit. We can't have you showing up late for work because of car trouble. Herman will give you a good deal. I'll see to it."

"Well," Marcie said, a sinking feeling in the pit of her stomach. All she needed was another monthly bill. "I don't suppose it would hurt to see what Herman comes up with."

Sarah picked up her pen, jotted another note, then looked at Marcie and said, "If that's all, we both must get back to work."

Marcie swallowed. "There's one more thing. I can't find the charts George kept on the residents."

"That's no concern of mine," Sarah said, waving a hand as if at a pesky fly. "You'll have to ask George."

"I did. He said he kept them in the top drawer of the file cabinet, but they're nowhere to be found. I was wondering, do you think Deborah might know where they are?"

"What makes you think Deborah would know?"

"She's the only other person who has access to the file cabinet."

Sarah leaned forward. "Listen carefully, Marcie. Don't bother Deborah about old business. And don't waste another minute searching for old charts. You're starting fresh. Is that understood?"

"Yes, ma'am," Marcie said quietly. Her other questions died in her throat.

CHAPTER 8

Feeling like a child who'd been spanked, it was all Marcie could do to hold her head up as she walked out of Sarah's office. She pushed through the outside door and made her way to the corner of the building. Sagging back against the brick wall, she put a fist to her mouth and held it there. Despite her attempt to hold them back, tears of frustration kept slipping out of the corners of her eyes. She swiped them away with her fingers. Fortunately, no one was around to witness her loss of self–control.

A strong breeze blew the hair back from her face. It felt like a caress. That, and a few deep-breathing exercises, helped her grow calm enough to think straight. No more running to Sarah for answers. She, Marcie Parker, the Executive Director of Port Victor, would handle difficult situations as they arose. She was a professional, after all. If Sarah wanted to know what was going on, she could come see for herself.

That decided she started walking across the cement yard the way she had come. Even though Sarah had told her to start fresh, she could not forget about the women's charts or the luggage. Like it or not, she would have to confront Deborah about both issues.

Someone called, "Hey! Wait up!"

The voice belonged to Roger McCandliss. He'd exchanged the clipboard for a blue hardhat and was jogging towards her.

Panting for breath by the time he reached her, he managed to ask, "Ready for that tour?"

Marcie ran a hand over her windblown hair. "How long will it take?"

"About ten minutes."

Marcie's face shaded over with concern. What would Sarah say if she saw the two of them traipsing off together? Would that constitute a scandal? Would she—

Roger interrupted her train of thought once again. "Sarah gave you a hard time, didn't she?"

Marcie winced. "How can you tell?"

"Sarah gives everyone a hard time. She's a damn good businesswoman. If it wasn't for her, this place would've gone belly–up a while back."

"Because of Grace?" Marcie asked.

"Oh yeah. Nothing was too good for Grace. The way Grace died and then Victor never should've happened. Considering what Sarah's been through, she's done a hell of a job. But she can be as crabby as a bulldog with hemorrhoids. Just don't let it get to you."

Marcie laughed at the wisecrack about Sarah.

Roger set the hardhat on her head and said, "Let's go."

Interested in what he found so "fascinating," she gave in. As they walked toward a metal building near the rear of the lot, Roger pointed out the differences between the types of brick. At first Marcie listened to every word, but then her mind wandered back to the missing charts. If Deborah denied any knowledge of them, she had one hope left. That George would remember enough details from the intake interviews and the daily progress notes for her to make up a brief chart on each woman who had resided there. Pearl knew first names; maybe George could summon up surnames. Full names were important because a woman who has left one program often ended up in another. Marcie could call other halfway houses and, with any luck, match a woman with her luggage.

"Here we are," Roger said, bringing her back to the tour.

They entered a huge hangar with a cement floor crisscrossed by a system of narrow tracks on which several carloads of bricks were traveling at very slow speeds. High overhead, air ducts large enough for a human to crawl through hung suspended from the ceiling. On an elevated platform a number of shirtless workers bent to the task of unloading bricks from the first car in line. Even though vents sent blasts of cool air, the workers' faces and bare chests glistened with sweat.

"This is where the bricks are fired," Roger said. He had to shout because of the clamor surrounding them.

"As in a kiln?" Marcie shouted back. She sniffed the air, expecting to smell smoke or at the very least a sooty odor. Oddly enough, the only scent she detected was that of Roger's sweet– and–sour mix.

"Yeah," he said, "but this kiln is not like any you've ever seen. This baby is seven-hundred and twenty-one feet long. Its interior temperatures reach up to two-thousand degrees."

A temperature of two-thousand degrees went well beyond Marcie's range of comprehension. Her oven only went up to five– hundred.

"Now for the best part, the kiln room," Roger said. "That's where the bricks start to rock 'n' roll." He started walking.

Marcie hung back. "No, un …. I'd better get back to work."

"You can't leave now!" He exclaimed. "This is the most fascinating part."

"Isn't there a rule against going into the kiln room? Didn't a worker by the name of Henry get fired because he went in there?"

"Henry was a goof–off. He snuck into the kiln room to drink a brown bag full of rotgut. That's why he got fired."

"But what if Sarah finds out that we've been goofing off?"

"Hey, I'm the yard manager. I'm taking a new employee on an official tour."

"That may be, but I was hired on a trial basis, and —"

He cupped her elbow with a firm hand and steered her across the series of tracks to solid footing. She could feel the temperature rise as they neared the kiln. Despite the heat, she shivered when the hairs at the back of her neck bristled.

Roger steered her along. Up ahead a glass and wood enclosure protruded from the wall of the kiln. A lone man bent over a desk.

"What's he doing in there?" Marcie asked.

"He's logging the heat readings. He's the kiln fireman and he's sitting in what's called the pyrometer house."

"Isn't he hot in there?"

71

"Nope. It's heavily insulated. Anyway, he spends more time out than in. As soon as he finishes logging the readings, he'll start checking the portholes again, all thirty-two of them. We have a fireman on duty around the clock. They all follow the same routine."

"Portholes? Like on a ship?"

"Not exactly. Here, I'll show you." He picked up what looked like an ordinary broom handle and used it to open a cast iron window in the wall of the kiln. "Bend over and take a look inside."

The roaring flames that filled Marcie's vision held her spellbound. It was like looking into the bowels of Hell. Frightening, repulsive, yet, yes, fascinating. Like the aftermath of a terrible accident. You see the gore, hear the screams, feel the heat—the sight makes your skin crawl and causes bile to rise in your throat, yet you can't look away.

"It takes ten tons of coal a day to keep that baby going," Roger said.

Marcie straightened. "It's incredible. Truly incredible." She stooped down again when Roger said, "Watch this." He pushed the broom handle into the opening. In the blink of an eye, it ceased to exist.

"Oh my," she said. She didn't have to look in a mirror to see that her face looked sunburned.

They continued past the pyrometer house and the last of the tracks. Roger kept spouting facts and figures: How many carloads of bricks went through the kiln every twenty–four hours, how long it took for the cars to travel from one end to the other, how many bricks were fired each week. Marcie didn't hear a word he said. She walked along in a daze, her head full of the burning Hell beyond the porthole.

Noticing the quiet, she looked around and found herself in a short hall enclosed on three sides. What's more, Roger was holding a steel door open and beckoning her to go through to the other side. "We're just in time," he said. "A load of bricks is ready to go."

Every instinct told Marcie to make a run for it. To get out this place and back to the safety of her office. Back to business. Compared to this, dealing with Deborah would be a joy ride.

"Watch your step," Roger said. "There's a drop."

How could she turn him down? He took such pride in the workings of the brickyard. She clutched the hand he offered and stepped inside a strange room. The door banged shut behind her. Both dismayed and startled, she flattened herself against the wall.

"What do you think?" Roger asked.

She couldn't speak. Her mouth had gone dry.

"About the kiln room," Roger said, watching her intently.

Standing on a platform about a yard wide and twelve feet long, overlooking a pair of tracks on which a carload of raw clay bricks traveled at a snail's pace, she licked her lips to work up enough saliva to answer him. "Well, it certainly is interesting."

"That it is," Roger said. "Now, keep your eyes on the opening to the kiln."

The kiln door reminded Marcie of a guillotine with a straight blade. The carload of bricks that crept towards it looked every bit like a funeral procession. The slowness of the action made her want to scream. The faster the action the sooner she could get out of there.

"Lean out so you can see inside the kiln," Roger said, demonstrating.

Still standing with her back and both palms pressed against the wall, Marcie said, "Un-un. Heights make me dizzy."

"It's only a four-foot drop."

"I don't care. I've seen enough."

"Here, I'll hold you so you can't fall." Before she could protest, he'd wormed his way behind her and was holding both her arms. With his feet planted on either side of hers, he took a step forward. Afraid she'd make both of them fall if she didn't follow his lead, she moved her feet along with his. When they reached the edge of the platform, he said, "Now you can see inside the kiln."

She glanced at the burning inferno, shut her eyes and turned her head the other way. Terrible images flashed through her mind. Like watching an old black-and-white movie with splotches of blood-red color. Except her characters and storyline were not make-believe— they were all too real.

"What's the matter?" Roger asked.

"I can't—"

"Sure you can," he said. "The bricks are getting close to the kiln now."

The images kept flashing. Half the town watching her mother go mad. She cried, "I've got to get out of here!" She tried to turn away, but Roger's body blocked hers.

"Hold on," Roger said. He pulled her back from the edge and turned her around so they were facing each another. "I didn't mean to scare you," he said. "I thought you'd like to see how bricks are made."

"I'm sorry," she said with downcast eyes. "Really. It's just that I … un … the fire reminded me of something I want to forget."

"Well then, we need to go." Roger turned to open the door. Now that she was free to leave, Marcie was filled with regret. If she had only been able to go along with him, Roger would still be holding her. She hadn't been held in a long time.

Expecting to go their separate ways once they were outside, Marcie was surprised when he said, "I'll walk you to the line."

"Do you think that's a good idea?" She looked over her shoulder. "What if Sarah sees us?"

"She won't see us unless she comes looking, and that's not likely to happen. If she wants me, she calls." He patted the cell phone holster on his belt.

"But Deborah might see us. I know she'd tell Sarah."

"Forget it. The mighty midget's watching her shows."

His confidence instilled her trust. That and the lingering warmth of his body next to hers.

"Well," she said, "if you're sure."

They strolled across the lot side by side. "Hey, don't let what I said about Sarah being a slave driver spook you."

"It's not what you said, it's what she said. That if I don't do everything she hired me to do, and that includes things out of the ordinary, she'll fire me."

"Don't worry about it. She threatens everyone that works for her."

Marcie changed the subject. He couldn't know how much the job meant to her. "Have you ever been inside the greenhouse?"

"Just while it was being built. What a joke. Victor didn't know a rose from a tulip but he just had to have a greenhouse. My guess is he built it as an excuse to stick even closer to Grace."

"He must have loved her very much."

"Grace could do no wrong. All she had to do was say 'Daddy' and he'd give her the moon. He was always wiring her money, bailing her and her drinking buddies out of jail. It drove Sarah nuts."

"I can imagine," Marcie said, but she couldn't imagine, not in a million years. Her own father had abandoned her the day of the fire, left her to deal with a crazy woman. That was thirty-one years ago. To this day, she had no idea if he was dead or alive.

"And he was nuts about the mighty midget," Roger said. "He carried her around all the time. Sarah told him she'd never learn to walk if he didn't put her down, but that didn't stop Victor. He had all of her furniture made to fit her. Same with her clothes. Ordered her shoes from some fancy place in Chicago. When I was just starting to work here, he would set her on the service counter and brush her hair, like a girl brushes her prized horse. It made me sick and it infuriated Sarah. It's a wonder she didn't pack up and leave."

Marcie mulled it over. It was hard enough to maintain a close and loving relationship with your husband without having him make a fool of himself over two other women. "But if she'd left, who would have taken care of the businesses?"

"Good point."

They stopped at the edge of the property line. One displayed square stacks of different colored bricks sitting on cement, the other a lush green lawn speckled with flowering shrubs and spreading shade trees.

Marcie looked up at him and asked, "Do you think Grace was on her way home when she broke into that Goodwill depository?"

Roger shrugged. "Probably. She would've been looking for a handout though. Grace hated Fleming's Hill with a passion. She'd have taken one look at the house Victor built for her and laughed in his face." He gazed off in the distance. "Funny how things work out." Marcie sensed he was thinking about more than Victor and Grace. He looked at her and said, "Well, I guess we'd better get back to work."

"Yes, I guess so."

Neither of them made a move to go.

"Thanks again for the tour," Marcie said. "I'm sorry I got scared in the kiln room. The fire and all … it was just too much for me to handle."

"No problem," he said, giving that crinkly–eyed grin. "Well, I'll see you later."

"Not at the brickyard, you won't. I'm not about to bother Sarah again."

"Can't say as I blame you. What about after work sometime? We could grab a bite to eat. That is, if you're free."

"If you mean, am I married or living with someone, I'm not. What about you?"

"Divorced going on three years now. Is your number listed in the book?"

"It's under M.E. Parker."

"What's the 'E' stand for?"

"Elizabeth."

"Marcie Elizabeth Parker," he said. "Nice."

"Actually, it's Marcella Elizabeth."

"Okay, Marcella Elizabeth. I'll give you a call sometime." He gave a little salute and headed back across the yard.

She watched him go, impressed by his easy, confident stride. He stopped and looked back. Spotting her, his face lit up. She smiled and waved, then set off with an extra spring in her step. If she wasn't careful, Roger McCandliss could get under her skin.

———

Marcie's steps slowed and her smile faded as she neared the greenhouse. The itchy feeling she always got when someone she could not see observed her struck with full force. Deborah was watching her, had probably been watching as she walked beside Roger.

She started to move on, then stopped to study the greenhouse. What appeared to be panels of hard plastic with white wooden frames rose from a white brick foundation. The panels went straight up and then curved inward, forming a peak. Some kind of shade material covered the lower panels. Trying to see inside was like trying to find a black dress in a dark closet. Once again, Deborah could see out but no one could see in.

Determined to confront Deborah, Marcie went to the front door and knocked. As she stood there, waiting for someone to answer, the itchy feeling grew stronger. Determined, she tried turning the regular sized doorknob. Locked. She bent over and tried a lower knob. Locked. She heaved a sigh and moved on. Maybe the itchy feeling was a guilty conscience playing a trick on her. She had no business following Roger around like a lost puppy. No business goofing off. The itchy feeling persisted all the way across the lawn to the back door. It left once she entered the house, adding more credibility to her suspicions.

Marcie rapped on the kitchen wall and said, "Hi Pearl, I'm back. What are you making?"

Pearl was rolling out dough on a cutting board fortified with flour. "Peach cobbler. I'll fix you a dish to take home."

"Oh, Pearl. You're going to spoil me."

"Pshaw" said Pearl, "A woman livin' alone. Her skin and bones. Looks like you could use a little spoilin'."

Marcie laughed. "You're right. I'll take all the spoiling I can get. May I fix myself a glass of your delicious iced tea?"

"Yessum." Pearl dusted her hands with more flour and resumed rolling.

Marcie wished she could roll dough like that. She never had the knack. Like so many things, playing golf, knitting, saving her marriage.

"By the way," Marcie said, "Do you know where Deborah is?"

"Miss Deb, she's prob'ly waterin' Mister Victor's flowers."

And spying on me, Marcie thought. She couldn't get over the fact that Deborah immersed herself in flowers out in the greenhouse, yet threw a fit if she found so much as an African violet inside the house.

Marcie said, "If you see her, would you please tell her I would like to talk to her in my office."

"Yessum."

"Thanks, Pearl. I'll see you later." She started to walk away, then, "Oh, I almost forgot. Did the phone ring while I was out?"

"No'um."

"Good," said Marcie. "If it rings when I'm not here, please answer it and take a message. I'll supply you with some notepads and pencils."

That got Pearl's full attention. Holding her floured hands to her chest, she looked at Marcie with a pained expression. "Miss Deb, she ain't gonna like that."

Marcie responded in a kindly manner. "Miss Deb is not the director of Port Victor. I am, and I would like you to start taking messages when I'm not here. I'm hoping to hear from referral agencies. We've got six empty beds to fill."

"Yessum," Pearl said, turning back to her dough, her head slowly shaking back and forth.

Marcie could imagine the thoughts running through her mind. Getting on Miss Deb's bad side, cooking for ten women. "It will all work out," she said. "You'll see."

"Yessum," Pearl muttered.

In her office, Marcie sank into the leather chair and leaned all the way back. Her feet hurt, her knees burned, and her head ached, but once ensconced in the sumptuous chair it didn't take long for the aches and pains to subside. She closed her eyes and let her mind go blank.

———

The cardinal that acted like an alarm clock was pecking at her bedroom window. Marcie tried to ignore him. She didn't want to wake up yet.

"Does your job description call for taking naps?"

Marcie jerked awake. She sat up straight, rolled the chair forward and shook her head to clear it. Except her head refused to clear. Why was Deborah standing in front of the desk? Comprehension dawned slowly. Tap, tap, tap went the pen in Deborah's hand. Thus, the sound of pecking.

"Please put the pen down." She could not believe it when Deborah did as she was told. "Thank you," Marcie said.

Minus the pen, Deborah twirled a lock of her silvery blonde hair while surveying the room. She didn't seem bothered by anything she saw. She didn't seem impressed, either. She just seemed content to stand there and twirl her hair. Of course she was dressed to perfection. A sapphire-blue corduroy jumper over a dove-gray silk shirt. Today she was wearing jewelry: A cluster of diamonds set in a gold ring, another gold ring set with pearls, a gold locket on a long, thick chain, and tiny sapphire studs in her ears. Odd, Marcie thought. Deborah didn't wear any jewelry the day of the interview. Because the little one didn't want Sarah to see what she had?

It was time to get down to business. Marcie gave herself a brief lecture. Maintain control. Be assertive. Look her in the eye. Speak coherently. You're the boss, not her.

"Thank you for coming in, Deborah. We got off to a bad start, and part of that was caused by my own … miscalculations. But we are charged with running Port Victor, so I'm all for trying to get along. I dearly hope you are, too." She waited for Deborah to say something.

Deborah was smiling, but not at Marcie, at some inner thought she was obviously not going to share. If her behavior was meant to be disconcerting, it was. Marcie carried on.

"I am so glad we are having this chance to talk. If you don't mind, I'd like to ask you a few questions. Wouldn't you like to make yourself more comfortable? Sit in one of the chairs?"

For an answer, Deborah picked up the pen and held it above the desk as if intending to start tapping it again. Marcie felt the same way when trying to talk to her son. He put up roadblocks, too.

Using a matter-of-fact tone, she said, "Deborah? Where are the resident's charts?""

The girl finally opened her mouth. It was as though she had been waiting for that particular question. "What charts?"

"You know what charts," Marcie said. "Doctor George kept them in the top drawer of the file cabinet. He was very disturbed to learn they are missing."

"Oh, *those* charts," Deborah said, as if there were many others.

Weary of the game, Marcie leaned over the desk and tried to look her in the eye. "Listen, Deborah, it's obvious you don't want me here, but if you would try to understand how much this job means to me. It means I can use my training to work with women who have lost their way. Women who need someone to help them find a new and better way. It means I can feel like a person with a purpose. It means I can pay my bills. It means I can trade my rattletrap of a car for a newer one. I know you can't appreciate such simple things. You've had everything you ever wanted, but if—"

"Have not!" Deborah shouted, her perfect features contorted into an ugly mask. "Your stinking charts are in the cabinet!" She ran out of the room.

Marcie sat perfectly still. If she sat that way for two minutes, Deborah would return and she could apologize for her last statement. Deborah may have had every material thing she ever wanted but she hadn't had what counts. She hadn't had a loving mother. She hadn't had a father. She had never lived in a home of her own. Never met another dwarf. Never had a romance. Never married. The "have not's" went on and on. Did that give her a license to be narcissistic? To be demanding and inconsiderate? Narcissistic, yes, given the way she had been pampered from birth by Victor Thornton. Demanding and inconsiderate, no. The way Marcie saw it, Deborah needed the right kind of love and caring. The kind two people shared, the usual give and take, the ability to communicate. She needed a friend. The two minutes and then some had passed. Out of the whole encounter, one bright spot gave Marcie reason to hope— Deborah had been listening.

She spent the rest of the afternoon trying to make sense of the charts. The intake and discharge forms were missing. Progress notes didn't match up. In short, they were useless. Deborah had done a good job of destroying every bit of useful information. Just as she'd done with the women's luggage. George was not going to be happy to hear about this. If only he had locked the file cabinet.

Under the best of circumstances, when a resident was released with the staff's blessing, the individual's plans and a forwarding address were duly noted on the discharge form. That didn't rule out a return to the treatment facility if life veered out of control again. Whether the resident left on her own or with a specific plan, three months must pass before the woman could be readmitted. But because of the question mark hanging over the women of Port Victor, Marcie would be deliriously happy to admit any of them at any time. A heavy sadness fell over her as she put the charts back where they belonged. She could not shake the feeling that some of the women had come to a bad end.

If George had realized early on that he couldn't do justice to the residents by running back and forth between Huntsville and Fleming's Hill, a distance of forty miles one way, Marcie could have gotten established before most of the women found reason to leave. George thought he was Superman, able to leap tall buildings to get from one town to the next.

The phone rang just as Pearl came into view carrying a tray laden with food for Marcie to take home.

Ignoring the phone, Marcie said, "Oh, Pearl, thank you so much. My goodness, you've given me enough to last a week." The phone rang again.

After setting the tray on the desk, Pearl backed out of the room as though the phone represented company. "I'll see you tomorrow morning," Marcie called to her. She heard a faint, "Yessum," in reply.

Marcie answered the phone on the third ring. "Rutledge here." George said.

"Well, hello there. How did your meeting go?"

He ignored her question and asked one of his own. "Did you find the charts?"

"I did. But they're worthless. Little Miss Deborah trashed the intake interviews and discharge papers. She also messed up the progress notes. I'm right back where I started."

George didn't respond right away. Then, "I should have left them with Sarah."

"Sarah told me not to worry about finding the charts, that I'm to start fresh. She obviously doesn't know how important the data was. But our dear Deborah did. Can you remember anyone's last name, where they lived, anything?"

"You know me. If I don't have a chart, I'm lost."

"The thing that bothers me most is the luggage hidden in the basement. I find it highly unlikely that the women willingly left their belongings behind."

"How much luggage are we talking about?"

"I didn't count the pieces, but it has to be at least five."

"That's serious."

"I don't know what to do about it. Deborah packed the bags and then told Pearl to put them under the stairwell. I'd like to question Deborah, but she's not very receptive."

"I advise you to do what Sarah said, start fresh."

"I suppose you're right, but this whole thing with Deborah makes it extra hard."

"You're a tough cookie, you can handle it."

"I don't know about that."

"Let me put it this way. If you don't, you'll be out of a job."

"Thanks for the reminder.

"Aside from all that, how did your day go?"

"It's been simply wonderful." She started laughing.

"Liar," George said.

That made her laugh even harder, a giddy, hysterical laugh that bordered on all-out sobs.

"Okay, Marcie," he said. "It's past five o'clock. Go home to Charley and your goddam clocks."

Tears streamed down her cheeks, her nose ran, her stomach ached, and still she laughed. Would tomorrow bring more of the same?

CHAPTER 9

Birds tweeted, pigs oinked, bells rang … the cacophony of clock sounds greeted her like an old friend. Marcie often wondered if they missed her when she was away from home, for they seemed to make more noise than usual when she returned.

"Hello, darlings," she called. "I missed you, too!" She looked down at Charley and added, "I missed you more." His tail beat the air and he gave her his happy grin. "Looks like we've got a mutual admiration society here," she said, then headed for the kitchen, where she put Pearl's cobbler on the counter and the chicken and dumplings into the fridge. From there she went to her bedroom and changed out of her work clothes and into a pair of jeans and a sweatshirt with the Alabama logo splashed across the front.

Exhausted by the trials and tribulations of her day, the bed looked awful inviting. She piled pillows against the headboard and grabbed her book off the bed table. In the process, she almost sent her Mickey Mouse clock flying. Her reflexes went into action. She tossed the book on the bed and on the rebound caught the clock. Handling Mickey ever so gently, she planted a kiss on his worn face and put him back on his special spot. From the day she received him on her eleventh birthday until she married David, his ticking had lulled her to sleep at night and his alarm had woken her in the morning. He was thirty-one years old now. His insides had long since rusted and one hand had broken off, but he was still her most prized possession.

Climbing onto the bed, she settled with her back to the pillows and opened her book. Charley flopped down in his usual spot. Now that she was home, he relaxed by putting his chin on his paws and closing his eyes. He deserved a break after being on guard all day.

Too tired to read, she set the book aside and scooted further down on the bed. No sooner had she closed her eyes than the flames inside the kiln roared back to life. Try as she might to shove the real life images into a dark corner of her mind, this time the horror of her family's disintegration refused to go away.

———

Life as Marcie had known it didn't end all at once. It started innocently enough with one friend trying to please another. Over a period of six weeks, a garland of satin ribbons became a string of twisted knots with frayed edges— worn fabric that snapped in two on a fateful day in mid-September.

Because the events leading up to that day were so painful to recall, Marcie pretended they happened to some other girl named Marcie Matthews with parents named Ed and Linda.

For that other Marcie, the summer of her eleventh year started out like any other. Life in a small Southern town was just that— small. From the time school ended in late May until it started again the Monday after Labor Day, children of all ages came out to play. Younger kids rode bikes, skated, jumped rope, climbed trees, flew kites, tossed hoops, swam in the local pool, played cowboys and Indians, hide-and- go-seek ... any game that could be played outdoors. Watching TV and playing board games kept them occupied on rainy days.

Some of the big boys held summer jobs, worked on their cars, pursued their dreams of becoming rock stars; others hung out on street corners or at the pool hall, cruised the streets, picked up girls, and threw beer parties at the old gravel pit on the outskirts of town.

Teenaged girls babysat, volunteered at the local hospital, served as camp counselors, daydreamed, talked about boys, went out on dates, and sharpened their bridge–playing skills. In that part of the country learning to play bridge was a rite of passage to prepare young women for grownup social events.

The only picture show in town changed its marquee every Friday night. The line of young kids waiting to buy tickets to the Saturday matinees, a double feature, two cartoons, the news of the day, and the current serial's next installment, stretched down the block and around the corner. Grubby little hands clutched bags of pretzel sticks, nuts, or candy bought at the dime store. Others waited to buy popcorn inside the lobby.

As soon as the lights dimmed, boys shifted from seat to seat, pausing just long enough to throw spitballs at favored girls. The objects of their affection huddled together, emitting delighted screams and giggles loud enough to bring the usher with his flashlight, which made them scream and giggle even louder.

The big kids waited until the nighttime showing. Instead of watching the movie, boys and girls paired off, sat in the back rows and progressed from holding hands to kissing. Partners changed almost as many times as the marquee.

At that delicate and frustrating age between childhood and young adulthood, Marcie and her girlfriends thought they were too mature for the matinee and their parents thought they were too immature for the eight o'clock showing. They were too old to play outdoor games and not old enough to go to the beer parties at the gravel pit. They were either too old or too young for just about everything.

Spending the afternoon at a corner table in Lester's Drugs and Ice Cream Parlor became a favorite pastime. Sipping vanilla–flavored Cokes and munching on cheese Nabs, they whiled away the hours by paging through the latest movie magazines and drooling over their favorite male stars. Every time the bell over the door tinkled, they looked up in the vain hope of seeing a cute boy. The only time older boys went to Lester's was when his mother sent him on an errand, and then he'd duck in and out as fast as humanly possible.

When the girls ran out of spending money they gathered in someone's bedroom, where they took turns fixing each other's hair in bold new styles and applying makeup "borrowed" from a mother or older sister while listening to their favorite D.J. play the hits of the day and giggling over everything and nothing.

After a prayer of thanks for their many blessings, they sat with their families at the dining table for home–cooked meals punctuated with talk of the day's events. After dinner, they went to their rooms to read, write in their diary, work on their scrapbook, and listen to the radio.

On Sunday mornings and Wednesday evenings they attended worship at the Methodist or the Baptist church. A friendly rivalry existed between the two churches, each bragging that their members were superior to the others. People of other faiths had to drive to Rocky Mount, thirty miles away, to attend the service of their choice. Marcie's family belonged to the Methodist church. She was active in the youth group; her mother taught Sunday school and sang in the choir, her father served as a deacon.

Excitement over the annual Fourth of July parade and the picnic that followed soon faded to a distant memory when the hot, muggy air of summer settled over the town like a vaporous cloak. Mosquitos hummed, bees buzzed, fireflies blinked, bullfrogs croaked, and cicadas screamed from the hedges. Men wiped sweat from their brows with linen handkerchiefs and women fanned themselves with cardboard cutouts from the funeral home. No one was in a hurry to do anything. When they moved at all, it was in slow motion.

On one such sultry night, when the simple act of breathing took every last ounce of energy, people sat on their porches watching for bats and inhaling fumes sent by citronella candles. Snatches of loud singing and shouting drifted in on a westerly wind. A religious revival had come to town the previous day and set up a tent in Parson's field on the outskirts of town.

Tent revivals were commonplace throughout the summer months. Signs nailed to telephone poles announced their impending arrival. The preacher and his crew would stay a week or two, work the worshipers into a fervor of "Amen's" and "Hallelujah's" and then move on. A short time later, another revival would take its place, much like the carnivals that roamed the countryside.

One night at the dinner table, Linda Matthews told her husband Ed and daughter Marcie that she planned to attend that night's tent meeting. She went on to explain that Joanne, her best friend, had dared her to go and since she'd always been curious about what went on out there she had taken her up on it. Don't worry, she told her family, Joanne was driving, and when she came home she'd tell them all about it.

"I don't think it's a good idea," Ed said. "You two women going out there by yourselves ... anything could happen.

"Daddy's right, Mom," said Marcie. "Please don't go."

"Nonsense," Linda said, tossing her head. "I already promised Joanne and it's too late to back out now."

So off she went. When she finally straggled in at nine–thirty, instead of regaling them with stories about what went on, she was thoughtfully subdued. Brushing off Ed's questions with non- committal answers, she climbed the stairs to get ready for bed.

The next night at dinner Linda told her family how inspired Joanne had been the previous evening and how much she wanted to go again. Since she was afraid to drive out there by herself, Linda had agreed to go with her. She couldn't disappoint her best friend, could she?

At the end of the two weeks, when the tent came down and the parade of trailers kicked up thick clouds of road dust, Linda and Joanne stood by to wave and blow kisses as their new friends rolled out of town.

The arguments between Marcie's parents started the following Sunday morning when Linda Matthews refused to get ready for church. No longer would she go to the Methodist church, she declared. No longer would she teach Sunday school, sing in the choir, participate in soup day, host circle meetings, make her special fudge for fund–raisers— she was through with that "bunch of hypocrites forever." From now on, she and Joanne would attend services at The Church of True Believers and Followers. Ed and Marcie were welcome to go with them, she said, but first she would have to seek permission from Brother Paul.

Dressed in his Sunday suit with a starched white dress shirt and a maroon tie, Ed threw up his hands and shouted, "Jesus H. Christ!" Then he slammed out of the house.

Clutching her mother's arm with both hands, Marcie cried, "Why are you doing this? Why, Mommy, why?"

"Never mind, Marcie Matthews," Linda said, snatching her arm back. "This is a free country. I'll go to whatever church I choose." She whirled around and stalked up the stairs.

Not knowing what else to do, Marcie ran after her father.

————

Located in a clearing surrounded on all sides by dense woods, The Church of True Believers and Followers held their thrice- weekly meetings in a ramshackle building that once served as a general store. Because someone had painted the insides of the windows black and because no one could gain entry without Brother Paul's permission, rumors about the goings-on at "that nasty place" spread through the county like kudzu gone wild. Some folks said they practiced witchcraft by casting evil spells on their enemies and setting fire to effigies. Some said they slaughtered animals and drank the blood. Others said they handled deadly snakes and drank poison. Still others said they held sex orgies. Richly embellished stories about what went on passed from ear to ear like an infection oozing pus.

Once word spread that Linda Matthews and Joanne Withers had "joined that evil cult," the status of the Matthews family slowly sank into a bottomless pit. Linda, because she had everything a woman could possibly want and it still wasn't enough; Ed for not having better control over his wife, and Marcie because her parents' blood flowed through her veins.

Where the Matthews were reviled, Joanne Withers garnered more sympathy than ever. Her young husband had been killed during an ambush in the jungles of Vietnam, and the pretty widow had been an object of pity ever since. Which meant Linda Matthews should be doubly ashamed of herself for leading poor Joanne astray.

In the midst of the furor, the Methodist minister called a meeting with both women at the Matthews' house. He spent an hour exhorting them to return to their home church. When he left the house, he was shaking his head in dismay and holding his hat in his hands.

Not only did Ed have Linda to deal with, his printing business suffered when local merchants and individuals stopped placing orders. The person who had been a loving father and a happy-go-lucky man became an angry, scowling human with a hair-trigger temper. Every night Ed and Linda yelled at each other while Marcie hid in her room with her hands clapped over her ears.

As if losing her fun-loving parents wasn't bad enough, Marcie lost all of her friends. Friends she'd known all her life, shared secrets with, friends she'd counted on having forever and ever. At first they were "busy" when she called on the phone or knocked on their door. If she accidently bumped into them downtown, they made up excuses and hurried past her. Her best friend finally told her the truth. All of the girls' parents had forbidden them to have anything to do with her. She was considered a "bad influence." These were the same parents that treated her as one of their own, parents who took her on family vacations— parents she thought of as aunts and uncles.

Little kids started to follow her everywhere she went, chanting awful ings in singsong voices: "Marcie's a wit–itch … she boils babies … eats them for dinner."

Boys her own age, boys she'd been friends with since their baby carriages and then their strollers were parked in a corner of Lester's Drugs while their mothers chattered, sipped Cokes, and smoked Lucky Strikes. Now, the boys used her as a target for stone-throwing and name-calling contests. For days on end, names like "Witch's bitch" and "Satan's girl" rang in her ears.

The torment heaped on her in the outside world followed her inside the house she used to call home, now a battleground of two strong-willed opposing forces. Ed started ranting about his problems the moment he walked in the door at night. Business at his print shop continued to decline. After laying off all his employees, he still struggled to pay the bills. If business didn't improve, he'd have to close the shop. Socially, he got the cold shoulder everywhere he went. Places he'd gone to since he was a kid, friendly places like the barber shop, where he could laugh and joke with ease, now treated him like he carried a deadly plague.

The shunning didn't stop there. Even the congregation of the Methodist church looked askance when he and his daughter sat down in their regular pew. The minister, a dear family friend, came to him with hands folded in supplication. It would be better for everyone concerned he said if Ed and little Marcie went to worship at the sister church in Rocky Mount until "this ugly mess blows over."

Oblivious to Ed's troubles, Linda's religious conversion had reached a feverish pitch. She cancelled her subscriptions to glossy magazines in favor of inspirational texts. All day long, the radio stayed tuned to a station that played nothing but gospel music interspersed with Scripture readings. At night, she paid rapt attention to the evangelical preachers on TV who healed the sick and shouted messages of eternal damnation for non-believers.

As Labor Day approached, Marcie pleaded with her parents to move to another town so she could attend a new school. The thought of facing the kids at her old one terrified her.

"Don't be silly," her mother said.

"We can't afford to move," groused her father.

On the Monday following the holiday, Marcie clutched her books to her chest and walked to school. Much to her surprise, she made it through the double doors and inside the main hall with only a few taunts shouted by loud-mouthed boys. Everyone else simply ignored her. Either the kids were bored with her or they'd found someone else to torment.

Her isolation, which was far easier to deal with, came to a startling end on the fourteenth day of September. On the way home from school that day she saw a black cloud of smoke billowing high into the sky. It looked like one of the bonfires at the high school pep rally before a football game. The only problem was, the high school was located in the opposite direction.

A funny feeling ate at the pit of her stomach when she saw people gathering behind a house on her block. Gaining ground, she saw that the smoke was coming from *her* house— from *her* backyard. Breaking into a run, she pushed her way through the crowd, and there, standing dangerously close to the flames that leapt into the air with a roar, stood her mother. Wearing a faded housecoat with her beautiful red hair twisted into a tight knot at the back of her head, she looked like a demented hag.

Boxes piled high with paraphernalia sat at her feet. Every now and then, when the flames started to die down, she reached into a box and pulled out something else to throw into the fire. Her personal possessions deemed to represent the secular world had been thrown out weeks before: Makeup, hair coloring, curlers, nail polish, party clothes, costume jewelry, and her so-called trashy high heels. Now, Marcie watched in horror as hats, handbags, photograph albums, books, scarfs, mittens, shoes, and slippers went flying into the flames, spikes of fire that rose each time they were fed.

Marcie recognized one of her own dresses as Linda flung it into the flames, and there . . . there was her father's brown worsted suit, the one he wore to church on Sunday mornings.

"NO!" Marcie screamed as she ran to her mother. She grabbed a hunk of fabric and tried to wrest the suit from Linda's grip. She could feel the fire's intense heat on her skin and feared both she and her mother would melt.

The harder she tugged and yanked on the suit the harder her mother tried to fight her. Linda kicked at her shins and ankles, jabbed at her chest and sides with crooked elbows, turned and twisted closer and closer to the flames. Still, Marcie clung to the fabric. The knot at the back of Linda's head came loose and her hair blew wild about her twisted face and glazed eyes.

Frantic, Marcie looked to the bystanders. "Help me! Please! Someone! Help!"

Unmoved by her pleas, the neighbor women stood about in whispering groups while the men cupped their hands to the sides of their mottled jaws and hollered: "Burn, Baby, Burn!"

Marcie flung her part of the suit at her mother, sending Linda tumbling backwards onto the ground and farther away from the fire. While Linda tried to recover, Marcie raced inside the house to call her dad at the print shop. He'd come home right away and put a stop to this madness.

A man she knew as uncle Denny answered the phone. He said he hadn't seen Ed and didn't expect to. Didn't Marcie know that he had bought the shop from her dad? "Yes, sir, old Ed decided it was a lost cause," said uncle Denny. "I been wanting to buy this place for the longest time and the chance finally came. Got me a—"

Marcie hung up on him and ran to the kitchen window to see if her mother had recovered. Maybe her dad had seen the flames from wherever he'd gone and had finally come home. Her father was nowhere in sight. But her mother was down on her knees, right there beside the flames, with her head bowed and her hands clasped in prayer. Marcie called the fire department.

———

She woke up in her bed. Though it was dark outside her window, the street-light filtering through the curtains allowed her to see a shape sitting in the straight-backed chair next to her closet. It must be her dad. She sat up, her stinging eyes squinting hard to make sure she wasn't dreaming. The figure rose from the chair and walked toward her. She knew by the flowing skirt it wasn't her father. Her mother?

The woman who sat down on the edge of the bed looked like Aunt Lillian, her father's sister. Why would she be here? She lived in Virginia. A vision of her mother praying beside the fire flashed before Marcie's eyes. She collapsed back on the bed.

The woman laid a hand on Marcie's forehead and brushed the matted hair off her face. "It's all right, darling. Everything's going to be all right."

Marcie sat up again. "Aunt Lillian?"

"Hush now, sweetheart. Just lie back and rest your eyes." Aunt Lillian gave her a gentle push. In a voice as soft as a kitten's fur, she began to explain what had happened.

The fire department extinguished the blaze and the crowd soon moved on. An ambulance took her mother to the hospital. She had suffered minor burns and lung damage from the smoke, but physically she'd be as good as new in a week or two. That didn't mean she'd be coming home. She'd be sent to a different kind of hospital, the kind of place where she could rest and heal her mind.

Near as anyone could figure, Linda started the fire about half an hour before school let out. Only she knew the real reason why, but the cause of her action centered on her husband Ed.

Earlier that morning, Aunt Lillian received a phone call from her brother. Ed told Lillian he was calling from a pay phone because he had packed his bags and left the house for good. He'd tried to stick it out for Marcie's sake, but he couldn't stand living with Linda another minute. He'd sold the business and was moving to Houston, Texas, where jobs were said to be plentiful. He hated to leave Marcie behind. Linda had made her life miserable, her friends had dropped her, and she was having a tough time in school. Could Lillian come and take his daughter home with her? Just till he could get back on his feet and come for her?

"It won't be for long, Lil," Ed promised. "Maybe a few months or so. It would do the girl a lot of good to spend time with you folks. You and Ralph are the kind of parents Linda and I used to be."

Leaving Uncle Ralph to look after their children, Lillian headed to North Carolina. She turned onto the Matthews' street moments after the fire truck arrived.

And so, Marcie had gone to live with her Aunt Lillian and Uncle Ralph and three cousins. Aunt Lillian was sweet and kind, and Uncle Ralph was always pulling practical jokes on people. Best of all, her cousins never breathed a word about her mother, and the new friends she made at school didn't either. Still, she ached to see her father.

Neither she nor her aunt and uncle ever heard a word from Ed Matthews. Not a telephone call, not a post card, not a birthday or a Christmas card—nothing.

As for Linda Matthews, she spent two years in a mental hospital. After her release, she returned to the house she'd once called home. By then The Church of True Believers and Followers had been more or less run out of town. No one knew what Linda did all day. She became a recluse.

Every now and then Lillian called to check on her. The conversations were mostly one-sided, with Lillian doing all the talking. After hanging up, she told Marcie the same story she always told. Her mother was doing all right. Not great, but all right. Before the conversation ended, Linda was supposed to have said, "Be sure to give Marcie my love." That was the only time Marcie knew her aunt to lie.

That other girl named Marcie? She may not have lived happily ever after, but she did more than survive. With a master's degree in Social Work, she chose to specialize in substance abuse. Addictions had interested her ever since her mother became so addicted to her church she willingly gave up her husband and only child.

CHAPTER 10

The following morning Marcie arrived at Port Victor a half hour early. Having retrieved the garage door opener the day before, she pulled in beside the van and entered the house through the storage room. The mouth-watering aroma of bacon hovered over the kitchen. Expecting to find Missy eating breakfast at the table, she was surprised to find only Pearl putting away the breakfast dishes.

"Hi, Pearl," she said. "How are you this bright and sunny morning?"

Pearl hung a clean coffee mug on the cup rack. "Alright, I reckon."

"I'll take one of those." Marcie reached for a mug and filled it.

She took a sip and said, "Ah, you make the best coffee."

"It ain't nothin' special. Just plain ol' Eight O'Clock."

Marcie took another sip. "Is breakfast over already?"

"Yessum. Missy, she likes to eat soon's she gets up."

"What about Deborah?"

"Miss Deb, she don't eat a proper breakfast. She likes them bars."

"Granola bars?"

"Yessum."

"Well that makes it easier on you. What's on your agenda today?"

"Iffen you mean what am I gonna do today, I'm fixin' to do the ironin'."

"I didn't think people ironed anymore. Oh, I get the iron out when I have to press cotton or silk, but I try to avoid it whenever possible."

"Miss Deb, she likes her things ironed."

Marcie groaned. "I was afraid you'd say that. Does she like them starched, too?"

"Yessum. Specially her sheets."

Marcie put a hand up as if to ward off a blow. "I'll see you later."

Standing outside Deborah's door, she debated whether or not to leave the note she had written. It was quiet inside the room, not surprising considering the early hour. What was surprising was the continued silence from Ginger. Maybe she knew Marcie was a friend and not a foe. Dogs sensed such things. Charley certainly did. She just wished Deborah did, too.

Careful not to spill her coffee, she tucked the envelope as far under the door as it would go, then continued down the hall to her office.

The note said:

Dear Deborah,

Please accept my sincere apology for saying you'd had everything you ever wanted. That is far from the truth. We can't change our pasts, we can only try to change the present. I know you are hurting, hurting badly, and I'd like to offer you comfort. Please feel free to come talk to me at any time.

Yours truly, Marcie.

Last night, after letting her own past invade the present, a mistake she would not repeat, Marcie had agonized over the best way to approach Deborah. She could use Pearl as a conduit again but that wouldn't be fair to Pearl. So she decided on sending the note. She only hoped Deborah wouldn't tear it up without reading it first.

Having finished her coffee, she went to the foot of the stairs and climbed halfway up. "Missy," she called.

The girl's reply came fast. "What?"

"I'm coming up."

At the top landing, with halls leading off both sides, the door to the fire escape was open. Fresh cigarette smoke filled the air. Marcie stepped out onto the wrought iron landing. The odor of cigarettes was much stronger out there. A telltale butt laid on the lawn below. Marcie went back inside and closed the door. Turning, she saw Missy huddled against a wall on her right. The girl's solemn face showed signs of distress.

"I know it's against the rules—" she started, averting Marcie's steady gaze.

Marcie waved a hand. "I don't mind if you smoke out there. Just keep the door closed and use an ashtray."

"I don't have one," she said quietly.

"Well, we'll just have to get you one. For now, go get that butt and put it in the trash before someone sees it."

Missy stared at her with obvious disbelief. "You sure are different," she said.

Marcie laughed. "Is that good or bad?"

"Good, I guess."

"Then we're making progress. I guess."

"I'll be right back," Missy said, making for the door to the fire escape.

Marcie followed her out. While Missy ran down the steps, Marcie looked at the landscape. It was another gorgeous spring day, the greens seemed greener, the sky seemed bluer, and now that the smell of cigarettes had dispersed, she detected the heavenly scent of honeysuckle. For some reason that brought Roger to mind. She had looked for him in the yard when she left last night and again when she arrived this morning. He said he would call. Did she really want him to?

Missy bounded back up the stairs, hiking up her long plaid gingham skirt so she wouldn't trip over it. With it, she wore a long-sleeved rayon blouse with ruffles on the collar and cuffs. Not the typical clothing for a girl her age.

Once they were back inside, Marcie said what she'd wanted to say at lunch the day before. "Listen, Missy, I'm not a psychotherapist. I deal with the present and the future by teaching coping skills, techniques you can use in everyday life. I also do private counseling. In addition, you'll be expected to attend three AA meetings a week and go through an evaluation process at vocational rehabilitation. They hold classes every weekday morning from eight until noon." She appealed to the girl with her hands held palms up. "Does that sound so bad?"

Missy seized on one topic. "What's the evaluation about?"

"Well, they give you a series of tests to determine whether you're college material or need help with job placement. If you didn't graduate from high school, they prepare you to get a GED."

"What kind of tests?" Missy asked, her eyes wary.

"The usual. You probably took them in high school. They measure your aptitude and intelligence level. "You can't fail the tests," she said. "I just wish Sheila and Tiffany had stayed long enough to give our program a chance."

"Me, too," Missy said, a wistful note in her voice. "I liked Sheila. She was my roommate."

Marcie felt a fluttering in the pit of her stomach. "Did you know she was planning to leave?"

Missy shook her head. "I had no idea. We went to bed at lights out. Then something woke me up. Like someone moving around. Then I heard giggling. It was Tiffany. She giggled all the way down the fire escape. It's a miracle Deborah didn't hear her."

"Do you think they were planning to leave for good or just for a few hours?"

"I know they weren't planning to leave for good. What I can't figure out is why Sheila went with Tiffany in the first place. They were total opposites. They didn't even like each other."

"How are you so certain they planned to come back?"

"Sheila might have left her things behind because she didn't have much, but not Tiffany, never Tiffany."

"Why not Tiffany?"

"She had two suitcases and a backpack crammed full of stuff. Every day she'd get her scrapbooks and show off her clippings. She was homecoming queen, May Queen, head cheerleader, Miss Petunia, Miss Steel City, and I don't know what all. Then she'd show us pictures of all her old boy friends, starting in third grade. Boys and her awards were all she talked about. After the first couple of times, Sheila and I would yawn all the way through it. Tiffany was so wrapped up in herself, she never noticed. And she had all these clothes and shoes. That girl really loved shoes. She was a pretty girl, but cheap. You know what I mean?"

Marcie could hardly contain herself. Turned out, Missy did talk, and talk and talk. This was more information than she had ever dreamed of hearing. "Yes, I'm afraid I do. I heard she met a boy at the AA meeting the night she snuck out of the house."

"Did she ever. She fell all over him."

"What about Sheila?"

"The boy Tiffany liked had a friend and he flirted with Sheila. I didn't think Sheila was the type to go out with some strange boy."

"You still think the girls were planning to come back."

"Definitely."

The fluttering in Marcie's stomach turned into a hard knot. Something bad had happened to those girls, she just knew it. "Were you in the room when Deborah packed Sheila's things?"

"Yes and no. She had me gather Sheila's things that were on hangers and put them on the bed. Then she told me to go downstairs. I went into the sunroom and read until Pearl came to tell me I could back to my room."

"How long did you stay downstairs?"

"About two hours."

"I see," said Marcie. "Can you tell me anything about the girls? Where they came from? What their last names were?"

"Sheila had a Southern accent like mine so she must have been from around here. She was neat and quiet. We got along fine. Mainly because we didn't poke our noses into each other's business." She gave Marcie a pointed look with this last.

"I caught it," Marcie said. "Please go on."

"Like I said, Tiffany talked about nothing but boys and her awards. She could be from Mars for all I know. I don't remember their last names. In AA we use first names only. I don't even know Pearl's last name."

"How did the girls get along with Deborah?"

"They didn't. We always stayed as far away from her as possible. I still do."

"Why is that?"

Missy looked all around and then leaned over the railing to look downstairs. Even though the coast was clear, she spoke in a hushed voice. "Deborah freaks us out. She's so beautiful on the outside but something's rotten inside. She has this look in her eyes, like she hates us and wants to be rid of us. Yesterday? When she came to the kitchen about the clock? She made me so nervous I almost threw up. You heard what she said. That she didn't care if I choked. All she cared about was the clock being too loud. If she had caught me smoking on the fire escape, she would have kicked me out so fast I wouldn't have had time to collect my things. I don't know how she got to be the housemother anyhow."

It was startling to know how frightened the residents were of Deborah. Of course Missy's perception about Deborah disliking them was right on target. Marcie owed the girl an explanation, but she had to think of one first.

"Miss Sarah, the lady who owns Port Victor, hired Deborah as the housemother. It's a complicated situation and my hands are tied. Just stay put in your room after lights out and all should be well."

"Don't worry. I'm not about to do anything stupid."

"Like leaving the door open while you were out smoking?"

Missy made a face. "That was pretty stupid. I should've gone down to the basement."

"Yes, you should. Now," said Marcie, "How about taking me on a tour of the rooms. We'll be admitting new residents and I want to make sure everything is in order."

"There isn't much to see," Missy said. "Except for different color schemes, the bedrooms are all alike."

"I'd still like to take a look around. Show me your room first."

Missy took a few steps down the hall and opened the door to a spacious bedroom overlooking the back yard. Moving inside, Marcie was immediately impressed by how fresh and clean everything looked. Painted a lovely lavender color with white trim, the two single beds with night tables on either side were also white. As were the two dressers with white-framed mirrors. Identical puffy comforters featuring clusters of violets on a white background covered the beds. White Priscilla curtains hung over white blackout shades, and the hardwood floor looked brand new. A large walk-in closet offered plenty of storage space. Most important, Marcie couldn't find a single sheet of plastic. "I'd kill for a room like this," she said.

Missy cracked a tiny smile. "I love it. It's the prettiest room I've ever seen. It's a thousand times nicer than the one I had at home. Sheila thought so, too. She loved this room. And she loved Pearl. That's another reason she planned to come back."

"Oh no," Marcie said. "I did it again."

Pearl lifted her eyes upwards, as though praying to be spared another shock.

"I swear," Marcie said, "I won't do it again." She placed the note pads and pencils in front of Pearl. "Keep these handy so you can take down the names and phone numbers of the people who call when I'm not here."

"Miss Deb, she ain't gonna like it."

"Miss Deb's out in the greenhouse half the time, and she doesn't want to be disturbed the other half. I'm expecting calls from people who want to send us residents." Miss Deb would probably hang up on them, she added to herself.

Pearl whined, "But I don't know how to talk to them people. Don't rightly know what to say."

"Well then, let's do a little role-playing. I'll pretend to be a referral agent and you'll be Pearl."

Pearl's eyebrows met in the middle. "How's that?"

"You'll be the one to answer the phone."

"But it ain't ringin'."

"It will be." Marcie then made a ringing sound with her tongue.

Pearl stared at her as if she had lost her mind.

"I'm pretending to be a phone," Marcie explained.

"Thought you was gonna be people."

"I'm going to be both. A phone and a person."

Pearl pulled a tissue out from under her shirtsleeve, blew her nose, and tucked the tissue back. "You ask me, this here is pure foolishness."

"Please, Pearl. Just go along with me, okay?"

"Yessum."

"Now, I'm going to call again," Marcie said. "This time you're supposed to say hello." She made the ringing sound once more.

"This here's where I say hello?" Pearl asked. Marcie nodded.

Both women practically jumped out of their seats when the phone actually rang. "You get it," Marcie told Pearl. "It'll be good practice for you."

With a stubborn set to her jaw, Pearl shook her head. She stood up, looked at the wall phone, then shuffled off toward the cellar door.

The phone rang again. Marcie said, "Wait" At last Pearl turned to look at her. "Listen and learn."

Marcie moved to the wall phone and lifted the receiver off its hook. "Port Victor," she said in a pleasant voice, "Marcie, speaking." A moment later, she said, "Can you hang on while I go to my office?" She motioned for Pearl to come to her. "All you have to do is hold the phone until I pick up the one in the office."

Pearl approached warily. "I don't haf'ta say nothin'?"

"Not a word. Here," she shoved the receiver into Pearl's fumbling hands, "I'll let you know when I get there."

"How you gonna do that?"

Marcie studied her worn and weary face and was struck by a sad possibility. Strange as it may seem in this day and time, Pearl might not be familiar with the workings of a phone. What with Sam and Junior in drunken stupors most of the time, they probably had no use for outside communication.

"You'll see." Marcie said. She made a fast exit and fairly flew to her office. Snatching up the desk phone, she said, "Okay, Pearl, you can hang up now."

A distant voice said, "Eh? What's that?"

Marcie raised her voice a notch. "Pearl. Please. Hang. Up. The. Phone." The wait to hear the telling click seemed to take forever.

When it finally came, she spoke to the director of the halfway house in Gadsden, Alabama, one of the many she had talked to yesterday about referrals. "Sorry about that," she said. "Pearl's a little hard of hearing. Now, about the woman you want to send us." While Marcie made notes, the director told her about a woman named Veronica Lake. Marcie recalled the actress by that name. She had worn her silky blonde hair in a peek-a-boo hairdo. This Veronica Lake had left the halfway house in Gadsden two months ago to take a job as a chiropractor's receptionist. Less than five weeks later she ran off with one of the patients, a married man who promised to divorce his wife and marry her. When his wife found out about the affair, she made hubby stop payments on the trailer he had bought for Veronica. So she hung out in bars, and went off with any man who paid her drink tab. Finally, with nowhere else to go, she went back to the halfway house. They couldn't readmit her because it hadn't been three months since her release. The director would make arrangements to get her up to Port Victor no later than three o'clock that afternoon. No, it wouldn't be by bus. Veronica couldn't be trusted to complete the trip.

If Veronica couldn't be trusted to arrive by bus, how could she be trusted to stay once she arrived? "That will be fine," Marcie said. "If you've got an extra minute, I'm trying to follow up on some former residents. All I have are first names." She read the list. The director's response was negative. She agreed to call Marcie if any of the women showed up on her doorstep.

After hanging up, Marcie went back to the kitchen. Remembering it was Pearl's day to iron, she opened the door to the cellar and called Pearl's name. When she heard the familiar "Yessum," she hollered, "I'm coming down."

Standing at an old wooden ironing board, Pearl was pressing a pink satin sheet. Deborah's, no doubt. Marcie saw no reason why they couldn't send Deborah's linens out to a laundry. Neither Deborah nor Sarah would have to know; she could pay for it out of petty cash. But, like so many things, that topic would have to wait.

"We have company coming," she told Pearl. "Her name is Veronica Lake."

Pearl's brow pinched together in a puzzled frown. "Here all this time I done thought she was dead and buried."

"You're thinking of the actress. This Veronica is thirty-seven."

"Huh," said Pearl. She was using an old, heavy iron that made the blue veins in her hand swell. No doubt it strained the tendons in her arm as well. Marcie made a mental note to buy her a new, lightweight one.

"Veronica should be here this afternoon. You can count on her for supper."

Pearl was silent for a moment, then asked, "Reckon she likes BLT's?"

"I think everyone likes BLT's." Then Marcie said, "Pearl, I want to apologize for my actions over the phone. Chances are you won't have to answer it, but in case you do, I want you to feel comfortable. That's why role-playing is such a great tool. We used it a lot where I used to work."

"Yessum," Pearl said with a total lack of enthusiasm.

"Did you and Sam have a phone?"

"No'um. My folks done had one way back. T'were a four- party-line an' you had to guard what you said. Made me as nervous as a cat in heat."

"Well, we have a private line. No one can hear what you say except the person you're talking to. We can go through all that later. I need to get back to work and leave you alone."

"Dinner's at noon."

"What are you cooking up today?"

"Potato pancakes, chick peas, pork chops, an' apple sauce."

Marcie gave her a warm smile. "You really are out to put weight on me."

"Yessum. You're too pretty to be so skinny."

Marcie laughed and said, "Thank you. I think."

Eager to get back to the office and prepare a chart for the new resident, Marcie climbed the stairs and quickly passed through the kitchen and formal rooms. When she turned the corner into the hall, she came to a dead stop. "Oh my God," she said with a hand to her throat. "I could've broken every bone in your body."

Looking like a little princess, as always, Deborah didn't seem fazed by the near collision. In a cool tone, she asked, "Veronica Lake?"

Flustered, Marcie's brain couldn't seem to process the question. Her eyes darted here and there, and then lit on the dog at Deborah's feet. Ginger was a Pomeranian all right, a tubby little thing with a heavy, puffball coat of golden fur. With her red velvet collar studded with rhinestones, she sat obediently at her mistress' tiny feet.

Marcie got down on her knees, looked the dog in the eye and said, "Well, hello. You're a pretty little baby." Even though Ginger's perky ears stood up and her tail wagged back and forth, Marcie knew better than to try to pet her. She had made that mistake once when she was about six years old. All it took was one pat on the bulldog's head for him to lunge and bite her on the chin. Because no one claimed ownership of the dog, the vet didn't know if it had had its rabies shot. Marcie not only had to get stitches in her chin— she still bore the scar— but also had to go through a series of rabies shots.

She sat back on her heels and looked from the dog to Deborah. "I'm sorry. What did you say?"

"This Veronica Lake. Where is she from?"

"You listened in," Marcie said.

"Naturally I listened in. In case you've forgotten, I'm the housemother."

Marcie pushed up from the floor. Standing tall over the little one, she kept her voice steady. "I wanted to talk to you about that. Perhaps you would like to get a private line so you won't be bothered with office calls."

"I'll do no such thing."

"But I can't have you listening to my conversations. That's an invasion of privacy."

"Pooh on your privacy. How do you expect me to know what's going on if I don't listen in?"

"I'll be most happy to tell you what's going on. I promise to report to you every time we expect a new resident."

"You may start reporting to me now. Who is this Veronica and where does she come from?"

"All I know is she's coming from Gadsden."

Deborah looked incredulous. "You're allowing this stranger to come to Port Victor without knowing anything about her?"

Marcie stood her ground. "What does it matter? Sarah wants us to fill this house and keep it full."

Deborah made a sour face. "I hate having all these women in my house."

Marcie lifted an eyebrow. "May I remind you that this is a halfway house and, as the housemother, your help would be greatly appreciated."

Deborah's eyes flashed with anger. "May I remind *you* that I'll do as I please." She tugged on Ginger's leash and turned to open her door.

Before she could get inside her room, Marcie said. "Did you read my note?"

"Yes," Deborah said and closed her door.

"It was nice meeting you, Ginger," Marcie called. At least Deborah hadn't torn up the note without reading it. As for the unpleasant exchange, it was still the best exchange they'd had.

CHAPTER II

Marcie heard the crunch of tires on shells before she saw the actual car. Which turned out to be not a car at all but a long, black hearse. What's more, the hearse appeared to be driving itself. Peering out the office window, she watched in amazement as a wizened old man in a visor cap and wearing Coke-bottle eyeglasses climbed out of the driver's seat. He shook himself as though trying to get his limbs to move and then went around to the passenger's door. That's when the show began.

A long, shapely leg sheathed in black hosiery revealed itself ever so slowly. The foot wore a high-heeled sandal with tiny straps wound round the slender ankle. The heels on the sandal had to be at least five-inches high. A few seconds later, the other leg joined its mate. In the process, the skirt rode up to expose a bit of white thigh and the black strap of a garter belt. Finally, a voluptuous blonde eased herself out of the car. Standing well over six-feet, she was wearing a slinky black dress with a plunging neckline. Once out in the open, the skirt fell to just below her knees. Standing proud, she fluffed the white feather boa at her neck and threw one end over her left shoulder. Then she took her time surveying the house from top to bottom and side to side. Marcie waved but Veronica didn't appear to see her.

The trouble started when Veronica attempted to step forward and her spiked heels caught in the crushed shells. If she hadn't grabbed the top of the hearse's door she would've pitched forward and landed flat on her face.

If ever there was a woman in distress, Veronica was it. Marcie made a bee-line for the front door. She met up with Pearl in the foyer.

"Don't she beat all?" Pearl said "I ain't never seen such as her."

Marcie said, "She certainly lives up to her namesake."

"Why's she so dressed up?"

"Maybe she thinks we're serving cocktails at five."

Pearl cupped a hand to her ear. "What's that you say?"

"Never mind," Marcie said, doubting that Pearl had ever heard of a cocktail party. "Right now she needs help getting to the front door."

Pearl started backing up. "I got to peel my taters."

"Can't it wait?"

"No'um. I'm a'feared that there hearse might carry me off." Pearl made a hasty retreat toward the kitchen.

Swell, Marcie thought. She stepped out on the porch and greeted the new resident with a smile. "Hello! Welcome to Port Victor. I'm Marcie Parker, the director."

Veronica put a hand to her ample breast and said, "Please don't mention that word. I've had it up to here—" the hand went to her chin "— with producers and directors."

"I'll keep that in mind," Marcie said. She looked for the driver and found part of him on the far side of the hearse. All she could see were his cap and goggle–like glasses. She called, "Welcome to you, too!"

Still hanging onto the car door, Veronica managed to lift her chin in a lordly manner. "Whoever decided to use shells for a driveway was either drunk or crazy. How did he expect a lady to walk on this stuff?"

"I'm afraid you'll have to take your shoes off until you get to solid footing."

"Absolutely not!" Veronica cried. "I'll have you know I paid good money for this pair of hose. They're pure silk."

Oh Lord, Marcie thought. Another Deborah. She assessed the situation. Even if Pearl agreed to go near the hearse, she couldn't help carry Veronica to the walkway that led to the steps. Veronica was at least two heads taller than Pearl, and Pearl had enough trouble carrying herself. But if Veronica would climb back in the hearse, and if the driver would pull all the way up to the walk, the lady could step directly onto it.

"I can't see for nothin'," the driver croaked when asked. True enough, Marcie thought.

"Would you mind if I drove her up?"

"Yes, ma'am, I surely would. This here's the only hearse we got."

Who was "we," Marcie wondered. Did the halfway house have a special need for a hearse? Were residents dropping dead like flies? She swallowed a laugh. The thought was too ridiculous.

Veronica looked at the driver and said, "Well, Simon, you'll just have to take me back to Gadsden."

Simon shook his head. "They told me not to bring you back no matter how hard you begged."

Veronica gazed at Simon from under a fall of hair. "Now, Simon, you know I'll be good to you."

Simon ducked down behind the hearse, but not before Marcie saw how red his face turned. She looked at Veronica, winked and said, "He's a cutie pie, all right."

At that, Veronica broke the haughty facade and howled with laughter. Greatly relieved, Marcie let her own laughter loose.

Missy appeared on the porch. "What's going on?"

Still laughing, Marcie looked over her shoulder at Missy and said, "Come help me get this long–legged woman into the house."

With Veronica sandwiched between them, her arms draped over their shoulders and her décolleté revealing mounds of unharnessed breasts, they managed to get her to the walkway. When she was standing there, a statu-esque, full–figured woman dressed in party mode, she said, "Well! I must say, this was not the entrance I had in mind."

"Sorry," Marcie said, remembering her spill into the foyer. "It happens to the best of us." She looked at Missy. "Now for the luggage." Simon popped up from his hiding place and opened the back door to the hearse, the very door where caskets entered for the last time.

"Oh. My. God," Marcie said, getting an eyeful of luggage. Stacked one on top of the other, Veronica had four matching Louis Vuitton bags.

"Careful!" Veronica called from the comfort of her perch. "They're expensive!"

Simon stood aside in a show of unwillingness, arms crossed, eyes focused elsewhere. Marcie couldn't blame him. One bag would break the ancient little man's back.

Missy grabbed the first suitcase and said, "Do I have to lug this thing all the way upstairs?"

Marcie nodded. "I don't know how else it's going to get there."

Missy whispered, "Please don't put her in my room."

Marcie looked back at Veronica. "Which color do you like best, pink or blue?"

"Pink," Veronica declared. "I've had more than enough of the blues."

Marcie pulled a suitcase out of the hearse and almost dropped it. "What have you got in this bag? Gold bricks?"

"Don't I wish," Veronica said.

"Put the bag down and wait right here," Marcie told Missy. "I remember seeing a dolly in the garage."

Veronica and Missy had been deep in conversation. They went noticeably silent when Marcie came back on the scene. She eyed them suspiciously. "What?"

"Nothing," Missy said.

"Yes, something," Marcie said.

Missy looked at Veronica. "Oh, she was just asking how I liked it here."

"And?" Marcie said.

"I told her she ought to make a run for the hills, that it was just awful."

"Very funny," Marcie said, but she was smiling when she said it. "Well, let's get this luggage unloaded so Simon can get back to Gadsden before full dark. He doesn't see very well." A major understatement if ever there was one. The man should have given up on chauffeuring live people and dead bodies a long time ago.

With the aide of the dolly, Missy was able to take two pieces of luggage at a time. Even though she knew she would regret it, Marcie volunteered to take the other two. Meanwhile, Veronica stood on the stoop, blowing Simon enough kisses to last him until he made it, if he made it, back to Gadsden.

Just as Simon was climbing behind the wheel, Deborah came storming into the foyer. "What is that hearse doing here?" Before Marcie could answer, Deborah looked up the stairs at Missy. "And why is she making all that noise?" Thump, thump, thump went the dolly. "It's enough to wake the dead."

The connotation hit Marcie's funny bone and she bent over laughing. "I... can... explain," she sputtered.

"Well, it had better be good," Deborah said, hands on hips.

Veronica stepped into the foyer and closed the door behind her. She took one look at Deborah and said, "Well, hello. How did you get to be so little? I was five-foot-eight in the sixth grade. You can imagine how it felt to be the tallest girl in my class. Especially when all the boys were little shrimps like you." She fluffed her boa, and added, "So I went for the big boys in high school."

Deborah looked Veronica over and then she said, "It is my dearest hope to never lay eyes on you again." She whirled around and strode away.

"Thanks! I love you, too!" Veronica called to Deborah's back.

Marcie had promised herself she would handle difficult situations as they arose. That this one was a humdinger would test her fortitude. Either that or drive her straight to the funny farm.

CHAPTER 12

For the first time in her life, Marcie was running late. She'd made the mistake of waiting till after work on Friday to shop for groceries. Not only were the aisles packed with people pushing loaded shopping carts but every check–out lane had long lines of disgruntled customers, even the express lane for which she qualified since she had less than twenty items. If George wasn't coming to dinner she would have bypassed the store as soon as she saw how crowded it was. The only solution was to buy Betty Crocker's au gratin potatoes and Mrs. Smith's cherry pie. If she ever made it through the checkout lane, she might make it home in time to get everything done.

What a week it had been. She couldn't wait to tell George all about it. Because he was a colleague and still associated with Port Victor, she could speak freely about the residents without breaking the rule of confidentiality. To anyone else, she couldn't even reveal the names of the residents, much less any information about them. Roger came to mind. She hadn't seen or heard from him all week. It made her wonder if Deborah told Sarah she'd seen them acting cozy. Maybe Sarah had a policy against her employees fraternizing with each other. She thought it odd that he'd seemed interested in her and now was not.

Having cleared checkout and loaded her groceries in the trunk, Marcie took off for home. After crossing the bridge, she was zigzagging down her road to avoid the potholes when she spotted a female turtle directly in her path. More delay, she thought, as she pulled over to the side of the road. Because she'd been peed on once, she picked up the turtle by its sides and turned the tail away from her. Then she carried her to the tall grass at the riverside of the road and set her down.

It was egg-laying season for the female turtles. They slowly and laboriously homed in on the place of their birth. The lucky ones didn't have far to go; others had to take a more dangerous route across roads and busy highways. Most drivers tried to avoid them, but squashed turtles were not an uncommon sight at that time of year. For the turtles who made it to their birthplace, nothing short of picking them up could stop them from digging mud holes in which to lay their eggs. They covered the holes and left the eggs to incubate themselves. When the baby turtles hatched, they squirmed their way to the surface and headed toward the water. Their tenacity amazed Marcie.

From the time she greeted Charley outside the house and her family of clocks inside the house, she was a flurry of activity. Sensing excitement in the air, Charley kept close watch on her, his ears pricked as if waiting for the doorbell to ring. When she told him his buddy George was coming, his tail beat the air and a toothy grin spread across his face.

It didn't take as long as she had thought to get everything prepared and either in the oven or simmering on the stove. With time to spare, she freshened up in the bathroom, changed into the outfit she'd worn for the interview, which George paid for, then poured herself a glass of red wine and took it and a bottle of spring water for George down to the dock. Charley happily loped alongside her. It was still a bit chilly outside but a lot warmer than it had been earlier in the week.

The lights on the boathouse flashed on as she neared the end of the dock, giving enough light for her to set up two plastic lounge chairs. The river was calm tonight; the current mild ripples. It shimmered where the lights hit the surface, creating an attractive silvery gray color. A half-moon and a dozen stars peered down at their twins reflected in the water. Most of the fishing boats had turned in for the night, the purple martins and swallows had yet to return from their winter quarters, and it was too early for the annoying buzz of mosquitos. It was utterly peaceful and quiet. She took a sip of wine and congratulated herself for completing her first week of work without having a nervous breakdown.

She felt George before she saw him. Each step he took on the dock set off vibrations under her chair. Charley jumped up from his spot beside her and trotted off to greet him. Marcie remained seated The vibrations stopped and George's voice echoed all around her. "Hey, pal," he said to Charley, "how you doing?" The movements started up again and then his shadow reached the light.

She smiled up at him. He started to bend over for their traditional peck on the lips, then stopped and said, "What the hell did they do to your hair?"

She remembered he'd given her money to go to a hair salon. "That's why I hate going to a stylist," she said. "You never know what they're going to do to you."

"Well . . . it doesn't look that bad."

"Thanks," she said, puckering her lips for a kiss.

He obliged her and then stood gazing up at the stars. She always forgot how tall and lanky he was until he stood still. Dark, almost black eyes, and brown hair beginning to recede in front, he was a good–looking man, a widower for some eight years. Whenever someone asked if he was ever going to marry again, he said, "I've already had the best woman a man could want."

His was the same sad story that happened to far too many innocent victims. A drunk driver ran a stop sign and plowed into the driver's side of his wife's car, killing her instantly. They had no children, so George lived alone.

He looked down at Marcie and said, "What's up?"

She said, "I thought we could catch up on the news. Or would you rather eat first and talk later?"

"I'm starving," he said.

"Right," she said. He was always starving and ate enough for two men without gaining an ounce of weight. She started to climb out of the chair.

"But I can wait a while," he said.

She settled back. "Good. I need some time to unwind." She handed him the bottle of water, then picked up her glass and took a big swallow. He sat down and uncapped the water bottle. George never imbibed. Whether or not he drank alcohol before his wife's death, she didn't know because she'd never asked.

Charley flopped down in his spot and promptly fell asleep.

"How was your week?" George asked.

"That depends on your point of view," Marcie said.

"Clarify," he said.

"Well, we now have four residents. Veronica Lake arrived on Tuesday and—"

"Veronica Lake?"

"Lake is actually her middle name. It seems her momma loved to watch the late night movie channels. One night, when Momma was nine months pregnant, she went into labor while watching, *I Wanted Wings,* starring none other than Veronica Lake. Apparently the contractions didn't bother her, because she stayed to see the end of the movie and barely made it to the hospital on time."

"That's quite a story," George said.

"I'm not finished," Marcie said. "Momma took it as an omen that someday her daughter would be a big star. Momma took Veronica to every Saturday matinee. After the movie, they would act out the main parts. Naturally, Veronica starred in all the school plays. Soon after she graduated from high school, Momma put her on a bus heading to Hollywood. Momma told her to wear tight sweaters and hang out at Schwab's Pharmacy. That's how Lana Turner got noticed, or so the story goes."

"Was she?" George asked.

"Noticed? Oh yes, but not for her acting ability. To sum up, our Veronica followed the same pattern as the actress with men and booze, but without the fame and fortune."

"What about Poppa?"

"He deserted them when Veronica was six years old. I guess he didn't like movies. Momma supported them by working as a waitress."

"So what's our Veronica doing in Alabama?"

"Her home is in Gadsden. When Momma died, Veronica came back for the funeral. She intended to return to the Coast but she got tied up."

"A man?"

"More like men."

"She sounds interesting."

"That she is, and very likable and funny. She's also difficult. I never know what role she's going to play next. At least she keeps the other residents entertained. All but Pearl."

"Why not Pearl?"

"Veronica makes demands that throw Pearl for a loop. For instance, Pearl keeps creamy peanut butter on stock and Veronica likes chunky. She eats it on toast for breakfast. Pearl doesn't have the keenest sense of humor. But I love that poor woman dearly. She's the cog in an otherwise rudderless wheel."

"Good. Keep training her to become the housemother."

"She already is. Most of the time Deborah's doing who knows what out in the greenhouse. And that's another thing."

George climbed out of his chair and said, "That's enough for now. Let's eat."

"Fine with me," she said.

When she stood up, George looked her over once again. "Nice dress," he said.

"You bought it for me," she said. "And the blazer that goes with it. See the shoes? You bought those, too." He'd given her three-hundred dollars to "fix yourself up" for the interview.

"And I bought the hair. Not bad, not bad at all."

She laughed and said, "Thanks. You ought to do my shopping more often."

"Very funny," he said, putting the chairs away.

Charley preceded them down the dock and up to the house, his tail wagging all the way.

———

For an educated professional, George's table manners were practically nonexistent. He hunched over his plate, arms on the table, scooping up his food as if someone might come along and snatch it out from under him. He ate one serving at a time and didn't like his portions to touch. He gave eating his all, refusing to talk or even look up until he cleaned his plate. Marcie had long since learned to keep quiet.

As on all nights at her house, various clocks serenaded them. She'd hidden the fire engine clock in her closet. The first time its siren went off, George jumped clear out of his seat. Marcie had to admit the clock took getting used to. It had cost twenty-five cents at a garage sale. Only later did she understand why the people sold it so cheap.

George pushed his plate away and leaned back in his chair. "There is nothing like a home–cooked meal."

"I'm glad you enjoyed it," Marcie said. If he only knew. "Are you ready for your cherry pie?"

"In a minute," he said.

She got up and started clearing the table. Her thoughts turned to tomorrow, a Saturday. She wouldn't have to curl her hair, put on makeup, or wear panty hose with a suit or dress. She actually looked forward to catching up on household and yard duties.

"How are the kids doing?" George asked.

Marcie turned away from the sink to look at him. "You would have to spoil our evening."

"I gather things aren't going too well."

She put the plates in the dishwasher, added the flatware, and closed the door.

Sitting down in her chair, she sighed and said. "You gather right. I hardly ever hear from them, and when I do, it's Julie telling me how much they love D.C."

"Maybe it's time to remind David that you have custody."

"He couldn't care less."

"Have you told Julie about your job?"

"Every time I call the line is either busy or I get the answering machine. Let's talk about something else. Like the luggage in the basement. According to Pearl, the pieces belonged to the women who left APA. She dragged them—"

George interrupted. "Why would they leave their things behind?"

"That's it exactly. Why? After Deborah pawed through everything, she told Pearl to take them down to the cellar. Imagine that. Poor Pearl, as bent over as she is, lugging those bags down two flights of stairs. Deborah ought to be spanked."

"None of it makes any sense."

"How well I know. I've been calling other treatment programs to see if I could match any of the women to their luggage, but so far I've run into a blank wall."

"Did you question Deborah?"

"You must be joking. Deborah doesn't respond well to questions."

"What about Sarah?"

"Before I could get a word in, she let me know in a hurry that she didn't want to hear any problems. Think of an explanation while I get the pie."

Marcie had baked Mrs. Smith's pie in one of her own pie plates to make it look homemade. She brought it and a knife to the table and set them down in front of George. "You do the slicing and I'll get the forks and plates." She also got his favorite mug out for coffee.

Marcie's thoughts went back to her kids while George attacked his pie. George tried to warn her not to sell the house in Huntsville and move the kids away from their friends. If she could take it all back, she would have listened to his warning.

The push to leave Huntsville began soon after New Start closed its doors. At loose ends, Marcie had turned to the kids for comfort. As usual, Davy gave grunts and shrugs to her attempts at communication, but Julie opened up to her. Marcie was horrified by what she heard.

A change in school districts had caused racial tensions. Younger girls like Julie were especially vulnerable to the older bullies who lurked about the halls, threatening kids into giving up their lunch money or whatever else they had of value. Julie also said that drug use was commonplace. Kids were smoking pot on school grounds, showing up for classes stoned. Julie worried about Davy because she knew some of his friends used drugs. Marcie became very worried herself.

Her ex was no help whatsoever. He was too busy playing house with his new girlfriend. When he finally listened to her fears, he discounted them, which only made her more determined than ever to get the kids out of that school.

She became obsessed with finding a safe place for the sake of her children. All of her married life, the United States Army had told her when to move and where to live. For the first time she could go anywhere she pleased. It gave her a sense of control.

Day after day, while the kids were in school, she visited small towns within a fifty-mile radius to Huntsville. One sunny afternoon, quite by accident, she discovered an empty cedar cabin set on a wooded acre alongside the Tennessee River. She fell instantly in love with it. She could picture the three of them snug and secure, fishing and swimming to their heart's content. The people at a nearby marina told her the place was for sale. Everything happened quickly after that. The owners of the cabin accepted her offer and a neighbor's uncle wanted to buy the house in Huntsville. The move was set for the week after school let out for the summer.

Bubbling over with excitement, she took the kids out for pizza. While waiting for their order, she broke the good news. Davy threw a fit. Knocked his chair over and slammed out of the restaurant. Julie burst into tears.

George told her to call it off. Said she was making a big mistake. Her ex echoed the same warning. She countered. The kids would adjust. Besides, the deal on both houses had been struck.

To mollify Davy, she promised that he and Julie could invite their friends down during the summer, and she would take them up to Huntsville whenever they wanted to go. All went well for a while. It was like a vacation. Marcie postponed looking for a job in order to be a full-time mother. She enjoyed fixing up the cabin, making her own imprint on it. She and Julie planted a small vegetable garden and set out flowering shrubs and several varieties of annuals.

Then school started. Fleming's Hill was a small Southern town where roots grew deep. The high school was riddled with cliques, kids who had known each other all their lives. Always before, Davy and Julie had other Army brats to bond with, but they were outsiders in Fleming's Hill. Because of her sweet disposition, Julie was eventually accepted. Her cocky brother was not.

The year was a nightmare of school conferences, temporary suspensions, temper tantrums, and tears. In the middle of it all, David was transferred to the Pentagon. Twice, Davy hitchhiked up to his father's condominium, only to be sent back to Alabama.

When school let out in May, Marcie took the kids to the airport. They were supposed to spend a month with their father. One month stretched to two. Two months stretched to three. Then Julie made that fateful call.

Now, here she was, still living alone, still lonely, and still aching to see her babies.

George lapped up the last bite of pie and shoved his plate aside. He looked at Marcie and said, "I've got to hand it to you. You make a mean cherry pie."

"Why, thank you, George," Marcie said with a sly smile. "Do you want to take your coffee into the living room?"

"Works for me."

He sat on the old corduroy sofa facing the fireplace. She settled in the wing chair cater-corner to him. "I've got one more report to make," she said. "The other new resident checked in on Thursday. Her name is Phyllis Webb. She's married with two kids in college and she's been suffering from empty-nest syndrome."

"Ah," said George, knowing that women who have devoted their lives to their kids sometimes go off the deep end when the kids leave home.

"Has she been in treatment before?" George asked.

"No. Her husband tried to get her into a program but she was in a heavy state of denial. She still is. The only reason she's at Port Victor is because he threatened to divorce her if she didn't do something about her drinking."

"Good for him," George said.

"She thinks he shipped her off so he can date other women. I'm going to give her plenty of time to clear the cobwebs out of her head." Marcie could relate to Phyllis. She knew all about an empty-nest, but knowing it would only make things worse, she didn't try to drown her misery in a bottle.

"You've got your work cut out for you."

"I know," she said. "So, how was your week?"

"Busy," he said.

"That's it?" Marcie said.

"The seminar went well, but then I had to catch up with my patient load."

She knew he'd be leaving soon. His heavy eyelids and slouched position showed how tired he was.

They sat in comfortable silence, him drinking his coffee while the clocks played their off–key tunes and Charley snored from his spot near Marcie's feet.

Setting his mug on the side table, he stretched and said, "Well, I'd better be going. You fed me too well and now I'm ready for bed." He pushed up from the sofa as if it took all the strength he had.

Marcie walked him to the door. Once there, they gave each other a quick kiss, and then George patted her on the shoulder and said, "Thanks for dinner. Keep up the good work."

"I don't know how good it's been, but I should get an A for effort."

After closing the door behind him, she went to the kitchen. She'd just started loading the dessert plates into the dishwasher when the phone rang. Maybe it was Julie! She answered with a breathless hello.

"Hi," said Roger. "Sorry it took me so long to get in touch with you. I've been coaching my youngest son's T-ball team three nights a week and my older son's Little League team the other three. By the time I finish putting all the equipment away I figured it was too late to call."

As he talked, Marcie felt a stirring around her heart. She didn't know Roger had kids, but she was happy to hear he continued to be active in the boys' lives. Which was more than she could say for her ex. David's idea of being a good father was to let the kids do whatever they pleased. No rules, no restrictions, just let them loose on society.

"How old are your boys?"

"Timmy is seven and Roger Junior just turned eleven. They're great kids and I love coaching them."

Her heart skipped a beat. She had talked Davy into trying out for a team. He went once and never went back, because the coach "expects me to hit a home run every time I'm at bat." Marcie knew better than that but she let it go.

"Good for you," she said. "I'm sure you're a terrific coach."

"I do my best." He paused, then, "So, would you like to go out for dinner tomorrow night?"

She'd suspected this was coming so was prepared. "Sorry, but I have plans." She planned to finish her book and go to bed early.

"That's what I was afraid of. Well then, how about a week from tomorrow?"

"Doesn't Sarah have a policy against her employees getting together socially?"

"Not as far as I know. Just in case, I'll take you to a place that has the best catfish in the state. It's out in the county and our Ms. Sarah wouldn't think of going there."

"I hate to sneak around," she said, tingling with excitement.

"You can call it sneaking. I call it going out for a good meal."

Doubt replaced excitement. "I don't know ... I'll have to think about it."

"Go ahead and think," he said.

She laughed and said, "If nothing comes up, I'd like to go."

"Great," he said. "Why don't I pick you up at six?"

"Okay. I'll see you then." She replaced the receiver without saying good-bye. Looking down at the dog curled at her feet, she said, "Wake up, Charley. Believe it or not, I have a date." Charley stood up on all fours, stretched his body out and yawned. "Try to control yourself, Charley," she said and laughed. She called to the clocks, "I have a date!" They showed their enthusiasm by chiming, tweeting, oinking, and winking. "Thank you, one and all," she said, taking a bow.

One thing she knew for certain, looking forward to a date with Roger would help her maintain a cheerful attitude throughout the week ahead.

Her smile faded when one of George's admonitions came back to haunt her: *Never be certain about anything.*

CHAPTER 13

Rested and refreshed after her weekend off, Marcie was ready to tackle whatever happened that day. First, she wanted a cup of Pearl's coffee. She opened the kitchen door only to find Pearl blocking her way to the coffee pot. Marcie tried to prepare herself for whatever bad news was coming her way. Pearl was practically tearing her apron apart.

"What's wrong?" Marcie asked.

"Them two's been at it this mornin', an' I can't do nothin' 'bout it."

Marcie took Pearl's hands into her own to quiet them. "Try to calm down, Pearl. Whatever it is, it's not worth raising your blood pressure over. Take a deep breath and slowly let it out."

Pearl sucked in a gulp of air and immediately started wheezing. The wheeze turned into a gasping cough. A pitcher of guilt poured over Marcie's head. She had forgotten that Pearl had been hospitalized with emphysema and didn't have the lung capacity to breathe deeply.

Marcie released Pearl's hands and gently patted her back just as she'd patted Missy's a week ago today. The difference was, Missy was young and healthy. Pearl was not. She continued to wheeze but the coughing finally stopped. She pulled a ball of tissue out from under her sleeve, turned her face to one side and coughed up the phlegm that had blocked her airways. She dropped the tissue in the waste can, then pulled out a fresh tissue and dabbed at her watery eyes.

"Feel better?" Marcie asked.

"I reckon," Pearl said in a choked voice.

"Are you going to get upset again when you tell me what happened?"

"Yessum."

"Then tell me one thing. Did any of the residents leave over the weekend?"

"No'um. But I'm'a sinner 'cuz I been prayin' one'a 'em would." Marcie said.

"You are not, nor have you ever been a sinner."

Pearl dipped her head down and said, "Iffen you say so."

Marcie lifted Pearl's trembling chin with a hand and looked her straight in the eye. "I say so because it's the truth. You are a good woman, Pearl, and don't you ever forget it." She gave Pearl another moment to compose herself. "Now, let me guess whom you've been praying about. Would she happen to be a tall, big–breasted blonde?"

"Yessum. Veronica, she's 'bout to worry me to death." Before Marcie could respond, Pearl said, "Speakin'a the devil." She scurried off to the hall bath.

Veronica swept into the room, a peacock–designed caftan billowing out behind her. Coifed and wearing full makeup, she spotted Marcie and gushed, "Oh, thanks be to God you're finally here. If I don't get relief, I am not long for this world." She put the back of a hand to her forehead, closed her eyes and feigned a near fainting spell.

"Relief from what?" Marcie asked.

Veronica opened her eyes and dropped her hand to her belly. "From the worst case of indigestion a human being could possibly have. I love Pearl's pinto beans, but they caught my insides on fire. I have a very delicate stomach, you know."

Marcie didn't bother asking why she'd eaten the pintos if her stomach was so delicate. "Would a couple of Alka-Seltzers help?"

Veronica reached out to her "You are divine. I've been trying to get relief for hours."

Marcie eyed her keenly. "Don't tell me you woke Deborah up."

A look of pure innocence crossed Veronica's face. "All right, I won't."

"But you did, didn't you?"

"Well," she dragged the word out. "I might have tapped on her door, but that selfish midget wasn't about to help a poor soul in need."

Pearl came out of the bathroom. Although she hung back, seemingly afraid to come forward, she wasn't afraid to speak out. "Veronica, she done more'n tapped on Miss Deb's door. She almost beat it down. Miss Deb, she hollered for her to go away, but Veronica, she just kept poundin'. Miss Deb's little dog, she was barkin' and carryin' on somethin' fierce. The ruckus woke everybody in the house."

"Swell," Marcie said, imagining the scene. She turned to Veronica. "You did it on purpose, didn't you? Deborah told you she didn't want to lay eyes on you, so you made up a reason to make her look at you."

Veronica took offense. "I did not make it up. I went to Pearl first, but she said only you and Deborah had keys to the medicine chest. Well, you didn't happen to be here at five o'clock this morning and I was about to explode with gas. What else could I do but go to Deborah?"

Marcie looked back at Pearl. "Did she ask for your help?"

"Yessum. I done told her to wait on you."

"And here you finally are," Veronica said. "May I please, pretty please with whipped cream and a cherry on top, have some Alka–Seltzers?"

"Follow me," Marcie said, stopping to pour a mugful of coffee first. She glanced back at Pearl. "You did the right thing, Pearl. I'll see you later."

"Yessum," said Pearl, with that familiar note of doubt in her voice.

As soon as they entered the dining room, Veronica started in on the decor. "I'd love to get my hands on these rooms. They could look so elegant without all this tacky plastic. What's it there for anyway? It's not like you raise cats. I have a good mind to tear it all off."

Marcie knew that it could cause trouble, but she said, "Go ahead. I'll help."

A mischievous gleam appeared in Veronica's eyes. "You will?"

"I've wanted to get rid of this stuff since day one," Marcie said. She set her coffee mug on the dining room table and started snatching the plastic covers off the chair seats. Meanwhile, Veronica was whipping plastic off the living room furniture, letting it fly in the air and float to the floor. The two women met at the settee, where the last piece of plastic lay.

"Be my guest," Marcie said with a little bow.

With a dramatic flair, Veronica pulled the plastic off an inch at a time and then waved it in the air above her head. "Now you see it and now you don't." She crumpled the plastic into a ball and then went around the room collecting the pieces on the floor.

Pearl poked her head around the kitchen door, slapped a hand over her mouth, then parted her fingers long enough to say, "Lawd'a mercy. I never seen the likes a you two."

Marcie looked at her and said, "When we host the AA meetings we want people to be able to sit on the cushions, not on cheap plastic. We want to be proud of Port Victor, not ashamed."

"Yessum," Pearl said and ducked out of sight.

When all the plastic had been rolled into a big ball, Marcie carried it out to the trash can in the garage. Passing through the kitchen on her way to rejoin Veronica, she caught Pearl as she was heading down to the cellar to do the laundry. "Pearl, if Miss Deb asks about the plastic, please tell her that I take full responsibility for its removal. Not Veronica, not the two of us. I'm the one who started and finished the job. Okay?"

"Yessum. Veronica, she done got on Miss Deb's bad side. Don't reckon she'll ever get off'n it."

Veronica is not the only one on Miss Deb's bad side, Marcie thought. Returning to the living room, she grinned at Veronica and said, "How's your indigestion?"

Veronica laughed. "I've been tooting all over these rooms."

"Maybe we ought to open a window." Knowing that she shouldn't, Marcie went to one of the window and tried to open it. She heaved, she grunted, she pulled, she gritted her teeth, but her efforts were all for naught. "I'll bring a putty knife from home," she said. "That should loosen the paint enough to open them."

Veronica said, "You are a genius. I don't even know what a putty knife is."

Marcie retrieved her coffee from the dining room table. "You'll find out tomorrow. Let's get you some Alka–Seltzer."

As they entered the hall, Marcie put a finger to her lips for silence. She didn't want to risk disturbing Deborah with Veronica in tow. Veronica made a show by lifting the hem of her caftan and taking mincing steps in her backless gold lame slippers.

They made it into the office without incident. Marcie closed the door and went directly to the medicine chest. She pulled out two packets of the desired tablets and added two packets of Goody's powder.

Turning around, she saw that Veronica had made herself comfortable by kicking off her slippers and spreading out in a wing chair, as if she intended to stay a while. She looked like a giant peacock with a yellow topknot.

"Oh no, you don't," Marcie said. "I've got work to do." She gave the packets to Veronica, rounded the desk and sat down in her chair.

"Aren't I work?"

"You most certainly are work," she said. "But I have phone calls to make, and after that I have a scheduled session with Missy."

Veronica pouted. "When can I have a session?"

"We'll see how the day goes. About those packets. Take one of them now and save the other for when you need it. Tuck the Goody powders away in case you come down with a terrible headache. I do not want you knocking on Deborah's door no matter what. If you make her unhappy, you'll make the lady who owns this house unhappy, and if she's unhappy, I'll be unhappy, because I'll be without a job."

"Well damn," Veronica said, leaning back in her chair. "You just took all the fun out of this place."

"Never mind about fun. This is a treatment program, not Disneyland. But I brought a few board games and decks of cards. They're in the sunroom."

Veronica's eyes lit up at the mention of cards. "I play a wicked game of Spite and Malice. I wonder if Phyllis or Missy plays."

"Stop wondering and go ask them. If they're not familiar with the game, you can teach them. Put some clothes on first. All residents should be dressed by eight o'clock."

"Yessum," Veronica said in a perfect imitation of Pearl. She retrieved her slippers and slid them on her feet.

"I have one more issue to settle," Marcie said. "You must stop pestering Pearl. The poor lady works like a slave around here and she can't be your private nursemaid or chef."

"But Marcie, Pearl's cooking is so country. Everything is fried in lard. Meat, fish, chicken, vegetables, all fried in greasy fat. And if it's not fried, it's cooked with fatback."

"I'm aware of that. But she works hard to put food on the table."

"Why can't some of us do the cooking? Phyllis talks about recipes all the time. You may not believe this, but I know a thing or two about cooking myself. I spent half my youth in the restaurant where my momma worked. Maybe we could get a grill. I can grill anything."

Marcie turned it over in her mind. "That is a great idea. For heaven's sakes, don't talk about this in front of Pearl. Once we have a plan, I'll lay it out for her."

Veronica preened. "Well, I'm glad to know I'm good for something."

"You're good for lots of things. Just keep the good girl image alive when you interact with Deborah and Pearl."

"Yessum," Veronica said, rising from her seat. She sauntered out the door in a whirl of peacocks.

Marcie knew that in the future she had to be more careful with her relationship to Veronica. She'd already gotten too friendly, and if she continued down that path it would not only alienate the other residents but deter Veronica from taking her treatment plan seriously.

The phone rang before Marcie could make the first call.

The man at the other end of the line introduced himself as Reverend Thomas. "I'm calling from Athens, Georgia," he said. "You may not accept patients from out of state. In that case, allow me to apologize for taking up your time."

Something about his voice and his good manners plucked at Marcie's heartstrings. "Have you tried the halfway houses in Georgia?"

"Oh yes. Georgia Lu has been in and out of a dozen facilities. Every time we place her, one or more of her brothers comes to rescue her. The brother's idea of a rescue is a stop at the nearest honkytonk. Since the accident, we believe it's in the lady's best interest to receive treatment elsewhere."

"Accident?"

"A very bad automobile accident. It's a miracle the lady survived."

They didn't have a rule against admitting women from out of state and Marcie wasn't about to make one up. "We'd be glad to accept your lady, Reverend Thomas."

"Bless you, Ms. Parker. More than likely, you've just saved a life."

"Heavens," Marcie said. "I haven't even met the lady."

"That's true, but by allowing us to bring her to Alabama, you've taken the first step."

For the next minute or so, the Reverend gave Marcie all of the data needed to open a new chart. When asked about the woman's expected time of arrival, he said, "I've looked at a map and I believe it would take five hours to drive her there. She should be there sometime this afternoon."

"I'll be waiting for her."

"Excellent. I'll have one of our deacons bring her over."

After hanging up, Marcie went to the file cabinet and drew out the proper forms. As soon as she put them together and wrote Georgia Lu on the tab, she went in search of Pearl.

Remembering that Pearl did the wash on Mondays, she headed down the creaky stairs and into the smell of laundry detergent and bleach. She rapped on the wall and said, "It's me, Pearl."

"Yessum," Pearl said without pausing in her work.

"You can plan on five for supper. We have another resident coming this afternoon."

At that, Pearl stopped folding towels and looked up. "What's this one like?"

"All I know is her name, Georgia Lu Dawson, and that she survived a bad car wreck."

"Huh," said Pearl. "Don't you reckon it's best iffen you was to know more 'bout these women?"

Shades of Deborah, Marcie thought. "I doubt if Deborah or Miss Sarah knew much about you when you first arrived."

"Yessum," Pearl said, and turned back to her towels.

"Oh, and Pearl. I'm having an extra key made to the medicine chest. From now on, you're allowed to dispense over-the-counter aides when I'm not here. That way we'll avoid any major disruptions."

Pearl dropped the towel in the laundry basket. "Un, un. I don't want them women wakin' me up of a night."

"I don't either. But someone needs access over the weekends, and I don't want another scene with Deborah. Trust me, Pearl. It'll all work out."

"Yessum," said Pearl.

Marcie looked toward the stairwell and sighed. "I can't stop thinking about the women and their missing luggage."

"It's a cryin' shame is what it is."

Marcie nodded in agreement. "I have half a mind to look through those suitcases myself. Maybe Miss Deb overlooked something."

"Miss Deb, she took her time with them bags."

"I'm sure she did." And she omitted everything that contained valuable information, just like she did to the charts.

———

Marcie had been hoping Missy would come to the office of her own accord. They'd gotten along well ever since the day Marcie caught her smoking. Missy had opened up to her about Sheila and Tiffany, she'd taken her on a tour of the upstairs, had helped get Veronica onto the walkway, and had taken the lady's luggage upstairs, no easy feat. Whenever they sat down to lunch, she'd joined the conversation, expressing her opinions about this and that. So Marcie was taken aback when Missy entered the office walking stiff-legged with her arms held close to her sides.

A veil of distrust slid over Missy's small brown eyes the moment she sat down. She chose the wing chair nearest the door, indicating she was ready for a fast exit. Dressed in a crisp brown shirt neatly tucked into a long beige wraparound skirt, her penny loafers shined, and a faint odor of soap lingered about her person.

Marcie decided to try humor. "You're going to have to start counseling me, Missy. I'm getting depressed over our lack of communication. Not about things in general, but about you and what you hope to gain by being here."

The girl didn't bat an eye. She stared at a spot on the wall somewhere behind Marcie's head.

Marcie flipped through Missy's chart, what little there was of it. She hoped the silence would trigger a response of some kind, any kind would do. After a while, the heavy stillness wore on Marcie's nerves. She never was any good at the silent treatment– except when she had too much to say.

"Maybe you'd rather talk to a man. Dr. Rutledge—"

The girl flinched at the thought. "No."

"All right," Marcie said soothingly. "I'm just trying to help you."

Missy's face returned to stone. "You can help me by leaving me alone."

Marcie laughed and said, "You know, this is really funny." A brief flicker in the girl's eyes encouraged her to go on. "All my life I've been the kind of person other people tell their secrets to. Friends and strangers alike have poured their hearts out to me. I've even had people tell me their troubles in a foreign language. I couldn't understand a word they said, but they were all smiles afterwards. Next to God, I probably know more private thoughts and deeds than anyone else." At the mention of God, a twitch appeared at the left corner of Missy's mouth. Marcie added, "And now, here you sit, all locked up inside yourself, and I can't find the key."

After a moment in which the twitch became more noticeable, Missy glanced at the wall clock and said, "May I be excused now?"

Marcie sighed. "Yes, you may. Just remember, a thousand people have trusted me. I'll be here when you're ready."

The girl rose like a statue and in three long strides was out the door.

Marcie scribbled 'none' on the progress page in Missy's chart. The girl was carrying a heavy secret around and it had to do with her relationship to God. Marcie could empathize. Her own relationship with God had ended some thirty-one years ago.

———

The sputter and clank of an ancient car grinded to a stop in front of the house. Marcie stood and went to the windows. A giant of a woman dressed in men's clothing lifted a battered suitcase out of the trunk of the car and hollered a goodbye that could be heard in the next county. The car rattled off in a cloud of exhaust and the woman turned toward the house. A look of wonder showed on her face.

Pearl peered around the doorjamb and said, "My, she's a big 'un."

"That she is. Would you please open the door and show her to the office."

Marcie assumed a business-like stance behind the desk, but when the huge woman barged into the room and said, "Howdy, ma'am," Marcie's efficient look dissolved into a wreath of smiles. "You must be Georgia Lu Dawson."

"That's right, ma'am. I come from down around Athens, Georgia. That's how come I got the name Georgia."

"Well, Georgia Lu, let's sit down and get acquainted. I'm Marcie Parker, the director of Port Victor."

"Pleased to meet'cha, ma'am." The chair springs groaned in protest as she settled herself. Large folds of fat bulged over a dark rawhide belt that sported a square silver buckle embedded with different colored gemstones. She looked all around and said, "This sure is a purty place you got here."

Marcie smiled. "Thanks. We think so, too."

Georgia Lu sat with her legs spread apart and a hand braced on each large thigh. She wore a man's short-sleeved work shirt and a worn pair of chino pants slung low on her hips. Aside from her size, the most startling thing about her appearance was a bright pink scar that snaked from the brow of her left eye, down her cheekbone and over to below her left ear, disappearing into her cropped iron-gray hair. When she smiled, the scar danced a jig.

"Georgia Lu, pardon me for asking, but how tall are you?"

The woman squared her broad shoulders. I'm six-three and a half and I weigh three-hundred and thirty pounds in the raw. I got five brothers and I'm the runt of the litter."

"Well," Marcie said, "I hope to keep you on my side."

"Don't you worry about that, ma'am. I 'preciate you taking me in and I'm proud to be here." She flashed a row of white teeth. "I know I can't never take another drop of liquor. It'll kill me sure as the world is round." She traced a fingertip down and around the scar. "I got this here in a bad wreck. I been in lots of wrecks but this one nearly took my soul. I got scars all over my body and they cut out my spleen."

"How long have you been drinking?"

"Since I was a youngun. My pappy kept a still out back. We always had lots of 'shine."

"Have you ever worked, Georgia Lu?"

She puffed out her massive chest. "I been workin' all my life. Mammy died when I was seven and I took over the house. After the boys growed up and Pappy died, I tilled fields, plucked chickens in a factory, picked peaches. I done most any kind of work there is."

"Very good," Marcie said. "Have you lived in Georgia all your life?"

"Yes, ma'am, 'cept for the time I lived in Oklahoma. Blackie was in the Air Force there. We had us a high old time." A sudden frown marred her sunny face. "Y' know they got bugs bigger'n birds out there."

Marcie stifled a laugh. "Who's Blackie?"

"He's my husband."

Marcie's brow went up. "Oh? Where is he now?"

"Don't rightly know. I ain't seen him in seventeen years."

Marcie sensed the disappearance of Blackie had left far deeper wounds than all the car wrecks. She stood up, came around the desk, and offered Georgia Lu her hand. "Welcome to Port Victor, Georgia Lu. You're going to make a pleasant addition to our little family."

Georgia Lu heaved herself up and grabbed Marcie's hand in a vise-like grip. She pumped it up and down, squeezing the knuckles together. "Thank you, ma'am," she said and finally released Marcie's hand.

Having swallowed a cry of pain, Marcie tucked her injured hand under her left arm to protect it from further abuse. She forced her features into a smile and said, "Now, let's go introduce you to the other ladies and then you can get settled." Settled where? Marcie asked herself. All of the rooms were occupied, which meant Georgia Lu would have to share someone's room. She decided to put her in with Veronica. The two tall ones should make a most interesting pair.

CHAPTER 14

"How did things go last night?" Marcie asked Pearl the following morning.

"Georgia Lu, she wants a garden. Says she'll do the hoein' and weedin'. Says there's nothin' like growin' our own vegetables."

"She's right about that," Marcie said. The more she thought about it the better she liked it. "Maybe we could get Jackson to till a spot out back." Jackson was Port Victor's lawn man. Marcie had only greeted him in passing and he seemed like a friendly sort. "He comes today, doesn't he?"

"Yessum. Ever' Tuesday, lessen it's rainin'."

"Good." She imagined he'd have to get permission from Miss Sarah, but better him than she.

"So the women got along all right?"

"Yessum. Miss Veronica, she got 'em in the sunroom and had 'em playing games."

"She didn't raise a fuss over her new roommate?"

"No'um. Georgia Lu, she follows Miss Veronica 'round like a big ol' hound dog."

"Well, I'm glad to hear good news for a change." The tone of Pearl's voice when she spoke about "Miss" Veronica indicated a definite warming trend.

"This afternoon, I'm going to get the women together for a group session. I hope you'll be able to attend."

"What time, you reckon?"

"Two o'clock. You should be able to take a break by then."

"Yessum. I got my ironin' an' my cookin' this mornin'."

"That reminds me," Marcie said, "what do you think about letting the women do some of the cooking?"

"Un-un. Them women'll make a mess outta my kitchen."

Here we go again, Marcie thought, from Deborah's house to Pearl's kitchen. "What if they clean up their mess and put everything back when it belongs?"

Pearl crooked her head to one side and squinted at Marcie, "What kinda cookin'?"

"Have you ever cooked outside on a grill?"

"No'um. I cook in the kitchen. That's what it's for."

"Well, besides grilling, some of the women, Phyllis, for example, would like to fix their favorite recipes."

Pearl thought it over. "Phyllis, she's right smart. I reckon she'd know a pot from a pan. Don't know about them others."

"I'm sure they've all had some experience in a kitchen. Just think about it, Pearl. You deserve to be waited on once in a while."

"Huh," Pearl said.

Marcie moved to the coffee pot, poured some into a mug and then headed for the door. "I'll be in my office if you need me."

"Yessum."

Two excellent ideas in two days. The women cooking and the planting of a vegetable garden. What would they think of next?

Marcie stopped in front of one of the tall windows. She put her mug on the floor and dug the putty knife out of her shoulder bag. With a little effort, she pried the paint off the bottom frame, unlocked the window and raised it on the first try. Cool, fresh air filtered through the screen and into the room. She tucked the putty knife into her bag, retrieved her mug and went merrily on her way.

Pausing outside Deborah's door, she left the note written on Sunday, requesting that Deborah get a private line so she wouldn't be disturbed by office calls.

Next, Marcie spent what seemed like hours calling other halfway houses to ask about the missing women. Not a single person recalled any of the names. The women seemed to have disappeared into thin air.

At eleven o'clock, Phyllis James sat across the desk from her, fidgeting with the pearl buttons on her cream–colored silk blouse. The natural aging process, usually accelerated by the heavy consumption of alcohol, had been kind to Phyllis. At fifty-two, she dressed her slim figure in trendy fashions and wore her sable– tinted hair in a pageboy. Her long, triangular face usually softened by artfully applied makeup, hadn't worked this day.

Marcie said, "From the look on your face I'd say you have a bad case of homesickness."

Phyllis's mouth turned down. "I feel like a child who's been sent to camp against her will."

"Think of the alternative. If you hadn't agreed to go to camp, Bill would have filed for divorce."

Phyllis's face tightened into a hard mask. "That's what he says, but the two-timing SOB will probably file anyway."

Marcie had met Phyllis's husband the day she came to Port Victor. Instead of letting her out at the walkway and then going about his business, he'd brought her suitcase inside the house and introduced himself. When he left, he'd hugged and kissed her and expressed his love for her.

"Bill seemed like a very caring and concerned husband," she said. "A man who wants his wife back sober and in good health and spirits."

"Oh, brother," Phyllis said. "Bill didn't get where he is in the company without slinging a lot of bull around."

"Do you put him down like that in front of your friends and acquaintances?"

Phyllis didn't have to answer the question. Her flushed face gave her away. "I may have. On occasion."

"When you were drinking?"

"I'm not the only one who drinks," Phyllis said. "Everyone does."

"Does everyone put their mate down?"

Phyllis shifted in her seat. "No... oh, I don't know. Lots of women complain about their husbands working late."

"In front of their husbands' colleagues?"

Phyllis didn't answer right away. "Well, no, I guess not."

"The thing is, Phyllis, when you've had too much to drink, you're uninhibited and you say things you'd never dreamed of saying when you're sober."

"I've found that the truth comes out when you're drinking."

"The truth as *you* see it. Has Bill ever given you reason to suspect him of womanizing?"

"Bill is a very handsome man. Women are always going up to him, teasing and flirting with him at parties."

"And how does Bill respond to that?"

"He usually laughs it off, but sometimes he lets it go on. The man loves being the center of attention."

"And how about you? Do men flirt with you at these parties?"

Phyllis crossed her legs, uncrossed them, sat up in her seat and then crossed her legs again. "Well, they ask me to dance, and some of them hold me too close."

"How do you feel when that happens?"

"I don't like it."

"Not at all?"

"Well, I can't help but feel flattered."

"So Bill feels flattered and you feel flattered, but that's as far as it goes. Right?"

"I guess so."

Marcie leaned forward and spoke in earnest. "Phyllis, you must learn to trust Bill. If he didn't care about your welfare, he would've dumped you long before now. The fact that he's hung in there, through all your binges and insults, not to mention your lack of companionship, tells me he's a man still in love with his wife."

Phyllis put her left elbow on the chair arm and held her chin in her hand. She studied the floor for several moments. Finally, she looked at Marcie and said, "I hear what you're saying, but I still don't believe it."

"That's why you're here. By staying sober, you'll have plenty of time to learn how to think rationally."

Phyllis gave a short laugh and said, "I'd kill for drink right now."

"That's only natural. We can't always have what we want. And, in time, the craving will go away."

"I doubt it."

"I've seen it happen. Many times. When I worked at New Start, most of our men wanted a drink in the worst way. It was all they could think about, but put a deck of cards in front of them and they forgot all about that drink. Being occupied with something, like reading a good book or knitting a scarf will help keep you from dwelling on wanting a drink."

"I do like to read," Phyllis said.

Marcie gestured toward the bookcase. "Help yourself." She got up and rounded the desk. At the same time, Phyllis rose and went to look at book titles.

"What do you like?" Marcie asked. "Family sagas? Mysteries? Love stories?"

"I just like a good story." Phyllis said.

Marcie pulled a book from the shelves. "Here's a great story by Cathie Pelletier. Her lead character might give you insights into the way a man's mind works." She handed her the copy of *Running the Bulls*.

Phyllis gave her a sincere look and said, "Thanks, Marcie. And thanks for being patient with me."

"I want you to heal, Phyllis."

"I know." She clutched the book to her chest and left the room.

Marcie returned to the desk and wrote a progress note in Phyllis's chart. She filed the chart, then sat down to rest until time for lunch.

As if she'd been waiting for Phyllis to clear the hall, Deborah stormed into the room, her face twisted in anger. "Just who do you think you are?"

In a calm voice, Marcie asked, "What's wrong, Deborah?"

The little one pointed a finger at her. "You know perfectly well what's wrong."

Marcie said, "Please sit down so we can talk about whatever's bothering you."

Deborah looked down her nose at the chairs. And no wonder. It finally dawned on Marcie that the chairs were designed to accommodate a normal-sized adult, not a little person. She thought about where she could find a chair to fit Deborah, thus being able to offer her a comfortable seat, which might lead to conversations rather than confrontations. Then she remembered the child–sized rocking chair up in her very own attic. Armless, and with a cane seat, she'd found it in an antique shop and had given it to Julie when she was about nine. Marcie smiled inwardly. The rocker would be a perfect fit.

"I can't begin to count what's bothering me," Deborah said. "First, you bring that dreadful woman into the house. Imagine what the townspeople are saying about a hearse parked right outside our front door. Then you take the plastic off the furniture so it'll get stained, and then you open a window in the living room. I could go on and on."

"Let's take one issue at a time. I'm sorry Veronica woke you yesterday morning. I can assure you it won't happen again. As for the plastic, imagine what the townspeople say when AA members tell them they have to stand up for meetings because they're afraid if they sit down they'll mess up the cheap plastic covers. And to be honest, Deborah, I'm confused about your allergic reaction to fresh air."

"Who said I was allergic to fresh air?" When Marcie didn't answer, Deborah said, "I'll bet it was Aunt Sarah. That woman doesn't know a fig from a leaf. I don't want the windows open because I don't want all that dirt blowing onto the furniture."

"Ah, so it's dirt you're worried about. Well you needn't worry any longer. I'm putting the women to work and Pearl will go after them to make sure they dust and sweep up every speck."

Deborah's face wore a look of surprise. "The women are going to take over Pearl's jobs?"

"Some of them, yes. Pearl is not well, Deborah. She needs more time to rest. Besides, taking on jobs around here will give the women a sense of accomplishment. Every single one of them is proud to be here. They love Port Victor and want to keep the house in pristine condition."

Deborah made a sour face. "They're a pack of slobs straight off the streets."

"Just the opposite is true. If you saw more of the ladies, you'd realize how neat and clean they keep themselves. Well, Georgia Lu might look a bit rough, but she does the best she can. In case you've forgotten, we have a rule that the residents must be bathed and dressed by eight o'clock." A rule Deborah broke every day of the week. "And none of them are off the streets, as you put it. I'm having a session this afternoon at two o'clock in the sunroom. It would be a nice gesture if you'd come meet our newest residents."

Deborah twitched her nose as if smelling something foul. "I suppose I'll have to meet them sooner or later."

Changing the subject, Marcie said, "Did you read my note about the phone service."

"I'm thinking about it."

"Good. I don't want you to be bothered by phone calls, most of which are for me anyway."

Deborah pursed her tiny lips and said, "I don't want to be bothered by anything, or anyone." She turned toward the door.

"Don't leave yet," Marcie said. "Can't we just talk? Say, about Uncle Victor's flowers?"

Deborah whirled around and demanded to know, "What about them?"

"Nothing. I was just wondering what kind of flowers they are. I have a garden—"

"It's none of your business!" She stormed out the way she'd stormed in.

It was almost funny to watch such a tiny person get angry, especially one as beautiful as Deborah. Even if she stomped her foot it wouldn't make any noise. Marcie's dearest wish was to have Deborah sit in on her assertive training session.

That was about as likely as having her kids decide to stay home.

———

Having been told at lunch that a group session would be held at two o'clock, the women had already gathered by the time Marcie went looking for Pearl. The reason they had arrived early became obvious when she entered the sunroom through the kitchen hallway. Veronica was regaling the women with stories about her life in Hollywood. Marcie didn't have the heart to interrupt. She slipped into a rattan chair at the back of the room. All of the women, including Pearl, seemed thoroughly engrossed in the show. All they needed were bags of popcorn.

The blonde stood center-stage in a stunning purple gauzy dress with a flared skirt. Her neckline, wrists, ears, and fingers dripped costume jewelry. Once more she wore spiked heels, black, toeless, pumps. She was a gorgeous woman, no doubt about it. Like Phyllis, the visible effects of alcohol abuse had been kind.

Veronica used a confidential tone as though she'd never confessed her experience to anyone. "I'd been out drinking and dancing till dawn. Simply having the time of my life. No thoughts or worries about tomorrow. A taxi driver I use when I've topped the hill and started a slow slide down, helped me into his cab, drove me home and put me to bed."

"Hot damn!" Georgia Lu shouted, slapping her knee and practically jumping out of her seat. "What'd he do then, Veronica?"

Veronica glared at her roommate and said, "He turned out the lights and locked the door behind him."

"Aw, shucks," Georgia Lu said, slouching back in her chair.

"Now, as I was saying before I was so *rudely* interrupted. I'd been out boozing all night and didn't get to bed until dawn. When I partied like that, I usually slept for twelve hours. Wouldn't you know, my agent woke me up at nine-o-damn-clock. I knew it had to be important because he knows better than to call me at such an ungodly hour. He had to repeat himself three times before my sluggish brain could figure out what he was saying When I finally did, I almost died." She clutched her chest and gazed up at the ceiling.

"What'd he say, Veronica?" Georgia Lu said. "What'd he say?"

Veronica spoke to Georgia Lu as if she were hard of hearing. "That's what I'm trying to tell you." She looked at the other women, rolled her eyes, and then went on. "He wanted me to audition for a part in a big musical." She licked her luscious lips. "A speaking part." A chorus of "Ahh's" rose up. "Oh, I'd done walk- ons and crowd scenes but I'd never had any lines. It was my golden opportunity. But…" The women leaned forward in simultaneous motion. "But the bad news was I had to be at the studio in an hour. An hour! Can you imagine?" She made a face of comical disbelief to which the chorus of "Ahh's" turned into "Ohh no's."

"My head was pounding like a jackhammer. My eyes were so red and swollen I could hardly see. I staggered into the bathroom and damn near drowned myself under a cold shower. Then I sat at my dressing table and surveyed the damage. When I looked in the mirror, an old, worn-out hag looked back at me."

"What'd you do, Veronica?"

Veronica silenced Georgia Lu with a fisheye. The chastened woman covered her mouth with a hand and held it there. Satisfied, Veronica continued her story. "My agent said they wanted a wholesome look. I put on a little pancake and some blush and it looked good. The trouble started when I tried to put on my mascara. My hand was shaking so bad I couldn't hold the wand steady. I kept getting black goo all over my eyelids, my nose, everywhere but my eyelashes. Then I'd have to get out the cleansing cream and start all over. And time was running out!"

The women shook their heads in sympathy as though programmed to act as one.

"I finally gripped my right wrist with my left hand to keep it steady. I was just beginning to stroke my lashes when an excruciating pain hit me right between my eyes. Everything went black! I thought God had struck me blind!" She held her head in both hands and rocked on her heels. "I told myself: You did it again, you stupid fool. You drank too much, you drank too much."

Mesmerized by her predicament, the women jumped in their seats when Veronica flung out her right arm and shouted, "I threw that damn mascara wand clear across the room! Then I stared at the hopeless wretch in the mirror. I thought of my momma's dream and I whispered, 'I'm never going to make it, Momma! It's too damn late!'" She gave a cry of anguish, her eyes tightly shut, hands balled into fists. Everyone in the room let out a gasp.

Veronica began to moan. "I fell to my knees and clasped my hands in prayer. God, please make it stop hurting... I promise I'll never take another drink." She peered at her audience through half-closed lids. After a breathless moment, she opened her eyes, fluffed her hair, and swung her hips. "Of course I've never been good at keeping my promises."

A hushed silence settled over the room, as if the women couldn't believe the story had ended. Then Georgia Lu, with her head humbly bowed, got up and went to Veronica. In a voice raw with emotion, she said, "Veronica, you'll always be a big star to me." She seized Veronica's hand and planted a kiss on it.

Veronica bestowed a benign smile on her biggest fan. "Why, thank you kindly, Georgia Lu."

Georgia Lu's mouth parted in a mammoth grin. "Tell us more, Veronica," she begged. "Tell us all about that there Hollywood."

The women cheered. "Yeaaaa!"

"Ah, excuse me, ladies," Marcie said, rising from her chair. "That was a stirring performance, Veronica, but alas, we have work to do." The women groaned as Marcie replaced Veronica at the front of the room while the latter and Georgia Lu took their seats.

Setting up the portable chalkboard in front of the French doors, Marcie decided to restrict all drunk-o-logues until after her session was over. Despite the fact that she enjoyed the drama the competition was too stiff.

She waved a piece of chalk in the air and said, "Thank you for your attention, ladies. Because Georgia Lu is new to us, we'll start with a review of the rules." Low groans made a humming sound.

Marcie turned to the blackboard and wrote, "No alcohol or other drugs are permitted." She looked at the women and added, "Violations of this rule results in immediate dismissal. Any resident punitively dismissed must wait ninety days before applying for readmission. All prescription drugs and over-the- counter medication, and that includes cough syrup, mouth wash, and yes, even Midol, must be kept locked in the drug cabinet and only dispensed by Pearl or myself."

Marcie turned back to the board and wrote, "No phone calls for the first two weeks. No weekend passes for the first month." She turned back to the residents with a glance at Veronica. "Passes must be earned and may be revoked at the discretion of the director. Any questions?"

Veronica made a face while the other shook their heads.

Back to the board, she wrote, "Lights out at eleven during the week and midnight on Friday and Saturday. No smoking in the main part of the house." She wrote on without interruption. Her shoulders began to ache from the difficulty of writing at an awkward angle. How did teachers do it? When she finally finished, she turned toward the women. "Any questions or comments?"

Veronica spoke up. "Why don't you just lock us in our rooms?"

"Funny you should say that," Marcie replied. "If you don't behave yourself, I just might do it. Speaking of behaving, I forgot to mention that you're not to disturb Deborah for any reason whatsoever."

Georgia Lu's arm shot up in the air again. When Marcie nodded, the big woman asked, "Who's she?"

Good question, Marcie thought. "Deborah was hired by Miss Sarah as Port Victor's housemother, but she's more like a guest."

All of a sudden, the women froze in their seats, all eyes focused on something beyond the French doors.

"I heard that!" Deborah called.

Marcie turned around and gave Deborah a big smile. "I'm so glad you could make it," she said. "Come and meet our newest residents." Even though she expected Deborah to stay clear, she moved the blackboard to a corner to make room for her.

Eyebrows rose in surprise when Deborah stepped forward, stopping just outside the doorway. None of the women made a move or said a word. "So this is what they look like," she stated flatly. She went on. "Let's see," she said. She pointed to Missy, Veronica, and Pearl in turn. "I've seen you and you and of course you. But not you or you."

"Let me introduce you to Phyllis," Marcie said. Phyllis stood up, gave a little wave and sat back down. "And our newest resident is Georgia Lu Dawson." Georgia Lu stood up but she did not sit back down. She went straight to Deborah and, without a word of warning, lifted her up to eye level. In unison, the women sucked in their breaths when Georgia Lu held Deborah out in front of her and said, "Why, you don't weigh no more'n a sack of potatoes."

Marcie had expected Deborah to start pounding on Georgia Lu's shoulders and demanding to be let down. Instead, Deborah appeared to be off in another world. An excited smile trembled at her lips as she looked all around. Her big blue eyes traveled from the sunroom to the living and dining rooms, the foyer, and back to the sunroom.

It struck Marcie then. For the first time, Deborah was seeing through the eyes of a tall adult.

Disappointment clouded Deborah's face when Georgia Lu set her down.

Oblivious to what had just occurred, Georgia Lu said, "I ain't never seen nobody as little as you."

Deborah busied herself with straightening her clothes. When she finished tucking and pulling, she looked at Georgia Lu and said, "I can use you." Without a word to anyone else, she turned and walked away.

Wearing a puzzled look, Georgia Lu stared after her.

"Whew," said Missy in a hushed voice. "I'm glad that's over."

"If that don't beat all I ever seen," Pearl said, pushing up from her chair and shuffling off toward the kitchen.

"The little shrimp," Veronica said. "Who does she think she is? Coming and going like a prissy princess."

Phyllis piped up. "I was so scared when Georgia Lu picked her up, I almost peed my pants."

At that, laughter rang out. Not a hearty, good-time laugh, but a laugh of sheer relief.

When the laughter died down, Marcie said, "Tomorrow we'll meet at the same time for a session on how to be assertive. Afterwards, Veronica can entertain us with another story."

Everyone cheered except Veronica's biggest fan. "Ma'am?" Georgia Lu said. "What'd she mean when she said she could use me?"

"I haven't the slightest idea, Georgia Lu. But I do know she enjoyed being held up where she could get a different view of her world." She looked at the women individually, and said, "What do you think?"

"I think she's a nutcase," Veronica said. "As for you," she looked at Georgia Lu, "I'll swear, woman. I thought I was unpredictable, but you take the cake."

Georgia Lu looked all around, "Cake? Did you say cake? I sure would like me a piece of cake."

Veronica said, "Sorry, Georgia Lu. It was a figure of speech."

"You mean there ain't no cake?"

Veronica huffed and said, "For heaven's sakes, Georgia Lu. Go ask Pearl." Georgia Lu loped off toward the kitchen.

"Lord," Veronica said, "she's about to drive me crazy. But I can't get mad at her because she'll do anything I ask of her." Then they all began to speak at once.

The roar of a lawn mower drowned out their voices. Marcie went to the window and looked out. "Excuse me, ladies," she said, "I've got to see a man about a plot of ground." She headed for the front door.

———

Jackson had a large upper body and short legs. He wore a pair of blue coveralls over a white shirt and a straw hat with a wide brim. The minute Marcie flagged him down he cut off the mower and sat waiting in the shade of a mulberry tree. She went up to him and said, "Hi, Jackson. I'm Marcie Parker, the new director. You doing okay today?"

He took off his hat and wiped the sweat from his brow with a bandana. He placed the hat on his right knee. "Doing just dandy. How about yourself?"

"I couldn't be better," she said. "What I want to know is do you have a tiller?"

"Sure do. I got about every piece of machinery there is."

"What would you think about tilling us a spot so we can plant a vegetable garden?"

He took a toothpick out of his pocket, stuck it in his mouth, chewed on it and then took it out. "I reckon a good spot would be out back between the two dogwoods. It gets full sun and the drainage is right. But I'd have to talk to Miss Sarah."

"Oh, of course," Marcie said. "I knew we'd have to get permission."

He nodded. "Seems like Miss Sarah would be proud to have a garden. It would save her lots of grocery money. Knowing Pearl like I do, she'd be canning everything y'all don't eat."

Marcie hadn't thought of canning the overflow. "Sounds wonderful," she said. "We could be eating home-grown food all year long."

"Yes, ma'am."

"We'd be glad to share with you and Miss Sarah."

"Don't worry about me. I got three acres planted."

"Wow," Marcie said. "That must be a lot of work."

Jackson fitted his hat to his head, an indication he wanted to get back to his mowing. "I got five growing boys, a wife, my mother, and two aunts to feed." He started the mower. "I'll speak to Miss Sarah after I finish here."

"Thanks, Jackson. Thanks a lot." He tipped his hat and roared off.

———

Talk about crazy days. This one had been a doozy, and it wasn't even over yet. She went inside the house, thinking to hide out in her office, but a booming voice stopped her. Much like her roommate, but without the glamorous image, Georgia Lu was holding forth in the sunroom. Marcie couldn't resist.

Georgia Lu said, "I had me this sorrel gelding named Red. In the summertime ole Red loved to go wadin' in the creek near the house. He'd prance around, swishing his tail and I'd splash water over him. One night, I was drunker'n a wobbly bicycle an' I decided me and ole Red oughta take us a dip in the catfish pond. It was a big old pond my daddy carved out in the back field. Twern't no catfish in it, we done caught 'em all. And everybody knowed that there pond was crawlin' with snakes. Redbelly water snakes, brown water snakes, banded water snakes, all the bad ones. Like I said, I was crocked to the gills, so I coaxed ole Red down the hill and into the pond. I was ridin' bareback an' grippin' ole Red's mane as we went deeper and deeper. The water got up to here." She put a hand on her hip. "That's when somethin' told me we'd gone too far. I started tryin' to get ole Red to turn around. We got halfway 'round an' ole Red must'a stepped in a hole, 'cause he stumbled and I tumbled into that black water. That sobered me up in a gol dang hurry 'cause I can't swim."

A chorus of "Oh no's" rose up. Georgia Lu went on. "I can't swim, but I sure can holler, and holler I did. I whooped loud 'nuf to wake everybody in

146

three counties. Didn't do me no good. I swallowed a lot of water while I was hollerin' and I started to sink. The more I fought that water, the more it wanted my hide. I was goin' down for the count when I felt somethin' bump up against me. I made a grab for it, prayin' it weren't no snake." She paused for a moment, her audience hanging on every word.

"It was ole Red!" she bellowed. The women let out audible sighs of relief. "Yes sir, ole Red saved my life. But it took all my brothers, three ropes, and Pappy's tractor to haul us outta that there pit."

The pleasant sound of laughter followed Marcie out of the room. For the first time she had a sense belonging, of having finally found her place.

CHAPTER 15

The post card featured a photo of the school Julie attended in Washington, D.C. Shot from the air, the campus showed a cluster of eight buildings with the traditional ivy clinging to their red brick walls, tennis courts, two playing fields, and an abundance of green lawn and far-reaching trees. None of it mattered to Marcie. What mattered was the message on the other side.

"Hi Mom. Mid-terms are over and a group of us girls are celebrating with a trip to New York. Hope to see you in June. I love you, Julie."

New York! Sixteen-year-old girls going to New York? To celebrate? Were they being chaperoned? If so, by whom? How long were they staying? *Where* were they staying? What was David thinking? He wasn't.

Standing there by the mailbox, she read the card again. Blinded by the news about New York; she hadn't caught the last line. Why had Julie written that she *hoped* to see her in June when she should've said she'd *see* her in June? That had been the plan all along. She slammed the mailbox shut and rushed into the house, barely noticing Charley and failing to greet the clocks. She went straight to the phone and dialed the number to David's condo. It was after six o'clock eastern time on a week night. With any luck, he'd be home.

"Hullo," said a grumpy-sounding Davy.

"Well, hello, yourself," Marcie said, surprised and delighted that her son had actually answered the phone. "How are you?"

"Okay."

"I got a job, Davy. A really good one."

"Yeah?" He couldn't have sounded more disinterested.

"I'm the director of Port Victor, a halfway house for women."

"What kind of name is Port Victor?"

"Well, the 'Port' part is like a port in a storm, and 'Victor' is after the man who built the house. This job is like the one at New Start, except I'm the boss and I counsel women instead of men."

"Huh," Davy grunted.

She changed the subject. "Are your mid–terms over, too?"

"Yeah."

"How do you think you did?"

"I don't know."

Even if he was her son and she hadn't spoken to him in a long time, she'd had enough of his sulkiness. "Is your sister there?"

"Nah."

"Has she already left for New York?"

"How do you know about that?" Marcie was amazed. He'd spoken a complete sentence.

"She sent me a post card from school."

"She's so lucky it sucks."

"I take it you're not going to New York?"

"Nah."

"Why not?"

"I don't have anybody to go with."

Marcie swallowed hard. That was a huge admission coming from him. It sounded like Fleming's Hill all over again. Julie made friends easily; Davy did not. Especially in a new environment.

"May I speak to your dad?"

"He's not here. He's never here."

That's why he'd answered the phone. The poor kid was lonely. "Oh, Davy," she said, wanting to reach out and pull him to her, "won't you please come home? I love you and I miss you and I'm here for you."

"I don't have a home. You sold it."

"I know, honey, and I'm sorry, but we can't buy it back. Our home is here on the river now, and if you'd just give it another try I know you'd come to love it as much as I do."

"Not a chance."

"Oh, Davy, please don't talk like that. It makes me feel like I'm losing you."

"I gotta go, Mom."

"No, wait! Are you coming in June?" Marcie heard the click on the other end of the line. A rush of tears blurred her vision. Her chin trembled. Her face collapsed. She ran to the bedroom, flopped onto the bed and sobbed.

She cried long and hard, both her nose and eyes leaking tears. Then she got the hiccups. Her stomach muscles ached and her head felt ready to explode. She managed to reach the box of Kleenex on her bedside table. She blew and blew her nose, crumpling up one tissue after another. Her skull throbbed each time she hiccupped. She tried holding her breath. She tried pinching her nose shut, taking in air and blowing it out. She hiccupped. Resigned, she just sat there on the side of the bed, waiting for the next one, and the next one after that.

How could a mother dislike her son one minute and love him with all her heart the next? Because he was still a child, a child in need of love and attention, a child who needed guidance, a child who had a lot of growing up to do.

As for Julie going to New York, Marcie would just have to trust her. The girl had a good head on her shoulders. No doubt the girls planned to attend a couple of Broadway shows, do some sightseeing, and shop. It would be a good experience for all of them. Marcie couldn't wait to hear all about it. Still, David should have called her. Consideration for others was not one of his strong suits.

Finally aware of Charley nuzzling her leg and whimpering sympathetically, she stroked the top of his head. "You're still my best buddy," she told him. His tail beat the air. "I'll bet you'd like your dinner, wouldn't you?" His ears went up and his tail beat harder. "Okay, but I've got to clean up first."

Charley followed her into the bathroom, where he stood guard while she washed her face and applied a moisturizer. Her eyes were puffed up like a frog's and her nose was as red as her lipstick. But it had felt good to purge all those pent-up tears. What's more, she'd gotten rid of the hiccups.

After feeding Charley, she went around the rooms saying hello to each of the clocks. It was probably her imagination but they seemed to respond by showing off their particular talent. She hated to think of stashing them when Julie and Davy came home. Maybe she'd just leave them in place and let them wind down. The kids *would* come home in June as planned, or else. Or else what, she did not know, but she'd figure something out.

As she walked through the rooms, her fingers trailed over treasured pieces. Except for the children's furniture and a few odds and ends, she'd arranged for David to dispose of the furnishings they'd shared. Then, piece by piece, she'd collected an eclectic blend of modern, Colonial American, and antiques found in out-of-the-way junk shops. Nothing she bought resembled the stiff and formal brocades she'd had before. Most of the pieces had to be refinished, a job she'd tackled with a sense of discovery. As each layer of paint or varnish, and sometimes both, was stripped a new surface emerged. Finally, down to the bare wood, she allowed the piece to breathe a while before rubbing in an oil-based finish to bring back its natural beauty.

She loved the smell and feel of wood. All of its hidden crevices, grooves, and ridges gave off a distinctively rich aroma depending on type. She had kept buying and scraping and polishing until the house couldn't hold anymore. Along with the usual array of cabinets, drawers, and appliances, the large country kitchen alone housed a pie safe, a freestanding cabinet with a flour bin, a hall tree, and a round oak table with four cane-bottomed chairs. When hunting for clocks, interesting pieces of furniture still caught her eye, but to date she'd managed to resist buying.

The house itself started off as a four-room cedar cabin. The former owners kept adding on as their family expanded, but Marcie still thought of it as a cabin. Three bedrooms, two baths, living room with a stone fireplace, kitchen, and a den. The front room, kitchen, half of the den, and Marcie's bedroom faced the river; the kids' bedrooms, their bath and the other half of the den faced the road and the hill that led up to the bluff, where Augustus Alexander Fleming's tombstone threw a long shadow over the others in the old cemetery. The founder of Fleming's Hill, he was Sarah Fleming-Thornton's great-great-grandfather.

Once a year a team of descendants held a cleanup day at the old cemetery. They cut the saplings, hacked at underbrush, cleared debris, hauled off rotted logs, raked the grounds, cleaned tombstones, and planted flowers and shrubs. Afterwards, they held a memorial service and then adjourned to Fleming's Park for a picnic supper. Marcie envied them. It must be wonderful to have a place to pay tribute to the dead.

Stories about ghosts in the old cemetery abounded. One female ghost in particular was supposed to wander the bluff in search of her lover who had been reported missing from his regiment after the battle at Antioch during the Civil War. According to legend, she believed he had been wounded and was trying to find his way home to her.

With flashlights in hand, Davy and Julie had hiked up to the bluff one night in hopes of spying a ghost or two. All they'd gotten for their efforts were burrs stuck to their socks and pant legs, a few scratches, and dozens of mosquito bites. Later, they had laughed about it.

Marcie smiled at the memory. If only the kids loved this place as much as they did back then, it would be paradise on earth.

———

The following morning Pearl and Georgia Lu were ready to light out for the Farmer's Co-op to buy seeds and plants for the garden. Sarah had given the okay and, true to his word, Jackson had not only tilled a spot, he'd fertilized it as well.

Marcie hadn't counted on taking them to the Co-op, but how else could they buy seeds? Because she couldn't leave the other residents alone— she considered leaving them in Deborah's care the same as leaving them alone— she called upstairs for everyone to get ready to go shopping.

After she'd gulped down a mugful of coffee and left a voice mail message on the phone, she climbed into the van. Situated behind the wheel, she took a deep breath and let it out in a whoosh. She'd never driven a van before and the thought of driving five women around town made her extremely nervous. If anything happened, it would be her head on the chopping block.

Georgia Lu and Pearl boarded next. Pearl still had her apron on. They settled behind Marcie on the front row and got into a discussion on the merits of planting all seeds or some seeds and some plants. After boarding, Missy and Phyllis sat in the second row. Phyllis was telling Missy about the book she was reading, *Running the Bulls.*

"This time it's the wife who has an affair. It's fascinating to see how the husband handles it, which so far is not very well."

"I need to check out the books in Marcie's library," Missy said. "I'm reading an old paperback over again, and I didn't like it the first time I read it."

"You really should. She's got quite a collection."

Marcie held her tongue for fear of turning Missy off the idea of borrowing a book. If she could get Missy to stay in the office long enough, she might be able to break down the girl's wall.

She looked at Georgia Lu over her shoulder. "Was Veronica almost ready when you left the room?"

"No, ma'am. She's in a world of fussy over what to wear. We got dresses strewed all over the place. It'll take me half a day to hang 'em all up."

"Swell," Marcie said. Just as she started to climb out of the van, the door to the storage room opened and Veronica came tripping out in a black linen suit with the requisite jewelry and spiked heels.

"Sorry I'm late, girls," she said. "I just couldn't decide what to wear." The skirt to her suit was so tight she had to lift it well above her knees to mount the steps to the van.

"Gol dang it, Veronica," Georgia Lu wailed. "That's the first dress you tried on."

"It's not a dress, it's a suit," Veronica retorted. "And I'll have you know it's an Armani." She sat down in the single seat to the right of Georgia Lu and Pearl.

Marcie said, "Is everybody ready?"

"Yes," sang the chorus. Marcie started the engine and put the gear in reverse. She'd been studying the instrument panel while waiting for Veronica, but she still didn't know how to turn on the lights or the windshield wipers. If the sun kept shining she'd be okay, but an April shower could pop up out of nowhere.

Having made it out of the garage, she steered the van in front of the house and down the far side of the driveway. As soon as traffic cleared, she turned left. Fortunately, her destination was a straight shot down Main Street to the other end of town.

As they passed the street that led to the town square, where most of the dress shops were located, Veronica said, "Oh, good, we're going to Huntsville." She leaned forward, "Marcie, please take me an exclusive shop. I need some dressy sport clothes for around the house."

Pearl cackled a laugh, Georgia Lu whooped, Phyllis and Missy giggled.

"Veronica," Marcie said, "I hate to disappoint you, but we're going to the Farmer's Co-op to buy seeds for the garden."

"What? You mean I got all dressed up to go to some dirty feed store?!"

Marcie said, "Tell you what. After we leave the Co-op, I'll stop by JC Penney's. They ought to have what you're looking for."

"You must be kidding. My momma used to shop there all the time. She'd buy these tacky little dresses for me to wear to school. They had ribbons and bows and were always too short. I swore I'd never shop there once I got out on my own."

Marcie understood only too well. While living with her aunt and uncle she often had to wear hand-me-downs that had belonged to her older cousins. "Maybe we could try Goody's," she said.

"Goody's? I never heard of it," Veronica said.

All the better, Marcie thought. "It's a ladies dress shop. You can at least take a look at what they've got."

"Oh, all right."

"We can't stay long. I don't know what Deborah might do if she wakes up and finds an empty house."

"Who cares?" Veronica said.

"I do," Marcie said. "My job could be on the line." Silence prevailed for the rest of the ride.

Marcie was glad to see that the Co-op had parallel parking. If she'd had to try squeezing the van in horizontally, she was bound to hit something. She parked a short distance from the front door to allow for ample space. "Okay, ladies, all out."

Veronica remained in her seat while the other women descended the steps. Marcie looked at her. "Aren't you joining us?"

"Heavens, no. I can smell the manure from here."

"Suit yourself," Marcie said and left Veronica stewing.

When Marcie caught up with the others, Georgia Lu and Pearl were filling a tray with a variety of tomato and pepper plants. Meanwhile, Phyllis and Missy were browsing up and down the aisles. Rather than buy the seeds in small packets, the two gardening experts chose to buy them by measuring cups. Okra, cucumbers, squash, eggplant, corn, and zucchini.

"Do we have room to plant all this stuff?" Marcie asked.

"Yessum," Pearl said. "We done studied on it." She pulled a diagram out of her apron pocket. On it, the two had drawn lines where each crop would grow.

"See here," Georgia Lu said, putting a fat finger on the drawing. "You don't want to plant the cucumbers next to the squash 'cause they'll grow a half breed. An' see here, most of the wind comes from the west—"

Marcie interrupted because time was limited. "Okay," she said. "You two know what you're doing so let's get on with it." She headed to the checkout lane. This would be her first purchase out of petty cash. She rounded up the women and, with Georgia Lu carrying the plants and Pearl carrying the seeds, they boarded the van.

"That was fast," Veronica said as the women returned to their seats.

"It don't take long when you come prepared," Georgia Lu said. "An' this here is a mighty good day to plant."

Marcie started the engine. "Next stop Goody's." More confident about driving now that she'd made it this far, she backed out of her spot and off they went.

Just getting away from the house had put the women in high spirits. They talked and talked, and laughed and laughed. If Marcie hadn't been so worried about what Deborah might do upon awakening, she'd be talking and laughing with them. She could kick herself for promising to take Veronica to Goody's.

If it took as long for Veronica to look at clothes as it had taken her to choose what to wear today it'd be lunchtime before they got back.

They made it to the shopping center and Marcie found a parking spot right in front of the store. She turned around to face the women. "Ladies, I think you'd better stay in the van while Veronica shops. We need to get back to the house as soon as possible."

Several moans hummed in the background. Marcie said, "We'll come back when we have more time." She opened the door and descended the steps.

Veronica soon followed. Halfway there, she stopped and said, "I don't know, Marcie. This place looks kind of tacky."

"Maybe so, but you won't know what they have unless you go inside."

Veronica traipsed off, her high heels clicking on the pavement. Once inside the store, Veronica sniffed her nose as she took in the scene. But she forged ahead to the ladies' section. She pawed through the racks and miracle of miracles pulled out an attractive velour sweat suit in a lovely teal–blue color. "This is what I've been looking for," she said, a bright smile on her face. "Here, hold my purse while I try it on."

"Please don't be long," Marcie said, slightly buckling under the weight of Veronica's purse. What did she have in there? Rocks? Five minutes later, Veronica returned to the rack of sweat suits. "It fits perfectly," she said. She then pulled out two more suits in the same style but in different colors, a deep rose and a white. "Summer's coming up so I'll need white."

The mention of summer brought visions of Marcie's kids sitting around the oak table, eating pizza and telling her all about life in Washington, D.C.

"Okay, I'm ready to go," Veronica said.

Marcie could not believe it. "Aren't you going to try those on?" She gestured to the rose and white pairs of sweats.

"I don't see why I should. They're the same size as the blue one. Besides, getting in and out of this suit is a royal pain in the ass."

Veronica charged the clothes and all went well until the clerk stuffed her outfits in a big plastic bag, hangers and all. "My dear," she said to the clerk, "you mustn't mess up a customer's new clothes. Don't you have a proper bag to put them in?"

156

The clerk popped her wad of chewing gum while sizing Veronica up. Then she said, "What's a proper bag look like?"

"It's a long— oh, never mind." She snatched the bag out of the clerk's hand, removed the clothes and flung the bag onto the counter. She shook and smoothed the suits and then carefully folded them over one arm and carried them out of the store with her head held high.

Marcie was proud of her. She, too, hated it when clerks stuffed her clothes in a bag but she'd never had the nerve to say so.

The women oohed and aahed over her purchases.

"Hot damn, Veronica," Georgia Lu said. "Now you'll look like the rest of us."

"Hardly," Veronica said, giving her roommate a look.

Marcie cut in before Veronica could say more. "Here we go, ladies. Fasten your seat belts." She looked in the rearview mirror for people or passing cars and caught a glimpse of Georgia Lu searching for her seat belt. "It was a figure of speech, Georgia Lu. The van isn't equipped with seat belts."

She heard Pearl mutter, "She's always pulling that figur'a speech thing on me."

"What's it mean?" Georgia Lu asked.

"Beats me," Pearl said.

"It means a phrase that's often used as a kind of joke," Phyllis said.

"What's that there 'phrase' mean?"

"It's a group of words that carry a single thought. Like telling you to fasten your seat belts when you don't have any."

Georgia Lu turned to Pearl. "What'd she say?"

"Beats me," said Pearl.

"It don't make no sense," Georgia Lu said.

"Don't pay 'em no mind," Pearl said. "Marcie, she uses them hifalutin' words all the time."

They made their merry way back to the house, Veronica happy to have found a few "snazzy outfits," Phyllis and Missy laughing over different figures of speech, Pearl and Georgia Lu on the subject of planting their garden, and Marcie relieved to be heading to her second home.

CHAPTER 16

Saturday morning broke gray and gloomy. Marcie opened one eye, peeked out the window and turned on her other side. Burrowing into her covers, she slowly drifted back to sleep. Even Charley had no desire to get up. Lying on the hooked rug beside her bed, she could hear his light snore.

She couldn't have slept long when her eyes snapped open. Roger! How could she forget about him? He'd be arriving at six to take her out to dinner! In the meantime, she had to shop for groceries, clean the house, wind the clocks … She didn't have time to lounge about. Throwing back the covers, she scrambled out of bed and made for the bathroom.

All she could think about while taking a shower and getting dressed for the day was her date with Roger. Why, oh, why had she agreed to go out with him? After the divorce, she'd sworn off romantic notions about men. Why set herself up for another rejection? Then Roger came along. She'd been swayed by his good looks and air of confidence. She'd also wanted to see what it was like to be in the company of a man other than George. That was then and this was now, and she wanted out. She wasn't ready to date. She might never be ready. Just the thought of making polite conversation gave her a headache.

She let Charley out to do his business, made coffee and put an egg on to boil. How could she in good conscience break the date on the very day they were supposed to go out? She couldn't. She would just have to suffer through it—no, wait. They didn't have to go to a restaurant, where they might run into someone Roger knew, and that someone might spread the word that he was dating Sarah's new hire. It was entirely too risky. She would prepare a meal for them to have at home. That way, no one would have to know they were having dinner, and when conversation ran out, he could leave and she could go to bed.

She'd make a meatloaf. David had loved her meatloaf. With baked potatoes, peas, and a green salad. She'd have to call on Mrs. Smith again. Maybe an apple pie this time. Although she didn't want to ply him with liquor, Roger struck her as a beer man. She would pick up a six-pack of Heineken, David's favorite, and a bottle of wine for herself.

That decided, she retrieved the morning paper from the mailbox. A light drizzle sprinkled her head and shoulders. A bank of dense fog curled over the river. She dreaded the thought of driving to town in this kind of weather. With any luck, the sun would break through and burn up any remains of this steaming pot of witches' brew.

Charley bounded up, his jaw parted in a satisfied smile. He'd checked his territory and apparently all was well. No skunks, no beavers, no foxes, no muskrats, no cats, and no stray dogs. He tagged along with Marcie and entered the house when she did. The usual cacophony of clock sounds hailed their arrival. As bells tinkled, chimes pealed, and guitars strummed, Marcie wondered how Roger would react to her family of clocks. She'd find out soon enough.

She took her time eating a soft-boiled egg on toast. Putting Roger out of her mind, she poured a second cup of coffee and perused the local newspaper. A silent auction and dinner to benefit the Methodist children's home was scheduled for a week from today. An accident on Red Leaf Lane had claimed the life of a fifty- two-year-old man on a motorcycle. The city council meeting had erupted into an argument between a council member and a developer who had been trying to get a zone change for more than eight months. A liquor license had been granted to Slyvie's Bar and Grill. The beautification council had awarded Yard of the Month to Mr. and Mrs. William Maier on Washington Street.

Marcie checked the obituaries in case the name of one of her missing women was listed. She read Ann Landers' column, and then her horoscope. It said: *Problems will stem from rationalizing matters rather than seeing issues in a realistic light. If you want a productive day, take off those rose-colored glasses.* What rose- colored glasses, she wondered? She'd packed those away with the divorce papers.

Pushing up from the table, she carried her dish and cup to the sink, gave them a quick rinse, put them in the dishwasher, and unplugged the coffee pot. One more trip to the bathroom and she'd be ready to go shopping.

The fog had lifted by the time she reached the bridge. First stop, Home Depot, where she looked at outdoor grills. Not wanting to mess with bags of charcoal, she splurged on a gas grill that had a separate heating unit for a pot of something. Then she looked at irons and ended up with a lightweight steam iron. The grill put a dent in petty cash but she didn't think Sarah would mind. A young, male clerk loaded her items into the back of her wagon and off she went to the grocery store.

———

She was dusting Elvis when it dawned on her. Roger had never asked for directions to her house. He'd never even asked for her address. It wasn't as if she lived in town. To get to "the road to nowhere," as her son referred to it, Roger would have to cross the bridge over the Tennessee River and make the first right turn onto Old Point Road, a deadend. Her cabin was the seventh on the left. Surely he would call before leaving his house. Still, he'd be taking a chance. She might be out in the yard or in the shower. At this point, she didn't really care. As a fellow employee of Sarah's, Roger was the wrong man at the wrong time.

Charley sensed something was up as she bustled about the house sweeping and polishing. He followed on her heels everywhere she went. She'd start to make a fast turn and there he'd be, stopping her cold. She was patient with him at first, saying "Hey, buddy, move it." But as the day wore on and she wore out, she was likely to snap, "For heaven's sakes, Charley! Go lie down!" He wouldn't. On top of that, he was shedding his winter coat everywhere the two of them went.

Finished with cleaning, she retired to the kitchen to prepare the meat loaf. She'd paid extra for ground round and now she wished she had stuck with plain hamburger. Music! She could use some music. She could also use something to sip. Thinking it too early for wine, she opened a bottle of Heineken.

With Charley banished outdoors and Michael Jackson's *Thriller* blaring from the stereo in the living room, she attacked the ground beef with a swing in her hips. It didn't take long for her spirits to lift. She started singing along with Michael, pausing now and then to do a little dance or take a sip of beer. The best part was, she was having fun all by herself. She didn't need a man in her life to make her happy. Roger could take a flying leap for all she cared.

Now that the food was ready to cook, it was time to dress. The sound of Eric Clapton playing on the stereo grew dimmer as she went to her closet. Veronica came to mind as she hunted for something to wear. Unlike Veronica, she didn't have time to dither, and she wasn't about to put on an outfit that required panty hose. Jeans and a sweatshirt? Slacks and a shirt? She decided on Levi's with her rose–colored cotton sweater over a white shirt. That would be both comfortable and casual.

By five-thirty Roger hadn't called for directions. He'd probably forgotten all about their so–called date. Oh well, she could eat leftovers all week long. Nothing wrong with that. And he'd saved her from making polite conversation. She retrieved her bottle of beer, put a Doug Kershaw tape on the stereo, and started two-stepping around the living room. Sensing that all was well, Charley finally flopped down in front of the fireplace.

Between the music and the clocks, she didn't hear the doorbell. But Charley did. He was up in a flash and charging the door. "Oops," she said gaily. "It looks like our guest has arrived." She set her beer on the coffee table and went to the door, mindless of the loud music and the clocks.

Opening the door wide, she said, "Well, I see you found me after all."

Roger put a hand to his ear and said, "What?" He held the other hand behind his back.

She said, "Just a minute!" Hurrying to the stereo, she turned the volume down. Back at the door, she looked at Roger, as if for the first time. Wearing a pair of khaki slacks and a black long- sleeved T-shirt; he was as good looking as she remembered. But he didn't seem quite as confident. And what was he holding behind his back?

"Come in," she said, stepping aside.

He glanced down at Charley. The big dog had pricked his ears but was not wagging his tail. "Is it safe?"

She thought he meant the clocks. "You'll get used to them."

"There's more?" He looked past her, scanning the area.

"Oh yes," she said, still full of good cheer, "there's thirty-two of them."

Frowning, he backed up a step. "Thirty-two?"

"Yep. You'll get to meet all of them."

"Thirty-two?" Roger repeated.

The smile faded from her face. This was not fun. "Are you coming in or not?"

He took a cautious step forward, then another, and another, all the while looking everywhere but at her.

Marcie closed the door behind him. He looked back at it as though wishing he were still outside. "Listen," she said, "there's nothing I can do about the clocks. If they bother you that much, you'd better leave now."

He grinned that special grin, and said, "I thought you meant thirty-two *dogs*."

A giggle bubbled up and out of her. "Heavens. I couldn't afford to feed that many dogs."

He pulled the hand out from behind his back and presented her with a bottle of Merlot. "I hope you drink wine."

"How did you know this was my favorite?"

"I didn't. I just guessed."

"Well, you guessed right. And that reminds me, how did you know where I live?"

"Your job application."

Shocked, she said, "You read my application?"

"I'm afraid so."

"You stinker! That's private information."

He grinned and said, "*Was* private."

"Well," she said, feigning indifference, "now that you're here, I suppose you can stay." She turned her back on him and, with the wine bottle in hand, strode toward the kitchen.

He either had to leave quietly or follow her. He followed.

Marcie put the meat loaf and the potatoes in the pre-heated oven and set the timer. The salad greens had been washed, wrapped in paper towels, and stored in the crisper. The yeast rolls could heat and the peas could cook while she tossed the salad. At the proper time, she'd bring Mrs. Smith's apple pie out of the laundry room. What was she forgetting? Oh, yes, Roger. She turned around, expecting to see him pressed up against a wall. He was nowhere in sight. Maybe the clocks had run him off, after all. Like children showing off for company, they had been especially noisy ever since the doorbell rang. Charley wasn't in the immediate area, either. What was going on?

After looking in the living room and the den, she found them on the screened porch, Roger looking at the river, Charley guarding the door. "Ah," she said. "I see you decided to stick around."

Roger turned to face her. "This is quite a spread you've got here. Great view, lots of land and trees. My boys would live on that dock. They love to fish."

Marcie started to say, "I wish my boy did," but thought better of it. Roger didn't know she had kids and for now she wanted to keep it that way. She gazed off in the distance. "I lose myself here… the birds, the peace, the quiet. Yet, I'm only ten minutes from town."

"Yeah, I could be content living here."

"Where do you live?"

"Not far from the brickyard, on Maple Street."

"Oh, I know where that is. It's a nice neighborhood." She had pictured him living in a trailer after giving his home to his ex-wife and kids.

"It's okay," he said. "One of these days I'm going to have a place on the river."

"Good luck," she said. "Would you care for a Heineken? Or would you rather have wine? I've got some cheese balls to munch on."

"Yeah, sure," he said. Once more, he followed her and Charley after him.

Standing at the refrigerator, she looked at him and said, "What will it be? Beer or wine?"

"What are you going to have?"

"Never mind what I'm going to have. If you'd rather have a soft drink, I've got Cokes and 7-Up."

"I'll take some of that wine."

"Ha," she said. "I thought you were a beer man."

"I'm not much of a drinker. Sometimes I'll have a beer after working up a sweat, like mowing the lawn. But tonight, wine sounds good."

She got the cork remover out of a drawer and took it and the bottle for him to open. Then she went to a cupboard and collected two wine glasses.

"I'm not very good at this," he said. "I'd better open it over the sink."

She made way for him, thinking this couldn't be the confident and gregarious man from the brickyard. But then, at the yard he was in charge. Here, she was. She decided to go easy on him.

Standing a few feet away, she watched as he tried to pry the cork out of the bottle. He was going about it all wrong, proof that he didn't drink much. Her fingers itched to wrest the bottle from his hands, but she resisted. He would figure it out eventually.

In an effort to take her mind off the cork, she started talking. "I suppose you're wondering why I have so many clocks." He glanced at her, then went back to his task. "It all started when I got a Mickey Mouse clock for my eleventh birthday. He was a windup and I was fascinated by how he worked. He doesn't tell time anymore, but I still have him. My ex is a career Army man. Every two years or so, he was transferred to another part of the country, which meant I was transferred, too. Anyway, I thought it'd be fun to collect clocks as souvenirs. Used clocks, never new. I hunted for them at garage sales, antique shops, junk shops. Finding special clocks soon became more than a hobby, it became a passion. I ran out of room for them a long time ago, but that didn't stop me, especially after the divorce. But now that I have the job at Port Victor, the urge to buy more clocks has gone away."

Roger managed to ease the cork out intact and pour wine into the glasses without spilling a drop. Grinning with pride, he carried the glasses to where she was standing and offered her one.

She accepted and then proposed a toast. "Here's to a lovely evening."

After clinking glasses with her, he said, "Here's to your clocks."

She laughed and held her glass out to his. "To the clocks." They took a moment to savor the wine.

"What do you think?" Roger said.

"Of what? The wine or the weather?" It was a form of hell trying to converse with someone you didn't know. David could finish her sentences. And George... More often than not, he anticipated her question and provided an answer before she could open her mouth.

Roger laughed and said, "Maybe you should turn the music up so we can forget the small talk."

She shook her head. "The clocks are making enough of a racket." She tipped her head back and cried, "Hush!" Maybe it was her imagination, but her plea seemed to work. Not that the clocks were silent, they were never silent, but at least she could hear herself think. She got out her tin of cheese balls and arranged them on a dessert plate. She looked at Roger and said, "If you don't mind the chilly air, we could drink our wine on the porch."

Roger insisted on carrying the plate along with his wine glass. They settled on matching wicker rockers with a glass-topped table in between. Once again, Charley sat on guard at the door.

Guilt washed over her. Except for feeding him his dinner, she had ignored him. Marcie called him over. Bending to him, she stroked the top of his head. "Forgive my bad manners," she told Roger. "I should've introduced you to Charley before now. He's my best buddy in the whole world."

"He's a good-looking Shepard," Roger said. "How old is he?"

She did the arithmetic in her head. She'd bought Charley as a puppy when Davy turned four. Davy was now fifteen. "Good heavens," she exclaimed, "he's eleven years old." She sat back, her mind filled with the terrors of her eleventh year. Well, she wasn't planning to go crazy over a church and she wasn't going to abandon him, so she and Charley would toddle around together in their old age.

"That's getting up there," Roger said. "Seventy-seven, in dog years."

"Don't remind me," she said, giving Charley a cheese ball. He swallowed it whole.

"Something sure smells good," Roger said.

"I hope you like it. I haven't made meat loaf in a long time."

Roger sat up straight and looked at her. "You're making it for us? I thought I was taking you out for dinner."

"I didn't feel like going out, so I decided to cook for you. I hope you don't mind."

"Mind? The last time someone cooked for me was Thanksgiving."

"I didn't know you were so deprived." She shoved the dessert plate toward him. "Here, have a cheese ball. They're home-made by Betty at the Bake Shop."

Roger laughed and proposed another toast. "To Betty."

Marcie added, "To Betty Boop, Betty Grable, Betty Crocker, Bette Davis—"

Roger chimed in. "Betty White, Archie's Betty—"

Marcie cut him off. "Oh, and what was the name of the woman that played Barney's girlfriend on, 'The Andy Griffith Show?'"

With a straight face, Roger said, "Betty?" They both burst out laughing.

Marcie cheered, "To all the Betties of the world!"

"Hear, hear!" Roger cried.

Charley stood before them, grinning and beating the air with his tail. It turned out to be a lovely evening, after all.

CHAPTER 17

Roger had been a perfect gentleman. After a pleasant evening of humor and harmony, he had given her a chaste kiss on the cheek and left with a promise to see her again. She'd been highly impressed by his casual acceptance of her clocks, and especially by his keen sense of humor. Whether or not their next date would go as well remained to be seen.

After a lazy Sunday at home, Marcie started the workweek in good cheer. As she pulled up to Port Victor's garage on Monday morning, she caught sight of Georgia Lu out in the garden. Oh for a camera, she thought. With her standard pair of Bib overalls rolled up just below her knees, her worn pair of cowboy boots, and a flannel shirt buttoned wrong, Georgia Lu wore a flowery sun bonnet on her head even though the sun had yet to show its face. Wielding her hoe like a sledge-hammer, she attacked whatever weeds dared to invade her patch. Smiling broadly, Marcie tapped her horn and gave a little wave. Georgia Lu never looked up.

Though the overwhelming odor of disinfectant assaulted her nostrils when she opened the kitchen door, she still managed to keep the smile on her face. Pearl took it upon herself to sterilize the glassware and dishes with Clorox once a month. "Gotta get rid of them nasty germs," she'd said.

Marcie rapped on the doorjamb and said, "Hi, Pearl. I'm here."

Pearl studied her for a moment and said, "You look right perky this mornin'."

"Thanks. I feel right perky. How did things go?"

"I reckon it went alright," Pearl said. "Folks from AA liked havin' them plastic covers off. I been waitin' on them boys to come back."

"I wouldn't wait on them. Chances are they're either in jail or another state by now. I'm waiting on the girls. Tiffany must be missing her photo albums."

"Reckon they'll ever show up?"

"All we can do is hope so."

The women fell into an uneasy silence. Then Marcie said, "I saw Georgia Lu out in the garden. Was that your hat she's wearing?"

"Yessum. Georgia Lu, she's a'feared of the cancer."

"Good for her," Marcie said.

"Yessum. Reckon I can get down to my washin'?"

Marcie gave her a gentle pat on the shoulder. "Yes, Pearl, you may be excused."

No sooner had Marcie settled behind her desk than the phone rang. She answered with her standard introduction: "Port Victor, Marcie speaking."

Words spilled out of a woman's mouth in a breathless rush. It was all Marcie could do to keep up with her. It seems the woman had rescued a girl from a barroom brawl last Friday night. Now that the girl had sobered up, the woman didn't know what to do with her. The girl didn't have a home to go to, and the bartender had told her she was a regular at his place. The woman feared the girl would go back there and get into another fight. She'd made some calls and someone, she couldn't remember who, had told her about Port Victor. Could she please bring her down there?

"Sorry, but I didn't catch your name," Marcie said. She didn't catch it because the woman hadn't offered it.

The woman remained silent for so long Marcie thought she'd hung up. Then the words came, slower now. "Do I have to tell you my name? I don't want to get in trouble because I took the girl home with me. She could charge me with kidnaping, couldn't she?"

Marcie said, "How old is the girl?"

"She says she's nineteen, but for all I know she could be fifteen."

"What's her name?"

"Cassandra. She calls herself Cassie."

"Where are you calling from?"

"Huntsville."

"Why don't you bring her down for an interview and we'll see how it goes."

"Can I bring a friend with me? In case, you know, she tries to jump out of the car or something."

"You may bring a friend," Marcie said, "but if Cassie doesn't want to come, call Alcoholics Anonymous and tell whoever answers about your predicament. They're listed in the phone book. We don't admit anyone against their will unless a judge orders it."

"Oh." Another long pause. "Then I should've let her get arrested, huh?"

"No. You did the right thing. Bring her on down and once she looks our place over, she'll probably decide to stay." Marcie gave her directions. "When do you expect to get here?"

"Is an hour okay?"

"That will be fine. I'm looking forward to meeting you." The woman hung up without saying goodbye.

Marcie sat pondering. If she admitted Cassie and the girl was quick to anger what would it do to the dynamics of their happy family?

She crossed to the other side of the house, opened the door to the cellar and called, "I'm coming down!"

"Yessum," Pearl said with a weary note in her voice.

Pearl stabbed out a cigarette and was in the process of putting the metal ashtray back on the shelf next to the box of Tide.

"Please forget the pine deodorizer," Marcie said. "I don't think I could survive it and Clorox in the same day."

"Yessum. But them there cigarettes sure raises a stink."

"It'll go away in a minute. I came down to tell you we might have a new resident sitting at your table today."

"When're we gonna know?"

"Two women from Huntsville are bringing her down in an hour. We'll know soon after that. Her name is Cassie and she's in a bad way."

"What kinda bad?"

"She got into a fight at a bar and I guess she took quite a beating."

"Mercy," Pearl said.

"She's also homeless."

169

"My stars, she is in a bad way. Reckon she'll stay?"

"Who knows? She could definitely use treatment. But she's just young enough to think she owns the world."

Pearl snorted. "Where're you gonna put her?"

"Probably in the room with Phyllis. Sounds like the girl could use some mothering."

———

As soon as she heard the family crunch on shells, Marcie went to the window. This time a shiny new Mercedes stopped in front of the house. Expecting to see three females climb out, her eyes widened in dismay when only one appeared. Worse, the girl was left standing there as the car pulled away. Thinking she could prevent them from leaving, Marcie raced up the hall. How dare they dump the girl out as if she was some stray they couldn't wait to get rid of!

The Mercedes had already turned onto Main Street by the time she opened the door and stepped out on the stoop. "I'll be damned!" Marcie said as she watched the car disappear into traffic.

"Think how I feel," the girl said.

Marcie looked at her then. Clutching a black plastic garbage bag to her chest, her face wore an ugly rainbow of colors: Black, purple, dark yellow, blue, red. Her high cheekbones especially had taken some hits as well as her swollen nose. No telling what kind of wounds lay beneath the Band–Aids that decorated her forehead. Or what condition her ribs were in. Despite her bruised and battered exterior, Marcie could see an All-American cheerleader waving her pompoms in front of the team.

"Come on in," Marcie said. "As Pearl would say, you need tending to."

"Who's Pearl?" Cassie asked as she joined Marcie on the stoop.

Marcie took the plastic bag from her arms and said, "She's your grandma."

"Very funny," the girl said. "My grandma's six feet under."

"How about your mama?"

"Who knows? She split a long time ago."

"And your papa?"

170

"He's got this new wife. They don't want anything to do with me. Like I care."

Marcie felt a tightening in her chest. Of course the girl cared. Very much so. "Well, if you stick around long enough, we'll adopt you into our little family."

The girl entered the foyer with Marcie following her in. The door closed behind them just as Georgia Lu came lumbering through the living room. She spied Cassie and bellowed, "Hot damn! What's the other fella look like?"

"Not fellows. Dumb broads," Cassie said. "Three of them."

"Atta girl!" Georgia Lu boomed.

That brought Deborah flying out of her room, a pink dressing gown flowing in her wake. She stopped short when she saw Cassie. "What on earth?"

Cassie looked from Georgia Lu to Deborah and then to Marcie. "What is this? A home for circus people?"

Stifling a laugh, Marcie said, "You could say that."

"I demand to know what's going on!" Deborah said.

Marcie held out her hands. "I can explain. Cassie here was in an accident, and Georgia Lu just came in from the garden. You can go back to your room now. We've got everything under control."

Deborah took a moment to think it over. Then, completely ignoring Cassie, she chose to address Georgia Lu. "Stop hollering. You sound like some crazed hillbilly."

Georgia Lu lowered her head. "Yes, ma'am. I'll try to do better."

"See that you do," Deborah said. With that, she took her leave. Marcie said, "Good morning, Georgia Lu. This is Cassie. Cassie, meet Georgia Lu."

"Howdy," Georgia Lu said. "Pleased to meet'cha."

"Hi," said Cassie, looking like a street urchin.

Voices on the stairway signaled that two or more of the women were coming down.

Marcie looked at Cassie and said, "This is your lucky day."

The two of them watched as Georgia Lu tried to pass the women on the stairs. It was a tight squeeze, but she made it up and they made it down. As soon as their eyes fell on Cassie, they flocked to her side, fawning and all talking at once.

Marcie interrupted. "This girl needs medical attention. If one of you will come to the office, I'll give you some supplies." Marcie started down the hall, unaware that she had three females following her.

Once they had all crowded into the office, Marcie told Cassie, "We'll skip the intake interview for now. It looks like you've already been adopted."

Cassie scanned the crowd and then said, "This is one big loony bin." Because of her wounds, her grin came out more like a grimace.

"You got that right," Veronica said.

"Amen," said Missy.

When everyone had left, Marcie plopped into her chair and heaved a big sigh. One thing about this job, it was never dull.

She pulled a note card out of a drawer and poised her pen over it. How to say what she wanted to say?

———

"Dear Deborah," she started. "So that you needn't be disturbed by the residents any longer, what would you think of giving up your job as housemother? Who would take your place? Since Pearl has maintained sobriety for the past seven months, she qualifies for the job. Please think this through and let me know the answer as soon as possible.

Sincerely, Marcie."

———

She read it over again. Satisfied, she stuck it in the envelope, sealed it, went to Deborah's door and shoved the note under it.

———

At the dinner table that day, the women paid rapt attention as Cassie recounted the fight she'd been in. "This dude asked me to dance. He wasn't that great to look at but he was tall and had a blonde ponytail. I like tall men and the

172

ponytail was a definite plus. I'd seen the guy around and liked his moves. An oldie by Fats Domino was playing on the juke box. So we were out there, twisting all over the floor. The dude could dance."

"You should see Blackie dance!" Georgia Lu called from her seat next to Veronica. "That man can spin like a top!"

Veronica turned an eye on her. "Who the hell is Blackie?"

"My husband."

Dropped forks clattered on plates as several women gaped at Georgia Lu.

"Since when did you get married?" Veronica asked.

"The day Blackie said I do."

"Of all things," Veronica said, "I never pictured you with a husband."

"Me, either," said Missy.

"Well, everyone's entitled to get married," Phyllis said.

"Exactly," said Marcie. "Now, let Cassie finish her story."

"I'll swan," said Pearl, obviously a delayed reaction to the news put forth by Georgia Lu.

Cassie continued. "Like I said, we were rockin' and rollin,' and all of a sudden somebody bumped me from behind. A hard bump. Sent me plowing into the dude, throwing me and him off balance. He yells, 'Hey!' Soon as I got my feet under me, I turned around to see who bumped me, and wham! Right in the face. The kind of punch where you see stars. Before I could see straight, wham! Somebody slapped me into the next world. People started yelling and cussing, hitting out at anything that moved. These three skanks are pounding me into the floor, the dude trying to pull them off me. It was Chaos City. Then some idiot fired a pistol. People hit the floor, then started jamming the door. Sirens came screaming our way. I felt somebody jerking me by the arm. I thought it was the dude so I went along. Next thing I knew I woke up in a bed. It was too fine to be a jail cot. This woman was standing over me. She got me up and we took a ride. And here I am."

"You are one lucky girl," said Veronica.

"Amen," said Missy.

"You couldn't have come to a better place," said Phyllis. Marcie's heart swelled with pride.

"Reckon you'll stay?" Pearl asked.

Cassie looked all around. "I'd be a fool not to."

In addition to the sound of clapping hands and cheers, Georgia Lu let out her special wolf whistle.

And so it was decided. Without an intake interview. Without knowing anything about her, Cassie became Port Victor's newest resident.

CHAPTER 18

The next day Pearl stood waiting by the kitchen door, her hands kneading the apron she abused when something had gone wrong.

"What is it?" Marcie asked, trying to steel herself for news she didn't want to hear. She set the gift-wrapped iron on the counter and poured a mugful of coffee. What with Cassie's arrival yesterday, she'd forgotten about the iron and the grill in the trunk of her car.

"My ham," Pearl said.

"Your ham?" Marcie said, relieved but confused. "What about it?"

"It done flew the coop."

"Pearl, what are you talking about?"

"'Member we had baked ham for dinner yesterday?"

"Yes, and?" Irritation began to simmer on the cusp of Marcie's mind. She wanted to be done with this ham business so she could give Pearl the package.

"I saved some back to make ham salad sandwiches an' somebody's done eat it up."

"Are you sure?" Marcie took a sip of coffee.

Pearl huffed and said, "I reckon I know what's what in my own kitchen."

"Okay. I believe you. But who would eat your leftovers?"

"Beats me."

"I'll speak to the ladies at group today. Tell them that raiding the refrigerator is off limits."

"Tell 'em not to be gettin' into the cupboards neither."

"I will. Maybe we ought to provide snacks in the afternoon. What do you think about having chips and dips or cheese and crackers after group?"

"Don't know nothin' 'bout no dips, but I got plenty'a cheese and crackers."

"Good. Let's hope that satisfies whoever ate your ham."

"Yessum. Sorry I got so riled."

Marcie nodded. "I understand, Pearl. While we're on the subject of food, Phyllis wants to make spaghetti one day soon. Is it okay if she talks to you about the ingredients?"

"I done thought about what you said. I reckon the women can cook some iffen they clean up their mess."

"Thank you, Pearl. The girls will be pleased to hear it." She exchanged her mug for the package on the counter. Holding it out, she said, "This is for you."

"Me? I'll swan. What have you gone and done now?"

"Open it."

While Pearl's gnarled fingers pulled at the wrappings, Marcie picked up her mug and sipped some more coffee.

Once the box was open and Pearl held the iron in her hands, her face became a web of deep furrows when she smiled. She lifted it up and down. "I'll be a pig's snout if this ain't somethin'," she said. "It can't weigh more'n a pound."

Although she knew the answer, Marcie said, "Do you like it?"

"I like it just fine." A worried frown replaced the smile. "You reckon it'll do the job?"

"Sure it will. Try it out. I can always take it back."

Pearl clasped the iron to her breast. "No'um, no call to do that."

"Okay, then. If you need me, you know where I'll be." She topped off her coffee and then left the room with a lighter heart than when she'd entered it. She'd get to the grill later on.

The peacock was waiting in the office. Draped in her flowing caftan and gold slippers, Veronica greeted her warmly. "There's my favorite person. My, my, you look absolutely stunning. Especially your hair. What color do you use to get that healthy shine?"

"Cut the bull, Veronica, and tell me what you want."

"Is that any way to say hello?"

Marcie set her mug on the desk and sat down in her chair. "No, it isn't. Please accept my apology. It's just that I don't do private sessions first thing in the morning."

"This isn't private and I don't want a session. I," she batted her eyelashes "have a special request."

"Please don't make me drag it out of you, Veronica. I just finished playing that game."

"Oh, all right. I have a gentleman friend. He's tall, white, and rich. And ... he's invited me out to dinner!" She fairly squealed this last.

"Whoa," said Marcie. "Where did you meet this friend, and who is he?"

"We've had coffee together at the AA meetings. His name is Thomas Winfield Black." She lifted her chin and added, "*Colonel* Black. Retired."

Marcie wondered why Pearl hadn'tmentioned this. Too bothered by her missing ham, no doubt. "I see," she said. "I presume he's single."

"Of course. I don't date married men."

"What about that last guy?"

Veronica's mouth turned down at the edges. "That bastard told me he was getting a divorce. But any port in a storm and all that crap."

"Like Port Victor?"

Veronica turned thoughtful. "You know, Marcie. I thought I'd die of boredom when I first got here, but then I started to enjoy myself."

"I'm glad you're enjoying yourself. But one day soon you'll have to get serious about treatment."

Veronica sat up straight, brows arched. "Serious? What do you call being sober for a month? I don't know about you, but for me, that's damn serious."

"You're right. Sobriety is number one. I congratulate you. I meant serious about planning for your future. We'll talk about this at group today. I have several announcements to make."

"Well how about making one now? Do I get to have dinner with the Colonel, or not?"

"I guess I have no choice but to say yes. When and where do you plan to go?"

"You sound like my mother, bless her dear departed heart. This Saturday night, he's taking me to The Rib Room in Huntsville. Oh, I can just taste that slab of rare roast beef." She ran her tongue over her cherry-red lips. "And that baked potato dripping with butter and sour cream. Lord, but it's been so long since I've had a decent meal."

Marcie's mouth watered over the thought of rare roast beef. She liked hers swimming in *au jus*. George owed her a dinner. She'd have to remind him. "That sounds fine to me," she told Veronica. "Just remember you have to be back here by eleven o'clock."

"Eleven? I thought curfew was midnight on the weekends."

"It is. For being in bed. It's eleven for being out."

"Oh pooh, you're no fun."

"As long as you don't drink before or after dinner, you can have all the fun you want by eleven."

"Not to worry. The Colonel has been dry for nine years. He's as bad about drinking alcohol as a raging teetotaler."

"That's the best news I've heard all day. Now go get dressed. It's almost eight."

At the door, Veronica turned and waved her fingers. "Ta-ta. Let's do lunch sometime."

Marcie played along just for the heck of it. "Today okay with you?"

"I'll check my calendar."

"Fine. Have your people call my people."

"I'll do that," Veronica said, her eyes twinkling.

Marcie got up and went to the file cabinet. She pulled out Veronica's chart and sat back down. Even though Veronica's date with the Colonel could hardly be called progress, she made a notation about it.

"Are you busy?" Missy asked from the doorway.

Marcie put down her pen and closed the chart. "Not at all. Please come in."

"I came to borrow a book. Do you mind if I look them over?"

"Help yourself," Marcie said. She got up, went to the file cabinet and put the chart back in its slot. Should she or shouldn't she confront Missy? The girl had resided at Port Victor for more than three months. Far too long to keep silent about her family life and any plans she may have for when she left the program. As far as Marcie knew, Missy had never received or made a phone call. No one had come to visit her. No one had written her a letter. All of which suggested something bad had happened to her.

Marcie moseyed over to where Missy was standing. "What kind of books do you like to read?"

Missy gave her a look and said, "I don't need any help."

"With selecting a book? Or with unburdening yourself?" There. It was out.

Missy turned on her, small eyes narrowed to slits. "You never stop, do you?"

"Not until I get some answers."

"You should've been a lawyer," Missy said. "Always minding other people's business. It's disgusting." She started to walk away.

Marcie took hold of her arm. "Don't run this time, Missy. Please. Whatever it is, you can't shock me. I've heard it all."

Missy fired back. "I get it. You want me to tell you my deep dark secret so you can kick me out."

Before Marcie could challenge the remark, Missy's anger dissolved into a well of sadness. Her eyes shimmered with sudden tears and her lower lip quivered. When she spoke, it was in a little girl's voice. "I thought you liked me."

Overcome with the emotion of the moment, Marcie blinked away her own tears. "Now listen carefully, Missy. I am going to lock the door so we will not be disturbed. After that, we are going to sit in the wing chairs, side by side, and you are going to tell me what's troubling you."

Missy nodded her assent. She went to the desk and plucked a Kleenex out of the box Marcie kept there. While she dabbed at her eyes and blew her nose, Marcie locked the door. When she turned around, Missy was huddled in the nearest chair. Marcie moved behind her, resisting the urge to pat her shoulder, and sat down in the chair nearest the windows.

The girl worried the wad of Kleenex in her hands. She plucked tiny pieces out one at a time and stuck them on her skirt, concentrating on making a circle. The circle grew larger. A symbol of her life, perhaps?

Marcie sat with her hands folded in her lap, quietly gazing about the room yet keeping tabs on Missy out of the corner of her eye. Sometimes the silent treatment worked and sometimes it didn't. She was prepared to sit there for as long as it took Missy to break the silence.

When the Kleenex was gone and Missy's skirt was littered with white flakes, she turned to Marcie with a belligerent set to her jaw and blurted it out. "I'm gay."

That was not what Marcie had expected to hear. "That's it? That's the deep dark secret?"

"Go ahead," Missy said. "Tell me to pack my bags and get out."

"Hold on," Marcie said. "What makes you think I'd kick you out for being gay?"

Missy averted her eyes. "Because… you know."

"No, I don't know. You're gay. So what?"

"So I can't be trusted. I might make a play for, say, Phyllis or Cassie."

"Have you made a play for Phyllis or Cassie?"

Missy twisted around in her chair, her eyes frantically traveling over the bookcase. Agitated, she said, "Where's your Bible?"

Marcie held up empty hands. "I don't have one."

Missy stared at her. "Not even at home?"

"Not anywhere."

"I've never known anyone who didn't own a Bible. What are you, an atheist or something?"

"Something," Marcie replied. "But never mind me. This discussion is about you."

Missy popped out of her chair and headed toward the door. "I'll be right back," she said, leaving a trail of Kleenex flakes on the carpet. Marcie shrugged. She would borrow Pearl's vacuum cleaner later on.

During the time Missy was gone, Marcie reminisced about her days at New Start. The few openly gay men who came through the program had been extra careful to keep their distance from the straight community. They knew if they didn't, they'd be bullied and bloodied in the dark of night. Marcie had tried to point out that regardless of their sexual orientation they were all in need of treatment in order to maintain sobriety. They must have listened, because one day when they were role-playing, the straights applauded the gays for playing the roles of Suffering Susan, Martyr Mary, and Pitiful Patty— the names given to the mothers, wives, girlfriends, and sisters who enabled the men to keep drinking. Unbeknownst to the men, the session was taped. After the director showed it at the monthly staff meeting, he hailed it as "an excellent example of the efficacy of role playing."

When Missy returned, she was clutching a black Bible. She locked the door and then took a position in the middle of the room. Holding the Bible aloft with her left hand, she placed her right hand over its worn cover. While gazing upwards, she said, "I swear on this holy Bible before Almighty God that Mary Ellen was— is— my one and only lover." Still holding the Bible, she took her seat.

Marcie said, "Why don't you start at the beginning."

"It's an ugly story," Missy warned.

"I've heard ugly."

"My father is a preacher," Missy said. "We're fundamentalists but we're not related to any other church. God speaks directly to my father. He tells him the rules we must obey. One of those rules concerns marriages within the church. Early on, boys and girls are sworn to each other, whether you like the person or not. No matter what your husband does— beats you, rapes you, treats you like a slave— you're wed for life. The only way out is to kill yourself or run away. I ran away."

"Oh, Missy," Marcie said, reaching out to her. She drew her hand back when Missy went on.

"When I was young and didn't know any better, I accepted the teachings of the church as the true Word. We lived, ate, and breathed church and the Bible. I had four brothers older than me. We were home-schooled by our parents. They worked us hard. If anyone got a bad mark or complained, Father would whip us with his belt. My mother always took his side, so we did as we were told and kept our mouths shut. No one laughed in our house.

"Things got really bad for me when my father's father came to live with us when I was ten. I had never liked him. He smelled like mothballs and he was always sneaking up on me. He gave me the creeps.

"One night I felt someone getting into bed with me. Then I smelled him. It was Grandfather. I started to scream, but he clamped his bony hand over my mouth and whispered. "No one will believe you. Everyone knows little girls lie." Then he took my hand and made me rub his thing. For the next four years he made me do all kinds of horrible things." A violent shudder shook the length of her body.

"My God," Marcie croaked.

Missy made a helpless gesture with her hands. "I wanted to tell someone so bad. I almost did, hundreds of times. I kept remembering what grandfather said. That no one would believe me. I thought I was being punished by God for every bad thought I'd ever had."

"The filthy bastard," Marcie hissed under her breath.

"Mary Ellen finally stopped him in a roundabout way. We'd been best friends forever. She always wanted me to spend the night with her. Her parents were members of our church and Mary Ellen was the brightest student in Sunday school, but my father still wouldn't allow it."

"Wait a minute," Marcie said. "Your father wouldn't let you sleep over at your friend's house, yet *his* father was molesting you right under his nose? That is unbelievable."

Missy laid a hand on the Bible and said, "I swear it's the truth."

"Oh, Missy, I don't doubt you for a minute. Most cases of sex abuse happen within families. Your grandfather should have been sent to prison. Inmates detest child molesters. They would have given him a very hard time."

Missy looked at her. "Really?"

"Yes, really," Marcie said. "Tell me how Mary Ellen stopped him."

"I finally got permission to spend the night with her on my fourteenth birthday. That's when I told her, and that's when we became lovers." Missy's cheeks turned crimson. "I'm so ashamed. It was all my fault." Her gaze fell on the Bible in her lap. She got up, placed it on the desk and sat back down. It was as if she wanted to distance herself from its teachings.

"We were lying in bed, talking about the boys we were promised to, and I couldn't hold it in any longer. I started crying and telling her about my grandfather. She put her arms around me and held me real tight. For the first time in my life I felt safe. It was so wonderful to know that grandfather wouldn't be climbing in my bed that night. So I kissed her on the mouth. She kissed me back." Missy gave a wistful sigh. "We kissed and kissed."

"That's all you did?"

"Yes."

"It's natural for girls to hug and kiss. That doesn't mean you're gay."

"But I love Mary Ellen and she loves me."

"That's natural, too. You were young and vulnerable. You'd been traumatized by your grandfather for four years. You said it yourself, Mary Ellen made you feel safe. Don't label yourself as gay just because you love her."

Missy wore a puzzled frowned. "I don't understand."

"It's difficult, I know, and I could be wrong. What happened next?"

"When I got home, I told my grandfather that Mary Ellen knew what he'd done and if he ever touched me again she would tell her parents. He got real quiet after that. Stayed in his room a lot. Then he caught pneumonia and died."

"I hope it was a very painful death," Marcie said.

"No. He just went to sleep and never woke up."

"Too bad."

Missy grimaced. "I'm positive he went straight to Hell."

Goosebumps crawled over Marcie's flesh. The image of him burning in hell made her think of her mother's dire warning. That she, an eleven–year–old child was "doomed to the fiery pits of hell" for not giving her soul to The Church of True Believers. Which was why Marcie didn't own a Bible.

Missy said, "I'd been promised to Howard. I liked him okay as a friend, but I didn't want to marry him. I prayed and prayed to the Lord to save me, but He didn't listen. Howard and I were married when I was seventeen. We went to Memphis for our honeymoon. On the way there, Howard stopped at a liquor store and bought a bottle of rum and a big bottle of Coke. I was shocked. Drinking alcohol was forbidden in our church. Anyway, when we got to the hotel, he fixed us drinks. He said it would relax me. He was right. After a couple of rum and Cokes, I didn't care what he did to me. From then on, every time Howard wanted sex, I had a few drinks first. It was the only way I could stand for him to touch me."

"How sad," Marcie said.

"He made me think of Grandfather. Sometimes I could even smell the old mothballs. Poor Mary Ellen. We talked to each other at church, but that was it. Howard was very possessive. He didn't like for me to have company. Then it came time for Mary Ellen to marry a boy named Douglas. She got very depressed, would hardly talk to me. She hated my being with Howard and she hated that I drank. Besides that, Douglas didn't want to marry her any more than she wanted to marry him.

"Things got better for Mary Ellen when she enrolled in college. She wanted me to go with her, but I had such a bad hangover every morning all I wanted to do was sleep. Finally, I couldn't take it anymore. One day, while Howard was at work, I took a bus to Atlanta. I was going to get a job and live on my own. No church. No Howard. No Mary Ellen. But when I got there and saw how big the city was, I got real scared. I didn't know where to go or how to get there. I called Mary Ellen to come get me.

"She'd heard about this place from the mental health center, and she convinced me to come here. She said we could start over together in a new town, but first I'd have to go through the program and learn a job skill. She's in her last year of nursing school."

Marcie said, "Is she still married to Douglas?"

"Yes, but they have an understanding. Each of them is free to do whatever they want as long as the church doesn't find out."

"Swell," Marcie said. "They get to be hypocrites."

Missy thought it over. "I guess you're right. But Mary Ellen doesn't want to hurt her parents."

"What about you?"

"As far as my father's concerned, I'm dead. I've shamed him in the worst way. Howard, too. He's a widower in the eyes of the church. He'll get married again. I hope the girl loves him."

Marcie went to her and pulled her out of the chair. With a wrench of tenderness, she hugged Missy to her breast. They stood there, holding on to one another, shedding silent tears.

———

Deep in thought over Missy's dilemma, Marcie heard the knock on the door. Too weary to get up, she told the person to come in.

The instant she saw who opened the door, she jumped out of her chair. "Oh, Sarah," she said, rushing to greet the mistress of the manor. "It's so good to see you. Please come in."

Sarah said, "Do you make it a practice to keep the door closed?"

"No, not at all. Only when I'm having a private therapy session. Missy must have closed it on her way out. Please, the desk chair is all yours."

"I can't stay long," Sarah said. "I shouldn't even be here." She sat down in a wing chair and put her purse in the other. "Now then," Sarah said, "congratulations are in order. We have six residents and not a single one has left since you've been here." Marcie guessed Deborah had told her how many women they had. "What's your secret?" Sarah asked.

It took a moment for Marcie to make the connection. At first she'd thought Sarah was asking about her date with Roger. "Just lucky, I guess."

"Nonsense," Sarah said. "It's something you do that George didn't. And don't tell me it was because he couldn't get down here often enough." That was exactly what Marcie had intended to say.

Marcie spoke off the top of her head. "Well, I've provided games and books for the women to enjoy. I listen and respond to their questions and comments. We have a group session every day, where the women feel free to express themselves openly and honestly without fear of condemnation. I try to see the bright side of the picture and keep a sense of humor. Three of the women are going to start Vocational Rehabilitation next week. They'll set goals for them to work toward. One of my goals is to keep them busy and involved in treatment. Probably the most important thing is, we like and respect each other."

Sarah beamed a smile. "Your credits are adding up."

"Thank you. I've wanted to see you, but I know how busy you are."

"I've meant to get over here before now, but something always comes up. How's your petty cash holding out?"

"Well, I ... un, I've made a few purchases." Marcie was quick to add, "But I have money left."

"How much?"

"One hundred and eighty-nine dollars and twenty-seven cents."

"That's not enough. I'll give you an additional five-hundred. That should last a while." Sarah reached for her purse and set it on her lap. She opened the clasp and pulled out a bulging wallet. After removing five bills from a fat wad, she placed them on the desk.

Marcie couldn't believe her eyes. Didn't Sarah worry about being robbed? "Do you always carry that much cash around?"

"Of course," Sarah said. "I don't like to write checks. You have to keep track of them and I've got enough to keep track of."

Marcie opened the desk drawer that held the petty cash box. She unlocked it and pulled out three scraps of paper. She reached across the desk in an effort to give them to Sarah. "Here are the receipts."

Sarah waved them away. "That's not necessary," she said. "I'm sure the money was well spent."

Marcie put the money and the receipts in the box. "Thank you very much. You're too generous."

Sarah said, "I took a look at the garden before I came in. Who keeps up with it?"

"Her name is Georgia Lu. Having grown up on a farm, she knows all about planting. She's out there every day scaring the weeds away."

"I expect you'll share the bounty with me."

"Yes, ma'am. We'll bring you baskets full."

"Now then, what's this I hear about you wanting Pearl to take over Bitsy's job?"

Ah, so she'd heard about that, too. "Well, the housemother's job is constant. Deborah likes her privacy and she doesn't like to be disturbed. When I'm off, Pearl is always there for the women. Besides that, she's qualified in every sense of the word."

"Bitsy doesn't see it that way," Sarah said. "She thinks you don't like her."

"But I do like Deborah. It's just that—"

"That's settled then." Sarah retrieved her purse and started to stand up.

Marcie couldn't let her leave without bringing up a subject dear to her heart. "Sarah, before you go, I have one more thing to ask of you. Would you consider giving Pearl a small stipend? She cooks, does the laundry, irons, orders the supplies, takes care of the women, and keeps the house spick and span. To put it simply, we couldn't do without her."

"I think it can be arranged," Sarah said. "We could give her the title of house manager and put her on the payroll."

Marcie clapped her hands together. "Oh, I can't thank you enough."

"It is I who thank you, Marcie Parker. You come up with some splendid ideas. Keep up the good work."

Both women stood at the same time. Marcie's heart was fairly bursting as she escorted Sarah out the door and up the hall.

In the foyer, she looked at Sarah and said, "Do you have time to meet our ladies?"

"I'm afraid not, dear. I'm on my way to a board meeting."

Marcie saw her out the door. "Thanks again," she called.

A driver was standing beside Sarah's car, ready to help her inside. Once seated, she gave a little wave. The driver slid behind the wheel and off they went.

"Well," Marcie said, closing the door with a sigh. "That's that." Her emotions had seesawed all day, and now she'd reached the calm that heading home always brought. The temperature had fallen several degrees and the wind had picked up. Although it was still light out now that they'd switched to daylight-saving time, she wouldn't be going down to the dock this evening. She might build a fire and settle down with her latest book and a glass of wine. Pearl had prepared a container of beef and barley soup for her to take home so she didn't have to cook. She'd be lazy tonight. Turn off the brain waves that often kept her awake till all hours of the morning.

Nothing could be done to erase Missy's past. Long in his grave, grandfather couldn't be resurrected to face the punishment he deserved. Even though her parents should be shaken until their teeth rattled, they would never accept their role in Missy's tortured youth. Marcie hoped the girl's brothers had enough sense to run away. Otherwise, another generation of pious preachers and detached fathers would be let loose on a naive community of followers.

What mattered now was Missy's immediate future. She had expressed an interest in counseling. Almost everyone in treatment leaned in that direction at one time or another but few followed through. Testing and classes at rehab would point to the path she would most likely follow.

In addition, Marcie wanted Missy to take a day pass to be with Mary Ellen. The two girls would benefit by spending time together. Eventually, they'd know whether they still loved each other more than just friends.

———

As usual, Charley was waiting for her. Smiling, she made the turn onto her driveway. Charley hopscotched all around the car as she pulled into the garage. "Watch out," she called when she couldn't see him any longer. Unscathed, he showed up at the car door, practically blocking her exit.

"What's the matter with you?" Marcie asked as he sniffed her up and down. "You been eating those berries again?" She laughed when he grinned and jumped up on her. "Get down," she told him. "You're acting like a puppy."

She lifted the container of soup off the floor on the passenger's side and set it on the workbench. Charley nipped playfully at her heels as she headed up the driveway to the mailbox at the edge of the road. Marcie couldn't figure out what had gotten into him. She opened the box, fully expecting to see an empty shell.

Her heart leapt at sight of the post card. At last! She snatched the card out of the box. Without moving a muscle, she read it fast and then read it again. She let out a joyous whoop. Charley jumped up on her again. "You knew it, didn't you? That's why you've been acting so frisky." Charley's tail beat the air so hard his whole body shook.

Flapping the post card in the air, Marcie bounced down the driveway. In the garage, she collected the soup and then entered the house with Charley bounding in behind her.

The clocks clamored for immediate attention. "Hello, darlings! I have good news! The kids are coming home!" She carried on with an extra swing in her step. The kids would be home on June 10. Only four more weeks! Reaching the kitchen, she put the soup on the counter and then headed for her bedroom, more than ready to get out of her work clothes and into jeans and a warm sweater. On the way, an unpleasant thought brought her to a sudden stop. If she and Roger were still dating when the kids came home, and she had a hunch they would be, how would the kids react? She imagined Julie would be glad for her. But Davy … he'd find any excuse to pitch a fit.

She was a single woman, after all. Free to go out with whomever she chose. Davy wouldn't see it that way. He had acted like the man of the house after his father left. Thought he could boss his mother and sister around. When they balked, he'd get angry and stalk off to his room, where he'd slam the door so hard Marcie feared it would split in two. Having a new man around would threaten his self–imposed status. He might even hitch a ride back to D.C.

Why must there always be complications? The joy she'd felt only moments ago now turned to sober realization. Reuniting with her children wouldn't be easy. Maybe she should break Saturday's date with Roger. Tell him she wasn't ready, tell him she was afraid Sarah would find out, tell him anything but the truth— that her relationship with her son was tenuous at best.

But she enjoyed Roger's company. They had fun together. What was so wrong with that? Was she not entitled to a life? She would have to give this some serious thought. So much for turning off the brain waves tonight.

CHAPTER 19

After a restless night of making and discarding decisions, she was happy to go to work the following day. Because the women of Port Victor always provided plenty of distractions, she could put both the kids' homecoming and her date with Roger at the back of her mind.

Ah, there was a distraction now. For some reason, Georgia Lu was waiting at the garage door. She hailed Marcie when she was halfway up the drive. Whatever she wanted must be important for Georgia Lu to tear herself away from the garden. She opened the car door for Marcie and started right in.

"Ma'am, I been thinkin' on this, and it ain't fair."

"What isn't fair?" Marcie said as she climbed out of the car.

"I don't see no good reason for me to go to that there rehab."

At group yesterday, Marcie had announced that Georgia Lu, Veronica, Phyllis, and Missy would be starting rehab next Monday. Cassie would start a week later. "But it's a wonderful opportunity, Georgia Lu. It's also a vital part of the program. Trust me, you'll do just fine."

"It's a waste of time, ma'am. I know what jobs I can do."

"That's just it, Georgia Lu. At rehab, you'll find you're capable of doing jobs you never dreamed of doing."

"I dream I'm wearin' a white uniform. What's that mean?"

Marcie thought it over. Although today's nurses wore scrubs of many colors, she said, "Maybe you're dreaming about being a nurse."

Georgia Lu fixed her gaze in the distance. "My aunt Bertie were a nurse. She wore white shoes, a white dress, and a little white cap on her head. She looked like an angel. She retired a few years ago, and don't ever wear white anymore. But she's still my angel."

"Did you ever want to be like her when you grew up?"

"Yes, ma'am. When I were a kid I used to play pretend nurse. I'd grab hold of a rabbit and wrap 'em up in gauze. They didn't like it much, and my pappy would get after me for usin' all the gauze."

"Well, if not a nurse, maybe you're cut out to be a nurse's aide. That's why you'd benefit from going to rehab."

"If I were a nurse's aide, would I get to wear white?"

"Yes, Georgia Lu, you'd get to wear white."

"Alrighty then. I'll go to that there rehab place."

"That's the spirit. It'll only take four hours out of your day. You'll still have plenty of time to work in the garden."

"Yes, ma'am. Sure am glad we had this here talk. I gotta get back to my weedin'." She lumbered off in her cowboy boots with the sun hat perched on her head.

Marcie knew rehab couldn't perform miracles, but at the same time, she thought Georgia Lu would be an asset at a hospital or a nursing home. She could lift and turn patients with ease, feed the ones who couldn't feed themselves, and entertain patients with her stories of life on the farm.

Another surprise awaited Marcie in the kitchen. It was only seven–thirty, the time Pearl usually did the breakfast dishes, yet she was huddled over the table with Phyllis and Veronica. Phyllis had dressed for the day; Veronica wore her fluffy pink caftan. Marcie went straight to the coffee maker. If ever she needed a wake–up call, it was now.

"Hello all," she said, walking to the head of the table. "What are you doing this early in the morning?"

Veronica looked up. "Oh, hi, Marcie." Phyllis looked up. "Good morning, Marcie." Pearl managed a grunt. They continued talking amongst themselves. Marcie bided her time taking small sips of hot coffee. Veronica was making a list of some sort on one of Pearl's notepads. The longer she stood there the more curious she got. "Is anyone going to tell me what you're doing?"

"Don't forget oregano," Phyllis said. Veronica wrote it down. "And basil," Phyllis added.

191

Missy wandered into the room and asked, "What are y'all doing?"

"Making a grocery list," Veronica said. "The man from Halsey's comes this morning."

"Well," Marcie said, "I'm glad somebody got an answer."

Missy looked her way and said, "Oh, hi, when did you get here?"

"A few minutes before you did. Where's Cassie?"

Missy slowly shook her head. "That Cassie, she's a case."

"What do you mean?"

"She gets up at the crack of dawn, sometimes before that. She runs in place for a while, then she does her workout, and then she runs in place, then she does her workout—"

Speaking loud enough for the others to hear, Marcie said, "Thank you, Missy, for having the good manners to answer my questions." She started for the door, expecting a smart remark, at the very lease a comment.

"Have you got plenty of chili powder?" Phyllis asked Pearl.

"Best you look in the spice rack," Pearl said.

Marcie felt like the invisible woman as she left the room.

Once settled in the office, she made notations in the charts belonging to Georgia Lu, Phyllis, Veronica, and Missy regarding the recent exchange. That done, she started making a list of chores for the women to perform. She would present it at today's group session and could already hear the moans that would ensue, especially from Veronica. When she put her pen down and closed the memo pad, she was startled to see Deborah standing near the desk. "Lord," she gasped, her heart thumping against her chest, "you scared me half to death. What are you doing up so early?"

"What were you writing about?" Deborah had become a pro at asking a question instead of answering one.

Marcie's heart slowly returned to a normal rhythm. "I was just making notes for our group session later today. We'd love to have you join us."

"No thanks," Deborah said. "I'll be busy this afternoon."

Doing what? Marcie wondered. "Well, we meet every day. You're welcome to attend anytime." She got up and rounded the desk. "I have something for you." At the closet, she opened the door and picked up the item she'd been keeping there. She bumped the door closed with a hip and looked at Deborah. "Where would you like to sit?"

"You brought that for me?" Deborah said, her big blue eyes sparkling like sapphires.

"None other," Marcie said, setting Julie's childhood rocking chair at an angle to the desk. "Try it on for size."

A smile trembled at Deborah's lips as she crossed to the chair. She sat down, wiggled around, looked up and said, "It fits. Let's leave it right here." This time her smile displayed an even row of tiny white teeth.

Marcie wished she had a camera. "You know," she said, taking her seat, "you're even more beautiful when you smile. You ought to do it more often."

"It was nice of you to bring the chair," Deborah said. Then she started rocking back and forth while twisting a lock of her lustrous blonde hair around and around her index finger.

That told Marcie it was time to get down to business. She said, "Now that we're sitting here together, what's on your mind?"

Deborah kept twisting her hair. "What you told Aunt Sarah."

It took a moment for Marcie to make a connection. "That I like you?"

"Yes."

Even as she sat there, quietly conversing with Deborah, Marcie couldn't believe it was happening. This was the first time the little one had entered the room without being angry about something. She hated to be a skeptic, but such a dramatic change in behavior sent out warning signals.

Deborah continued. "I've been so mean to you. How could you possibly like me?"

"Because underneath all that anger and frustration, there's a sweet and lovable person dying to get out. Oh, Deborah, you have so much to offer. I wish you'd consider going to rehab along with the women." Oh-oh, Marcie thought when Deborah stiffened in her seat.

"Oh, so you think I'm just one of the girls. That I need therapy and rehab like some drunken old whore."

Marcie's initial instinct was to defend the women, but that would be a mistake. Instead, she decided to go deep into the well of Deborah's anger. "This may be a painful question," she said, "but it would do you so much good to talk about it. Were you truly referring to our residents when you called them drunken whores? Or were you referring to your mother?"

Deborah's head jerked up. "What do you know about my mother?"

"I know she left you for your grandmother to raise. I know she was a drunk like Sarah's daughter Grace. I know you never knew your father. I know you've never traveled, never met a person your size. I know your beloved Uncle Victor wrapped you in a safe cocoon, and I know how angry you are now that he's gone."

Deborah seemed to shrink into herself. Marcie went on. "You're still young. You have a life ahead of you. It can be a good one or a bad one, it's up to you."

"What should I do?" Deborah asked in a timid voice.

"Talk to me. Be open and honest. What's said in this office stays in this office."

Deborah kept rocking and twisting her hair. Marcie sat patiently waiting for whatever came next. She had an appointment with Cassie at nine o'clock. She could postpone it if Deborah decided to open up to her.

Deborah stopped rocking and flung her hair over her shoulder. Practically spitting out the words, she said, "I hate my mother! And I hate Aunt Sarah!"

"That's understandable," Marcie said. She leaned over the desk. "You've just taken a giant step toward recovery."

"Oh, so now we dig into my past," Deborah snapped. "Who did what, when, and where? Is that how it goes?"

"No. To paraphrase the Serenity Prayer, we try to accept the things we cannot change and change the things we can. That doesn't mean we can't talk about the past. I'm always prepared to listen."

Deborah tilted her head to one side and asked, "Did you hear all that stuff about me from Aunt Sarah?"

"No, I did not. She said you could be difficult, but you already know that."

"*I* could be difficult? What about her? She threw me out of the big house. Made me move in here to play nursemaid to all these strangers. If that's not being difficult, I don't know what is."

"Were you happy living in the big house with your aunt?"

"No, but it was better than being stuck here."

"Are you sure about that? Here, you're your own boss. You can watch TV whenever you want, water your uncle's flowers …. Seems to me you're much better off here."

Deborah strained forward, the tiny veins in her neck turning blue. "What do you know about Uncle Victor's flowers?"

"Just that you water them fairly often."

"You want me to be honest? Well, here's the truth." She paused, then cried, "Uncle's flowers are dead! They're nothing but scraggly brown stems. The crazy thing is I water them anyway. Oh, I know uncle's frowning down on me. He made me promise to take care of them if something happened to him. I tried! Oh, how I tried." She sat back and breathed a shuddering sigh. "I guess I tried too hard."

"We often do when we try to live up to promises. The dead flowers weigh you down with guilt each time you water them. It's time to get rid of them. I'll help if you want me to."

Deborah put the back of a hand to her forehead and closed her eyes. "I'm tired," she said. "I have to rest now." She pushed up from her chair and walked out of the room as though in a trance.

Marcie didn't try to stop her. They'd made great inroads this morning, far more than she'd ever expected. But it was only the beginning. For such a small person, Deborah carried a ton of anguish.

Marcie checked her watch. She had twenty minutes until Cassie's session. Time to start a chart on Deborah.

"Ma'am? We got troubles."

Marcie looked up. Pearl was abusing a new apron. Except for a different flower pattern, this apron was in the exact same bib style. Marcie wondered how long it would survive.

"What kind of trouble?"

"My hunk of cheese is gone. I was gonna slice it for that snack you want, but some rat done got into the icebox and ate it all up."

Marcie knew better than to ask if she was certain the cheese was gone.

Cassie poked her head inside the room and said, "Oops, I didn't know you were busy. I'll wait at the end of the hall."

"No," Marcie said. "Come on in and have a seat. Pearl and I are about finished." She looked at Pearl and said, "Give me some time to think and I'll catch you later."

"Yessum," Pearl said and turned toward the door, her shoulders sagging.

"Hi, Pearl," Cassie said in passing. Pearl said nothing. Cassie took long strides into the room as if she couldn't wait to get started. At the first chair, she kicked off her flip-flops and sat yoga-style, making Marcie wince. Even in the best of times, she could never sit in that position. The girl wore cut–off jean shorts and a red T–shirt that proclaimed in bold white letters: GRASS IS CLASS. Marcie hoped she didn't wear it to AA meetings. In her experience with the men at New Start, straight alcoholics thought dopers were zoo material.

"So," Cassie said, "what's new with you?"

"That's funny," Marcie said, "I was getting ready to ask you the same thing."

Cassie shrugged. "Nothing's new with me."

"I'd say there's a lot new with you. Counting the weekend at the woman's house, you've been sober for six days. Your cuts and bruises are healing nicely; you have a real bed to sleep in, a lovely environment and three good meals a day. Do you think you'll stick around long enough to go to rehab?"

"You bet. I like this place. It's cool."

"Excellent. Now then, do you have anything you'd like to discuss? Like your father's new wife?"

Cassie set her elbows on her knees and cupped her chin in her hands. "No, not really. She's a bitch, but my mother was an even bigger bitch."

"How?"

Cassie sat up, her arms resting on her thighs. "She ran around on my dad. One time I caught her and this bearded dude doing the nasty right there on the living room couch. Talk about gross."

"Did you tell your father?"

"No way. He thought my mother was a saint. Until he came home early one day, sick as a dog, and went upstairs to go to bed. Oh, hello there. His saint turned into a devil."

"That's so sad," Marcie said.

"I couldn't cope with all the drama so I flopped at a friend's house."

"Then what?"

"I flopped anywhere I could."

"You were how old when your parents started divorce proceedings?"

"Sixteen."

"When did you start drinking?"

"I started sneaking into my parent's liquor cabinet when I was fourteen. Drinking made everything cool. You know what I mean?"

"Yes, I know. Have you gotten to know the other residents? Played cards with any of them?"

"Un–un. I've got to stay in shape, you know?"

"From where I'm sitting, you're in great shape. How do you do it?"

"Push-ups, sit-ups, crunches, stuff like that. I can't wait till you let me run outside. It's hard work but it's worth it, you know?"

Marcie laughed. "Exercise is a dirty word in my vocabulary. Oh, I do stretches and breathing exercises, but you won't catch me running."

"Breathing exercises?"

"Yes. You'll learn how to do them in one of our group sessions. Listen, Cassie, I do wish you'd take time to socialize with the other residents. It's not healthy to isolate yourself."

"Missy does it all the time. She gets dressed and then lies around reading some book."

Marcie smiled and said, "She's exercising her mind, you know?"

Cassie gave her a blank look. Then she said, "You're putting me on, right?"

"Right," Marcie said. "Now go find someone to play cards with."

"Cool!" Cassie cheered. She uncrossed her legs, grabbed her flip-flops and left in a flash.

In Cassie's chart, Marcie wrote, "Obsessed with exercise. Doesn't interact with other residents. Too cheerful and compliant to be believed. Shrugs off parents' behavior. Carrying a lot of pain around. Hiding something." Aren't we all, she mused.

The phone rang just as she started to put Cassie's chart back. She answered it before the second ring. "Port Victor, Marcie speaking."

"Rutledge here."

"Well, so you're still breathing."

"Don't give me a hard time. I've been traveling."

"You're supposed to keep me informed of your comings and goings."

"Sometimes even I don't know until the last minute."

"Excuses, excuses. But never mind that. Are you ready to hear some good news?"

"I'm always ready to hear good news."

"The kids are coming home. On June 10. Can you believe it?"

"It's about time. Let's talk it over at dinner Saturday. I owe you one."

She hesitated. Should she tell him she had a date with Roger? "Saturday's not good for me, but I'm free on Friday. I could meet you at your office after work."

"No can do," he said. "I promised a guy I'd teach his psych class Friday night."

"Can you do a Sunday brunch?"

"Sounds good. Meet me at the Hilton at 1100 hours."

"I'll be there."

"See you then." The line went dead.

Marcie smiled. She had so much to tell him.

It was past time for a glass of iced tea. She set off for the kitchen, but turned back when the phone rang. It was Sarah's secretary, Rebecca calling.

"Oh, hi," Marcie said. "I've been meaning to ask if you want to come over here for lunch sometime. We eat at noon."

Rebecca said, "Lunch? What's that? I haven't had lunch in years. I munch, all day, here at my desk."

"Sarah works you that hard?" Marcie asked.

"Harder. Maybe we can get together for a drink after work. That's if I get off before the bar closes."

"Good grief. I hope Sarah pays you well."

"There's not enough money in the world to pay me what I'm worth. But that's another story. I called to tell you that Pearl is officially on the payroll. Sarah's paying her minimum wage. She'll get her first check this Friday. Hey, that's tomorrow. Do you want to tell her or should I?"

"I'd love nothing better than to tell her."

"Great. Well, I'd better run. We've got to get together."

"I agree."

"Okay. Talk to you later."

"'Bye."

Once again, Marcie set off for the kitchen. She smiled when she saw Cassie playing cards with Missy. She paused at their table for a moment, watching the contrast in the girls' body language. Intense and cautious, Missy held her cards up to her face. She took a lot of time before making a play and changed her mind several times before discarding. On the other hand, Cassie was open and impulsive. She held her cards loosely, waving them around while she talked about nothing in particular. She made quick moves when her turn came. The irony was Cassie won the hand. Obviously, it didn't pay to be too cautious.

The delicious aroma of Pearl's chicken gumbo wafted out to greet her as she entered the kitchen. "Ah, you're just the person I wanted to see," Marcie said. She proceeded to tell Pearl the good news.

"No'um," Pearl said. "I don't want that job. I like things just the way they is."

"What do you mean you don't want the job?"

Pearl took the pot of chicken gumbo off the burner. She turned to face Marcie and started in on her apron. "What am I gonna do with more money? I don't spend half what I get from the Social Security. 'Sides, being a house manager would put more work on me."

"No, it wouldn't. As of today, each woman will take on a specific chore so you'll have plenty of help. Don't you see, Pearl, being the official manager means you're the boss when I'm not here."

"Miss Deb, she goin' somewheres?"

"No. She's still the housemother, but you know as well as I do that you're in charge."

Pearl shook her head. "It just don't seem right takin' money from Miss Sarah."

"Your salary won't come out of Miss Sarah's pocket, it'll come from her corporation."

"What's that?"

"A big company that encompasses all of her properties. The money she collects from her businesses pays her employees' salaries."

"I ain't never seen a paycheck. What am I gonna do with it?"

"Good point. I'll bet half the women here have never received a paycheck or had a bank account. I'm going to ask one of the ladies at my bank to come over and give a talk on money management. In the meantime, I can either cash your check for you or you can save it until we can go to the bank and open an account."

"I reckon I'll save it. What' a 'bout my cheese? How're you gonna find out who stole it?"

"I'm going to talk about it at group today. I'm hoping whoever took it will get the message this time."

"What if they don't?"

"Then we'll have to put a lock on the refrigerator door."

Pearl's voice turned whiny. "An'then I'd hafta carry a durn key around."

"I hope it doesn't come to that, Pearl. It'd be a last resort."

"Yessum." Pearl moved to the stove and put the pot back on the burner. She turned the heat on and picked up her stirring spoon.

Marcie headed back to her office. She needed time to think about her session with Deborah. What would the little one confess to next?

CHAPTER 20

Marcie left the chalkboard in the corner. She placed the sheaf of papers on a nearby chair and then stood before the group. "Ladies, I have a lot of things to cover today, so let's get started."

"What kind of things?" Veronica asked.

"The first order of business is the pilfering of food."

Georgia Lu raised her hand and said, "What's that there 'pilferin' mean?"

Veronica turned to her and said, "It means stealing. Someone has been stealing food."

"Thank you, Veronica, but I wouldn't exactly call it stealing. It's more like taking food to eat in private."

"Same thing," said Veronica.

Marcie began to ramble on about trust and honesty. Soon, even to her own ears, she sounded like a mother scolding her children for getting into the cookie jar. The women were either fidgeting or looking bored, and she didn't blame them, so she tried a different approach.

"I realize you don't have the foggiest notion of what it takes to keep a house like this going, but let me tell you, Miss Sarah pours a bundle into this place every month. The electric bill alone is staggering. So, if food continues to disappear, you are going to go hungry because I am not going to ask Miss Sarah for more grocery money." Marcie paused. She didn't expect anyone to confess, she hoped no one would. She just wanted the thefts to stop.

"Speaking of food," Veronica said, "when are you going to buy us a grill?"

Marcie wanted to throw up her hands and retreat to her office. "For heaven's sakes, Veronica, haven't you heard a word I've said?"

Veronica drew herself up, looked around the room and started reciting verbatim in a perfect imitation of Marcie's voice. "Ladies, I have a lot to cover today, so let's get started." "What kind of things?" "The first order of business is the pilfering of food." "What's that there pilfering mean?" "It means stealing. Someone is stealing food." "Thank you, Veronica, but I wouldn't call—"

"Okay, that's enough," Marcie said. "I must say that your talents have no bounds."

Veronica preened. "A great actress learns to memorize everyone's lines."

"Hot damn!" Georgia Lu shouted. "I done told you she was a great actress!"

"Thank you kindly, Georgia Lu."

Marcie said, "As for the grill, I forgot all about it. It's in the garage. We can unpack it and set it up after group." Cheers and clapping ensued.

As soon as everyone settled down, Cassie raised a hand. What now, Marcie wondered as she gave her the nod.

"Is group like this all the time?"

"Yes," Veronica, Phyllis, and Missy said in unison. Then, like little girls who had spoken aloud in church, they giggled into their hands.

"Cool," said Cassie.

"So, as I was saying, ladies, the pilfering of food must stop." For once, everyone remained quiet. Marcie went on. "Now then, I have an important announcement to make. Miss Sarah has hired Pearl as our official house manager. Isn't that wonderful?"

"Hot damn, Pearl!"

"Congratulations, Pearl," said Phyllis. "You certainly deserve it."

"Amen," Missy said, then darted a look at Marcie. Only the two of them knew the significance behind Missy's reference to prayer.

Veronica stood up, turned to where Pearl was sitting. "May I say that Miss Sarah couldn't have done better if she'd hired someone with a Ph.D."

Pearl and Georgia Lu looked at each other. "Veronica, don't she sound like our Marcie?" Pearl said. To which, Georgia Lu replied. "All them hifalutin' words sets my head on fire."

Even Marcie had to laugh. Then she said, "Now, I have one more order of business before we start our lesson for the day."

"You mean we'll have to sit through a lesson after all this?" Veronica asked.

Ignoring the remark, Marcie gathered the sheaf of papers and started handing them out. When she got to Pearl and Georgia Lu, she passed them by. Back in her spot, she said, "I want you to take a look at this list of chores and decide which one you want to do. I'll give you ten minutes to discuss it between yourselves and then I'll expect your answers."

"What if we don't want to do any of them?" Veronica said.

"Never mind," Marcie said. She left the room and went to wait in the kitchen.

Pearl soon followed. "Who done stole my cheese?"

"I checked for signs, Pearl, but none of the women looked the least bit guilty."

"I been studyin' on this." Pearl said, "Cassie, she's gotta be the one."

Marcie frowned. "Cassie? What makes you think that?"

"That Cassie, she's the newest one. Nobody took food before she come here. If that's not guilty, I'm a cross-eyed raccoon."

"Then we'd better get your eyes checked, because Cassie's the last person I'd suspect. She's so weight conscious she works out most of the time."

Pearl wagged a finger at her. "You wait'n see."

Marcie checked her watch. "Well, it's time to go back in."

"Do I hafta?"

"Yes."

"Are you ready, ladies?" Marcie asked as she returned to the front of the room.

"I am," Phyllis said, waving her paper in the air. "I took the bathrooms because no one else wanted them."

"All three of them?" Marcie said.

"Yes."

"Well, if you're sure...Ladies, did you hear what Phyllis said?"

"Yes." "Un-huh." "Yessum."

"Good. I'm going to count on each and every one of you to clean up after yourself. That means folding your towel and putting it back on the rack, putting the cap on the toothpaste, wiping any soap residue out of the sink and tub. And if you happen to make a mess in the toilet, don't wait for Phyllis to clean it up."

"We already do most of those things," Veronica said.

"I want you to do *all* of those things. Who's going to vacuum the carpets?"

"Me," said Cassie.

"Great. And the dusting?"

"I am," said Missy.

"Fine. That leaves you, Veronica."

"I'm not trained to do housework. Anyway, I might break a nail." She held up both hands so everyone could see her long nails painted with pink polish. "It's taken me forever to get them looking this good."

"No excuses, Veronica."

Veronica heaved a dramatic sigh, and then turned to Missy. "Could you switch to another chore? I suppose I could dust without breaking a nail."

Missy looked the list over again. "I guess I could do the storage room."

Cassie spoke up. "I could do the storage room."

"Thank you, Cassie," Marcie said, "but you already have a job."

"No problem. I can do both. It's good exercise."

"That it is. So, Missy, that leaves sweeping the walkway and the garage."

"I'll take it."

"Okay then." She read off the list of chores and assigned a name to each one. Settled at last, she sighed with relief. Then Georgia Lu raised a hand.

"What is it, Georgia Lu?"

"Everybody has a job but me and Pearl."

"That's because the two of you already have jobs. Pearl's the house manager and you're in charge of the vegetable garden."

"Hot damn!"

Marcie went on. "Now, for those of you who'll do housework, you'll start cleaning this Saturday morning and every Saturday morning after that. With all of you on the job, you can whip this house into shape in no time. That will leave the rest of the day for R&R."

The hand shot up. Marcie didn't bother asking what Georgia Lu wanted. She simply explained that R&R meant rest and relaxation.

204

"Does anyone else have a question?" She paused briefly. "Today we're going to talk about goal setting." Before the hand could go up, she rushed on. "Please save your questions until I've finished. Setting a goal means you are working toward something you want to achieve. Why do we need to set goals? Without them we're just drifting along, floundering, not getting anywhere, or getting into trouble. Like the life you led before coming to Port Victor. Since your first day here you've achieved a major goal. You've maintained your sobriety. Which means you're on the road to the ultimate goal of being able to live a fulfilling life in the outside world minus the use of alcohol.

"This is how it works. Say you set a goal to lose five pounds. You concentrate your energy on achieving that goal. Once you reach your desired weight, it's time to set another goal. Like reading a book. You finish the book and then you set another goal. On and on we go until we get to bigger goals. Like finishing rehab." She looked at Missy. "Let's say you go to college. You set a goal to attend classes and study hard so you'll get a passing grade. You do that with each of your classes with the bigger goal of graduating." She turned her attention to the group as a whole. "In a job situation, you show up for work on time, do your job to the best of your ability, with a goal of getting either a raise or a promotion or both. Maybe you want to take a vacation but you can't afford it, so you set a goal to save enough money to take that trip. Or maybe you're saving to buy a car. I can think of a zillion goals. The point is you're always working toward something. That gives you a sense of purpose, which in turn builds self-esteem." She paused, and then called for questions.

As usual, Veronica was the first to speak. "Like I set a goal to get my fingernails to a certain length."

Amid a few titters, Marcie said, "That's right, you did, you just didn't know it at the time. Now you need a new goal. Georgia Lu set a goal to rid her garden of weeds. She didn't know it either, but now she does." She looked around the room. "Anyone else?"

Phyllis said, "I've set a goal to cook you all a delicious dinner."

"And I can't wait," Marcie said. "Once you've prepared your meal, what do you do?"

"Set another goal?" Phyllis asked.

"Exactly."

"I could stand to lose five pounds," Missy said. "That and doing well at rehab are my goals."

"My goal is to run five miles a day," Cassie said. Then she added, "Outside."

"Can you run on shells?" Marcie asked.

"I can run on nails."

"Well, as long as you stay within sight of the house, you can run up and down the driveway."

A wide grin showed Cassie's dimples. She pumped a fist in the air and said, "Yes! You're the best!"

Marcie laughed and said, "Just don't come running to me if you break a leg."

Veronica looked at Cassie and said, "Girl, you're crazy to run on those shells. I couldn't even *walk* on them. Missy and Marcie had to carry me from the car to the house."

"Were you wearing spiked heels?" Cassie asked. When Veronica looked away, she said, "There you go. I couldn't even *walk* in your heels."

"Okay, ladies. We've done enough work for one day. Veronica, I turn the floor over to you."

Cheers and applause followed that announcement. Marcie exchanged places with Veronica and settled in for the show.

Dressed to the nines, as usual, Veronica wore a short, black party dress with a layered ruffle skirt. Her hands, arms, neck, and earlobes dripped diamonds or zircons, Marcie couldn't tell which, and the spiked heels with straps showed off her slender ankles. Today, she wore a peek–a–boo hairdo like her namesake. It covered the right side of her forehead and part of her right eye.

Veronica started by saying, "Girls, are you ready?"

The women leaned forward in their seats, eager for the show to begin.

Veronica fixed her eyes on her roommate. "I will not tolerate any interruptions. Is that clear?"

A chastised Georgia Lu sat back in her chair, her large hand covering half of her face.

"Picture this, my dears," Veronica said, gazing upwards as though at the scene laid out before her. "A large open-air restaurant perched on a cliff overlooking the Pacific Ocean. A dark sky blinking a million stars over Ensenada, Mexico. A band playing samba music sweet and low. The surf pounding the rocks below. Well-dressed ladies and gentlemen sitting at candlelit tables eating abalone and lobsters. Talking and laughing. Drinking gallons of Margarita. My date is a dreamy part-time actor and professional dancer. We listen to the sounds echoing into the night sky. We drink, we eat, we dance, we sigh." She paused.

Like the rest of the group, Marcie thought half the fun of listening to one of Veronica's stories was watching her facial expressions and hand gestures. If she hadn't followed her namesakes lead and gotten hooked on booze— who knew? Sober, she might have become a leading lady.

Georgia Lu couldn't contain herself any longer. "What kinda dress you got on, huh?"

"A silk print in shades of purple, orange, and lime green on ivory. It had tiny spaghetti straps and deep slits up the sides. Very sexy. My skin glowed with a golden tan and my hair and makeup were *perfecto.* And my purple dancing shoes had silver glitter sprinkled on them."

"Hot damn! Bet you was a sight for sore eyes!"

Veronica went on. "My date wore a black suit with a black and white striped dress shirt and an ivory-colored tie with black squares. We were the best-looking couple there, if I do say so myself."

"Did'ya take pictures, huh, Veronica, huh?"

"Certainly not. Only tourists carry cameras." Her violet-blue eyes glittered as she went on. "The energy level was high and we were feeling no pain. We got up to dance. Everyone, even the waiters, watched us twirl around the floor. Dancing with a great partner was like dancing on clouds. Pure heaven. Oh, we'd stop now and then to have another drink. And the band took an occasional break. That's when you could hear the surf below. It couldn't have been more divine." She paused for a moment, holding the women captive. Then she flung out her arms and cried, "But the best was yet to come."

"The band started playing music from the film, *Gilda*. You may not remember the movie, but my mama and I used to watch it over and over again on the movie channel. It starred my second favorite actress, the beautiful and incredibly sexy, Rita Hayworth. She had flaming red hair and was every man's pin–up girl. They named her the 'Love Goddess'. Anyway, the band leader looked over at me and tilted his head toward the dance floor. He meant he wanted only me out there. Not my partner, not any of the other guests, only me. So I took to the floor. There I stood, in the spotlight, playing the part I was born to play, and my audience started clapping before I could take a single step.

"Get ready, girls, because here goes." Veronica pretended to put on long, elbow–length gloves. A gloved hand went to her skirt, her waist, her breast, and up to her hair. Then she began to sway in rhythm to some inner music, hips moving in concert with her shoulders. A humming sound came from deep in her throat. She swayed and hummed, arms gracing the air like a ballerina. And then on just the right note, she started to sing in a throaty voice.

"'When Mrs. O'Leary's cow kicked the lantern that burned the town down, that was the story that went around, but here's the real lowdown. You can put the blame on Mame, boys. Put the blame on Mame.

"Mame kissed a buyer from out of town, that kiss burned Chicago down, So you can put the blame on Mame, boys, put the blame on Mame.

"Remember the blizzard back in Manhattan in 1886, they say traffic was tied up and folks were in a fix. That's the story that went around, but here's the real lowdown. Put the blame on Mame, boys, put the blame on Mame. Mame gave a chump such an ice-cold no, for seven days they shoveled snow. So you can put the blame on Mame, folks, put the blame on Mame.'"

Barely pausing for breath, Veronica sang the lyrics again while performing a mock striptease. She didn't remove a single article of clothing to plant the idea of stripping in your mind. Accompanied by bumps and grinds, she sang on, first pretending to peel off one glove at a time, twirling it in the air and then throwing it for the women to catch. They actually tried to catch an invisible glove. Next came each piece of jewelry, then the spiked heels. She turned her back on the women and slowly pretended to unzip her dress. "Put the blame on Mame, boys." She turned back around and shrugged out of one shoulder at a time. She brought the dress down over her hips and then let it fall to the floor. After stepping out of the dress, she tossed it to the group. Again, they tried to grab hold of empty air. Veronica then ran her hands across an invisible bra. She snapped the band on her bikini panties with her thumbs. The women giggled. Veronica pretended to unsnap her stockings from a garter belt. "Put the blame on Mame, boys." She slowly eased the stockings down each leg, drew them from her feet, rolled each one up and threw it to the crowd. "Put the blame on Mame."

Marcie checked her watch. It was after four. "Un, Veronica, ladies," she said, standing up, "as much as I hate to interrupt such a stirring performance, it's time to take a break."

"But I'm just getting started," Veronica said. "I haven't told you about the standing ovation I got. Everyone, even the members of the band, stood up when the number ended. They clapped and shouted and whistled. All for little old me. It was one of the best nights of my life. I finally got to play *Gilda* in public." She hugged herself, eyes shimmering.

Marcie went to her and put an arm around her waist. "I wish I could have been there, Veronica, I truly do. You painted a superb picture of what it was like." She looked around the room and said, "Ladies, what do you say?"

They rose as one and gave her a standing ovation with applause and cheers for "More! More!" Phyllis surprised everyone with a screeching whistle and Georgia Lu kept hollering, "Woohoo! Woohoo!" Marcie stood aside while Veronica took her well-deserved bows.

When everyone quieted down and a few of the women started moving the chairs to the game tables, Marcie wished Deborah could have witnessed Veronica's performance. Maybe she would have been impressed. Then again, she might have thought the faux striptease went beyond the bounds of decency and called Sarah to tell her how Marcie conducted her group therapy sessions. Deborah probably wouldn't approve of Marcie playing cards with the women, either. She looked around the room and said, "Who wants to try to beat me in a game of Spite and Malice?"

CHAPTER 21

Marcie braced herself for a long, hard day. Tempers usually ran short on Fridays. Little problems that had festered all week suddenly burst like boils. A sense of urgency seemed to sweep through the house, as though the residents had one last chance to solve all of life's problems. She often wondered if the women resented her freedom on weekends and deliberately set out to punish her for leaving them to fend for themselves.

As she turned onto Port Victor's driveway, she saw Cassie running down the other side. Wearing short shorts, a T-shirt with something written on the front, and a headband, she looked like any other high school runner. Except Cassie dropped out of school in the tenth grade, which meant rehab would put her in a class with other dropouts so she could work toward earning a GED. Marcie tapped the horn and waved. Cassie beamed a big smile back at her. Nearing the garage, she tapped the horn again and waved at Georgia Lu. The master gardener never looked up.

As usual, she knocked before entering the kitchen. The aroma of cooked sausage filled the air. Pearl's hands were deep in a sudsy sink. A perfectly good dishwasher built into the cabinet near the woman's right thigh went unused because Pearl didn't trust "that newfangled machine" to get things clean.

Marcie filled her mug with steaming black coffee. She looked at Pearl and said, "How did things go last night?"

Pearl kept her eyes on the sink, "I don't rightly know how to tell you."

"Just spill it out, Pearl."

Pearl lifted her hands out of the sudsy water and dried them on a dish towel. When she started in on her apron, Marcie knew the news wasn't good. "That talk of yours flew right out the window. Somebody done stole my carrot cake."

"The whole cake?"

"The whole dang thing. An' it bein' froze."

"I don't get it," Marcie said.

"Y'know how I always makes two cakes so's I have an extra. That cake went into the freezer. This mornin' when I come down, the cake was gone."

"Damn," Marcie said. "That means the person snuck down here after lights out."

"Yessum."

"You don't suppose it could be Deborah, do you?"

"Sometimes of a night, Miss Deb, she'll fix her and that dog a ice cream sundae with chocolate syrup, but she always washes the bowls an' leaves 'em for me to put up." Pearl frowned and added, "Funny thing, Miss Deb, she ain't eat a sundae since you come here."

"Maybe her taste has changed and she prefers cake."

"No'um. Miss Deb, she likes her cookies and her ice cream."

"How does she reach the freezer?"

"See that stool over yonder?" Pearl pointed to a two-step stool sitting in the corner between the windows and the door to the dining room. Marcie had always thought her powers of observation were fine-tuned, but she had never noticed the stool.

"Well, I guess we can scratch Miss Deb off the list. I'm so disappointed. You'd think after my talk yesterday, no one would dare take any more food."

"Yessum. An' here's somethin' else. My bread's been goin' too fast. I'll open a fresh loaf and 'fore I knowed it, I hafta open a new one."

"Maybe the thief made a ham and cheese sandwich with the cake for dessert."

"You reckon?"

"I don't know, Pearl. I was half kidding. But it's not funny."

"No'um, it sure ain't. What're you gonna do?"

"What I should have done in the first place. Call the women into the office one at a time and ask them if they took the food. Even if they deny it, they may reveal some twitch or tic that shows they're guilty."

"Good idea," said Pearl.

"By the way, how long has Cassie been outside?"

"Cassie, she's been out there since I started fixin' breakfast. She wouldn't come in to eat."

"Well, I'll let you know how the question and answer sessions went."

"Yessum," Pearl said and went back to her dishes.

With her coffee mug in hand, Marcie headed for the front door. She opened it and stepped out on the porch. Cassie was halfway up the west side of the driveway. When she neared the front of the house, Marcie waved her in. Cassie stopped and jogged in place, a baffled look on her shiny face.

"It's time to come in," Marcie called.

Cassie slowed her pace and then started a series of stretching exercises. Marcie watched, understanding the process. The girl's body glistened with a healthy sheen of sweat. Finally, Cassie took a deep breath and let it out. Then she said, "I was just getting warmed up."

"Since dawn?" Marcie said.

"Yeah," the girl said, grinning.

Marcie opened the door and stepped aside for Cassie to enter. "Before you do anything else," she said, "I want to see you in the office."

"Okay," Cassie said, still bursting with energy. Marcie wished some of it would rub off on her.

After removing her running shoes and socks, Cassie took her usual yoga position in the chair. She looked at Marcie and said, "What's up?"

"It's not a good idea to skip breakfast, Cassie. It's a long time before we eat lunch."

"No problem," Cassie said. "If I try to run on a full stomach, I feel like I'm going to barf, you know?"

"But won't you get hungry between now and noon?" Marcie said.

"Not really," Cassie said. "I don't think about food when I'm working out, you know?"

"There's such a thing as overdoing it, you know."

Cassie seemed to think it over. "See, if I don't work out, I hate myself. It's like I've got to do it, you know?"

"Yes, I know. You're obsessed with it."

Cassie sat up straight and beamed a wide smile. "Right!"

"Sorry, but I don't find it amusing," Marcie said. "Your behavior is out of control. Whether you like it or not, we need to work on this."

"Whatever you say," Cassie said with a shrug.

Marcie leaned forward with an earnest expression. "Cassie, did you take the food?"

Cassie reared back in her chair. "Me? No way. I'm not that into food."

Marcie sat back. "Okay, you may be excused. For now." Cassie lost no time in gathering her shoes and socks. Marcie went on. "Your assignment is to find an activity to do apart from working out."

"That's cool," Cassie said as she made a beeline for the door.

A worried frown creased Marcie's brow. Obsessive- compulsive disorders were one of the hardest anxieties to treat. A combination of cognitive behavioral therapy and medication were normally used. She made a note to talk to George about it.

On her way out to the garden to talk to Georgia Lu, she found Pearl kneading dough instead of her apron. She rapped on a cabinet.

Pearl's head came up. "Who done it?"

"At the moment, all I know is who didn't do it. Cassie is innocent."

Pearl narrowed her eyes. "How'd'ya know that gal didn't do it?"

"It's hard to explain, Pearl. Mainly, it's the look in a person's eyes that tells me when he or she is lying. My kids never had a chance when one of them did something wrong. I always knew when they were lying."

Pearl's head jerked up. "You got kids? How many you got?"

Marcie sighed. The bit about her kids had just rolled off her tongue as if she talked about them on a regular basis. Pearl was waiting to hear what she had to say. It was high time to tell the truth.

"Yes, I have a girl and a boy, Julie and Davy. They're teenagers and they go to a private school in Washington, D.C. That's where their father lives. In a few weeks, they'll be out of school for the summer and they'll spend it here at home."

"I'll swan," Pearl said. "You got kids." She shook her head. "An all'a this time I thought you was alone."

"Well, with the kids away at school, I am alone. Except for my dog, Charley. Oh, and I have thirty–two clocks. They're a lot of company, too."

At mention of the dog and the clocks, Pearl's mouth dropped open. It was still hanging open when Marcie finished speaking. It was as if she was waiting for more big news.

Marcie moved toward the door to the storage room. "I'm going out to talk to Georgia Lu now. See you when I come back in."

Pearl craned her neck to watch her go, her mouth still hanging open.

Marcie chuckled to herself. She'd never seen Pearl completely speechless. But then it was the first time she'd talked about her family situation.

———

Standing slumped over in the garden's middle row, Georgia Lu had her hands wrapped around the top of the hoe and was resting her chin on them. She seemed to be waiting for a weed to dare show its face. Either that or asleep on her feet.

"Yoo Hoo! Georgia Lu!" Marcie called.

Georgia Lu stood up straight and peered in Marcie's direction. Whether she actually saw her or not was debatable. It looked like she was peering into space. Since she didn't seem inclined to make a move, Marcie walked across the lawn to the edge of the garden. "Georgia Lu? Can you come here for a minute? I'd like to talk to you."

In slow motion, Georgia Lu lifted one booted foot, set it down, then lifted the other foot. She continued the routine until she was about two–feet away. "You seem tired, Georgia Lu," Marcie said. "Why don't you take a break?"

"I was takin' one till you showed up."

"Sorry, Georgia Lu, this won't take but a minute. Did you or did you not take the missing food?"

Georgia Lu came alive. She ripped the sun hat off her head and threw it on the ground. "Gol dang it! I done told them harpin' hens I didn't take it an' here you are thinkin' I did."

Marcie held up her hands. "No, no, no. I never said I thought you took it. I'm asking everyone the same question. Please believe me."

Georgia Lu bent over, snatched the sun hat out of the dirt and set it on her head. She looked at Marcie and said, "Ma'am, I don't know who took that there food, but sure as the owl's gonna catch the mouse, I'm gonna find out who did."

Marcie nodded. "I believe you will, Georgia Lu. I believe you will." She headed back to the house.

Her dough left in a bed of flour on the counter, Pearl was lying in wait when Marcie walked in. "Did I hear right? You got thirty- two clocks?"

"You heard right," Marcie said. She opened a cupboard, selected a glass and took it to the refrigerator to get some iced tea. "I started collecting clocks as souvenirs right after David and I got married. One thing led to another and now I have a house full of them."

"Mercy," said Pearl. "One clock's more'n 'nough for me. I hate it when that alarm goes to bleetin'. Sounds just like a lamb at shearin' time."

"As a matter of fact, I happen to have a lamb clock, but it doesn't bleat, it goes baa–baa. I have all kinds of clocks and I never set any of their alarms."

"I'll swan," Pearl said. "If that don't beat all."

Marcie laughed. "Someday I'll have you over to meet my little family of clocks."

"Don't rightly know if I'd like that."

"What? Coming over to my house? Or meeting my clocks?"

"Meetin' that dog of yours. I'm afeared'a dogs."

"Oh, Charley's just a big old pussy cat. He wouldn't harm a flea."

Pearl went back to her dough.

Marcie lingered at the door to the dining room. "Pearl, I'd appreciate it if you kept the information about my kids to yourself. I really don't want my personal life to be tonight's topic of conversation."

Pearl kept her eyes on the dough. "You oughta know I don't talk to nobody less'n I have to."

"I do know, Pearl, but sometimes our mouths are bigger than our brains." Like mine was a few minutes ago, she added to herself. "And, by the way, you should be happy to hear that Georgia Lu is not guilty."

Pearl looked up. "Sure 'nuff?"

Marcie nodded. "She swears she's going to catch the person red-handed."

Pearl grinned. "Georgia Lu, she always does what she says she's'a gonna do."

"I pity the guilty party," Marcie said. "Well, I've got three more women to ask. I'll give you the results when I finish."

Upon returning to the office, Marcie pulled the women's charts out of the file drawer and laid them on the desk. She first wrote a report in Cassie's chart, then Georgia Lu's. When she looked up, Phyllis gave a tentative wave from the doorway, as if asking if it was okay to come in.

"Oh," Marcie said, glancing up at the clock. "It's time for our session, isn't it? Please have a seat. I got sidetracked about this missing food business."

"Do you know who took it?" Phyllis asked.

"Not yet. Did you take it?"

Phyllis put a hand to her stomach and jiggled the little pot belly she had acquired. "Do I look like I need more food?"

Marcie smiled. "I take that as a no."

"Absolutely," said Phyllis. "If I wanted something extra to eat, I'd ask Pearl."

Marcie leaned back in her chair. "Are you excited about seeing Jim tomorrow?"

Phyllis sighed. "I'm excited and scared at the same time."

"Let's talk about what scares you," Marcie said. "Being with Jim after a month away from him?"

"I don't know what to say, I don't know how to act. It's like I'm going out with a stranger."

"Well, in a way you are. You'll be that sober girl Jim fell in love with. It'll be awkward at first, but if I were you I'd let him take the lead. If he wants to take you some place nice for lunch, go along with him. If he wants to see a movie afterwards, let him choose which one. Try not to argue about anything. It's a waste of precious time and it'll only cause hard feelings."

"Oh, I know, but if he starts talking about the job ... well, I don't want to hear it."

"Then change the subject. Tell him about our treatment program. Tell him you're going to start rehab on Monday. Tell him about the books you've read. Think of all you've accomplished and be proud of yourself. Jim will love the new Phyllis just as much, if not more, than the young Phyllis that attracted him the first time around."

"It's going to be hard to do."

"Things that are worth working for usually are." Marcie paused. "Phyllis, didn't you used to teach school?"

"I taught second grade for five years and that was more than enough."

Marcie said, "Okay. Humor me, I'm thinking out loud. You already have a degree in education. Maybe you'd like to pursue a degree in something else."

"Go back to school? I don't think so. I'm too old to be sitting in a classroom."

Marcie said, "It's my belief that one is never too old to learn new tricks. But we'll leave it at that. What are you going to wear tomorrow?" Phyllis always dressed like a professional woman on her way to work. Someday, in the not-to-distant future, Marcie hoped she would be just that.

"I've changed my mind a dozen times," Phyllis said. "I'll probably end up wearing the red dress with the wide black belt. It's Jim's favorite."

"Good girl. Go get 'em, tiger."

Smiling, Phyllis rose and said, "Here I go, I'm ready to roar." "While you're at it, roar in Veronica's direction. I'd like to see her down here in about ten minutes."

"Will do."

"And Phyllis, I sincerely hope you have a great time tomorrow."

"Thanks, Marcie. So do I."

As soon as Phyllis cleared the room, Marcie opened her chart and started writing. It bothered her that Phyllis seemed to want to go back to her old life. Staying home without goals would eventually lead her straight to the bottle.

"You rang?" Veronica said in an exaggerated Southern drawl. She had struck a pose against the doorjamb, one shoulder and hip thrust out, a hand at her waist. Wearing a purple frock with patent leather heels, she looked ready to go dancing. Marcie surmised she had some wild tale to tell the women after group later today.

Marcie played along with the Southern accent. "If you aren't a sight for these poor old eyes. Come on in and set a spell."

"Don't mind if I do." Veronica took mincing steps across the carpet and lowered herself into the chair by the window.

"Are you practicing how to act on your date with the Colonel tomorrow?" Marcie asked

Veronica gave a throaty laugh. "Honey, I don't have to act around that man. He just loves looking at me."

"Veronica, you're a mess and a half."

"Don't I know it."

"What time is the Colonel picking you up?"

"Five o'clock, the cocktail hour."

"Don't you dare," Marcie said.

"Not to worry. The Colonel detests liquor in all forms."

"I'd like to meet him sometime."

"Well, all you have to do is be here tomorrow when he picks me up."

"Sorry, but I have—" she caught herself in time "other plans."

Veronica eyed her knowingly. "Would that mean you have a date?"

Marcie could feel the heat on her cheeks. "Not really. I'm just going out for dinner."

"With whom, may I ask?"

"No."

"Why not? You've asked me about the Colonel. Why can't I ask about your date?"

"Never mind," Marcie said. "We're getting way off track. I called you down here to answer one simple question. Did you take the missing food?"

Veronica raised a brow. "You've never specified exactly what kind of food is missing."

"You're right, I haven't. But if you took it you'd know what kind."

"Well then, you have your answer. I don't know because I didn't take anything."

"Okay, I believe you. Now go, get out of here, and tell Missy I want to see her." Veronica didn't budge. It seemed she was prepared to stay as long as she liked.

"Why are you still here?" Marcie asked.

"I'm waiting to hear about your life. You do have a life outside this house, don't you?"

It took a moment for Marcie to decide how to reply. "Veronica, I'm going to make you a deal. One of these days, after you've completed treatment, we can sit down and talk like girlfriends do. Until then, my life is my business."

"Girlfriends," Veronica said, rolling the word around on her tongue. "I never had a real girlfriend. All the girls I've known ended up being jealous of me."

"I can see why that could be a problem, but I haven't noticed any jealousy from the women here at Port Victor. In fact, you're very popular."

Veronica smiled. "I love it. These women make the best audience I've ever had."

"I hope that some of you will remain friends beyond Port Victor," Marcie said.

"I hadn't thought about that. It'd be nice to keep in touch with some of the girls. I hate that Georgia Lu is going back to Georgia. She's the best friend I've ever had."

This didn't surprise Marcie. Georgia Lu adoration for Veronica was obvious to everyone. "Maybe she won't go back. Maybe she'll make Fleming's Hill her home. Especially if you're here."

"But I don't know what I'd do around here. It's such a small town. No action that I know of."

"Seems to me you've had more than enough action. The kind that got you in trouble."

"Well, I'll have to admit it's been nice not to be tempted. That's what I love about going out with the Colonel." She laughed and added, "Of course the fact that he's rich and good looking doesn't hurt."

"I should've known that was coming. Well, I hope you have a wonderful time. Now please go tell Missy I want to see her."

Veronica dragged herself up out of the chair. "If you insist."

"I do."

Veronica flicked a wrist. "Ta–ta."

"See you later, alligator."

Marcie felt good about the conversation she'd just had. She opened Veronica's chart and started writing.

"You wanted to see me?" Missy asked a few minutes later. As usual, the girl was spit and polished clean from the roots of her hair to her shiny penny loafers. She crossed to the bookcase and inserted one into a slot. It was Barbara Kingsolver's, *The Poisonwood Bible.*

"How did you like it?" Marcie asked.

Missy said, "Oh, and to think I've wasted so much time reading trash when I could have been reading books like this." She tapped the novel's spine, then moved to her usual chair and sat down. "I loved it. It was the best book I've ever read. It made me sad, it made me angry, it depressed me, but that's because it was so real. I could identify with every one of the female characters. I got so mad at the preacher I wished someone would choke him. Oh, and those poor natives. They tried to warn him, but did he listen? Never."

Marcie said, "He reminded you of your father, didn't he?"

"They could be twins. Never wrong, never listen, never care! How could Miss Kingsolver know all that?"

"She's a great writer who probably did extensive research. Perhaps someone in her family did missionary work. Now it's time for you to pick another book. Since you're interested in psychology, I have an old paperback on the third shelf, *I Never Promised You a Rose Garden,* by Hannah Green. It's just as relevant today as it was when Ms. Green wrote it. You can get it on your way out."

Missy settled back in her chair. "But first," she said.

"What?" Marcie said.

"Isn't that what you were going to say? 'You can get it on your way out, but first'. Veronica said you wanted to ask me if I took the food. I just thought I'd

WHERE ARE THE WOMEN

save you the trouble. I did not take any food. I'm trying to lose five pounds, remember?"

"Yes, I remember. It's one of your goals. I didn't think you'd taken the food, but I had to ask. And just so you know it appears the ghost of Port Victor took it because none of the residents claim they did."

Missy crooked her head to one side and said, "What about you? We all know how you love the containers of food Pearl gives you to take home. Maybe you wanted that extra goodie and decided to take it. Who would ever know? Right?"

"You're just full of yourself today. Is it because you're going to see Mary Ellen tomorrow?"

"I guess so. It's been so long I've almost forgotten what she looks like. We have a lot of catching up to do."

"What time is she coming?"

"As soon as we finish cleaning the house. About one."

"Are you going anywhere special?"

"I thought we might go downtown and shop around. We could sit in the gazebo on the square and watch the world go by while we talk."

"Sounds like a good plan. Being organized and planning ahead will take you far in this world."

"I hope so."

"It will," Marcie said. "Just look at me. How organized and efficient I am. It's taken me to the top of the ladder at Port Victor." She laughed. "I hope you know I'm kidding."

"But you are organized," Missy said. "You have to be to take on a bunch of crazy women. I'd love to be in your shoes someday."

"Well, I'll take that as a compliment, Missy. I'm sure you'll accomplish whatever you set out to do." Marcie glanced up at the clock. "You'd better scoot. It's getting close to lunchtime."

Missy rose and went to the bookshelf. Her fingers skimmed over the titles until she found the right one. She pulled the book out, tucked it under her arm, and straightened the other books on the shelves. Organized and efficient. That was Missy.

Marcie opened the girl's chart and filled in five lines of progress notes. Despite the fact that no one had owned up to taking the food, it had been a productive day, so far. She still had more than half a day to go.

She picked up her glass of iced tea and took a long swallow. Lunchtime was a half hour away. She leaned back in the chair and clasped her hands over her midriff. Something kept nagging at her, something she was supposed to do. Then it came to her. She'd promised to give Pearl a full report after the last interview. The woman wouldn't rest until she heard the outcome, and then she wouldn't rest because the culprit hadn't confessed. It had to be one of the women, but which one?

It was then that Deborah breezed in. "We've had quite a parade up and down the hall this morning," she said. "What was so important that everyone had to see you?"

The little one looked more angelic than usual in her lily–white shift with a brilliant blue belt. It was hard to believe that she could switch from angel to devil in a nanosecond.

"We've had a problem with missing food," Marcie said, "and I thought it best to speak to the residents in private."

Deborah settled in her special chair. "So, who did it?"

"I have no idea."

Deborah said nothing, then, "I've been thinking a lot about what you said. That I should talk about the events that really bother me. But before I tell you, I want to make sure you won't ever repeat it. I'd like you to sign the confidentiality agreement with me."

"Good idea," Marcie said, getting up and going to the file cabinet. Once she had the form, she gestured for Deborah to join her at the desk. When the little one stood beside her, Marcie caught a whiff of perfume. It smelled like jasmine, reminding her of the Carolina jasmine that climbed a trellis at her family's home. She wondered if it was still alive.

Both of the women signed and dated the agreement. With it in hand, Deborah returned to her chair. "I'll keep this in a safe place," she said. "I feel so much better now."

"I'm glad," Marcie said. "Now you're free to tell me what's been bothering you."

Deborah looked at her and said, "This has been on my mind for a long time. Someone murdered my mother's new husband."

Marcie blinked. Was this a fantasy of hers? A bad dream, perhaps? "When?"

"Twenty-two years ago today. I was thirteen at the time. His name was Bill Thompson. He was stabbed to death with an ice pick."

The little one's voice and demeanor rang so true, Marcie halfway believed her. "Tell me what happened from start to finish."

"Well, Lila brought Bill home to meet Granny and me. Lila was so proud of herself for finally catching a husband. Bill fell in love with everyone and everything in Fleming's Hill, especially me. He was always picking me up and hugging me. He told Granny he was going to adopt me, have me live with them. Lila threw a fit. She hated Fleming's Hill and the last thing she wanted was for me to live with them. She railed at me, called me every ugly name she could think of. I thought she was going to kill me. Turned out, her Bill was the one who got killed." Deborah gave an odd little smile, more like a twist of her lip.

She went on. "Lila disappeared not long after that. Some people thought she was so distraught over Bill's death she jumped off the bridge. It was quite a circus. Dozens of boats out searching for her. Newspaper and TV reporters everywhere. What a joke." Condemnation hung in the air like an all-encompassing fog.

Marcie's heart went out to her. "How sad that you had to go through all that at the tender age of thirteen."

Deborah sighed. "I almost had a daddy. He was killed the day before he was to sign the adoption papers. Everyone in town thought the sheriff had something to do with it. He'd been in love with Lila ever since they were kids. He kept hoping she'd take him seriously. But when she brought Bill home ... well, some people thought he snapped."

"Good grief," Marcie said. "Do you think the sheriff did it?"

Once again, Deborah gave that twisted smile. "I have it on good authority that he did not."

"Do you know who did?"

With utter calm, Deborah said, "Uncle Victor."

Before Marcie could summon speech, Deborah leaned over and picked up the agreement. She stood up, her chair rocking back and forth by itself. "There," she said. "I've gotten that off my mind now." She made for the door.

"Wait!" Marcie cried, reaching out to stop her. "You can't go yet. Why did your uncle do it?"

"To save me." Deborah said. Then she was gone, leaving a stunned Marcie gaping after her.

CHAPTER 22

The morning had gone so well and then Deborah set off a minefield of explosive charges. Could they possibly be true? Could Victor Thornton, a devoted husband and father, who adored his ward, be capable of committing such an act of violence? What had Bill Thompson, a new husband and ready-to-be stepfather, done to precipitate such rage? And why an ice pick? Why not a knife, or a gun? Marcie shook her head to clear it. She couldn't think about that now. She had to go about her business as usual; otherwise, nosy people, like Veronica, would start asking questions. At the moment, her business was lunch.

A delicious aroma of tomatoes mixed with spices drifted out of the kitchen. Much to everyone's delight, Phyllis had prepared her special spaghetti with a garden salad and garlic bread. Ordered to sit while Phyllis and Marcie served the plates, Pearl kept casting anxious glances their way. Once she'd taken her first bite, a rare smile creased her wrinkled face.

"My stars," Pearl said. "I ain't never tasted such as this."

"I've been hungering for this ever since we wrote out the grocery list," Veronica said. "Phyllis, it's superb."

"Amen," Missy said.

"Um–huh," murmured Cassie.

"Thank you one and all," Phyllis said. "I made enough for two meals."

"Hooray," said Georgia Lu.

Except for Georgia Lu slurping long strings of pasta into her mouth, everyone else ate quietly and savored every bite. The garlic bread disappeared as did the salads. Pearl insisted on clearing the table while Phyllis served cheesecake for dessert.

After storing the leftovers, Pearl said, "Iffen any of you touch this here container, I'll tan your hide with this here wood spoon."

"If I don't catch the varmint first," said Georgia Lu.

"I wish the guilty party would confess," Veronica said. "This food business is getting on my nerves."

Missy looked at Pearl and said, "Would you tell us what was taken?"

"Aw, well, it don't 'mount to much," Pearl said, "but it's the prin— how do you say it, Marcie?"

"It's the principle of the thing. That means no one should take food out of this kitchen without asking Pearl first. As to what was taken, it started with a hunk of leftover ham, then a big chunk of cheese, an entire cake, and a lot of bread. Pearl's going to have a nervous breakdown if her stock keeps missing."

"Well," Veronica said, "you're right about one thing. It doesn't amount to much."

"Still," Phyllis said, "I understand why Pearl's upset. When my boys lived at home, they ate everything they could get their hands on. Money was tight back then and it really galled me when they'd pass out treats to all their friends. I'd try to make them understand that if they ate it all the first few days, they wouldn't have any treats for the rest of the week. It made absolutely no impression on them. Then they'd whine that there was nothing to eat."

Marcie could have told her own story. Like the time Davy didn't want Julie to have any of the bananas she'd bought so he hid them under his bed. She'd found half of them when they started to rot. Turned out he'd forgotten they were under there. So much for not sharing.

"I'm glad I never had kids," Veronica said. "They're nothing but selfish little beasts."

"Well, I wouldn't say that," Phyllis said. "They're selfish all right, but I can't imagine a life without them."

"Me and Blackie wanted kids," said Georgia Lu, "but we was havin' too much fun. That Blackie could dance like a whirlwind. Wish y'all coulda seen us flyin' around them dance halls. We were really somethin'."

"How did you meet him?" Missy asked.

"Do tell," said Veronica.

Georgia Lu scooted her chair back a few inches as if she needed more room for her story. "I was sippin' whiskey at this ole honkytonk. It was early in the evenin' and nothin' much was goin' on. Then ole Blackie sashayed in. He caught my eye 'cause he weren't but about five–feet–four and he was wearin' a uniform. I didn't know the Army took runts.

"Ole Blackie hoisted hisself on a stool next to the town whore. 'Course he didn't know she was the town whore 'cause he was a stranger. He bought her a drink an' just as they was cozyin' up to each other the gal's ex-boyfriend showed up with two of his rowdy friends. They was all big men with muscles out the yahoo. I fixed my eyes on 'em 'cause I smelled trouble.

"The boyfriend strolled over to the bar, grabbed the whore's arm and yanked her off'n the stool. Snarling like a mad dog, he told Blackie to get lost. Well, sir, Blackie didn't take to that too well. He stood up an' told the bruiser to get lost himself. The bruiser shoved Blackie into the barstools. But ole Blackie bounced back an' went to dancin' and jumpin' around like a bandy rooster, taking quick jabs at the bruiser's kidneys. The bruiser was drunk as a skunk and couldn't land a punch, so his rowdy friends stepped in to help him out.

"Did Blackie back off? No, sirreee, he took 'em all on. That's when I fell in love with him. He danced and jumped all over the place. The bruisers tried their best to catch him but they kept trippin' over their own feet. Pretty soon ole Blackie started to slow down. All that dancin' done wore him out. That's when I charged in. I laid all three bruisers flat, hoisted Blackie into my arms and carried my hero out the door. We got wed a week later."

"Way to go, Georgia Lu!" Cassie cried.

"You are something else," Veronica said.

"Mercy," Pearl said, "you coulda been kilt."

"But I weren't," said a proud Georgia Lu.

While she listened, Marcie didn't know whether to laugh or cry. It was pitiful yet hilarious at the same time, like a tragicomedy. But such was life. At least Georgia Lu had fond memories to sustain her.

———

Marcie set the chalkboard up as the women started drifting in for a refresher course on assertiveness. As soon as she had the women's attention, she started the lesson for the day. "Who can tell me the three basic types of behavior?"

Phyllis raised a hand. Receiving the go–ahead, she enunciated each word clearly. "Passive, assertive, and aggressive."

"Very good." Marcie said. "Now, Phyllis, can you tell us what each type means?"

"Passive behavior means taking no action, assertive means taking positive action, and aggressive means taking offensive action."

"Excellent," Marcie said, printing each definition on the board. She turned back to the women, her eyes scanning the group. "Does everyone understand what has been said so far?" The silence told Marcie that some women did and others did not.

"Our behavior is how we act and react. Most people are passive–aggressive. When something happens that we think is unjust, like the boss telling us we haven't earned a raise, instead of standing up for ourselves we don't say anything but we burn inside. Over time, our anger festers. And then one day some little thing happens, like our spouse forgot to take out the garbage, and we pitch a fit. It's not because of what our spouse did, it's because we didn't stand up to the boss. Does that make sense?"

The women murmured a few "un-huhs."

"All right then, who can give us an example of all three basic types?"

Veronica spoke up. "I've got a good one." Marcie gave her the nod. "Okay, you're standing in line to buy a ticket to see me appear on the silver screen."

Georgia Lu slapped a thigh and said, "Hot damn! I like this game!"

Muffled laughter and chuckles swept around the room. Veronica held up a hand and the room grew quiet. "You've been standing in line for hours waiting to see yours truly in a starring role. It seems like you've been waiting for days. Then some jerk cuts in front of you. If you're passive, you burn inside but you don't say a word. If you're aggressive, you punch him and yell, 'Get the hell out of my way'. But if you're assertive, you look him in the eye and say, 'Excuse me, but I was here first. You'll have to go to the end of the line.'"

"Woowee!" Georgia Lu bellowed. "This is some kind of fun."

Marcie looked at Veronica. "And what do you do if he won't budge?"

Veronica gave a wicked grin and said, "You stomp the shit out of him."

This time the room erupted into laughter. Even Marcie, who was too weak to fight it, laughed till tears rolled down her cheeks.

The laughter came to a sudden stop when a familiar voice called a hello from the foyer. Marcie ran a finger under each teary eye, sniffed her nose and turned to face her boss.

Sarah was not alone. Standing next to her was a tall, nice- looking man about Marcie's age. Sharply dressed in a yellow and brown plaid open–necked shirt and tan gabardine trousers, he had a salt–and–pepper beard and a head full of dark curly hair.

"Excuse me a minute," Marcie said to the women. Murmurings followed her as she walked toward the foyer on shaky legs. Had they heard what Veronica said and the laughter that followed?

Sarah was all smiles. "Hello, dear. I'm sorry to interrupt, but I have someone I'd like you to meet. Marcie Parker, this is Jacob Horner. He's the new pastor at our Lutheran Church. I've told him all about Port Victor and the work you do. He's very interested in your program and would like to give the girls a class on spiritual enrichment one day a week. Isn't that lovely?" She fairly chirped.

Marcie stared at the man in disbelief. A preacher? Doing a weekly group at Port Victor? Impossible. She swallowed with great difficulty.

"I'm very pleased to meet you," the pastor said in an amiable voice. "I admire the work you're doing and would like to play a small part in it."

Sarah added, "We don't want to interfere with your routine, dear, but what day would be most convenient?"

Marcie's mind went blank. This couldn't be happening. She must be hallucinating. But there they were, Sarah and the preacher, both of them staring at her. "Well, ah, let's see ..." In an effort to put him off as long as possible she decided on a week from today. By then she might be able to find a way out of this intrusion. "Un," she said, "how about next Friday?"

Pastor Horner's piercing blue eyes searched her face as though reading her mind. After a moment, he said, "That's fine with me."

Sarah clapped her hands together. "Wonderful! Now, Marcie, you take care of the introductions and then I want to see you in the office." She lowered her voice and added, "I need to speak to you on a private matter."

Marcie managed a nod. Her feet moved like they were made of lead as she preceded the preacher. Reaching the porch, she gave a forced smiled and said, "Ladies, I'd like you to meet Pastor Jacob Horner of the Lutheran Church."

Georgia Lu bounded out of her chair and grabbed the pastor's hand. "Glad to meet'cha, preacher."

He met her grip with a firm shake and said, "Thanks, I'm happy to be here."

Georgia Lu shoved the chalkboard out of the way, lugged a chair from the nearest corner and set it in front of the women. "Park it right here, preacher."

Marcie said, "I've just learned that Pastor Horner will be holding a group meeting each Friday." She noticed Missy blanch.

"Jacob," the pastor said. "Just call me Jacob." He lifted the sharp creases in his trousers at the knees and sat down. Surveying the women from right to left, he said, "I guess we'd better begin by getting to know each other." He nodded at Veronica and said, "What's your name and where are you from?"

With that mischievous glint in her eyes, Veronica drawled, "I'd rather hear about you, Jacob honey. Are you married?"

"Hot damn!" Georgia Lu said. "Ain't she somethin'?"

Except for Missy, whose pale cheeks turned crimson, the others tried to muffle the giggles.

Marcie turned on her heels and stalked toward the office, cursing herself as she went. Why hadn't she taken a firm stand? Why hadn't she let it be known that indeed he would be interfering? But it had been so unexpected and had happened so fast she hadn't been able to think straight. Then the irony of the situation struck her. She'd been teaching the women how to assert themselves yet she hadn't followed her own lesson. She must have looked like a fool. Determined to be assertive when facing Sarah, she lifted her chin and squared her shoulders when entering the office.

"Please close the door, dear," Sarah said from behind the desk. Marcie did as she was told and sat down in a wing chair. What was so important that Sarah had to speak to her in private? It must be about her and Roger.

Sarah leaned forward and spoke in hushed tones. "This concerns Veronica." Faint with relief, Marcie almost laughed out loud. She willed her facial features not to betray her as Sarah went on. "I've had complaints from the wives of a few of our AA members. They say Veronica is a terrible flirt and her behavior disrupts the open meetings. At the last one, she wore a see-through chiffon dress with a plunging neckline. The ladies said she spent half the night bending over with her breasts practically popping out of her dress, while she fussed with the straps on her high-heeled shoes. They can't imagine what she does at the closed meetings when they're not there to keep an eye on her."

With a straight face, Marcie said, "I'll speak to her. Tell her to dress more appropriately, but. I'm not promising anything. Actresses act, and the way Veronica dresses and makes herself up are all a part of her act. Please tell the ladies that she's not interested in their men. She's only interested in one man, the Colonel. In fact, she has a dinner date with him tomorrow night."

Sarah's brows pinched together. "*Our* Colonel? Colonel Black?"

"That's the one."

"Well!" Sarah huffed. "I didn't know he had such bad taste."

"Oh, Veronica's not that bad. Despite the way she dresses and carries on, she's actually a very nice person and a lot of fun."

"But she's an actress," Sarah said, as though uttering a dirty word.

"That's true, but she's done very well since she's been here."

"Oh dear," Sarah said. "A woman like Veronica going out with our Colonel." She held up a hand as though she couldn't bear to hear another word about "our" Colonel, which Marcie translated as "my" Colonel.

"Well," Sarah said, "what do you think of our pastor?"

Marcie hesitated. She decided to tell Sarah the truth. "I don't think his coming here is a good idea. Some of the women suffer a lot of guilt because of their ingrained religious beliefs. Alcoholism and moral dogma don't mix too well."

Sarah said, "Oh, Jacob won't preach to them. He just wants to raise their spiritual consciousness."

"They get that at AA, Sarah."

"It's not the same. He hopes they'll start attending our church. Wouldn't that be wonderful?"

Marcie said, "Let's see how it goes."

"Oh, I'm sure it will go just fine. We're lucky to have Jacob. Our old pastor put people to sleep. Jacob raises our consciousness. He's a modern man with a lot of pep. You'll grow to love him." She stood up. "Well, I have to be going." At the door, Sarah paused and shook her head. "I can't believe the Colonel picked Veronica." She clucked her tongue. "What a terrible waste of a good man."

After Sarah left the house, Pastor Horner was still in the sunroom. She could hear occasional bursts of laughter echoing down the hall. Each time it happened her muscles tightened and her pulse raced. Being assertive with Sarah hadn't worked. It appeared she was stuck with the preacher.

Just as she reached a point where she couldn't stand another second of it, she heard the familiar crunch of tires on shells. From the window she saw a carload of black people and it looked like an argument was taking place. Then one of the black women got out of the car and it took off in a cloud of exhaust.

Marcie hurried to the door. Upon opening it, she saw a one-armed woman wearing a white-toothed smile and carrying a battered blue suitcase. Not wanting to attract the attention of the group, she gestured for the woman to come in. Marcie put a finger to her lips and hustled her to the office. After closing the door behind her, Marcie introduced herself. In a lilting voice, Clara Young did likewise. And so Port Victor had its first black resident.

Above a flawless nutmeg–brown complexion, Clara wore a bouffant–styled wig the color of burgundy wine. Gold hoop earrings dangled from pierced ears and a string of red beads encircled her neck. She was dressed in a neat black–and–white checkered pantsuit with a white shirt. Someone had folded her left jacket sleeve at the elbow and pinned it under her shoulder.

After the preliminary questions were over, Marcie felt a growing rapport with the jovial woman. With a direct look at the empty sleeve, she said, "How did you lose your arm?"

Clara answered in a singsong. "It got tangled in a mangle."

"How long ago?"

Clara puckered her generous lips and wrinkled her smooth brow until the answer came to her. "It's been close to seven years. I had me a real good job at the mill, but after the accident, they wouldn't let me work no more. They put me on the disability."

"When did alcohol become a problem?"

"I started seein' the bootlegger about six years ago. We been keepin' steady company ever since."

"Damn!" Marcie exclaimed. At Clara's startled look, she said, "Sorry, but I get ticked off when they, whoever *they* are, judge an able–bodied person as disabled and then send her a reminder every month in the form of a check. Just look at you. Off the top of my head, I can think of a dozen jobs you could do, more with therapy and training. But instead of being productive, you've been paid to sink into oblivion."

Resignation showed on Clara's face. "Preacher Henry says it's the Lord's will. I got five sisters, three brothers, and oodles of kin all over the county, but they's all too selfish to care for Mammy. She's crippled up with the ar-thur-i-tis and needs looking after. Preacher Henry says I was the chosen one. The Lord done made me a cripple so I can stay home with my crippled mammy."

Here we go again, Marcie thought. Another preacher deciding a person's fate. "Oh?" she said. "Did the Lord also lead you to the bootlegger?"

At first, Clara didn't seem to know what to say. Then her roly–poly body began jiggling with silent laughter. "I reckon the Devil had a hand in that."

Marcie leaned forward and said, "Listen, Clara, it was the whiskey that crippled you, not the loss of your arm. You can't look after yourself, much less your mother, when you're drunk."

"That's the plain truth. Last week I passed out with a cigarette in my hand and burnt a hole clean through the mattress. Mammy's scared I'm gonna burn the house down. That why they brought me to this place, to get cured up."

"Who dropped you off?"

"Uncle Pervis drove us. He was the only one with a car."

"So what was the argument about?"

Clara's big eyes widened. "How you know about that?"

"I was watching from the window and it seemed like everyone was talking at once."

"They surely were. Gave me a headache. They thought my sister Sally should bring me in and she wasn't budging."

"Well, Clara, we don't usually admit people without prior notice, but we just happen to have an empty bed and you're welcomed to it." Marcie got up and walked to the front of the desk. "Come on, I'll show you around."

Leaving the suitcase at the foot of the stairs, Marcie saw that the preacher had left and the women were playing cards or reading.

"This is some fine place you got here," Clara said. "Is it yours?"

Marcie laughed. "No. I have a little cabin on the river. A lady named Sarah Fleming–Thornton owns this house. It's named after her late husband, Victor."

"Miss Sarah, she's a saint."

Marcie thought it doubtful that any of her employees would agree. She said, "She's also very generous."

"Is she gonna care about me being black?"

"Not at all. Black, white, pink, or purple, she wants to keep the house full."

They sidestepped around the sunroom in favor of the kitchen. Marcie thought Pearl should be the first to know about their new resident.

Pearl was searching for something in the refrigerator. Marcie rapped on the wall as usual. Without looking up, Pearl said, "Thought you was gonna get back to group."

"We'll take up where we left off tomorrow. We have a new resident."

"Huh?" Pearl said. She closed the refrigerator and turned to face Marcie.

Noticing Clara, she said, "Lawd'a'mercy, where'd you come from?"

"Up near Hazel Green," Clara said. "Uncle Pervis dropped me off."

Marcie said, "Pearl, this is Clara Young, our new resident. Clara, meet Pearl, our house manager."

Pearl squinted her eyes at Marcie. "Did you forget to tell me 'bout her?"

"She just showed up about a half hour ago. Her family doesn't know how lucky they are that we have an empty bed."

Pearl shuffled forward, then stopped and gaped at the empty sleeve. "Mercy," she said, putting a hand to her throat.

"It's all right, Miss Pearl," Clara said. "I'm used to people's staring. I still got one good arm and I swear I won't cause you no trouble."

Pearl said, "I'm from out your way. Did you shop at Maier's?"

"Sure did."

"How they doin'? I ain't seen none of those folks in a long while."

"Mrs. Maier, she's got the cancer real bad. The Mister's doing the best he can."

"That's a durn shame. What about that boy of theirs? He helpin' his daddy at the store?"

"No'um. He got so mad about the cancer he left home. Said he couldn't stand to see his mama in pain."

"I don't reckon his mama can stand it neither." Then Pearl said, "You wanna cup of coffee?"

"That sounds mighty fine," Clara said. "My family has done wore me out." She moved toward the table. "Did you know we got a new mailman? Old Clyde retired and this new one's always late."

"Well," said Marcie, edging for the doorway. "I'll leave you two alone."

"Thank you for taking me in, Miss Marcie," Clara said.

"You're welcome. I'll see you later."

Still smiling at how well the two women had connected, Marcie couldn't wait to write a report in Clara's chart. With her mind occupied, it startled her when Deborah opened her door.

Quickly recovering, she said, "Hello, I'm happy to see you."

Looking up the hall and back, Deborah spoke in a hushed voice. "What's that colored woman doing here?"

At the use of the word "colored," Marcie knew that Deborah was living back in the days when black women were servants.

"She's our newest resident."

"What?" Deborah said. "You can't be serious."

"But I am. Clara's a lovely person and we're past the age of discrimination."

"Maybe you are but I'm not!" Deborah shouted. The door closed in Marcie's face.

Would complications never end?

CHAPTER 23

Marcie looked over at Roger and said, "Why don't I ever see you around the brickyard? I look for you every time I drive by." They were sitting on the porch nursing bottles of Heinekens, with Charley lying on the floor between them.

Roger grinned at her. "You might not see me, but I see you." "Really?"

"Yeah. I have your routine down pat. Except for yesterday. I had just come out of the office when I saw you roaring off. I started to call you last night to see if you were okay."

Marcie averted his gaze. "Something happened at work and I reacted exactly like my son would." She'd been angry with herself for not telling the preacher to stay away from Port Victor, and angry with Deborah for her bigoted stance against Clara.

He twisted around in his seat as if to take in the whole of her. "You have a son?"

She nodded. "His name is Davy and he just turned sixteen. My daughter's name is Julie. She's seventeen. They go to private schools in Washington, D.C. Their father is stationed at the Pentagon and they live with him."

"You lost custody?"

"No. Never. Not for one minute. They chose to live with him. Of course he's never there." She heaved a sigh. "So they're free to do as they please." She added, "Even when he's there, he's not really there. Know what I mean?"

"Sounds like you got a bum rap."

"Something like that. The kids are coming home in a few weeks. They're supposed to stay for the summer, but if I have anything to say about it, they'll stay forever." She snorted a laugh and added, "Teenagers aren't what they used to be."

"I'll drink to that," Roger said. They clinked bottles and tipped them up to their mouths.

"Why didn't you tell me you had kids?" Roger asked.

"It's a sore subject."

"I believe it. If my ex tried anything funny with our boys, I'd haunt her for the rest of my life."

Glad to change the subject, she said, "How are your boys? They still loving baseball?"

"Baseball, soccer, hockey, swimming, rock–climbing, anything their friends are doing."

"You're lucky to be able to enjoy them while they're still young enough to be excited about things, and happy to have you around. I hope that never changes."

"Me, too. But the oldest one keeps one eye on the girls. Or I should say the girls keep their eyes on him."

"Does he look like you?"

"He's got his mother's nose but, yeah, he looks like me."

Marcie smiled. "No wonder the girls are after him."

He grinned. "Thank you, ma'am. I'll take that as a compliment."

"And well you should."

They sat gazing out at the river, taking sips of beer now and then. Comfortable, without the need for conversation.

A while later, Marcie said. "I wasn't kidding about the girls being after you. I'll bet you've had lots of dates since the divorce."

"I've gone to a few parties as an escort, but I honestly don't have time to date. Between Sarah keeping me late at work and coaching, it seems like I'm always running behind myself."

"So, you don't call what we're doing a date?" She teased.

He gave her a blank look and said, "Where am I? Who are you?"

She laughed. "You're fast."

He turned serious. "Yes, I do consider this a date. Last week, too. I hadn't had a home–cooked meal in months, and you sure know how to cook."

Me, Betty Crocker, and Mrs. Smith, Marcie thought to herself. "I'd say we get along fairly well. So far, at least."

"We dress well, too." They had both worn Levi's with blue button-down shirts.

Upon seeing him, Marcie had said they looked like the Bobbsey Twins. "We must have ESP going on," she said.

"Are you as hungry as I am?"

Marcie laughed as she stood up. "I'll feed my buddy here and then I'll be ready to go."

Ears pricked, Charley stood up and stretched, forelegs extended, body curved, and back legs kicking out one at a time. Then he started wagging his plume of a tail.

"Smart dog," Roger said. "He knows when it's dinnertime."

"Indeed. He's smarter than I am." She picked up the beer bottles and carried them into the house with Charley at her heels.

Roger called, "I'll wait out here."

"Help yourself," she answered.

While preparing Charley's dinner, she congratulated herself for how she'd handled the subject of her kids. Hopefully, she didn't come across as a bitter bitch, even if she felt like one. And she liked the way Roger reacted. She liked Roger, period. He was easy to be around. He had a great sense of humor. He didn't invade her privacy. He was handsome and, yes, he was sexy.

She made a potty stop, washed her hands, freshened her lipstick, and went out on the porch. "I'm ready," she told Roger.

"Wow," he said, "that was quick." He looked her over. "Where's your purse?"

"I'm not taking one."

"You'd better take your wallet in case they card you."

"Very funny." She locked the screen door and then went into the house with Roger right behind her. "See you later, Charley." To the clocks, she said, "Take a break."

"Do they ever?" Roger asked.

As if knowing they were being talked about, the clocks started tweeting, oinking, bonging, chiming, coo–cooing, and strumming a guitar.

She laughed and said, "There's your answer."

The restaurant was rustic in every way. Located out in the boondocks, it squatted next to a large area of backwater from the Tennessee River. With a corrugated tin roof, cedar plank walls outside and in, squeaky wooden floors, and rooms branching off in all directions, it looked like it had been put together in fits and starts. Their table for two showed a wavy view of the water through the heavy-duty sheets of plastic that served as windows. Despite the lack of intimacy, the place had a homey feel, as if everyone was related in some way.

Marcie picked up the hand-written menu and looked it over. "Should I have the whole catfish or the filets?"

"Definitely the whole," Roger said, "and I recommend you start with the small platter. Believe me, it's a lot of food."

She found the item on the menu. The small platter came with two whole catfish, cole slaw, country-fried potatoes, black-eyed peas, and hush puppies. "Then that's what I'll have."

"You want a beer? They don't have imports, so think Bud, Miller—

She cut him off. "Stop right there. I'd like a Miller Lite."

He laid a warm hand on her forearm. "I can't believe how easy you are."

She laid her hand on top of his. "That's because of the company I keep." They lifted their hands and sat back when the waitress showed up.

The girl flashed a brilliant smile and said, "Hi, how y'all doin'? What can I get y'all?"

Roger winked at Marcie and then looked at the girl, "We're doing just fine, thanks. The lady will have a Miller Lite and I'll take a Bud. The beer will whet our appetite for some of your best catfish platters. The lady wants a small but you can set a large one in front of me."

"Got it," the girl said, flashing another smile. Wearing cutoff jean shorts and a sleeveless shirt with its ends tied over her midriff, showing the stud on her belly button, she reminded Marcie of Cassie.

"Where were we?" Roger asked.

"I believe we were sort of holding hands."

"We can do better than sort of." He took her left hand in his right and gave it a squeeze. "You look real pretty tonight," he said. "I like that you don't wear a lot of makeup and jewelry."

She started to say something about Veronica wearing enough for both of them, but caught herself. Breaking the confidentiality code was taboo. Too bad. She would love to tell him Sarah's reaction to the news about Veronica and the Colonel.

"Thanks," she said. "I've never been the flashy type." She blushed and added, "Except for the current color of my hair."

"I like your hair."

"It was an accident, but I've gotten used to it." Just last week she'd touched up her roots. "My natural color is dishwater blonde." My, wasn't she being honest tonight. Next thing she'd be telling him about the birthmark on her upper thigh.

Their beers arrived with frosted mugs. "Allow me," Roger said, and poured hers from the side so as not to end up with a foamy top.

"The service here is impeccable," she said when he handed her the mug, handle side out.

He grinned and said, "Wait till you taste the food."

Marcie looked around. It seemed as though the restaurant had segregated the customers according to size. Families with children were set off in one room, partygoers in another, and couples away from all the noisemakers. It was a sensible arrangement. She and Roger could carry on a conversation without loud music blaring or kids screaming and running around.

"I don't care what the food tastes like, I'm glad you brought me here. It's a neat place and I'm feeling very comfortable."

"I like it because nobody knows you yet it feels like they do."

"Let's hope nobody knows you. I'm still afraid Sarah will drop the hammer on us."

"Don't worry," he said. "I asked her if she had any objections to me taking you out to dinner and she said it was fine with her."

Marcie stared at him. "You're kidding."

He shook his head. "No, I'm serious."

She fell back in her seat. "Here I've been worried sick about her finding out. Why didn't you tell me?"

"I just did."

"You stinker," she said, sitting up and punching him lightly on the arm.

Their platters arrived and what sized platters they were. Marcie took one look and said, "I'm full already." She looked up at their waitress and said, "You might as well bring me a take–home carton now."

"Don't do it," Roger said. "I'll bet you she eats every bite."

"No way," Marcie said.

The girl laughed and said, "Y'all enjoy. Holler if you need anything."

"Thanks," they said in unison, then looked at each other and laughed. "We're dangerous," Roger said. "We dress alike, we like the same drinks, the same place, and now we're saying the same thing."

"Beats arguing," Marcie said.

"You got that right," said Roger. "That was my ex's favorite sport."

"Never mind the exes," said Marcie. "Let's eat." She scooped up some slaw and put it in her mouth. Next she tried a slice of potato. Both were excellent. Noticing how Roger ran his fork down the side of the fish to separate the meat from the bones, she did likewise and took her first taste of fish the same time he did. Lightly breaded, it was the best catfish she'd ever had. No need for a squirt of lemon or a dab of tartar sauce, it was fine by itself.

Too busy eating to talk, George popped into her head. Funny how people she knew kept creeping into her mind. Maybe subconsciously she wished they could see her now. Out on a date with a terrific guy, sitting in a place they probably never heard of, eating a delicious meal… having the rest of the evening ahead of her.

———

They'd left the restaurant and were walking side–by–side over the graveled parking lot to Roger's car when all of a sudden he turned to her, took her in his arms and kissed her. His lips were so warm and soft she felt the kiss all the way to her toes. He broke for air and then kissed her again. This time she pulled her head back. "I'm afraid," she whispered.

Loosening his hold on her, Roger said, "Of what?" His voice had turned husky.

"Of what I may do."

"What would that be?"

"Give in to you."

"I don't expect that. I just want to hold you and kiss you. I like you a lot, Marcie."

"I like you, too, Roger. Very much."

"Then why—"

"Because you turn me on."

He smiled. "Is that so bad?"

"Yes."

"Then it's your call."

She wrapped her arms around his middle and raised up on her tiptoes. "One more, please." When his lips touched hers, happy tears leaked from her closed eyes.

———

The following day the Hilton's lobby was abuzz with people. Guests of the hotel were checking in and out, others had formed a line to speak to the *concierge*; others were waiting for the cashier, and still more were entering or departing the restaurant. From the looks of the crowd, a lot of whom had no doubt just come from church, Marcie was thankful she'd taken extra care with her appearance. She wanted to feel comfortable in her own skin.

Buoyed by the last night's date with Roger and now the prospect of having brunch with George, she followed the path that led to the restaurant. Early, as usual, she had the *maître d'* show her to a table, where she'd wait for George while watching the people. The *maître d'* pulled out a chair at a lovely table for two. She sat down and felt duly pampered when the man helped her scoot her chair up and draped a linen napkin over her lap. When told that she would be joined by Dr. Rutledge, the *maître d'* informed her that the doctor had already been seated.

An acute case of self-consciousness replaced the comfort she'd felt on arrival. She imagined everyone looking at her with critical eyes as she and the *maître d'* paraded all the way across the room. She ignored George when he stood up to greet her and remained tight-jawed until they were alone.

"You could've waited for me," she hissed across the table.

"I did," George said. "Are you ready to eat?"

This irritated her, too. She was bursting with news and ready to talk a while. "Why do you always have to *eat*? Why can't you ever *dine*?"

With a bemused look, he said, "Why can't I do both at the same time?"

"You're impossible," she said, shaking out her napkin and draping it over her lap. Apparently the *maître d'* only did that favor once.

Their waiter appeared. He introduced himself and asked for their drink order. Because she was annoyed at George, Marcie ordered a Bloody Mary. Normally, she would have had iced tea. George stuck with water.

"I'm going to the buffet," George said.

"Fine."

He left her sitting there waiting for her drink to arrive. She was still waiting when George returned with a plate full of food. It made her nauseous to watch him eat, arms on the table, wolfing it down, and of course the no-talking rule in effect. She couldn't help thinking how vastly different this meal was compared to last night's dinner with Roger. But then she didn't have romantic notions about George.

Her drink finally arrived, garnished with olives and a stalk of celery. She ate the olives and put the celery on her butter plate. Then she took big sips from a straw. The liquor went straight to her head, making her woozy. She hadn't eaten breakfast and knew she'd have to give in and go to the buffet. That or fall out of her chair.

George had cleaned his plate by the time she returned to the table. Knowing him, he'd make a trip for seconds, giving her plenty of time to finish a cheese and mushroom omelet with a side of fresh fruit.

Between the Bloody Mary and the food, Marcie was feeling quite mellow by the time the bus boy removed their empty plates. "You were right about one thing," she said. "Roger is a nice guy."

"Correction," George said. "I'm right about most things," He lifted his cup for a gulp of coffee.

"Don't you want to know how I know you're right?"

"Marcie, it doesn't take a member of Mensa to figure it out. You've obviously gotten to know him."

At that, Marcie allowed her happiness to bubble forth. "He's more than nice, and he likes me, George. A lot."

"I'm glad to hear it. So you're seeing each other?"

Omitting the kisses, Marcie described the two dates they'd had. She also told him how involved Roger was in his children's lives. How she wished, David had been that way with Julie and especially Davy. She told him about Julie going to New York City without David letting her know and about Davy spending so much time alone at home.

"How can I make them understand they'd be better off living with me?" Marcie asked.

George took on his professional demeanor, leaning slightly toward her and speaking earnestly. "Listen closely to whatever they have to say and think of a positive response. With Davy, establish your rules right away and stick to them. He's going to bait you every chance he gets. Don't allow yourself to bite. Summon every ounce of patience you have and then some. Remember they'll suffer from culture shock at first. Fleming's Hill is no match for Washington, D.C."

"Thanks, George." Her mind returned to Roger. "What should I do about Roger? We've established an ongoing Saturday night date. Should I put him off while the kids are here?"

"From the sounds of it, he'd be a good influence on them. The first time you might consider making it a foursome. If Davy balks, don't force it. Make it a threesome. Their father dates, he might even have a live-in. It shouldn't affect them adversely if you're seeing someone."

"I don't know about that. It seems that single fathers can do whatever they want and nothing's said about it, but mothers are supposed to remain celibate for the rest of their lives."

George appraised her. "Have you remained celibate?"

"That, my dear sir, is none of your business." She paused, then added, "But as a matter of fact, I have."

"Well then, as long as you and Roger aren't hopping in the sack every half hour the four of you ought to get along just fine."

Aware that the brunch crowd was beginning to clear out and still having a lot to talk about, Marcie suggested finding a quiet spot in the lobby to continue their conversation and George agreed.

While he waited for the check, she scanned the lobby and found an ideal spot behind a giant potted palm tree. She started to retrace her steps to find George, but he was weaving his way toward her.

"Nice," he said, settling in one of the overly large club chairs across from her.

"I'm dying to get to work tomorrow," Marcie said as an opening. "Missy, Veronica, and Phyllis took day passes yesterday and I can't wait to hear how things went. Oh, and Sarah paid me a visit Friday. Some of the AA member's wives have complained about the way Veronica flirts with the men at the open meetings. You know how Sarah hates gossip about Port Victor. By the way, I think she has a crush on Colonel Black. She was aghast to hear that he'd asked Veronica out for dinner. She kept calling him 'our' Colonel. I could hardly keep a straight face. Oh, and she had the nerve to bring a preacher to Port Victor. He's going to do a weekly program on spiritual enrichment. Can you believe it? A preacher taking an hour of my treatment plan. It's just—"

"Slow down," George said. "You're chattering like a magpie."

Marcie took a deep breath and let it out. "I know. But if I told you every-thing that's happened we'd be here all day."

"Focus, Marcie, focus," he said.

The most important news she wanted to share with him was about the murder of Bill Thompson but that was off limits. Since Deborah was not an official resident, the confidentiality code they'd signed could not be broken even for George.

Wound down now, she shrugged and said, "I'm finished."

"What about Sarah and this Colonel?"

Backing off, she said, "I was only guessing about her having a crush on him. She may have had a friend in mind."

"I see," he said, eyeing her skeptically. "You don't have any real news except that you're seeing Roger."

Her eyes lit up at mention of Roger. She smiled and said, "You're so good at narrowing things down. I suppose that's why I like your company, despite your bad manners."

"Bad manners?"

"Yes. You could have waited for me before you sat down. I felt like a fool traipsing through the restaurant a second time."

"It's not what happens to you—"

She finished for him. "It's how you react." Reminded of her behavior when the preacher took over her group session, she said, "Sometimes you can't help how you react. If something in your past has poisoned your mind against a set group of people, and then you come face to face with one of them, it seems only natural to blow a fuse."

"What set of people would you be talking about?"

"Preachers."

"Who or what poisoned your mind against preachers?" She hesitated. He knew nothing about that part of her life.

"Marcie?"

"Oh, all right." She told him the story from beginning to end. "That's a tough one," George said when she finished.

She said, "Intellectually, I know all preachers are not like the two that destroyed my family. But emotionally, I dislike all preachers."

"Dislike?" George said. "Or fear?"

She had to think about it. "Maybe I do fear them. Religion in general scares me. It turned out my mother was right when she said the Methodists were hypocrites. Shunning my father and me because of her affiliation with another church was not the Christian way. We needed love and support from the congregation. Instead, they turned their backs on us. I don't know about my father, but that was the end of my church–going days."

"I can't wave a magic wand and make it all right," George said. "But you could plan to do other things, like running errands when the preacher is there. What kind of preacher is he?"

"His name is Jacob Horner. He's the new pastor at the Lutheran Church. He seems like a regular guy, and he must have a sense of humor because the women were laughing a lot. It's just that I don't want him there."

"And there's nothing you can do about it because Sarah wants him there."

"Exactly."

"If you're asking for advice, I'd treat him kindly but I'd make myself scarce. You can do it, Marcie. You've already come through the worst."

"Oh, if only that were true."

"It's not what happens to you—"

"Never mind," she said. "It's tattooed on my brain. But sometimes our reactions don't go according to plan. What do we do in cases like that?"

"Punt."

CHAPTER 24

Monday rolled around right on time. Before reaching Main Street, Marcie admired the masses of hydrangeas showing their large blue and pink flowers. The combination of gardenias and magnolia blossoms sent heavenly scents wafting through the air. A profusion of pink, red, and yellow roses hid their prickly stalks. Tiger lilies favored hilly spots. Clusters of Jacob's ladder leaned against wooden wishing wells. All a prelude to summer and the kids coming home.

She looked for Roger as she passed the brickyard but he was nowhere in sight. The mere thought of him brought on a wave of longing for more of his kisses. Did she feel like this when she fell in love with David? She couldn't remember.

Cassie was out running but she missed seeing Georgia Lu in the garden. No doubt, she, along with Missy, Veronica, and Phyllis were getting ready to go to rehab. That meant Marcie would have to wait until afternoon to hear about the women's Saturday pass. It also meant she'd have to find a parallel parking place downtown. She hadn't figured on that until now.

Parking as far away from the van as possible, she turned off the ignition and climbed out of the car. Before she could reach the door to the storage room, Pearl came rushing out as though the house was on fire.

"The thief has run amuck." Pearl said in a choked voice. She started wheezing in an effort to catch her breath.

Marcie patted her on the back. "Calm down, Pearl. It's not worth you having a heart attack."

"But it's eatin' me alive," Pearl said.

"Tell me what happened."

"Ever since my stock went missin', I been watchin' my supplies real close." That was an understatement, Marcie thought. Pearl had practically taken up residence in the kitchen. "I been so busy checkin' the icebox and the freezer, I done forgot all about the storage room 'cause nobody goes in there lessen I tell 'em to. Well, I should'a been thinkin' 'bout it 'cause yesterday I went in to get some tuna to put in the kitchen. Y'know how I always like to keep six cans of everything handy so's I don't hafta go back and forth."

"Yes, I know, Pearl. Please get to what's missing."

"The minute I looked at them shelves the hair on the back of my neck stood straight out. That varmint's been stealin' me blind. Crackers, cereal, my canned goods. I'll hafta get me another order slip for Halsey's. Miss Sarah's not gonna like it."

"Good grief. I had no idea."

"You ain't the only one. What we gonna do now?"

"Let me think," Marcie said. Then, "Let's use what we've got on hand for now. I'll pick up a deadbolt to put on the door. You'll have to carry the key but that's better than losing more stock. I just can't figure out who among the women is so starved she has to keep taking food."

"I done told you who it is."

"But we have no proof it's Cassie. Or anyone else, for that matter."

"Maybe not, but I'd point a finger at her in any lineup. 'Member she's the one cleans the storage room."

"I'd forgotten about that. Let's go inside. I could use a cup of coffee before heading out to rehab."

As they walked through the storage room, Marcie saw empty spaces where canned goods and staples would normally sit. She knew she must do something about it, but what? Putting locks on every door would be ridiculous. This wasn't a prison, it was a treatment center. The only solution was to catch the person in action. But how?

As they entered the kitchen, the homey aroma of fresh-baked biscuits lingered in the air. A tray with four leftover biscuits sat on the stove. Marcie passed them by. She'd gained just enough weight to give her body shape. A cup of black coffee would have to do.

Pearl turned the faucets on. Hot water poured into the sink. She squirted a fair amount of Palmolive liquid into it. When suds began building up, Pearl started loading dishes into the mix.

Marcie said, "Did the ladies on pass get back here on time?"

"Yep. All 'ceptin Phyllis."

"What about Phyllis?" Marcie's first thought was that she'd come back early because of an argument with Bob.

Pearl's busy hands stilled. "'Bout nine last night, Phyllis, she called and said to tell you she wasn't comin' back. Said she and Bob talked it over and there weren't no sense to it."

"What!" Marcie slammed her coffee down and started pacing around the room, waving both arms in the air. "She and Bob talked it over, did they? That's just swell. Sarah will be thrilled to know that I cured Phyllis of an addiction that took years out of hers and Bob's lives in only four weeks. I'm sure that sets some kind of record."

"Don't know why you're gettin' so riled," Pearl said. "Phyllis, she'll be back."

Marcie looked at Pearl and, instead of the usual deep wrinkles and caved–in cheeks she saw the face of a wise old crone. She pulled a chair out from the table and sank into it. "You're probably right but she could've called me. She was supposed to start rehab today. I was so hoping they could lead her in the right direction."

Pearl went on with her dishes. "Phyllis, she'll finish next time."

"She'll have to wait three months before she can reapply, and I guarantee she'll be deep in the sauce before then."

"Who's deep in the sauce?" Veronica asked as she sauntered in.

Marcie took one look at her and almost laughed. Veronica wore a slinky purple dress with a slit up one side, and an abundance of jewelry. Not exactly the attire one usually wore to rehab.

"Never mind," Marcie said. She stood up and retrieved what was left of her coffee. "How was your date with the Colonel?"

Veronica closed her eyes in a dream-like state and said, "It was divine, simply divine." She opened her eyes and added, "I can't wait to tell you all about it." Glancing at Pearl, who wasn't paying the least bit of attention, she whispered, "Some things are best said in private."

Marcie wasn't so sure she wanted to hear about those "things" but she said, "I can imagine."

"Too bad about Phyllis," Veronica said.

Marcie felt a headache coming on. "Don't remind me. Are Missy and Georgia Lu ready to go?"

"Missy's been ready since six o'clock. Georgia Lu's trying to get dressed. I told her to wear something besides those nasty Bib overalls. She's trying to squeeze into her old pair of trousers, but she'll probably pop all the seams." Better to wear Bib overalls than a sexy party dress, Marcie thought but didn't say.

Looking freshly scrubbed, prim and proper, Missy entered the room. "I can't wait to go to rehab."

"That's my girl," Marcie said.

Georgia Lu straggled in. Just as Veronica had predicted, her pants strained at the seams. Still, she smelled fresh and clean.

Marcie herded the women out to the garage and into the van. No sooner had she pulled onto the driveway than she had to stop to avoid running over Cassie. She shoved the gear into park and climbed out of the van. "Go into the house," she told the girl. "I can't have you running around while I'm gone. We have to set some time limits." Leaving a quizzical-looking Cassie behind, she climbed into the van and took off down the driveway.

She had to drive around the town square three times before finding an empty parking place. Successfully maneuvering the van into it, she accompanied the women into the building. With introductions made and the ladies safely ensconced in a classroom, she walked down the street to the hardware store on the corner. An affable salesman helped her pick out a dead bolt lock. She bought two, just in case.

Once again she looked for Roger on her way up the driveway. She felt like a twelve-year-old with her first crush. Roger was the last person she thought of at night and the first person she thought of in the morning. Did he think of her in the same way?

She left the locks in the kitchen with Pearl. Georgia Lu could install them when she got back. Settled at last in her office, she pulled out the women's charts and prepared to make notations in each one. She would have to fill out a closed case report on Phyllis, her very first one, and it hurt, especially since Phyllis hadn't had the courtesy to call her.

She'd just completed the report when Cassie came bounding in on the pretext of finding a book to read. The way she kept glancing over her shoulder told Marcie she had other things on her mind.

"Sit down, Cassie. I was getting ready to call you in for a session anyway. You can look for a book, if you really want one, after we finish."

The girl practically leaped into a chair. With a sunny expression, she asked, "Am I in trouble?" The girl's skin glowed with a deep bronze tan.

"No," Marcie said. "But we have to set some ground rules for your runs. How does an hour three times a day sound?"

Her expression didn't change. "I guess I can live with that."

"And no skimpy clothing. All I need is for Miss Sarah to bawl me out because you're running around half-naked."

"Okay," Cassie said, still too cheerful to be believed.

"Now then, what's on your mind?"

"I'm supposed to start rehab next Monday, right?"

"Right."

"I've been wondering… What goes on exactly? I mean, is it a bad scene or what?"

"It's not bad at all. You sit at a desk in a classroom and complete different tests and projects designed to measure your aptitude, motor skills, and things like that."

"Like a regular school, huh?"

"Pretty much."

"Well, un, does a teacher watch you every minute? Can we leave the room whenever we want?"

Marcie peered at the girl. "What's the problem, Cassie?"

252

"Nothing. I mean, the thing I hated about school was being watched all the time."

"Who watched you?"

"Everybody. The teachers, the kids. Every time I turned around someone was staring at me."

"Did you feel that way in places other than school?"

Cassie thought about it. "Not really. I just hate being tied down. I have to be free to move around and take a break when I need it."

Marcie nodded. "You do have a high level of energy."

The girl's face lit up even brighter. "That's it! I have a high level of energy."

The way Cassie latched onto the term further aroused Marcie's suspicion that she was hiding something.

A rap sounded on the doorjamb. Marcie looked that way. The last person she wanted to see poked his head around the corner. "Am I interrupting?" Jacob Horner asked.

Marcie snapped, "As a matter of fact, you are." The moment the words were out of her mouth, she remembered George telling her to treat the pastor kindly. "Give me a few more minutes," she told him. "There's coffee in the kitchen."

"Right," he said, ducking his head back.

Marcie gave the preacher enough time to clear the hallway and then she looked at Cassie. "I want to discuss your need for breaks, but it'll have to wait till our next session. Don't worry. I'll ask your rehab counselor to give you time off between assignments."

"Cool!" The girl was out of the room in a flash, the book she'd come to borrow forgotten.

Marcie sat back. Cassie had been candid about most things, but in the telling she'd acted as if her barroom brawls and flopping from one place to the next were perfectly normal. Something wasn't right about this fear of being watched. Marcie ruled out paranoia. It had to do with unacceptable behavior. Could Pearl be right about her being the thief?

She returned to the file drawer, this time to get Cassie's chart. When she turned around, there stood the preacher wearing an open-necked Western shirt with a pair of Levi's that looked right off the rack. He held a coffee mug in each hand. "I thought you might like some," he said, setting a mug on the desk. Then, without waiting for an invitation, he sat in the chair closest to the windows, crossed his legs and moved a pointed–toed cowboy boot up and down in slow motion.

A wave of British Sterling cologne drifted under Marcie's nose when he sat down. It had been David's favorite. Hers, too. She willed herself to keep her cool as she returned to her seat. She looked across the desk and said, "Well, to what do I owe the pleasure of your visit?"

"That girl who was in here? Cassie? She's just a child."

Surely he hadn't come to talk about Cassie. "Yes, a child of nineteen going on forty."

"You'd never know," he said. He produced a squashed pack of cigarettes from a hip pocket. "Mind if I smoke?"

"I don't mind, but Sarah does. Smoking is forbidden in this house."

"Oh, sorry." He tucked the pack of Lucky Strikes in his shirt pocket. "I don't smoke that much," he said, giving her a lopsided grin. "Just when I get nervous."

Marcie snorted. "You don't seem like the nervous type."

"Oh, but I am. I get very uptight when I'm with someone who wishes I'd disappear into the woodwork. Especially if it's someone I want to impress."

She averted his steady gaze but not before noticing that his deep blue eyes showed bright flecks of yellow, like sunshine dancing on water. She looked down at Cassie's chart, then up. "I was in the middle of a session. We have a very tight schedule here and I don't have time to entertain people who drop in."

"I suspect you don't want me here at any time."

She was mentally prepared to tell him his suspicion was correct, but an image of Sarah passed before her eyes and she wore a severe frown. Marcie cleared her throat before responding. "About yesterday... I'll have to admit the interruption caught me off–guard. It can be hectic trying to squeeze every-thing in and we were in the middle of a very productive therapy session."

He uncrossed his legs and leaned back with a self–assured air that belied his professed nervousness. "Tell me about your routine."

She took a deep breath. Maybe if she told him he would take the hint and leave her alone. She went on, making some stuff up as she went. "Appointments with rehab personnel, doctors, dentists, Social Security, potential employees, and so on. We have individual therapy sessions, like the one I was having with Cassie, in the morning, and group sessions in the afternoon. New admissions take time, as do making progress notes in the women's charts. And the phone…" She lifted a hand and dropped it in her lap. "Some days it doesn't stop ringing."

"I had no idea."

"Most people don't. They think we sit around and watch TV all day. Some halfway houses operate that way, but we don't." She went on in a rush of breath. "The laundry, housework, shopping, cooking, and gardening have to be done. The women need time to read, write letters, fix their hair, do their nails . . . attend at least three AA meetings a week." His eyes seemed to be mocking her. She stopped speaking abruptly.

"It sounds busy, all right," he said with an amused expression. His attitude caused her adrenaline to start pumping and the vow to be calm and agreeable dissolved. "It might interest you to know that a lady called here last week and asked if her church circle could visit the inmates."

He laughed. Then he said, "Sounds like one of my flock."

She glared at him. "Well, instead of holding a group here you might put your time to better use by educating your flock."

Instead of being offended, he seemed delighted. He slapped the arm of his chair and said, "I like a sassy woman who speaks her mind."

She shot back. "Preachers bring out the worst in me."

His bemused expression turned to sober contemplation. He leaned forward, his hands on his knees, his eyes sorrowful. "You've been hurt by the church."

She gazed into his eyes without seeing them as attached to his face. They were deep pools of velvety water, beckoning her to bare her soul. She managed to look away. In a voice that strained to speak, she said, "I've paid my dues."

"Maybe you'll tell me about it someday."

His words broke the spell she'd fallen under. "I don't think so." She shoved her chair back, got up and went to the filing cabinet on a pretense of collecting needed forms. Over her shoulder, she said, "Excuse me, but I've got work to do."

"Give me two more minutes. I want to know how I can best help the women."

She slammed the file cabinet drawer and returned to her seat with blank forms in hand. So he intended to continue his groups. She couldn't stop him, but maybe she could set him straight. She met his gaze with a direct look. "Some of the women think they're doomed to the fiery pits of hell because of all the Bible–thumping, Scripture–spouting preachers in their past. We don't need any of that around here."

"Please don't throw us all into the same pot. We Lutheran's believe in a loving God, a God that offers mercy."

"You believe in the Bible, don't you?"

"Yes, of course."

"Well then, we could discuss your God's mercy for days. How about the Book of Job. Do you consider what God did to Job an example of His mercy?"

He grinned. "Ah, a Bible scholar."

Marcie glanced at her watch. "Your two minutes are up."

He raised his hands in a gesture of surrender. "I'm going, I'm going." At the door, he turned and said. "Do you remember my name?"

"Let's see …" She put a hand to her brow in a mock attempt at remembering. "Oh yes, *Pastor* Jacob Horner."

"Would you call me Jacob?"

"No."

He saluted her with his right hand. "Okay, Marcie Parker, call me whatever you'd like. I'll see you this Friday."

"Not if I can help it," she muttered under her breath. Then she snatched the forms off the desk and, with a hard yank, ripped them in half.

CHAPTER 25

Please, ladies, let's don't have any unwelcome surprises today, Marcie said to herself on her way to work. No residents going AWOL, no thefts of food, and especially no drop–in visitors. Still annoyed by the preacher's unexpected visit yesterday, she was in no mood for any nonsense.

As usual, she looked for Roger as she passed the brickyard and as usual he wasn't out. Nothing odd about that. What struck her as odd was, she didn't see Cassie out running. Maybe she pulled a muscle or sprained something. She'd soon find out.

Odder still was the sight of Pearl standing in front of the refrigerator with her arms tightly crossed and a self–satisfied smirk on her face.

"What's going on?" Marcie asked, certain that Pearl couldn't wait to tell her.

"I done told you but you wouldn't lissen." She pointed a bent finger across the room where Cassie sat cringing at the table with Georgia Lu towering over her like an old–time sheriff.

"Caught her red-handed!" Georgia Lu boomed. "She was stuffin' cans in her duffel bag.

Talk about unexpected surprises! Marcie stared at the girl. "Cassie?" The girl slunk farther down in her seat.

"I hunkered down behind the table after lights out," Georgia Lu said. "I would'a squatted there all night if I'd had to, but long 'bout midnight I saw that flashlight weavin' its way to the kitchen. That's when I knew I had the varmit by the tail." She gave a triumphant grin that sent the scar on her face dancing a jig.

Cassie seemed to be melting into the floor. Marcie found her voice. "For God's sakes, Cassie. What on earth—"

Georgia Lu raised a hand and said, "You want me to pound her into the ground, ma'am?"

Marcie hurried to Cassie's side. "No, un, Georgia Lu. I think I can handle this. Thanks very much for your help, though." To Cassie, she said, "Wait for me in the office." The girl slithered out of the chair and dashed out of the room.

Marcie turned to Pearl and Georgia Lu. All she could think to say was, "Well."

"You should'a seen that gal's face when I came up on her. It's a wonder she didn't shit her britches," Georgia Lu said. She gave a hearty laugh and added, "Funniest thing I ever did see."

"Wish I could'a been there," Pearl said. "I'd'a swatted her backside with my wood spoon."

"Well," Marcie said again, heaving a sigh. "At least it's over. I guess we should be grateful for that."

Pearl tilted her head to one side. "Why you reckon she did it?"

"I have no idea," Marcie said, moving to the coffee maker. Her mug filled, she looked at Georgia Lu and said, "Are you ready for rehab?"

"Yes, ma'am. What sleep I got was in these here clothes."

Marcie couldn't tell the difference. The oversized shirt and tight trousers always looked like they'd been slept in.

"Okay," Marcie said. "I'm going to have a talk with Cassie. Be back shortly."

"Let us know what she says."

"I will," Marcie said and hurried out the door.

Cassie sat crouched in a wing chair looking like a frightened kitten. Marcie found it hard to believe that this was the same bouncy cheerful girl that normally sat before her. Of course that girl had been hiding something.

"Okay, Cassie," she said, "it's time for the truth to come out."

Cassie nodded dumbly. "It's a long story."

"I don't have time for the long version now, just give me a briefing.

In a little girl's voice, Cassie said, "I've got bulimia."

Marcie blinked. "What?"

"Bulimia," the girl repeated. "You know, the eating disorder."

The diagnostic description in Marcie's mental health manual appeared before her eyes.

Bulimia: Characterized by recurrent episodes of binge eating ... termination of such eating episodes by self-induced vomiting ... awareness that the eating pattern is abnormal and fear of not being able to stop eating voluntarily.... There was more but that was enough.

The girl began to crack her knuckles. Marcie winced each time a knuckle popped. "How long?"

"About ten years."

"Good heavens."

"It's ruined my life," Cassie said, tears welling in her eyes.

"Tell you what," Marcie said. "I've got to take the girls to rehab so go ahead and do your run until I return. Stay in the backyard this time."

"Cool," said a suddenly happy Cassie and off she went.

Marcie stayed put, her mind whirling about the best way to handle this latest news. Bulimics and anorexics needed specialized treatment, usually given in a hospital setting. But that took either insurance or money and Cassie had neither. She decided to give George a quick call.

As soon as Diane answered, Marcie said, "Is he with a patient?"

"Yes," Diane said.

"Okay, here's my message. Our newest resident has bulimia. Does he know where she can get free treatment? Thanks. Got to run."

She pushed up from the desk and headed toward the kitchen. Missy, Veronica, Georgia Lu, and Pearl waited, high expectations written across their faces. "Cassie has bulimia," Marcie told them. "It's a serious eating disorder. She's compelled to binge and purge food."

"What's that there binge and purge thing?" Georgia Lu asked.

"Missy? Can you tell them what it means?"

Missy turned to the women and said, "Bingeing is when the person eats an enormous amount of food. It doesn't matter what kind of food it is or what it tastes like as long as its food. Purging is when the person throws it all up afterwards."

"That's disgusting," Veronica said.

"That gal's sick in the head," Pearl said.

Marcie said. "It is a sickness, Pearl. As for you, Veronica, I imagine you were pretty disgusting when you were hanging your head over a toilet because of too much booze."

Veronica sniffed and said, "Well at least I didn't waste perfectly good food. Stolen food, at that."

"Okay, ladies, it's time to hit the road."

Pearl caught sight of Cassie running past the bay window. "What's that gal doin' out there?"

"I thought running for a while might make her feel better."

"Feel better? She oughta be locked up!"

"Where? In the storage room?" Marcie said in an effort to lighten the mood.

Missy giggled. No one else thought it was the least bit funny. Marcie knew she would have trouble convincing some of the women that bulimia, if left untreated, could cause serious bodily harm. But now was not the time or place to discuss it.

"Come on, ladies. We're going to be late if we don't leave right now."

Moments later, Marcie was driving over the shells. She noticed a movement on her right. She looked that way. It was Roger, waving from the front of the office building. Her heart leapt at the sight of him. Grinning, she waved back.

"Who's the hunk?" Veronica asked.

Keeping her eyes on the road, Marcie said, "You never miss a thing, do you? He's Miss Sarah's right–hand man."

"Un huh," Veronica said. "And your date on Saturday night." "So what if he was?"

"Aha, I just knew you had a hot date."

"Correction. A very pleasant date."

"Sure it was," said Veronica.

"Speaking of dates, I have yet to hear about yours. We'll have a private session after lunch, okay?"

An empty parking spot opened up directly in front of the building. "Can y'all make it to your classroom without me?" A chorus of yeses rang out. As the ladies departed, she said, "I'll see you at noon." Anxious to get back to Cassie, she backed out and headed down the street. Passing the hardware store, she regretted not bringing the dead bolts with her. They would not need them.

This time Roger was out in the middle of the yard waving his hardhat in the air. Oh, how she wished they could take time off to talk a while. She'd gladly follow him into the kiln room where they could sneak a few kisses. With one last wave, Roger started walking toward the office building. Did they have to wait until Saturday to be together? Today was only Tuesday. She'd have to wait four more days. Heaving a sigh, she parked the van, then rounded the side of the house and flagged Cassie down. The girl came jogging up to her. "Take a few minutes to cool down," Marcie told her, "and then come to the office."

"Okay," Cassie said, seemingly back to her old self.

Marcie entered the kitchen as quietly as possible. Pearl would be down in the cellar ironing and that's where Marcie wanted her to stay. She filled her coffee mug and tiptoed out of the room.

As she passed Deborah's door, she wondered how the little one was faring since her big confession. Marcie had written her another note. It didn't say much; just that she was thinking about her and would welcome a visit at any time. Deborah's story about the murder of Bill Thompson had preyed on her mind. All she could figure was that Bill Thompson had tried to harm her in some way and Victor had stopped him. But how and where? Then again, the whole story could be a hoax. Deborah wasn't the most reliable person she'd ever known.

She pulled Cassie's chart out of the file drawer and settled at her desk. Was it only yesterday that the girl had said she hated being watched? That she needed freedom to move around? Now Marcie knew why.

Cassie bounced into the room and took her usual position in the chair. She looked at Marcie and said, "This means a lot. Everyone I've ever tried to talk to has shot me down."

Marcie leaned back in her chair. "People tell me I'm a good listener. Start at the beginning."

Cassie wiggled around in her seat and finally found her comfort zone. "Looking back, it really started when I was a baby. My mom was only sixteen when she had me and didn't know how to raise a kid. She read somewhere that a chubby baby was a healthy baby so she stuffed food in my mouth all day long. Cookies ... God, I can still taste Animal Crackers.

"So I grew and my tummy grew and grew. In school the kids called me 'Dumbo' or 'Hippo' and I'd run crying home to Mama. She'd give me ice cream or a candy bar and I'd be happy again. By the time I was twelve I'd ballooned way past the chubette stage. I was fat. Even Mama started nagging me about my weight. My dad was a job shopper in construction so he wasn't home much. When he was, he'd yell at Mama to do something about me. Put me on a diet, starve me, something.

"Mama tried to keep me on a diet but I snuck food into my room. I always had a stash hidden somewhere. Then, in sixth grade, I fell in love with this really cool guy. I knew I had to lose weight to get him to notice me. So I went to the library and read everything they had on weight control. Counting calories, low carbs, ketosis, fasting, swallowing cotton balls, you name it. But the method that a lot of models used caught my eye. They ate what they wanted and then threw it up. I tried it and it worked. I started losing weight. Mama and Daddy were so proud of me.

"Then things got out of control. My mind said I could eat all I wanted, so I'd take a gallon of ice cream into the bathroom and gorge on it till I threw up. It got to be a game, me seeing how much and how often I could binge. Mama couldn't figure out where all her food was going since I was losing weight. It drove her crazy. I felt bad about that but I couldn't stop. By that time I was doing it at school, at my friends' houses, anywhere there was a bathroom. It wasn't a game anymore. I had no control over it.

"By the time I turned fourteen I looked terrific. I weighed around a hundred and ten pounds. But I couldn't vomit automatically anymore. I had to stick my finger down my throat." She extended both hands and indicated the thick calluses that ran the length of her index fingers. "Sometimes I threw up blood. I never got my periods, I was failing in school... I got scared, real scared.

"A guy I knew turned me on to speed. It helped a lot at first. I got down to two binges a day, but the guy kept raising the price and I never had enough money. I sold my jewelry, my record collection, my clothes, and finally myself.

"It all blew up one night when a lady I'd babysat for accused me of stealing her diamond broach. I broke down and told Mama all about the bingeing and the drugs. She got hysterical and called Daddy to come home. He became furious with both of us.

"They sent me to a shrink. I really wanted help so I poured my guts out, and he said I needed treatment for drug addiction. He wouldn't even discuss bulimia. I was in and out treatment programs, saw shrinks and counselors and none of them took my eating disorder seriously. One guy even laughed. Can you believe it? He laughed and said, 'Maybe that would help my wife lose weight'. My parents got fed up. With each other and with me, so they split. I've been on my own ever since."

Marcie expelled a long sigh. Never had she expected to hear such a story. It left her speechless.

Cassie continued to pour out her surrealistic tale. She'd stolen food from homes, supermarkets, written bad checks to buy food, forged prescriptions and sold the drugs to buy food, and sold her body for food. The full ramifications of the disorder sent Marcie's mind into a tailspin.

Cassie inched forward in her seat. "Are you going to kick me out?"

"Of course not. I did leave a message for Dr. George to look into treatment programs specifically designed for eating disorders. If we find such a program and they'll admit you as an indigent, I'll arrange for a transfer."

Cassie fell back with relief. "Jeez, you're the first person to take me seriously."

"It's serious all right, damn serious."

Cassie gripped the chair arms and leaned as far forward as possible. She looked Marcie in the eye and said, "I've lived like an animal, scavenging for food and cramming anything that was remotely edible into my mouth. If I could sit at a table and eat three meals a day like a normal person, I'd be the happiest girl alive."

Marcie went to her then. She pulled her up and held her close. "Cassie, I'll do everything in my power to help you." She released her. "Now scram, I've got work to do."

Cassie beamed a smile and said, "You're the best!" Then she was gone.

It took quite a while for Marcie to write a comprehensive report on Cassie, a report she never dreamed she'd have to record. How could Port Victor function with a bulimic in its midst. What could she do? Provide her with a stash so she wouldn't steal Pearl's stock. That would be a temporary solution to the problem, but the ultimate goal would be to find a place to send her.

———

Missy's movements were stiff and disjointed as she approached the first wing chair. Keeping her eyes on the floor, she sat down on the edge of her chair as if she didn't intend to stay long.

Marcie couldn't figure it out. The girl had been fine that morning, had even explained the aspects of bulimia to the others, but she'd been subdued all through lunch, and now she seemed to be reverting to the closed-mouthed Missy of old.

"What's wrong?" Marcie asked. "Did something happen at rehab?"

"No," Missy said, still not looking up. "It's just that I've been dreading this."

"This session?"

"Yes."

"Why?"

"Because you're going to ask me about Mary Ellen. Where we went and what we did."

"Well, let's get to it then. What did you and Mary Ellen do?"

"We rented a motel room."

"Ah. Well, what's wrong with that?"

"We sinned against the church." She looked up, pain etched on her face. "My father would die if he knew."

Marcie's mind stumbled over Missy's dilemma. She tried to imagine being gay in an anti–gay society of evangelists but she couldn't come close. "Your father has already disowned you because you left the church, and there's nothing you can do about it. Remember when we talked about the Serenity Prayer? 'Accept the things you cannot change'. You can't change your father's beliefs any more than you can change your love for Mary Ellen. At least not now. Therefore, you must continue to live your life as the good person you truly are."

"You think I'm a good person?"

"I know you're a good person. You've done nothing to show me otherwise. You have taken this program seriously, you have set goals for your immediate and distant future, you're honest and trustworthy, kind and helpful... oh, Missy, you have so much to offer."

"If only I could get over this feeling that I'm sinning by loving Mary Ellen."

"If only we could wipe out the word *sin*," Marcie said. "A person is either good or bad and you're good."

They sat in contemplative silence for several moments. Then Marcie said, "So what's the plan? Are you going to be seeing Mary Ellen on a regular basis? Is she going to leave her husband?"

"We don't have an actual plan."

"That's just as well," Marcie said. "Seeing each other over time will give you both the opportunity to decide what's best."

Missy said nothing. Then, "You won't tell the others, will you?"

"That's up to you. What have you told them so far?"

"That Mary Ellen's a good friend of mine."

Marcie smiled. "And that's the truth."

At a few minutes past one-thirty, Veronica dragged herself into the office, her eyes still puffy with sleep from the nap she took after lunch. She had changed into her peacock caftan, which was a startling relief from her party clothes.

Marcie laughed. "If anyone needs a nap around here it is me, myself and I."

Veronica said. "If we didn't have to get up at the crack of dawn to get ready for that damnable rehab, I wouldn't have to take naps."

"What's so damnable about rehab?"

"All those 'which word best describes a dwelling' and then they give you four choices. And those math tests. 'If Mary went thirty miles an hour—'"

"Never mind," Marcie said. "You'll be thankful for those tests once you've finished. They'll help you with job placement."

Aghast, Veronica pointed at her chest and said, "*Mot*? A job?"

"How else do you plan to support yourself?"

Veronica tossed her head. "I'm an actress, remember?"

"How could I forget?" Marcie said. "But as I recall you didn't make a living at it."

"I did all right."

"With a little help from your friends. That is how you ended up here in Port Victor. I don't want to belabor that point. I want you to become an independent and productive member of society, and that will take learning a skill."

Veronica smiled a secret smile. "Not if I marry the Colonel."

"Oh, Lord, please don't tell me you went to bed with him."

"What do you take me for? Some kind of hussy? The Colonel has too much respect for me."

"I'm glad to hear it."

"He said I made him feel young again. That he loved my spunk."

"I love your spunk, too. If you'd put as much time and energy into rehab as you do to look sexy, you could be through with the tests in no time."

"Oh, pooh."

"I know. I probably sound like your mother back when you were in school, but you're a grownup now and it's time to face reality."

"Well," Veronica huffed. "If I have to get a job, reality sucks."

"That's true. Some of the time. Other times it can be wonderful. Just like your date with the Colonel."

"Yes, I have to admit it was lovely. A very romantic setting with linen tablecloths, flowers and candles. And the food was to die for." She turned up her bottom lip in a pout and added, "The only thing missing was a bottle of champagne. Oh well, I guess that's part of the reality you're talking about."

"Bravo, Veronica. You're finally catching on."

"Okay," she said, "I've told you about my date so now it's your turn."

"Well, Roger took me out to this really neat place in the woods and we stuffed ourselves on catfish. Then he took me home."

"Catfish! Out in the woods? How unromantic can you get?"

Marcie winked. "Says you."

CHAPTER 26

Marcie had tried to explain bulimia to the group and had asked for questions. "We're going to provide Cassie with a stash. It won't come out of your stock, Pearl. I'll take care of it."

"That's the craziest thing I ever heard," said Veronica.

"That's a durn fact," said Georgia Lu, her arms crossed and jaw set.

"We either provide her with food or let her steal whatever she wants. Which would you prefer?"

"Why does she have to have it in the first place?" Veronica asked.

"I told you why. Cassie is addicted to food the same way you were addicted to alcohol. Coupled with the fact that she has to have food to sustain life, she has to binge and purge until we find a treatment center for her. In a hospital, she won't have access to food the way she does here."

"Why can't we put them locks on the doors?" Pearl said.

"We could. But then she'd be compelled to go out somewhere and either steal food from a grocery store or rummage through trash cans."

Everyone seemed to be thinking it over. Then Missy spoke up. "I vote we provide Cassie with a stash."

"I guess we don't have a choice," Veronica said.

"Gol dang it," said Georgia Lu. "All that trouble for nothin'."

Marcie looked at her. "If you hadn't caught Cassie, she'd still be taking our food and we'd still be tearing our hair out. This way it's out in the open so we can all support Cassie until she can get the help she needs."

"Cool," said Cassie.

"Okay, enough said. Today we're going to do a session on problem solving."

"Didn't we just finish doing that?" Veronica said.

"Yes, but that was different. This is a formula that you can use in everyday life."

She turned and wrote these words on the board: PINPOINT THE PROBLEM. She turned back to face the women. "Pinpointing the problem is the hardest part of this exercise. Let's say a woman goes to see a marriage counselor. When asked what seems to be her problem, she says, My husband. The counselor asks, What about your husband? He's a slob, she says. The counselor asks, How is he a slob? He won't pick up after himself. The counselor says, Won't pick up what? The woman says, His clothes, his towels, his pajamas, his jacket ... He just drops everything on the floor and expects me to gather his dirty clothes to put in the hamper and hang his clean clothes up. The counselor says, You do that every day? Yes, she answers. And I work in the school cafeteria from seven until three. Then I go home to our twin boys, they're eight, and help them with their homework. At five o'clock, I'd better have dinner on the table when their father walks in the door."

"Isn't that just like a man?" Veronica said.

"Remember when I said the hardest part about this exercise was pinpointing the problem? The counselor had to ask the woman five questions before he could try to figure out what the woman was actually telling him. His next step is finding a solution. But first, who do you think has the problem?"

"The slob!" Veronica said.

"How many of you agree with Veronica?"

Every hand went up except for Missy's. "What's your deduction, Missy?"

"The wife has the problem."

"Tell us why, Missy?"

"Because she picks up after him every day."

"Correct," Marcie said. "Not only does she allow him to treat her like a slave but she's teaching her sons to be tyrants like their father."

"I don't get it," Georgia Lu said.

Marcie said, "The wife has spoiled her husband by constantly picking up after him, so naturally he has no motivation to do it himself. Do you understand?"

"I reckon."

"It will become clear as we go on." She addressed the group in general. "So now that we know what the problem is we have to find a solution. The next step in the formula is to make a list of every solution you can think of. It's okay to let your imagination run wild. Once we have our list, we'll test each solution by asking four very important questions." She wrote all four on the board: Is it doable? Is it safe? Is it legal? Is it reversible? Murmurings came from behind. She turned to face the group.

"Veronica, what would you tell this woman to do?"

"Kill the SOB." Bursts of laughter and giggles swept around the room.

Marcie wrote KILL THE SOB on the board. Then she turned around. "Okay, Veronica, let's look at the four questions you must ask. Is it doable? Yes. Is it safe? Yes and no. Is it legal? No. Is it reversible? No. We have to scratch that solution." She drew a line through Veronica's answer and then looked at the others. "Anyone else?"

Georgia Lu raised her hand. Marcie gave her the nod. "I'd whip his ass till it was raw."

Marcie wrote, WHIP HIS ASS. "Okay, so here we go with the four questions. Yes, it's doable. Yes, it's safe. Yes, it's legal. No, it's not reversible. He won't be able to sit down for a very long time." More laughs. "So we have to scratch that one."

Missy raised a hand. "Yes?" Marcie said.

"The woman should stop picking up after him. She should let his stuff lie on the floor until he finally picks it up."

"Sounds good, Missy." She wrote STOP PICKING UP AFTER HIM on the board. "Let's see how the questions go. Yes, it's doable. Yes, it's safe. Yes, it's legal. Yes, it's reversible. Okay, it passes the test. Anyone else?"

"I'd play a joke on the fool," said Clara. "I'd put his dirty things back in the drawer. Let him wear his nasty shorts a few times."

"Hooweee," Georgia Lu cried. "Ole Blackie would wave his BVD's in the air like a flag and then shoot 'em toward the hamper. Gol dang it if he didn't make a basket ninety-nine percent of the time!"

Once again, laughter swept around the room.

When everyone had settled down, Marcie said, "That's an interesting solution, Clara. Let's see how it checks out. Yes, it's doable. Yes, it's safe. Yes, it's legal, and yes, it's reversible."

"Anyone else?" Marcie asked. When the women remained silent, she turned to the board. "Okay, we have two possible solutions and now we have to rank them in order of preference. How many of you think the counselor should tell the woman to try Missy's?"

Pearl, Cassie, and Missy raised their hands. That left Veronica Georgia Lu, and Clara. "Thank you, ladies. By using this method, the counselor would probably tell the lady to leave her husband's things on the floor." She added, "*But* if that option fails, he could tell her to try putting his dirty things back where they came from. Each solution has its merits. It works best if you have more than one that passes the test. Be thinking about problems you want to try solving and we'll work on them tomorrow."

Georgia Lu heaved herself out of the chair and said, "I gotta water my garden. It's as dry as old bones."

Marcie said, "It won't be long before we'll be reaping the benefits of your hard labor."

"Yep. Them squash and cucumbers are 'bout ready to eat."

Pearl trailed along behind Georgia Lu. Marcie looked from one to the other of the four women and said, "Who wants to try to beat me at cards?"

"I play a mean game of poker," Cassie volunteered.

Delighted that Cassie was finally willing to join in the games, Marcie said, "Poker it is. We can use kitchen matches for chips."

"I don't know how to play poker," said Missy.

"We'll teach you," Cassie said.

How good could things get? Marcie thought. The only thing missing was Phyllis.

———

Before leaving work, Marcie decided to give Phyllis a call. The phone rang and rang. She was about to hang up when a breathless voice answered. After hellos, Phyllis said, "Oh, Marcie, I meant to call you yesterday but I've been so busy cleaning up this filthy house. I don't think Bob changed the sheets the whole time I was gone. You wouldn't believe the mess he made."

You made a far bigger mess by leaving the program, Marcie thought. She said, "I wish you'd talked to me before you decided to leave."

Phyllis gave a light laugh. "I knew better than that. You would've tried to talk me out of it." She went on in that breathless voice. "Bob and I... well, it's like a second honeymoon. It's like we're discovering each other all over again."

"I hate to pop your balloon, Phyllis, but honeymoons don't last."

"Ours will," she stated firmly. "We'll be just fine."

"Phyllis, I hope you know how important it is for you to continue going to AA, and by all means bring Bob to the open meetings. We miss you and want to keep in touch."

"Oh, I will, Marcie, I promise. Just as soon as I get this house in order."

"The house can wait. Maintaining your sobriety can't."

"Please don't worry about me. I'm sober today and I'll be sober next year."

Fat chance, Marcie thought. She said goodbye and replaced the receiver. How long would it take for the honeymoon to end? And then what would Phyllis do, alone in that big house all day? Drink, that's what.

After clearing her desk of papers and charts, she started to retrieve her purse when a rap sounded at the door. When she looked up, hoping to see Deborah, there stood Jacob Horner with a fat grin on his face.

"I'm glad I caught you," he said. "Mind if I come in?"

"Yes, I mind. I was just leaving."

"Then maybe we could go somewhere for a cup of coffee."

"You've got to be kidding."

"Not at all." He started inching his way into the room. He was wearing a royal blue polo shirt and a pair of tan Western–style trousers. "You give me a fresh perspective of religion per se and I like talking to you."

Marcie remembered that George had told her to be kind to the man. But kindness only went so far, and it didn't include going out for coffee with him. "Sorry, but I'm all talked out. It's been a very busy day."

"Oh? How so?"

"It's really none of your business."

"Hey," he said. "I'm just an ordinary guy."

"Aren't you married?"

"Divorced. Going on four years now. Ginny couldn't take the demands of a pastor's wife."

Tempted to say she didn't blame her, Marcie said, "Pearl always keeps a fresh pot of coffee going. If you want some, you'll have to go get it."

"I really don't want coffee, I'd just like to sit and talk to you."

She gave up on trying to get rid of him. "Then sit."

He did, lifting his trousers at the knees, as usual. His fastidiousness and manner of dress made her wonder about his upbringing. She asked, "Where are you from?"

"The high country in Colorado. Steamboat Springs. Ever been there?"

"No, but I've been to Colorado Springs, Pueblo, and Denver." She and David had lived at Fort Carson for two years and it was a post Marcie loved.

"Well, if you ever get a chance to go back be sure to visit Steamboat Springs. It's great country full of great people."

She couldn't stop a smile. "Oh, so now you're telling me you're great."

He grinned and raised a brow. "Among other attributes."

"Wow. I can't believe how lucky I am to have you sitting here."

"No," he said, appraising her with those deep pools of blue that beckoned her to dive in. "I'm the lucky one."

To cover her embarrassment, she said, "You asked about my day."

"Yes. I'd like to hear about it," he said.

She told him about the missing food and how all of the residents denied taking it. How Pearl worried over having her stock disappear. How Georgia Lu took matters into her own hands by hiding out in the kitchen last night. How she caught Cassie in the act of stuffing food in her duffel bag.

"Turns out that Cassie has bulimia. She's had it since the age of ten and despite her parent's attempts to find treatment, every effort failed. But I can't fail her. We have to find a treatment center that will accept her as an indigent. Do you happen to know of one?"

"Does the location matter?"

"No. Her father and stepmother live in Huntsville, but since they don't get along with Cassie, she's essentially homeless."

His expression turned sorrowful. "The dear, dear girl," he said. "To have suffered so much at her young age. Have you tried talking to her father?"

"Not yet. I'm waiting until we have a plan."

"I'll get right on it. I know quite a few doctors, both here and at my previous churches. I'll contact my neurologist friend tonight."

Her estimation of him underwent a change. He seemed to really care what happened to Cassie. She said, "I can't thank you enough. The sooner we find a place the better for all of us."

"What are you going to do in the meantime?"

"Provide her with extra food from my stock, not Port Victor's."

He nodded. Then, "I hope you don't think I'm going to tell Sarah about this."

"The thought crossed my mind."

He shook his head. "Marcie, Marcie, Marcie. When are you going to start trusting me?"

She didn't answer right away. Maybe she could like him, but trust? "I don't know."

"Is your hesitation because I'm a pastor?"

"Yes."

He leaned forward, the bottomless depths of his eyes roaming over her face. "Tell me who hurt you."

Before she knew what was happening, the words spilled out of her mouth.

She ended with, "Religion destroyed my family. My mother ended up in a mental hospital and my father sent me to Virginia to live with my aunt and uncle. That happened thirty-one years ago, and to this day, I have neither seen nor heard from my parents."

He had paid rapt attention, his expression changing from sad to angry and back to sad. "Gracious Lord," he said. "Your pastor's actions were unconscionable. He should have received a severe reprimand from his district superior."

"I doubt if his superior knew. We lived in a small town with tunnel vision."

"Sort of like Fleming's Hill," he said. Heaving a sigh, he stood. "I'll let you be for now, Marcie. Please give this some thought. One sorry preacher doesn't mean we're all that way."

"But it's not just one sorry preacher. We hear about the famous preachers and there are thousands just like them. Right now, here in this house, a resident is grieving her heart out. Why? Because her preacher father disowned her for leaving his fundamentalist church. On top of that, she's scared to death he'll find out that she's gay."

He lifted the crease in his pants and sat back down. "You're right. I'm ashamed to say there are a lot of bad pastors. I'm not one of them. How can I help the resident who's grieving?"

"You can't."

He studied her for a long moment, then, "Do you want to hear my take on homosexuality?"

"That should be interesting," she said wryly.

"I had an affair with a homosexual when I was fourteen. It lasted a year. Does that shock you?"

"It's not what you said that shocks me but the fact that you said it to me. I wasn't expecting you to be so candid."

He appraised her. "You're a counselor, aren't you? Doesn't everyone tell you their innermost secrets?"

She smiled at him. "Yes, but you're my first preacher."

"It happened when I was attending a Christian boarding school. He was two years older and I was easy to seduce. He had smuggled some obscene material into our dorm. I was a hick kid who'd only seen animals mate and I devoured the stuff. He noticed.

"One day he asked me if I wanted to watch real people make out. He led me through a field and into the woods, all the time describing what we'd see when we got to a shack he knew about. It was heady stuff and I got excited just listening to him.

"The shack was deserted when we got there and I expressed my disappointment in a very un–Christian–like way. The next thing I knew he was unzipping my pants. I didn't try to stop him.

"Even though I knew it was wrong we carried on until he was expelled for seducing several other boys, one of whom told on him. For years, I felt guilty. I kept waiting for God to punish me." He smiled and added, "He finally did when He called me to the ministry."

Nonplussed, Marcie didn't know what to say.

He said, "So, what do you think? Did I sin beyond redemption?"

"Please don't talk to me about sinning. I think you were a normal, healthy boy with an exceptionally curious mind. How does that experience affect your feelings about homosexuals today?"

"The ones I've known have been lonely people crushed by guilt and isolation. I counseled a black man in Mississippi. He was brilliant, Ph.D. in physics, and he literally drove himself crazy. He said, 'Try to imagine what it's like to be a black homosexual living in a rural Southern town full of Baptists and you'll know what Hell is'. He tried to go straight. Even dated a white woman for a while in the hope she could help him. Eventually, he suffered a psychotic break. As far as I know he's still institutionalized."

"What a terrible waste," Marcie said. "But his story reinforces my need to help Missy." Damn! She'd inadvertently told him who the resident was.

"I knew it was Missy," he said softly. "Her face turned chalk white when I asked her about herself. Do you want me to talk to her?"

"Not unless she agrees to talk to you. Before I ask her, I'd like to know how you interpret certain Scriptures that deal with homosexuality. Romans, for example."

He leaned back. "Ah, yes, Romans. Good old Paul telling everyone off. That Book has a lot of juicy stuff in it. Paul, a Jew, was speaking about the Greek practice of giving up heterosexuality for the pleasures of bisexuality. The Greeks made love to women yet they kept young boys as concubines. Paul called it a perversion and I agree."

Marcie's impression of this man had gone up another notch. Maybe they could be friends, after all. "So I take it you don't think homosexuality is evil or wicked."

"It's tragic."

Overcome with an emotion she had never felt before, Marcie had difficulty breathing. That she might be able to trust and have faith in a man of the church was unthinkable, yet she was thinking it all the same. Frightened by her thoughts, she stood up and lifted her chin. "I really need to be getting home," she said. "I appreciate your honesty and candor, and I'll speak to Missy. If she agrees to talk to you, I'll let you know."

He remained seated, those eyes locked on hers. "I hope I haven't offended you."

"Not at all. Really." She glanced at the clock. "It's time to feed my dog."

With obvious regret, he got up. "I'll let you know what my doctor friends have to say about Cassie, and I'll be available whenever Missy is ready to talk to me."

"Good. Fine. Thank you."

He must have sensed she would not be leaving the house with him so he simply said, "I'll see you later."

As soon as he left the room, she sank down into her chair. She was shaking all over and her heart was flopping around in her chest. Something extraordinary had happened this past half hour but she couldn't define it. Whatever it was, it gave her no comfort, only a mind filled with chaos. She would have to be very careful in her future meetings with Pastor Jacob Horner.

CHAPTER 27

Marcie couldn't stand the continued silence emanating from Deborah's room any longer. She'd written the little one another note requesting a meeting, but nothing had come of it. The possibility that Victor Thornton had murdered a man had preyed on her mind. It was past time to learn the truth.

She went to Deborah's door and knocked. No response. She knocked harder and shouted, "Deborah! Talk to me!"

"Go away!"

"No! I've missed seeing you. I've been worried about you."

Ginger began to bark. Not a menacing bark, a friendly bark. For some reason, that worked. Deborah opened the door and Ginger came running out with her tail wagging and her nose working overtime sniffing Marcie's feet and ankles.

"Good girl," Marcie said to the dog.

"Well, I hope you're happy," Deborah said. "You've caused a ruckus again."

"Did you read my note?" Marcie asked.

"Yes."

"When are you going to come see me?" Ginger danced around her feet.

Deborah hesitated. "I'm not dressed," she said.

"So what? You're all covered up." She wore a white velvet robe. Again, Deborah hesitated. Then, "I'll be there in a little while."

"Great," said Marcie. "See you later, Ginger." She continued on her way, hoping that Deborah meant what she said.

While waiting at her desk, Marcie looked out the window. Still no sign of rain, not even a gray cloud on the horizon. That was good for the boys and their ball games but not for her and Roger. They had planned to get together if the boys were rained out, but now they'd have to wait until their scheduled date tomorrow. She would serve a wine pot roast with potatoes and carrots. Rolls, a tossed salad, and maybe a chocolate cake.

Oh no, if tomorrow was Saturday that meant today was Friday and Pastor Jacob Horner would be coming to do his group. In order to avoid him, she would take off early. She'd certainly earned some time off what with all the overtime hours she put in. She could do her grocery shopping before the rush hour.

But if she left early, she wouldn't be able to tell Jacob that Missy had agreed to talk to him. And what was the latest on his efforts to find a place for Cassie? He said he knew a lot of doctors. That was Tuesday. Surely he knew something by now. And why hadn't George gotten in touch with her?

She had a bad feeling that neither of the two men had found a place that accepted indigents. Which meant Marcie would have to continue to provide Cassie with a stash each day. It wasn't helping Cassie reach her goal to stop bingeing and purging, and it was becoming more expensive. One day she'd given her a jar of peanut butter and half a box of crackers. Another day she'd bought a giant bag of popcorn and a bag of pretzels. Today she'd given her two apples and a large cluster of grapes. She'd also left bananas, peaches, the other half a box of crackers and a hunk of cheese for Pearl to give her over the weekend. Trying to think of healthy foods that didn't need cooking was becoming more difficult. It made her feel like an enabler. But what choice did she have?

Thoughts of Cassie flew out of her mind when Deborah walked in looking like a living doll in a dainty pink shirt with a ruffled collar and a white pleated skirt.

"I'm so glad you made it," Marcie said. "I've been concerned about you. What do you do all day?"

Deborah took a seat in the rocking chair and slowly rocked to and fro. "I stay busy doing this and that."

"Have you gotten rid of Victor's dead flowers?"

"I can't bring myself to throw them out. I keep hoping that if I water them, they'll come back to life."

"I think you're wasting your time."

Deborah's eyes flashed. "Nothing I do is a waste of time."

"I just wish you'd come to our group sessions. We do a lot of good work. This week we've been solving problems by using a special formula. The women have enjoyed it and I think you would, too."

"Why would I want to hear about the women's problems?"

"Because you might have one of your own."

"But I don't have any problems, and if I did I wouldn't discuss them in front of those women."

"You don't have any problems? Well then, consider yourself lucky, because most of us do."

Deborah settled back in her chair. "What's *your* problem?"

"Oh Lord," Marcie said with a laugh. "I have so many."

"Pick one," said Deborah.

If sharing one of her problems would further their relationship, Marcie was all for it. But which problem? Her car was falling apart, and apparently Sarah had forgotten to tell her friend to be on the lookout for a good deal on a replacement. Then there was Roger and their blooming relationship. And always the kids. She settled on this last.

"My children, a girl and a boy, chose to live in Washington, D.C. with my ex-husband. I won't go into how it happened, it just did. The kids are coming back to Alabama in a few weeks to visit me and I want them to stay until they go away to college. My problem is how do I convince them?"

Instead of focusing on the problem, Deborah said, "How are they getting here?"

"They're flying. I'll pick them up in Huntsville."

Deborah leaned forward in her chair. "You mean your ex–husband is letting your kids fly on an airplane all by themselves?"

"They're not little kids, they're teenagers, and they've done it before," Marcie said. "Buses take forever, and their father won't take the time to bring them down here."

Deborah sat back. "Then he should be shot."

She said this with such decisiveness and finality, Marcie believed she was serious. "That's a bit drastic don't you think?"

"No. He's an evil man who should be punished."

"Well," Marcie said, "he's insensitive and selfish but I wouldn't call him evil."

"He caused you pain, didn't he?"

"Yes."

"He's done harm to your family, hasn't he?"

"Well, yes." Marcie said.

"Then he's evil. You should get your children away from him. He's not fit to raise a pig, much less your children."

How strange it was to hear these things from a woman who had never married or borne children. Who had never known her father and never known a mother's love.

"Believe me I've given that a lot of thought. But my son and I have a… you could say, a difficult relationship. I've done everything I can to win him over and nothing has worked. I'm afraid if I started a legal battle, I'd lose him forever."

Deborah started rocking again. "You know what they say: 'The apple doesn't fall far from the tree'."

Marcie hadn't made that connection. Davy had been an obstinate child practically from birth. He'd grown worse as time went by. When she tried to discipline him or when she said no to something he wanted, he went to his father, and David always overruled her. Now that she thought about it, she had to wonder if David had been raised the same way.

Marcie said, "How do you know all this stuff?"

"From my soaps."

"For heaven sakes," Marcie said. "You're giving me advice based on the characters in your soaps?"

"I am. Those characters have more problems than you or your women could ever imagine."

Marcie had never watched soap operas on TV but she'd heard enough about them to know that someone like Deborah, who'd never been out in the world, could learn plenty from them. "All right," Marcie said, anxious to change the subject. "Thanks for the advice. Now it's your turn. How and why did your uncle Victor kill Bill Thompson?"

"You're going to bring that up again?"

"I certainly am. The last thing you said to me was that your uncle killed him to save you. I have lost sleep and spent countless hours thinking about how and why. Please don't keep me hanging again."

Deborah sat back, stilling the rocking chair. "Do you remember me telling you that Bill wanted to adopt me?" Marcie nodded. "He was always picking me up, hugging me, and telling me how he couldn't wait for me to be his little girl." She paused a moment. "The way he treated me ... well, it wasn't natural, but I fell for it all the same.

"The night before the adoption papers were to be signed, he wanted to take me to the movies and afterwards we'd have pizza, just the two of us. Lila had a fit, but it didn't do her any good. Uncle Victor didn't like the idea, either. But I got excited about seeing a movie, and Granny thought I should go.

"Instead of going straight to the picture show, Bill wanted to take me to see this waterfall. He said it was one of the prettiest places around. He pulled off on a bumpy dirt road and we rode and rode. Then he stopped and said we'd have to walk the rest of the way. It was as hot as hades and Bill started sweating and breathing hard. He said we needed to stop and rest. He found a nice spot covered with pine needles and I sat down cross–legged. He sat next to me and started tickling me. No one had ever done that and I was giggling and slapping at his hands. He was laughing, too. Then his hands started going all over me. He kissed my cheek, my neck, and my hair. He told me I tasted as sweet as honey. Then he started unbuttoning my blouse. He said he wanted to see if I was beautiful all over. I started crying and begging him to stop. But he just kept on. He took off my blouse and started to unzip my skirt when all of a sudden he keeled over.

"I thought I was hallucinating when Uncle Victor told me to put my blouse on, that Bill Thompson would never touch me again. When he told me to close my eyes and not open them until he said so, I did. I heard him grunting and I heard a sound like someone pounding a stake in the dirt. Then Uncle picked me up and carried me to his car. When he said I could open my eyes, I saw Bill all crumpled up in a heap. Then I saw the ice pick on the floor of the car near Uncle's feet. We left Bill there. On the way home, Uncle said if I told anyone what happened he'd go to prison and never get to see me again. I've kept his secret all these years. But now that he's gone, it feels good to finally tell someone." She gave Marcie an icy stare and added, "If you tell Aunt Sarah, I'll kill you."

Marcie let out a long shaky sigh. Except for the ticking of the schoolhouse clock, all was silent.

Finally, Marcie said, "I wouldn't dream of telling Sarah. It would break her heart. It's a wonder it didn't break yours. You were just a child, and a little one at that. And then your mother disappeared. I don't know how you stood so much trauma at such a young age."

"Oh, my mother didn't disappear. Uncle Victor got rid of her, too."

Marcie flinched, as if a cold fingertip touched her cheek. "You mean he killed your mother?"

"He had to. She was evil, and sooner or later she'd bring another evil man home with her."

Marcie's heart hammered against her chest but she knew better than to show alarm. "How did he dispose of... the body?"

"Simple. He knocked her out and put her through the kiln. There wasn't a trace of her left."

"Oh my God," Marcie said as the roaring flames flashed before her eyes. "How could he?"

"How could he not?"

"But you were only thirteen years old!" Marcie cried. "How did he expect you to understand his warped reasoning?"

"Oh, I understood, all right, and I was glad."

"Glad?"

"Yes. From then on it was just Granny and Uncle and me."

"And Aunt Sarah."

"No, not her, never her."

Marcie's mind was whirling like an out of control top. What to say? What to do?

"You can't ever tell anyone," Deborah said.

"I know," Marcie said. Even if she could, who would she tell? George? Jacob Horner? What good could it possibly do?

Deborah stood up and made for the door. "I'm very tired. I have to rest now."

As soon as she cleared the doorway, Marcie let out the breath she'd been holding. Leaning back in her chair, she tried to process what she had heard. She believed the story about Bill Thompson. The man was obviously a pedophile who desired to own Deborah in every sense of the word. But did Victor actually kill Lila, or was it wishful thinking on Deborah's part?

She tried to clear her mind by doing a Stop–Think exercise. She was no longer in her office at Port Victor. She was lying on a beach of sugar–white sand. Gentle waves lapped at the shore, sea birds cried overhead, the air smelled like salt and kelp. The sun warmed her bones. A myriad of tiny stars from the sun's rays flickered on her eyelids. A breeze blew her hair from her face and stirred the ruffles on her swimsuit. No one came to her with problems. Her own problems vanished. She had never felt more relaxed.

"Marcie? Is this a bad time?"

Her eyes popped open and she bolted upright. When the fog in her brain cleared, she saw the preacher standing in the doorway. "I must have dozed off," she said. "Come in."

She watched him amble over to the chair in his Levi's, boots, and an open-necked shirt. Wide awake, the reality of Deborah's confession came crushing down on her. She wanted to go to the preacher, fall on her knees and tell him everything.

Jacob said, "I found a place for Cassie but it's in Montana."

"Oh, how wonderful," she said. "I don't care if it's in Timbuktu as long as it's a decent place that treats bulimics."

"It's a fairly new treatment center that specializes in eating disorders. Cassie will be accepted gratis as a case study. She'll have to sign a waiver of confidentiality because they'll probably publish their findings."

"Oh, Jacob, I could hug your neck."

"Do you realize that's the first time you've called me by name?"

"Really? Well, from now on, Jacob will be on the tip of my tongue."

He grinned. Then he said, "Do you want me to call her father or would you rather talk to him?"

"I'll call him. But if he gives me any trouble, I'll gladly hand the job over to you."

"Fine by me. I've had a lot of practice with phones lately. I made nine calls before I found the right doctor. But it was worth it. Cassie will get the treatment she needs, and in time she'll be able to eat her meals like the rest of us."

"Oh, Jacob. What can I say? You pulled a miracle out of your hat."

He turned serious. "The Lord guided me all the way."

At that, Marcie changed the subject. "Onto other business. Missy has agreed to talk to you. Let me remind you that her father is a strict fundamentalist who is anti–gay."

He said, "Did I offend you?"

"Offend me? In what way?"

"By using the Lord as my guide."

"You didn't offend me. It's just that people either blame the Lord when something bad happens or praise the Lord when something good happens. I've never understood that. He gave us free will, didn't He?"

"But His presence is always with us. We need only to open our hearts to Him as our Lord and Savior."

Marcie shifted in her seat. "When do you want to see Missy? Now or some other day?"

He sighed. "Now will be fine."

"Sit right there and I'll send her in."

He stood when she did. "Will I see you afterwards?"

"No. I have an errand to run."

His eyes were tinged with sadness. "You're running away from me."

"I'll see you later, Jacob." She rushed out the door and up the hall.

CHAPTER 28

Cassie's father had not only agreed to buy her ticket to Butte, Montana, scheduled to leave at two o'clock on Sunday, but he would pick her up and take her to lunch at the airport. Cassie's excitement had spilled over to the other residents and everyone was joking and laughing as they played poker in the sunroom. Whether the women were happy because she'd be receiving the proper treatment or whether they were glad to get rid of her was hard to tell. Marcie thought it was probably half and half.

Before Jacob Horner's expected arrival, Cassie sat across the desk in her usual lotus position. Marcie said, "I wanted you to know I won't be here when your dad picks you up."

"That's cool," Cassie said. "I still can't believe he bought my ticket and is taking me to the airport."

"Believe it. He sounded as excited as you are. He really cares about you, Cassie."

For the first time the girl turned pensive. "I guess he does."

"When you become a parent you'll understand how hard it is to see your child suffer and not be able to do anything about it."

"I'm never going to have kids. All the ones I know are always in trouble."

Marcie gave a knowing smile. "You might change your mind once you're well enough to think about something other than food. Enough about that. I called you in here to see how you really feel about going to Montana."

"I love it," Cassie said, back to her sunny self. "I'm finally going to get help. I'd go anywhere for that."

"You're not afraid of going to a strange place?"

"I can't wait. I mean, you've done all you can and then some, but this will be a treatment center for people like me. I'll love you and Pastor Horner for the rest of my life for finding this place."

"You will keep in touch with us, won't you? We all want to hear how you're doing."

"I'll write every day if they'll let me."

Marcie got up and went to the closet. She grasped a gift-wrapped box from the shelf and then presented it to Cassie. "This might come in handy."

Cassie ripped the wrappings off and opened the box of stationary that also contained two books of stamps. "Oh, you shouldn't have," she gushed. "You've given me too much already. I promise to pay you back for my stashes." The girl untangled her legs and stood up.

"And I promise to hold you to it." The two of them came together in a hug. Marcie murmured, "I'll miss you, dear girl." When they stood back, Cassie seemed overcome with emotion. Tears glistened in her eyes and her lips trembled.

"Go, get out of here," Marcie told her. "This will be your last session with Jacob so make the most of it."

Cassie grabbed her shoes and ran out of the room. Marcie heaved a long sigh. How she wished she could accompany the girl to Butte to make certain the hospital was as nice as Jacob said it was. She would just have to trust him. Then it occurred to her. That was exactly what he'd been wanting all along—her trust, and now he had it. She couldn't wait to tell him.

Having finished filling in Cassie's discharge paper, she placed it in a special folder marked for residents who left the program with the director's blessing. When she turned away from the file cabinet, there stood Deborah.

"Congratulations," Deborah said.

"For what?" Marcie asked.

"For getting rid of that girl who's been running around half-naked. She's disgraced this house long enough."

Marcie decided against trying to defend Cassie. Unless Deborah had learned from her soaps how devastating bulimia could be, she'd never understand. "She's going to another treatment center."

"I don't care where she's going, just so she's leaving here."

A shiver caught Marcie unaware. The word *leaving* brought the hidden luggage to mind. This was the moment she'd been waiting for; the time had finally come where she could question Deborah about most anything.

As soon as the little one took her seat in the rocking chair, Marcie said, "I've been meaning to ask you about a mystery that's plagued my mind ever since I started working here. Do you know anything about the women who snuck out after hours and never returned?"

"Of course," Deborah said. "Every time someone trips the wire on the fire escape a buzzer goes off in my closet."

Marcie knew she had to choose her words carefully and keep a neutral expression on her face. One wrong move and Deborah would be out the door. "Whose idea was that?"

"Mine. I told the Fire Marshall what I wanted and he sent an electrician over. How else was I going to keep track of the women's comings and goings? And when they broke the rules, I had to punish them."

Deathly afraid of the answer she might get, Marcie still had to ask, "How did you punish them?"

"I got rid of them," Deborah said, almost cheerfully.

Marcie kept her voice steady. "Like uncle Victor got rid of your mother?"

"Something like that."

"But how could you? You're so tiny."

Deborah gave a sly smile. "That's why my trick worked. I may be little but I'm strong."

"How many women are we talking about?"

"Four. I waited for the others but they never came back."

Marcie leaned forward. "You're telling me you killed four of our former residents?"

"That's what I said."

Trembling all over, Marcie sat back. She tried not to show her fear, but her voice came out shaky. "Do you remember their names?"

"Certainly. I have an excellent memory. Jenny was the first one to leave. She took her suitcase and didn't come back. Louise and Carol snuck out together.

They pulled the same stunt. Kept me waiting almost all night. Margaret was easy and so was Darlene. I felt kind of bad about having to punish Sheila, but she shouldn't have gone out with that tramp Tiffany. Getting rid of Tiffany was a pleasure."

"But how could you take on two women at a time. Didn't one of them fight back?"

"Well, knowing how nice Sheila was, I hit Tiffany first. When she fell over, Sheila did exactly what I expected her to do. She forgot all about Ginger and bent over Tiffany to check on her. That's when I knocked Sheila out."

Marcie's brain tried to process the information. One thing she knew for certain. The little one sitting before her was a dangerous sociopath. She licked lips gone dry and said, "Well, you certainly know how to take care of things."

Deborah gazed at the far wall and said, "I've kind of missed all the action since you've been here. Ginger and I had fun hiding by the greenhouse. We'd lay in wait for the evil one to return. As soon as Ginger caught the scent, she let me know with a low growl. Then we went through this little routine. When the evil one tried to pass, we'd pop up out of nowhere and scare the bitch half to death. It was funny how they all said and did the same thing." Deborah's voice turned mimicking. "They had trouble sleeping and decided to take a walk. They promised never to go out again. They begged to be allowed to go back to bed. Blah, blah, blah." She shook her head, a look of disgust on her face.

"They all tried to get back on my good side by making a fuss over Ginger. I'd tell them they could pet her but first they had to wash their filthy hands, that there was a sink in the greenhouse and to follow me inside. It was pitch dark and they were scared silly but they followed me anyway. They washed and dried their hands and then I gave them permission to pet Ginger. She'd wag her tail and look up at them as if she couldn't wait to be petted. As soon as they squatted down or bent over, I'd hit them on the head with the brick. Then I'd hit them again and again and again. After it was all over, Ginger and I would come inside and I'd fix us ice cream sundaes."

"But look at the size of your hand. It's too tiny to hold a brick."

"Oh it wasn't a whole brick, more like a half of one, but it did the job."

Marcie tried but failed to imagine the scene. The tension she had felt had reached the base of her skull and the pain was now affecting her eyesight. Deborah was fast becoming a blur. It was time to end this horror story. "Do you have anything else to share?" Marcie croaked.

"Uncle would be proud of me. I may have let his flowers die, but I gave him four new ones."

Oh my God, Marcie thought. She couldn't bear to hear another word.

Deborah said, "I could tell you all the details but I'll save that for another day. I need to go rest now."

"Yes, you must be exhausted."

"I am. I truly am." Deborah got up from the chair. "Remember, you can't tell."

"I know," said Marcie. "Don't worry."

"It's you who shouldn't worry. I wanted to get rid of you when you first came here but I've grown to like you."

"Thanks," Marcie said, giving a tight smile. "I like you, too." The little one disappeared from view.

Marcie held her head in her hands and closed her burning eyes. She knew she should get up and take a couple of Goody's powders, but she couldn't make herself move. All she could think was, Oh my God, oh my God, oh my God. What was she going to do? She could keep Uncle Victor's secret, but oh my God, the women. Never mind the confidentiality code, she must tell someone about the women.

But who? If she called the police, what could she say? That Deborah murdered four women in cold blood. They would probably take one look at the little one and laugh in her face. She must see George. He had an answer for everything

CHAPTER 29

George just sat there, hands laced under his chin, no emotion showing on his face. She'd tried to keep the hysteria out of her voice, but he knew her too well. It didn't help that she'd pushed Diane out of the way when she tried to stop her from barging into his office, where a startled patient jumped up from a chair and rushed out of the room. That had been smoothed over, and Marcie had told George what happened.

The headache was on the verge of starting up again. She couldn't seem to keep her hands still. They fluttered from her clothes to her hair to her face. The silence became deafening. "Say something, dammit!"

Very slowly and deliberately, George began to speak. "I think the stress of the job and worrying about the kids coming home has been too much for you. A few days off would give you a fresh perspective."

She came halfway out of her seat. "This isn't about me, George! Didn't you hear a word I said?"

"Yes, I heard. But Marcie, think about it. How could Deborah possibly murder four grown women? They would overpower her at the slightest threat."

"She took them by surprise, George. She said that being little made 'her trick' work."

"What trick might that be?"

"I told you it involved Ginger. They hid out near the greenhouse. When the woman tried to pass on her way back to the fire escape, Deborah would show herself. The woman would promise to never sneak out again and then she'd make a fuss over Ginger. Deborah would lure her into the greenhouse and when she leaned down to pet the dog, Deborah would hit her in the head with a brick."

"And you're telling me she did this to four women?"

"That's exactly what she did. I can't imagine it but she did it."

"And you don't think she was making it up?"

"She was dead serious, George. I told you about the trip wire that sets off the buzzer. She knew the names of each woman. Who tried to get back inside and who did not. It all adds up. The luggage is still down in the cellar. Deborah thinks the women were evil, and in her mind, evil people have to be destroyed. What are we going to do, George? We have to report this to someone."

"Hold on, Marcie. The luggage doesn't prove anything. What we end up with is your word against hers. Whom do you think the authorities, not to mention Sarah, are going to believe?"

"But we can't let it go, George. We have five residents. What if one of them sneaks out and tries to come back? She'll kill again."

"Let's go back a bit," George said. "What did she do with the bodies?"

Though tempted to tell him about the murders Victor committed, Marcie knew he wouldn't believe that, either. Besides that was a secret she had decided to keep. "Deborah was coy about that. Maybe she dug graves in the greenhouse. She keeps it locked up tight and you can't see in. Who knows what's in there? She told me she gave Victor four new flowers. Maybe she's watering the bodies with acid." The thought made Marcie shudder. She wrapped her arms around her middle and held on tight.

She jumped when his buzzer went off. Over the speaker, Diane announced that his patient had arrived. George got up and came around his desk. "Time's up, Marcie. We need evidence. Try to find out what she did with the bodies. Be very careful. Let me know what you discover and we'll take it from there."

Standing face to face with him, she said, "Do you believe me?"

"I'll believe you when you can show me something concrete."

Marcie snapped her fingers. "Concrete! Maybe that's how she got rid of the bodies."

"Come on, Marcie. You can do better than that."

"Thanks a lot. I came to you for help and what do you do? You brush me off like I made it all up."

He put his arm around her shoulders and led her to his private door. "Call me if you find anything we can show the authorities." He opened the door and, like a sleepwalker, she passed through it. "Don't do anything foolish," he said and closed the door.

Standing alone in the hall, his words pounded in her mind.

What was she supposed to do now?

She sat in her car for quite a while, waiting for the Goody's powders she'd brought to take effect. While taking another swig of her bottled water, a few drops dribbled down her chin. She never felt a thing.

Paranoia swept through her as she contemplated her next move. She'd told Pearl she had errands to run and was taking the rest of day off. What if Deborah came looking for her? She said she'd save the details for another time. And though Marcie dreaded the thought, she needed to hear those details in order to gain evidence.

She fired up the engine and backed out of the lot in front of George's office building. The grocery shopping could wait. She didn't think she could stand being around a lot of people anyway. Her emotions were seesawing all over the place. So far she'd kept the tears for the dead women in check, but that didn't mean she could hold them back forever. She turned the wheels in the direction of Port Victor.

A burst of laughter came from the sunroom. Then she heard Jacob's voice. Her timing couldn't be better. She could do what had to be done without interference. She tiptoed across the kitchen with a flashlight in one hand and opened the door to the cellar with the other. Hoping the stairs wouldn't creak, she descended slowly.

As she made her way under the stairwell, she waved a hand in front of her face to brush away the cobwebs. Pulling out the first suitcase she laid a hand on, she backed out of the well. After carrying the case into the recreation room, she set it on the card table and positioned the flashlight to shine on the contents. Treating the items with the utmost care, she found the usual female paraphernalia: Clothing, nightgowns, underwear …. nothing to identify the owner unless you'd known her, and unfortunately Pearl never paid attention to what anyone wore, except for Veronica's low-cut dresses.

Setting that suitcase aside, she went back for another one. She knew right away that the bag had belonged to Tiffany. It was filled with photo albums and scrapbooks. Missy had told her Tiffany had more than one bag. Though curious about the albums, Marcie closed the lid. She didn't have time to linger. The next suitcase showed nothing of value. The same with the next. Then she hit the jackpot. A small pocket-sized address book was tucked into a zippered side pocket of the suitcase. Deborah must have been in a hurry and overlooked it.

With her heart beating erratically, Marcie looked at the first page. Listed under Personal Information was the name Sheila Blevins. It also gave an address and a telephone number! Marcie stood with the book in her hand, gazed up at the ceiling, and whispered, "Did you lead me here, Lord? If you did, I thank you from the bottom of my heart."

She stuck the address book inside her bra, closed the suitcase and hauled it back under the stairwell. Hurrying as fast as she could, she did the same with the other bags. Then she retrieved her flashlight and started up the stairs, carefully placing one foot and then the other. At the top step, she cracked the door open and listened for sounds. Veronica's voice drifted in from the sunroom. Other than that, she heard nothing. She opened the door and then made a beeline for her car. Once she'd backed out of the garage, she expelled a long breath. She headed for home where she would have complete privacy to call the Blevins.

Reaching the house, she feigned normalcy. She gave Charley his pats and called a cheery hello to the clocks, then buried herself in her bedroom with the door locked. The area code listed was two-oh-five, which meant Sheila had lived in the Birmingham area. Marcie's fingers shook as she dialed the number. The phone rang once, twice, and then a third time. She didn't think she could stand to hear an answering machine. Worse, no answer at all.

"Who's callin'?" The voice sounded like a male version of Pearl's, gravelly and wheezy.

Marcie hesitated. What to say, what to say? "Hello. Mr. Blevins?"

"You got him. But he ain't talkin' to nobody he don't know."

"I'm calling about Sheila, Mr. Blevins."

His voice turned sharp-edged. "What about her? Who is this?"

"My name is Marcie Parker. I'm the director of a halfway house called Port Victor. It's up—"

The man hollered so loud, Marcie had to hold the phone away from her ear. "Mother! C'mere! Lady on the phone wantin' to know about Sheila!"

Marcie heard a woman shout, "Our Sheila? Land's sakes alive."

A rustling sound could be heard as the phone exchanged hands. The woman said, "What's this about Sheila?"

"Oh, Mrs. Blevins, I'm so sorry to disturb you and the mister. Sheila was a resident at our treatment center here in Fleming's Hill, and—"

"That place called Port Victor?"

"Yes, ma'am. She—"

"How's she doin'?"

Marcie drew a deep breath. She didn't have the heart to tell them she was dead. And what if she wasn't? What if Deborah had made it up? "That's why I called, Mrs. Blevins. I never had a chance to meet Sheila because I hadn't started working at Port Victor when she was there. But I've been told she went out one night and no one has seen her since."

Mrs. Blevins gasped. "Pappy, come quick. Sheila's gone missin'."

Mr. Blevins' voice came over the line. "What did the sheriff say?"

As much as she hated to admit it, Marcie said, "I haven't talked to the sheriff."

His voice rose to a higher pitch than Marcie thought possible. "You ain't reported her missin'?"

"Mr. Blevins, I know this comes as a terrible shock, but I just found your number today."

"How long's she been missin'?"

"Since March."

"An' you ain't called the sheriff?!"

"I understand your—"

"Lissen, missy, you don't understand nothin'. I'm callin' the sheriff right now." The receiver banged in her ear.

As if he could still hear her, Marcie said, "Good for you." She laid back on the bed and tried to think what to do next. Should she call George and tell him about Sheila Blevins? No, not yet. She still didn't have any solid evidence.

Lying there, thinking, she finally knew what she had to do. She shot up from the bed and, within seconds, was back in the car, racing towards town.

Pulling directly onto the brickyard's lot, she parked in front of the building, hoping against hope that Sarah would be inside, and that she wouldn't run into Roger. One look at him and she knew she'd throw herself into his arms and start bawling.

Her mind filled with dread, she opened the door to the building and went directly to Sarah's office. Without bothering to knock, she opened the door and stepped inside the room.

Sarah looked up from her desk. "Why Marcie, what on earth?"

Marcie stood before her, a hundred opening words flitting through her mind. A dizzy spell caused her to sway in place. Fearing she would fall, she perched on the edge of a chair.

"What is it, dear?" Sarah asked. "Did something happen to Pearl?"

Marcie blinked. Then the words tumbled out of her mouth. "I don't know how to tell you this … Deborah has confessed to murdering four of our former residents."

Sarah rolled her chair back and stood up. She placed her palms on the desk and leaned over it. "Whatever are you talking about?"

"Did you know she had the fire escape wired so that a buzzer would go off in her closet whenever any of the women snuck out after hours? She and Ginger would wait by the greenhouse and when the woman passed on her way back to the fire escape, they'd surprise her. Then Deborah would lure her into the greenhouse on a pretense and when the woman bent over to pet Ginger, Deborah would hit her in the head with a brick. She'd continue to hit her until she was dead. The only reason she killed four instead of seven was because three of the women didn't try to return."

"How do you know all this?" Sarah asked.

"Deborah told me. I signed a confidentiality form with her so she thought she could tell me anything. We have the women's luggage in the basement. According to Pearl, Deborah packed up their things and then had Pearl drag them down to the cellar and hide them under the staircase. But Deborah overlooked a small address book in Sheila's suitcase. It had her parents address and phone number. I called them. They didn't know Sheila was missing. The mister got very upset and said he was going to call the sheriff. They live in the Birmingham area so it would be the Jefferson County sheriff. Sheila is dead, but I didn't have the heart to tell the Blevins."

Sarah slumped down in her chair and started speaking in a soft voice. "I always knew there was something bad wrong with that girl. She had that look about her. Like she was thinking wicked thoughts. What she needed was a good spanking whenever she misbehaved, but we couldn't lay a hand on her because of her delicate bones. She'd deliberately drop one of our china figurines and then smile in a twisted way. When I'd scold her, Victor would come along, scoop her up in his arms and tell her it was all right.

"After Victor died, she was impossible. She came at me once with my silver letter opener. If I hadn't wrested it away from her, I shudder to think what might have happened. From that point on, I was afraid of her. I was always looking over my shoulder, and I kept my bedroom door locked at night. I couldn't wait to get her out of the house. But ... I never expected ...." Her face collapsed. "Oh, those poor darling girls. How could she?"

Marcie went to her. She leaned down and kissed Sarah's cheek. All she could think to say was, "I know, I know."

Sarah twisted around and grabbed Marcie's right hand as if it were a lifeline. "We must be calm," Sarah said. "We must proceed. I'll call Tom Jr. Tell him to get in touch with the sheriff down in Birmingham. You go back to Port Victor and wait for me to call you. Deborah will be watching her soaps. If she should come out of her room, treat her as you normally would. Keep the women involved in something. We'll take it one step at a time. Oh, and Marcie, thank God you caught her."

Marcie expelled a great sigh of relief. Sarah believed her. Sarah was going to get an investigation started. "Tell the sheriff to search the greenhouse first," she said. She left the office as quietly as she'd entered. Fortunately, no one saw her. It would be impossible for her to play friendly with Rebecca or anyone else. But she had to pull herself together by the time she got to Port Victor.

CHAPTER 30

The chief investigator had requested she be present when they arrived at Port Victor around midnight to conduct their search.

Marcie went home as usual at five o'clock. She followed her normal routine, greeting Charley and the clocks, then changing into jeans and a long-sleeved T-shirt. She fed Charley but she couldn't eat a thing. The knots in her stomach were tied as tight as a bowline. She thought about putting a record on the stereo, she thought about reading her latest book, she thought about going down to the dock. She ended up pacing around the house. Knowing something was up, Charley followed her every move. As she paced, the clocks seemed to get louder and louder. For the first time ever, she put her hands over her ears. Would this night never end?

She returned to Port Victor at eleven-thirty. Creeping through the house like a jumpy cat, she settled in her office with the door closed and only a desk lamp lit. Ears on the alert, she listened for cars coming up the driveway. She waited and waited. Midnight passed … one o'clock passed … finally at two-thirty in the morning, the familiar crunch of tires approached.

Marcie waited on the porch, watching as the cars rolled up. Her mission was to try to prevent any undue noise. The last thing she needed was for the women to pour down the stairs with questions on their tongues.

One of the uniformed men motioned her to come forward. Since the alleged crime had taken place in the city, the man turned out to be the Chief of Police. He introduced himself and she shook his proffered hand. "I'm Marcie Parker, the Director of Port Victor."

"Pleased to meet you," he said. "You can come down to the station to make an official statement later, but go ahead and tell me what you know."

They were standing on the driveway next to his police car. He and the other three investigators had turned their car lights off. Since the cars were as black as the night, chances were slim that a passerby would notice. While she told him about Deborah's confession, the others stood nearby, ready to start searching for evidence as soon as the Chief gave them the word.

He listened patiently to what Marcie had to say and then asked a few questions. When he was satisfied with her answers, he thanked her and said he'd be in touch.

She asked, "Should I stay here until you've finished?"

"Yes. If we find enough evidence, we'll arrest Deborah tonight. I may need some help with her."

"You must know her."

"I grew up knowing about Deborah but not really knowing her. My dad was Victor Thornton's cousin. We'd better get started."

"Try to be as quiet as possible, okay?"

"Will do." He turned and signaled to the others. They all headed toward the greenhouse.

Back inside the house, Marcie stood in the foyer for several seconds listening for sounds. All was quiet. She only hoped it stayed that way. She crept back to her office and sat down at her desk. How long would it take? She didn't think she could stand waiting all night.

Uppermost in her mind was the question: Had Deborah been making it all up? For the missing women's sake, she hoped so. She hoped the investigators would find nothing but dead flowers and cave crickets. It would be okay with her if she looked like a fool. Better that than finding dead bodies.

And she worried about Deborah. Even if she'd been lying about her uncle killing Bill Thompson and her mother, and about the four murders she supposedly committed, she still needed to be put in a hospital under a psychiatrist's care.

The evidence combined with Marcie's story soon proved that she had not been lying.

Like thieves in the night, the investigators swooped in, broke into the greenhouse, and found all the evidence they needed: Bones and teeth, containers of dry lye, drain cleaners, paint remover, lead aprons, safety goggles, chemical–resistant rubber gloves, halves of bricks stained with traces of blood, and more. Dozens of cave crickets hopped about the area while field mice scattered across the dirt floor. That dainty little Deborah could spend so much time in such an environment played havoc with the mind.

Two investigators entered the house through the garage door and stealthily removed the luggage from the cellar. The residents, fast asleep upstairs, were unaware of the events taking place below them. Only Marcie was wide awake and alert to every sound.

Deborah was taken into custody at three–fifteen that morning. Instead of barging into her room, the Chief knocked on her door. Ginger started barking immediately. When Deborah opened the door, he read her rights and then told her to get dressed.

Marcie stood by at the end of the hall in case she was needed. Ginger ran to her, tail down and ears pinned back. Marcie picked the dog up and held her in her arms. Looking to see where Ginger went, Deborah poked her head beyond the doorframe. She spied Marcie, and, in an unnaturally quiet voice, said, "You weren't supposed to tell."

Marcie appealed to her. "I had to. You need more help than I can give you."

"Oh well," Deborah said, flippantly. "I never liked this house anyway."

Marcie couldn't believe how calm she appeared to be. She'd expected Deborah to start screaming, kicking, and fighting when told to get dressed. Then ... when she looked at Marcie, those big blue eyes should have flashed red with anger and accusations should have exploded from her mouth. But she seemed resigned, as if she knew this would happen sooner or later.

————

Sarah won an appeal from the judge that would decide the case. Rather than taking Deborah to a holding cell, she was swept away to the psychiatric unit at a Huntsville hospital. There, she would be interrogated by the police and evaluated by a psychiatrist.

Marcie finally went home at four o'clock. Not knowing what else to do, she took Ginger with her. The dog traveled well. She sat in the front passenger seat like a little lady, seeming to accept going to a new home.

Even though she was mentally and physically exhausted, Marcie took time to introduce Ginger to Charley. She put out a bowl of kibble and one of water. Any other time she'd wait until Ginger found a spot to sleep on, but this night she was too tired.

She woke at ten the next morning. Ginger had found a bed on the floor next to Charley. Despite the circumstances that had brought the Pomeranian to her home, Marcie had to smile at the two dogs lying peacefully together. She took a shower and got dressed. Then she woke the dogs and let them out, trusting that Charley would keep an eye on Ginger. She plugged in the coffee maker, put an egg on to boil, and then called Sarah.

As soon as Sarah heard her voice, she said, "Praise the Lord, she confessed."

"That didn't take long," said Marcie.

Sarah said. "According to Phillip, she bragged about how simple it was. How she'd sprinkle the bodies with caustic chemicals and how she liked going out to the greenhouse to watch them decompose. Oh, it makes me sick to my stomach to talk about it. Victor would die all over again if he knew."

Marcie had her doubts about that. "Where did she get the chemicals?"

"From Jackson. The first time she asked him to bring her some lye, he checked with me and I told him to give her whatever she wanted. He'll be devastated when he finds out what she used them for."

Poor man. He'll have nightmares for years, Marcie thought.

Sarah went on. "The magistrate, the Chief, and the district attorney are old family friends. Bless their hearts; they agreed to skip sending the formal complaint to the grand jury. They also agreed to skip the preliminary hearing. She'll appear before the judge in his chambers for the arraignment. He'll sentence her then and there. Then she'll be taken back to the hospital for further evaluation. After that, they'll decide where to send her. Oh, I'd hate for her to be put in a state facility for the criminally insane."

"Me, too. I don't think she'd last long in such a place."

"I'll never forgive myself for moving her into Port Victor."

"Don't blame yourself, Sarah. There's no way you could have predicted what would happen."

"I know, but I can't help it. I knew she was a bad apple but I never—" She broke off.

Marcie could hear a choking sound. "I'm going over to Port Victor," she said. "I can't leave the women, especially Pearl, in limbo all weekend. I thought of telling them that Deborah's gone to a hospital for treatment. Or would you rather I told them the truth?"

"Give me a moment to think about that." Marcie kept quiet. Then Sarah said, "Since Deborah confessed and will be sentenced privately, I'll do my best to shut the media out for now. But when the parents of those girls find out what happened to their daughters ... well, it'll be headline news and we'll have reporters and TV crews camping out on our doorstep. Of course I'll be sued and that will be reported. All in all, I think it'd be best if you told them the truth. You can also tell them I have no intention of closing the doors of Port Victor. I survived one scandal, I can certainly survive another."

Marcie's heart went out to her. Sarah knew as well as she did that Port Victor would never be the same. Still, she wanted to keep it going. "Sarah, you are the bravest and most generous lady I've ever known. It's a privilege to work for you."

"Thank you, dear. I don't know what I'd do without you."

They ended their conversation several moments later. Marcie knew a firestorm of bad publicity would soon ignite, but for now she would go about her business as usual. She put a slice of bread in the toaster, ran cold water over the egg while she cracked and peeled it, then poured a cup of coffee. Standing at the sink, she took a sip while wondering how to tell the women what had happened right under their noses.

———

By the time she got to Port Victor, the women had almost finished their Saturday morning chores. Marcie waited in the kitchen, sipping coffee and watching Pearl peel and slice potatoes. A pot of pinto beans simmered on the stove.

"Why can't you tell me what you're doin' here?" Pearl said.

"Because I don't want to tell it twice. You'll just have to wait until the women finish their jobs. Then we'll gather in the sunroom and I'll tell everyone at the same time."

"Dont't'cha know that curiosity killed the cat? You don't want me dyin' on you, do you?"

"You'd better not die on me, Pearl. We'd all starve to death." Of all the subjects in the world, why were they talking about death and dying? As if Marcie hadn't heard enough about death recently. "Did you hear anything unusual last night?"

"Was I 'spose to? I slept like the dead."

Ouch, Marcie thought. They couldn't seem to get off the subject. "How's the garden coming along?"

"Georgia Lu, she says it's dyin' 'cause of no rain. She waters most every evenin' an' it looks good to me."

"Well, according to the weatherman we're going to have thunderstorms tonight and most of tomorrow." Tonight! What with all that had gone on till the early hours of the morning, she'd completely forgotten about her date with Roger. Unless she was able to take a nap this afternoon, she couldn't possibly gather enough energy to fix dinner and carry on even a semi-intelligent conversation. She made a mental note to call him knowing that she'd probably forget about that, too.

Missy poked her head around the doorjamb. "We're ready, and you'd better hurry up. Veronica's griping about having a session on Saturday."

"I'll be right there," Marcie told the girl. Then she looked at Pearl. "You'll have to finish your potatoes later."

"Be there directly. If I don't put 'em in cold water, they'll turn as brown as a black baby's bottom."

Where did Pearl come up with these sayings? Marcie wondered. She and Georgia Lu could win a contest for the most descriptive but slightly off-center remarks. She continued on to the sunroom.

"This had better be important," Veronica said to her. "I've got to set my hair and do my nails."

"Hello to you, too," Marcie said. "You've got all afternoon to do those things. This is very important, so please be quiet and let me tell you why I called this meeting together."

"I'll slap a hand over her mouth," Georgia Lu said, then gave a hearty laugh.

"That won't be necessary, Georgia Lu. Now, listen closely. The Chief of Police arrested Miss Deb early this morning. She has confessed to murdering four of our former residents."

"Oh my God," Veronica gasped.

The rest of the women sat in shocked silence, staring at Marcie as if she had lost her mind.

Then everyone began to speak at once. "Why?" Clara cried. "Are you serious?" Veronica asked. "What were their names?" Missy wanted to know. "You mean they took her away *this* morning?" Veronica said. "Oh dear Lord," Pearl said, fanning her face with a hand and slumping further down in her chair. "Names, please," Missy said. "Why did she do it?" Clara said. "Were you here when they took her away?" Veronica said. Georgia Lu slapped a thigh and bellowed, "Gol dang it, I missed the whole durn thing!"

Marcie held up a hand for silence. "I can imagine what's going through your minds. This whole thing is very upsetting, to say the least. I've been a nervous wreck ever since Deborah confessed her crimes to me. I didn't know whether to believe her or not, so I went through the pile of luggage stored in the cellar." She looked directly at Missy. "I found an address book hidden in Sheila Blevins' suitcase. I'm sorry to tell you that she was Deborah's last victim." Sheila had been Missy's roommate.

Marcie took a deep breath and went on. "I called the Blevins' phone number. Her parents didn't know she was missing. Mr. Blevins was going to report it to the sheriff. I thought I'd better warn Miss Sarah. Everything happened so fast after that ... well, it didn't seem fast at the time. I was here until almost four this morning. But—"

"You were here? In this house?" Veronica said.

"Yes. The Chief of Police questioned me and then they started searching the greenhouse. They also came in and took the luggage away. Fortunately, they went about their business quietly so as not to wake you all up."

"Gol dang it!" Georgia Lu boomed.

"The names of the dead women are Jenny, Margaret, Sheila, and Tiffany. The others who left after hours, Louise, Carol, and Darlene didn't try to sneak back in."

"But why?" Clara repeated. "Why did she do it?"

"Because she's a dangerous psychopath. She has no conscience. It's a severe mental disorder. She killed those women to punish them for breaking a rule. In her mind, she thought they were evil and should be destroyed. No one ever suspected how sick she was because of her size and because she acted halfway normal. You hear about someone who shot and killed eight people and the neighbors can't believe it. He was such a nice, quiet fellow, they say. But it was real. He actually did the terrible deed. Well, Deborah also did the terrible deed."

"How could she do it?" Missy asked. "Physically, I mean. She's so little."

Marcie gave them a brief summary of Deborah's actions outside and then inside the greenhouse.

Hearing that, Pearl broke down crying and left the room. The others stayed glued to their seats, their eyes still wide with shock.

"Deborah did one good thing. By confessing she saved Miss Sarah and the parents of the deceased from going through the agony of a trial."

"And you were here through all of that?" Veronica said. She couldn't seem to think straight and Marcie couldn't blame her. She herself couldn't believe she was standing here on a Saturday morning telling the women about the grisly murders their housemother had committed.

"Yes. And I was here when they took Deborah away."

"What happened to her little doggie?" Missy asked.

"I took Ginger home with me. She and my dog Charley seem to get along well so I guess I'll keep her."

Wide-eyed, Veronica said, "You're going to keep a murderer's dog?"

"The dog didn't murder anyone," Marcie said.

"Yes, but she played a part in it. She witnessed everything."

WHERE ARE THE WOMEN

"Well, if it'll make you feel better, I'll take her to my Vet and ask him to check her out." Could an owner's mental illness transfer itself to a dog's brain? Could Ginger turn into a mean dog who would fight when slightly provoked?

"Are we safe now?" Missy said.

"Yes, you're all safe. Thank God none of you snuck out and tried to sneak back in." A thought occurred to her. "Just because Deborah is gone doesn't mean you can safely sneak out and back in. Someone will hear you, and that someone had better tell me right away."

"Yes, ma'am," said the chorus.

For the first time, Cassie spoke up. "I almost snuck out one night. I was hungry and thought about eating some stuff in the garden."

"Good lord," Marcie said. "It's a darn good thing you didn't."

"Don't I know it."

"If you don't have any more questions or comments, I'm going home and crawl between the sheets."

"Thanks for being honest with us, Marcie," Missy said.

"Miss Sarah and I wanted you all to know before the story comes out. But please keep this information to yourselves for now." She looked at Veronica. "Whatever you do, don't tell the Colonel."

"But he'll find out sometime," Veronica whined.

"You can wait until sometime arrives. Do I have your word?"

"Oh, all right," she said grudgingly.

"And Cassie, please don't tell your father. Just pretend that everything is normal. We'll keep you posted on the news so you'll know what's going on."

"It's hard for me to relate, you know. I didn't know her."

"Okay, girls, I'll see you on Monday."

In the kitchen, Pearl was standing with her back against the sink. She had a tissue to her nose but she'd stopped crying. Marcie went up to her and put a hand on her shoulder. "Are you okay?"

"I reckon."

"Oh, Pearl, I'm so sorry. We were so afraid something had happened to the missing women. We just didn't know what." She paused. "Now, sad to say, we do."

———

Charley, with Ginger at his side, was waiting as usual. They looked like an odd couple, one large and hairy, the other small and very hairy. She knew she'd think of Deborah every time she laid eyes on Ginger, but that was okay. Despite everything, she still liked Deborah. The little one never had a chance to live a normal life.

Marcie made a fuss over both dogs. They all entered the house and she called a hello to the clocks. The cacophony of bells, chimes, and animal sounds that met her ears sounded sweet to her now that she was home for the rest of the weekend. It would probably be the last weekend of peace and quiet for a long time. Not only would the murders consume the press, but her children were due home a week from tomorrow. The timing couldn't be worse.

As much as she wanted to fall into bed, she was too stimulated by all that had happened. She straightened the house, putting things back where they belonged, running a dust cloth over the tabletops, and mopping the floors. It was far from her usual cleaning job but it would have to do. Instead of having one dog getting in her way, now she had two. Ginger was going to have a whole new lifestyle.

She finally laid her head down at two o'clock. Both dogs found their spots on the floor beside her bed. It still took time for her mind to settle enough to fall asleep. When she did, it was a deep sleep.

She woke at four–thirty, still groggy. At four–forty–five, she sat up straight. She hadn't called Roger and she hadn't gone grocery shopping, which meant she wouldn't be able to prepare a meal. Besides, she barely had time to freshen up. First, she had a call to make.

Roger's cheerful voice came over the line. "Hey, I'm on my way."

"How did you know it was me?"

"Caller ID."

"Oh. Well, if you want something to eat tonight how about stopping by KFC and picking up a bucket of chicken and two sides."

"Okay." He said this with a question mark in his voice.

"We had an incident at Port Victor and I stayed there till four this morning. I went back today. Anyway, I didn't have time to shop for groceries."

"No problem. I happen to be a KFC fan. Is everything okay at PV now?"

"Yes. Everything's fine." White lies didn't count.

"Good. I'm on my way. You'll be able to smell me coming."

She gave a little laugh. "The dogs will smell you first."

"Dogs? Did you get a new one?"

"You could say I acquired her. She's a tiny Pomeranian named Ginger."

"Does she bite?"

"We'll find out when you get here."

She had just come out of the bathroom when she heard the doorbell. True to their nature, the dogs had already gathered at the door, wagging their tails and licking their chops. As soon as she let Roger in, they started sniffing. Roger held the bag of food high above his head as he tried to avoid stepping on a paw. The instant he set it on a kitchen counter, he turned to Marcie and took her in his arms.

She said, "I love the way you say hello."

He found her lips and kissed her. Lightly at first and then harder and deeper. Her body tingled all the way to her toes. Finally, gasping for breath, she pulled away from him. "Goodness," she said. "Talk about sweeping a girl off her feet."

He held out his arms to her. "Come here. I want more. You taste so good and I've missed you so much."

"If we have more now, we'll never get to eat our dinner."

"Who cares?"

"The dogs do."

He looked askance. "You're not going to feed them chicken bones, are you?"

"No. I'm going to put a little meat in their kibble. They can wait. Let's have a beer and sit out on the porch."

"No more hugging and kissing?"

"Yes more, but later."

"You're killing me, Marcie."

Deborah flashed through her mind. "Please don't mention the word killing. It spoils the mood."

He held up his hands in surrender. "Whatever you say. You're the boss."

"The boss wants you out on the porch. I'll bring the beers." He sighed, turned and started walking that way.

Marcie went to the fridge and pulled two beers from the bottom shelf. She uncapped them and headed for the porch, then stopped in mid–stride. How was it possible for her to be deeply involved in a horrible murder investigation just hours ago and now be prepared to spend a wonderful evening with a man she adored? She must be blocking it out. But it was there. All there. Just below the surface.

She stepped out on the porch, welcoming a lovely breeze from the river, and handed Roger his beer.

"Thank you, boss. It's nice out here. I love sitting on your porch."

Marcie sat down in the twin rocker. "And I love having you sit on my porch."

He grinned at her. "Then we've got something in common."

"Next time we'll have to sit on my dock."

"I'll sit anywhere you're sitting."

She looked at him. "What has gotten into you tonight?"

"What do you mean?"

"Well … you're more … romantic than usual."

"I told you. I missed you."

"I missed you, too."

"What are we going to do about it?"

"I don't have a clue."

"I've got a guy who'll substitute coaching for me a couple of nights a week. Could you stand seeing me that often?"

She lifted her chin and turned her face toward the river. "I'll have to think about it."

A second later, he said, "Have you thought about it yet?" She laughed.

His expression sobered. "This incident at Port Victor. Can you tell me about it?"

"Not yet. It's not that I don't want to. I can't. But you'll find out about it soon enough." How she hated that he would. How anyone would.

"Whatever you say. Just so everything is okay. I don't want my best girl getting home at four o'clock in the morning."

She looked at him. "Best girl?"

"My only girl."

"That's better," she said and smiled.

They sipped their beer in silence, both gazing out at the river.

Marcie looked down at the dogs curled at her feet. It was strange how natural it seemed to have Ginger here. Never, in her wildest imagination, had she thought she'd end up with Deborah's dog. Of course she never imagined Deborah would murder four women, either.

The beer made her woozy. The tiredness in her bones was creeping up on her. She ached all over. This was going to be an early night. Roger would be disappointed but she couldn't help it.

On impulse, she said, "If you don't have other plans, bring the boys over tomorrow afternoon and we can go fishing. I'll make potato salad and we can grill hamburgers."

"Sounds great." He set his beer on the table, went to her, pulled her up out of her chair, and gave her one of his dreamy kisses. She stood on tiptoes and wrapped her arms around his neck as they kissed again and again. Then she came to her senses and backed away.

He stood there with his arms hanging at his sides and said, "I'm falling in love with you, Marcie."

"And me you," she said.

He grinned. "I just told a lie."

She looked up at him. "You're not falling in love with me?"

"I never believed in love at first sight but that's what happened. I took one look at you and I was a goner."

"Really?"

"Yes, really."

She wrapped her arms around his middle, closed her eyes and laid her head on his chest. They stood that way long enough for her to drift off into a deep sleep.

"How do you like that?" Roger said loud enough to wake her. "I tell the girl I love her and she falls asleep!"

Marcie opened her eyes and looked up at him. "Oh, Roger, please forgive me. It's just that—"

He pressed a finger to her lips. "Shush. It's okay. I understand. Come on let's get some food into you." He led her into the kitchen, talking as he went. "I know you're an independent woman, but tonight I'm going to take care of you." She didn't protest.

He sat her down at the table, then got busy doling out chicken, mashed potatoes with gravy, and cut green beans.

Marcie shook her head. She was in love with this man and too tired to do what came naturally.

CHAPTER 31

Marcie hadn't known boys could be so polite. Fresh-faced, eager, and curious, Roger's sons were a joy to be around. They loved the dogs, the cabin with all its clocks, the big front yard, and the dock over the river. What's more, it didn't seem to bother them that their dad was seeing another woman.

"It's like being at a park, Miss Marcie," Timmy had said, his eyes glowing as he looked all around.

"It is, isn't it," she'd said.

"If we catch enough fish, can we eat them for dinner?"

She gave him a serious look. "Do you know how to clean and fry fish?"

"No, but my dad does."

She laughed and said, "Then we'll have fish."

Standing nearby, Roger said, "I heard that." He'd been trying to untangle his oldest son's fishing line.

"Good," she said. "Then you'll be prepared when we catch a ton of fish."

Roger Jr., whom they called Rog, said, "I can't wait to get started. Hurry up, Dad. It can't be that hard."

Without looking up, Roger Sr. said, "Patience, son, patience."

"I have a suggestion," Marcie said. "Why don't you cut the line and start fresh?"

Rog said, "Great idea!"

Roger gave Marcie a sideways glance, grinned and said, "When I start something, I finish it."

Feigning ignorance at the double meaning, Marcie looked up at the clear blue sky, the sun a giant orange ball on the western horizon. "I know we need rain," she said, "but I'm glad the weatherman was wrong about storms rolling in."

"It'll rain on Tuesday," Rog said. "That's when we have our big game against New Hope."

And so it went. Good-humored bantering among the four of them. No pouting, no talking back, no stalking off, no disrespect. Marcie had reveled in it. And they did, indeed, catch a lot of fish. Bream, mostly, but Rog caught a couple of catfish and Timmy reeled in a large-mouthed bass.

When everyone got hungry the boys had their choice of grilling hamburgers or cleaning and frying the fish. Much to Roger's relief, they decided to release the fish back into the river in favor of burgers. It had been a most delightful and carefree day, just the tonic Marcie's battered senses needed.

———

Earlier that morning, she'd called to check on Sarah.

"I'm afraid the hospital won't keep her," Sarah said. "She's started making demands. She wants her own bed, she wants a menu to choose her meals from, she wants her own clothes … the list goes on."

"I suppose that's to be expected. Is there anything I can do?"

"No, dear. I wish we could undo what's already been done. If Victor could see the result of his smothering … well, I don't know what he'd do."

Marcie wondered if, through a more thorough investigation, Victor's murderous deeds would make the news. "It's possible that Deborah carried a bad seed," she said. "After all, we don't know anything about her father."

"That's true," Sarah said thoughtfully.

Marcie went on. "For all we know he could be in prison himself."

"That's right. I'd forgotten about him. Whoever he is."

"Please don't blame Victor or yourself. Considering the circumstances, you both did the best you could."

"I suppose so."

"Try to get some rest, Sarah."

"Thank you, dear. I'll do my best."

————

Now, here it was Monday. How long would it take to identify the remains and release the names of the victims to the next of kin? She pushed it all to a corner of her mind. She had live women to think about.

Pearl was looking extra peaked and her movements as she washed the breakfast dishes were slower than ever.

"Are you feeling all right?" Marcie asked.

"Nothin's right. All them women talk 'bout is the killin's. It's drivin' me batty."

"That's only natural, Pearl. They'll get over it soon. Then everything can get back to normal." Would things ever be normal again? She seriously doubted it.

The moment she reached her office, the phone rang. "Did Cassie get off all right?" Jacob asked.

"Yes. She and her dad had a wonderful reunion. He even bought her a winter jacket."

"Bless them," Jacob said, and Marcie could picture the smile on his face.

She said, "I think you're converting me. I've been thanking the Lord a lot lately. And I'm finally able to put my trust in you."

"That's what I've been praying for," he said.

"Me, too," she said meekly. Then, "How did things go between you and Missy?"

"Fine, for a start. As you know, the girl is full of angst. It'll take time to make any real headway."

"Of course."

"Well," she said, desperately wanting to tell him about Deborah. "I'll see you on Friday."

"Right," he said. They hung up.

315

She picked up the receiver again and dialed George's office number. She'd deliberately waited until the quarter hour when he'd be with a patient. When Diane answered, Marcie said, "Hello, this is Mrs. Parker. Is the doctor busy?"

Diane paused for a beat. "Marcie Parker?"

"Yes."

"The doctor is with a patient, Mrs. Parker. Would you like to leave a message?"

"Yes. Please tell him that Deborah pled guilty to four charges of first degree murder. She's currently being held at an undisclosed location. Bye 'bye now." She placed the receiver in its niche, crossed her arms and waited.

Within minutes, the telephone rang. "What the hell's going on?" George wanted to know.

"Oh, nothing much," she said. "The investigators found more than enough evidence in the greenhouse. Deborah was taken into custody. She'll be arraigned and sentenced any day now."

"And you didn't call me?"

"I haven't had time, George. It's been a bit busy around here."

"Jesus," he said. "I can't believe it."

"Believe it, George. By the way, thanks to Jacob Horner, Cassie's safely ensconced at a treatment center in Montana. I have to go now. I'll talk to you later."

"Wait."

"Can't. Bye."

She hung up, looked at the phone and said, "Serves you right."

On her way up the hall, she paused in front of the grandfather clock. It took a while to set his chimes to the correct hour and she knew she'd probably be a few minutes late picking up the women from rehab. But once they heard him show his stuff they'd know it was worth it.

The women had been too sleepy to talk this morning, but they'd gotten charged up at rehab.

"Are they going to send her to Tutweiler?" Veronica asked. Tutweiler was the name of the women's prison in Alabama.

"I hope not," Marcie said. "She needs to be in a hospital setting."

"What if they give her the death penalty?" Missy said.

The thought made Marcie shiver. "Surely they won't."

"Why not?" Veronica said. "She killed four women, didn't she? Seems to me, they ought to kill her."

"Veronica, please don't talk like that in front of Pearl. She's grieving over Deborah."

"Don't know why," Georgia Lu said. "She won't have to tote and fetch for that crazy midget no more."

"That's true," Marcie said. "Still, she had feelings for the little one."

"Feelings, my ass," Veronica said. "She was as scared of that midget as the rest of us. Nobody ever knew what she was going to do next."

Marcie said, "It's hard to explain, Veronica, but sometimes a person can be relieved and grieving at the same time."

"Well," Veronica huffed, "you won't see me shedding any tears."

"That's fine for you, but please show some consideration for Pearl. By the way, she'll be moving into Deborah's suite as soon as we get new furniture."

"If I was Pearl," Missy said, "I'd have horrible nightmares every night. Who knows? The ghost of Deborah could linger for years and years."

"Lord, Missy, don't mention that in front of Pearl. I had a hard enough time talking her into it."

"It's no wonder," Veronica said. "You couldn't pay me to move into that room."

Marcie said, "Maybe one of you could help Pearl pick furniture out of a catalog."

"Me!" Veronica said, shooting her hand in the air.

"I don't think so," Marcie said. "You'd pick out the most expensive pieces you could find."

"So what? Miss Sarah has tons of money."

"See there? That's what I mean. You can be a consultant, but I'd like Missy to help Pearl."

Veronica huffed again. "What's Missy got that I haven't got?"

"Good judgment."

"Just for that," Veronica said, "I'm not going to tell you about my date with the Colonel."

"Okay."

"What do you mean okay? Don't you want to know he's talking wedding bells?"

Marcie jerked her head around to look at Veronica. "For the two of you?"

"Who else?" Veronica said. "Of course for the two of us."

"Don't you think it's a bit early for that kind of talk?"

"He doesn't want to elope tomorrow. He just wants to know how I'd feel about it."

"And how do you feel about it?"

"In a word: Marvelous!"

"I thought so," Marcie said. "I've got to meet the Colonel. Let's see, the next AA meeting is tomorrow night. Oh, oh, I can't make it."

"Another hot date with Roger?"

"I'm going to watch him coach one of his son's ball games."

"Un-oh," said Veronica. "That sounds serious."

"Maybe you can have a double wedding," Missy said.

"Maybe we can," Veronica said as if she was already planning it in her head.

"Forget it," Marcie said.

"We'll see," Veronica said.

"Gol dang it," Georgia Lu bellowed. "I better not miss that!"

"Y'all hush," Marcie said. "Can't you take a joke? I'm not getting married. That is, anytime in the near future."

"Ha!" Veronica said.

Back at Port Victor, Pearl served pimento cheese sandwiches, and canned beef and barley soup.

Veronica said, "This tastes good for a change, Pearl. Can we grill pork chops and veggies from the garden tonight?"

"Iffen you'll clean up your mess."

"That's the best thing about grilling," Veronica said. "It doesn't make a mess."

"Sure 'nuff?" said Clara.

"You can watch me and see. That's what they ought to do to Deborah. Grill her ass."

"Never mind," Marcie said through tight lips.

Veronica put down her sandwich and said, "Y'know, Marcie, I'm getting tired of your *never minds*."

Marcie sighed. "Y'know, Veronica, I'm getting tired of all the questions and statements about everybody's business but yours."

"Girls," said Pearl from the head of the table. "Eat your dinner."

"Yes, ma'am," said Marcie.

Veronica mumbled something under her breath.

"Wish y'all would quit your fightin' and carryin' on," Georgia Lu said.

"Me, too," said Missy.

"Me three," said Clara.

Everyone but Pearl broke out laughing. Better to laugh than talk about Deborah.

CHAPTER 32

DWARF MURDERS FOUR blared the Wednesday morning headline. Marcie had known to expect this but it still came as a shock. Riveted to her spot next to the mailbox, she read every word a reporter had written. Apparently, the police were keeping mum on how the murders were committed, because the story lacked details. The victim's and their next of kin were identified, even their home addresses given. Strangely enough, a description of the alleged killer was omitted.

The dates the women had gone missing were approximated. Port Victor was named as the dead women's last known residence. Described as a half-way house for recovering alcoholic women, it was owned by Sarah Fleming–Thornton, who was also the alleged killer's guardian. A local woman, Marcie Parker, was employed as Port Victor's director; however, Parker was not working there at the time of the victims' disappearance.

Folding the paper in two, Marcie slowly walked down the driveway with the dogs at her heels. She and Sarah would be hounded by reporters, as would all of the residents of Port Victor. Thank goodness, Cassie was tucked away in Montana, and even though Phyllis might be drinking again, Marcie was glad the woman would be spared the spectacle to come.

First, she called Pearl. "It's time to get serious," she told her. "The story about the murders is in today's newspaper."

"Lord help us," Pearl said.

Marcie went on. "That means reporters and TV cameras are going to be swarming around like bears after honey. Tell the women not to open any windows or doors and to close all the drapes. Tell them to stay inside and out of sight. I'll be over as fast as I can and we'll talk more about it then." If she hurried, maybe she could beat the reporters to Port Victor.

A dozen thoughts crowded her mind as she headed toward the bridge. Had Sarah seen the morning's headlines? Should she take the women to rehab? Would reporters still be buzzing around when her kids arrived? If so, how would Davy and Julie react when they learned their mother was embroiled in four grisly murders? What about Roger? Would he be upset with her for not warning him ahead of time? And Jacob. She'd talked to him two days ago and hadn't breathed a word about Deborah's confession. Did Mr. and Mrs. Blevins blame her for not telling them their daughter was dead? It was all too much.

Once she reached Main Street, she kept her eyes straight ahead. If anyone wanted a photograph they'd get her profile. It relieved her to see only two reporters standing on the sidewalk in front of Port Victor. As soon as she turned on to the driveway, they made a dash for her car. Ignoring them, she pushed the button to open the garage doors. Surely, they wouldn't follow her in. It was private property, after all. Safely inside, she closed the garage doors, leaving the reporters and their questions hanging.

Feeling as limp as an old stalk of celery, she climbed out of the car. Her feet didn't want to move forward. Oh, how she dreaded this day. She'd rather be home in bed with the covers over her head. And this was just the beginning.

The women had gathered like a flock of squawking hens. She held up a hand for silence. "I have to call Miss Sarah and then I'll come to the sunroom." She spied leftover strips of bacon and two biscuits on the stove and asked Pearl, "Mind if I help myself?"

"Saved 'em for you," Pearl said. "Them women are gonna wear you plum out."

"Thanks," Marcie said, making a bacon and biscuit sandwich. She filled her coffee mug and headed for her office. Before calling Sarah, she took time to eat her breakfast and drink some coffee.

Energized, she placed the call to Sarah. When questioned about the headline, Sarah's tone sounded woeful. "Yes, I've seen them. The Huntsville and Birmingham papers are much worse than our local. They dug up the story about Grace. I've filed an injunction to keep those people off our properties. That includes your house."

"Oh, good. Charley, my German Shepherd and Ginger are standing guard."

"I'd forgotten all about Ginger," Sarah said. "You're keeping her?"

"I am. She and Charley are getting along famously."

"If we ever get to visit Deborah, she'll be pleased to hear it."

Visit Deborah? Marcie hadn't given it a thought. No doubt, she'd be the last person Deborah would want to see.

"Marcie," Sarah said, "we're in for a ton of bad publicity. Female serial killers are rare enough, but a female dwarf who murdered four grown women is unheard of. The AP will be pick up the story. It could even go international."

The sandwich Marcie had eaten turned into a hard lump of dough. She swallowed and said, "Please, let's not think about it, let's just hope for the best."

"That's the spirit. How are the residents handling this? Has Pearl picked out her furniture yet?"

"I'm about to have a talk with the women. And yes, Pearl has picked out a nice suite from Penney's catalog. Do you want me to order it?"

"That would be good of you, dear. Just tell them to charge it to my account. The sooner we get Pearl settled the better. I want to sweep all traces of Deborah away."

Marcie saw flames before her eyes as an image of Deborah's mother, Lila, going through the kiln and not leaving a trace. Deborah had been glad to get rid of her, which showed how sick the little one was even at the tender age of thirteen.

Sarah said, "We'll get through this, Marcie. We have no choice." I do, Marcie thought. I could change my name, dye my hair black, and move to Vancouver.

The moment she hung up the phone it rang again. When Roger's voice came over the line, she could have wept with relief. "Oh, I'm so glad you called," she said.

He asked, "How are you doing?"

"Not so good. Sarah said the story could hit the national and international news and the prospect scares me to death."

"I'll be right over."

"No, not yet," she said quickly. "I'm about to have a group session with the women."

"Oh, okay. But for you to go through such a horrendous experience all by yourself ... I still can't believe it. How that squirt managed to kill four women is beyond me."

"I'll tell you how when I see you."

"That'll be at five o'clock. I'm going to follow you home tonight whether you like it or not. I'm your new bodyguard."

"You won't get an argument from me," she said. "Thanks for being so understanding." She'd been dreading leaving work. Through her office curtains she could see that more reporters and two news stations had gathered in front of the house.

"Hey, I wouldn't be much of a man if I didn't understand."

"You're a man all right, a wonderful, handsome, and compassionate man."

"Is it five o'clock yet?"

That got a laugh out of her. "No, but I'll see you then."

They wrapped up their conversation and then Marcie pushed up from her chair. The thought of seeing Roger boosted her spirits and made her ready to face the women.

Before she could make it through the door, the phone rang again. It was a reporter wanting a statement. "No comment," she said and hung up. Then on she went to the sunroom.

"It's about time," Veronica said. "We've been waiting forever."

"A half hour at most," Marcie said. "Now, for a briefing on our situation. It's almost time to go to rehab. We may be pestered by reporters—" The phone jangled again. She decided to take it in the kitchen. It was probably another news–hound seeking a statement.

"Mrs. Parker, this is Linda Galloway at Vocational Rehabilitation."

Surprised, Marcie said, "Oh yes, we were just discussing whether or not the women should come today."

"That's why I'm calling. We all wish to express our condolences on the troubles you've had, and we want to ease your situation. We have a back door leading in from the alley. Normally we keep it locked but we'll leave it open for your girls. That should assure your safety."

Marcie's heart swelled with gratitude. She wanted to reach out and hug everyone at rehab, especially Linda Galloway. "I can't thank you enough," she said. "We appreciate everything you and your counselors do; in fact, I wouldn't have much of a treatment program without you."

"Then we'll see you shortly?"

"We're on our way." She went back to the sunroom and said, "That was Mrs. Galloway. They're waiting for us. Let's go."

Once they were all in the van, Marcie gave them a short lecture. They were to ignore the reporters and TV cameras as if they didn't exist. They were to put a hand up to their face so as not to be identified. That said, she backed out of the garage and drove down the driveway.

As soon as she reached the sidewalk, the reporters swarmed around the van like the birds in Alfred Hitchcock's film. Refusing to heed Marcie's warning, Veronica smiled and waved as if she were riding on a float in Macy's Thanksgiving parade.

By the time Marcie returned to Port Victor the sidewalk was packed with microphone and camera–wielding maniacs. In hot pursuit, some of them pounded on the van in an effort to get her to stop. She roared up the driveway scattering shells and media hounds in her wake.

Inside the house, Marcie commenced her breathing exercises. Pearl stood by wringing her apron. When Marcie's heart returned to its normal rhythm, she poured a glass of iced tea. Only after she took a couple of sips did she speak to Pearl.

"It's getting rough out there."

"I peeked through the drapes. You done good, girl."

"Thanks. I dread to think how many more will be out there when I go back to pick up the women."

"Do what you already done," Pearl said. "They ain't wantin' to get run over."

"You could have fooled me," Marcie said. "I'll be in my office. If anyone starts peeking through the windows, let me know."

"That there phone has done wore itself out ringin'. Me, I let it ring."

"Good for you. See you later."

Marcie settled at her desk. The thin Priscilla curtains didn't offer much protection from prying eyes. She swiveled her chair around so her back faced the windows. Then she called Jacob.

As soon as he heard her voice, he said, "Are you all right?"

"I am now."

"Bless you, Marcie. What a tribulation you've been through. I would have been over there by now but one of my flock had surgery this morning. I couldn't think of anything but how you were faring."

"Thank you, Jacob. The last time I talked to you it took all of my will power to keep quiet about Deborah's confession."

"I wish you had told me. I could have offered you a prayer."

"I know, and that would have been a great comfort."

"I'm going to visit Sarah today. She wasn't at church on Sunday and now I know why. The poor lady. To think she took care of Deborah all of those years. It's a shame I never got to meet the child. I'm a fairly good judge of character and it's possible I would've seen her evil spirit."

"It would have been too late, Jacob. She murdered the women last winter. You hadn't moved to town yet and I hadn't started working here."

"But you got to know her."

"Not at first. She hated having me here and showed it every chance she got. We eventually became friends. That's when she started telling me her secrets."

"And you had to sit there and listen. How sad."

"It's going to be much harder on Sarah than on me."

"Bless you both. Know that I'm praying for you."

"And I'll be listening with all my heart."

They said their goodbyes and Marcie replaced the receiver once more. So far she had Roger, Jacob, Sarah, and the rehab staff on her side. She gazed upwards and pressed her palms together. "Thank you, Lord."

The phone rang again. Without thinking, she answered with her usual greeting.

"Jesus, Marcie," George said. "What have you gotten yourself into?"

It shocked her to hear the outrage in his voice. "Let me remind you that Deborah had a hand in the mess I'm in."

"Your name will be mud. You'll be forever connected to those murders. Why couldn't you leave well enough alone?"

"I can't believe you said that."

"Reputation is everything in our business."

"Now that you mention it, I'm worried about yours. That you would have me overlook Deborah's confession to save my reputation staggers the mind. I have to go now. Goodbye."

She was shaking all over when she hung up. George had not only been her mentor, he'd been her best friend. Or so she'd thought. How he could take such an attitude when she was stressed nearly out of her mind was beyond her. She wanted his support, his understanding, his companionship. What had he give her? Worse than nothing. She pulled the telephone jack out of its socket.

———

At ten minutes to five, a shiny yellow Ford Mustang zoomed up the driveway and came to a stop in front of the house. A reporter wouldn't dare come this close. She rushed to the door, peered through the peephole and then swung the door wide open.

Roger entered the house without hesitation. He took her in his arms and swept her off her feet. Then he put her down and kissed her soundly.

Conscious of voices and giggles coming from the sunroom, she pushed against his chest to free herself. "The women are watching," she whispered.

"Who cares?" Roger said. "I've been waiting all day for this."

"Well you'll just have to wait a bit longer." She took his hand and tugged on it. "Come, I want my ladies to meet you."

Marcie was relieved to see that Veronica wasn't in the group waiting for Pearl to call them for supper. "Ladies, I'd like you to meet Roger McCandliss. He works for Miss Sarah, and he's also my boyfriend."

Georgia Lu lunged forward and grabbed Roger's hand. The handshake lasted longer than normal; it seemed like a contest to see who would let go first.

"Okay, you two," Marcie said, "that's enough." Adhering to the code of anonymity, she introduced Georgia Lu as "our five star master gardener."

Georgia Lu smiled a broad smile and said to Roger, "You're the first man since Blackie that could shake like that. I'm honored to meet'cha."

"And I you," he said.

The rest of the introductions went smoothly and then Veronica appeared "Well, well, well, what have we here?" She sized Roger up from head to toe and said, "My, my, you are a hunk and a half."

"Ain't she somethin'!" Georgia Lu bellowed.

Marcie rolled her eyes and said, "Roger, this is our resident actress."

Veronica made a little curtsy and said, "It's my pleasure."

"The pleasure is mine," Roger said with a bow.

Pearl called from the kitchen. "Supper's ready!"

"Oh pooh," Veronica said. Still ogling Roger, she thrust out a hip, gave him a come-hither look and sashayed away. The rest of the women filed out of the sunroom without comment.

When they were gone, Marcie looked at Roger and said, "What's with the car?"

"I can't wait to see you behind the wheel," he said, grinning like a fool.

"What do you mean?"

"It's registered as a company car but it's officially yours. How do you like the color?"

Her stomach churning, she backed up a step. "I can't drive a car like that. What if I get in an accident?"

"It's insured, Marcie. And yes, you can drive a car like that. Be happy, honey. It's a special gift from Sarah to you."

Holding her head with her hands, she said, "I can't believe it."

"Believe it," Roger said. "Here's the deal. I'll follow you home in the Mustang. Then we'll take her out for a test drive and tomorrow we'll switch cars."

Her eyes widened. "Does that mean you're spending the night with me?"

"Yep. I'll sleep on the sofa."

"You'll do no such thing. I have two extra bedrooms."

He grinned and said, "Three, counting yours."

Blushing, she changed the subject. "Back to the car. You're going to follow me home in it, right?"

"Right."

"Then what are we waiting for?"

CHAPTER 33

Nothing could bother Marcie today. Not more headlines, not media hounds, nothing. Last night had been heaven on earth. Hers and Roger's passion had swept them into another world. She was still floating inches off the ground, and she couldn't stop smiling. Driving her new Mustang to work only added to her pleasure.

The reporters didn't recognize the car. Then she heard someone shout, "It's her!" With flashbulbs popping all around and cameras aimed her way, she kept her eyes straight ahead as she continued up the driveway. That the horde stopped at the sidewalk told her the injunction was in force.

"Good morning!" she exclaimed as she entered the kitchen.

Pearl squinted at her. "Mercy, what's gotten into you?"

Marcie giggled like a naughty little girl.

Pearl went on. "That boyfriend of yours was all them women talked about. Hear he's real handsome. How come you didn't bring him to the kitchen?"

"Sorry, Pearl, but we were in a hurry. Miss Sarah gave me a new car to drive and I was eager to try it out."

Pearl's eyes widened. "Miss Sarah, she done give you a new car?"

"Yes, ma'am. You want to see it?"

"Sure do."

Out they went to the garage, where they looked the car over from hood to trunk. "Isn't it sharp?" Marcie said.

"Sure is. How come her to do that?"

"My old heap was falling apart and she didn't want it conking out on me."

"I ain't never seen a yella car."

"I love it," Marcie said, patting the hood. "It's so bright and cheerful."

The two women went back to the kitchen. Missy was sipping coffee while waiting for Georgia Lu and Veronica. "Did you have fun last night?" Missy asked.

Marcie smiled and said, "As a matter of fact, I did."

As usual, Veronica entered the room with a question on her lips. "*Now* can I tell the Colonel?"

Marcie sighed. Veronica could be quite dense at times. "I'm sure he knows by now. It's in all the papers. But you'll find out at tonight's AA meeting."

"If anybody comes," Missy said.

"Oh, that's right," Marcie said. "They'll have to run the gamut of media types."

Veronica said, "Not to worry. The Colonel will tell them where to shove it."

Anxious to get going, Marcie said, "Where is Georgia Lu?"

"Changing out of her Bib overalls," Veronica answered.

"Oh," said Marcie. Georgia Lu had continued to tend her garden. Not a single reporter had bothered her. The big woman carried a hoe.

"Here she is," Veronica said.

"Good morning, Georgia Lu," said Marcie. "Let's go."

As soon as the women's eyes lit on the yellow Mustang the questions started. Marcie was beginning to feel like an encyclopedia. "Get in the van and I'll tell you all about it."

Today Veronica wore a slinky red dress with a low décolletage. She positioned herself at the window to give the crowd a good view. Marcie didn't try to stop her. What the heck, she thought. It was the highlight of Veronica's day. She just hoped a photo of her boobs wouldn't make it to the front page.

———

Several minutes after Marcie returned to Port Victor, the phone rang. Expecting to hear a reporter on the other end, she was surprised to hear Phyllis's voice.

"Oh Marcie," she said, slurring the words. "I feel so terrible about the murders. How could that little imp do such a thing?"

"Hello, Phyllis. It's good to hear from you."

"Are you okay?"

"Yes. Are you?"

"I'm not doing too well. I couldn't help it. Bob and I had a fight and I found where he hid the Scotch. What am I going to do?"

"You're going to have Bob bring you back to Port Victor?"

"You'd take me in?"

"Yes."

Phyllis let out a sob. Then she started crying in earnest. As long as the line remained open, Marcie hung on. It took a couple of minutes before Phyllis could speak. "Can I come tomorrow?"

"Why wait? I'll call Bob. I'm sure he'll agree to bring you back today."

"But I've been drinking."

"Go take a shower and put on a nice dress."

"Call Bob," Phyllis said and hung up.

Bob's secretary answered. Marcie told the woman who she was and that she was calling about Bob's wife. Bob came over the line a second later. Marcie decided to forego the niceties. "Is there any chance you could bring Phyllis back to Port Victor today?"

"I was going to call you, Marcie. Phyllis has been acting strange lately. She won't speak to me, she won't go anywhere, she just paces around wringing her hands. Whenever I ask her what's wrong she says 'nothing'. This morning she got angry when I asked her. Said I was smothering her. Said a lot of other things I won't repeat."

"She's been craving a drink, Bob. This morning she got angry with you so she could justify having one. She just called, slurring her words and weeping. I hope you can bring her back soon."

"I read about the murders, Marcie. How are things going over there? Is it safe?"

"You'll have to pass all the reporters but I'll have the garage doors open for you."

"I'll have her there within the hour."

"See you soon."

Marcie leaned back in her chair. Pearl scored a big point. She predicted Phyllis would be back. Funny how things had a way of working out. Now that Cassie was gone, Phyllis could move into her old room with Clara.

———

A strange thing happened on Marcie's way to pick up the women. Once she'd made it past the reporters, traffic came to a stop on both sides, allowing her to turn onto Main Street without incident. As she waved her thanks to the drivers involved, she wondered what precipitated their courteous behavior. Whatever it was, she was most grateful.

Phyllis was sleeping it off in her room when Marcie and the women returned to the house. It wouldn't take too long before she sobered up enough to face the women. Meanwhile, Marcie decided it would be a good time to take Georgia Lu shopping for a white uniform. She'd wanted to go ever since her rehab counselor said she could probably get her a job at the nursing home.

"Yahoooo," hollered Georgia Lu.

"Do they sell bras?" Veronica wanted to know. "I need a new one in case the Colonel wants to feel my titties."

"Y'mean he ain't touched your titties yet?" Georgia Lu asked.

"That's what I mean. He's treating me with respect. I say, enough respect already, I want him to get down to business."

Marcie said, "Maybe he wants to wait until you're married."

"Hell, that's too late. What if I don't like it?"

Marcie shrugged. "That's the chance you take."

Veronica eyed her. "I'll bet you aren't taking any chances."

A blush started on Marcie's cheeks and went all the way to the roots of her hair.

"Ha!" Veronica said. "I knew it!"

Marcie said, "If you want to go shopping, you'd better finish your lunch."

"Oh pooh," said Veronica.

"Yes, I know," Marcie said. "I'm no fun."

At five o'clock Roger pulled up in his truck. Rather than come inside, he chose to wait with the motor running. Marcie couldn't tell the women good-bye fast enough. She backed out of the garage in her flashy new Mustang. The two lovers exchanged waves and off they went for another night of pure bliss.

———

The next day, Pearl baked a cherry pie for dessert in honor of Missy's graduation from rehab. The girl had applied to the local college for the upcoming summer quarter. Rehab would pay for her books and tuition as long as she remained a resident of Port Victor.

Before eating her slice of pie, Georgia Lu changed clothes. She'd worn her white uniform to rehab, grinning all the way. Not wanting to spill pie on it, she put on her overalls. Under them, she wore a man's shirt with two buttons missing. A spot of pie would add flavor to her outfit.

"I wish ole Blackie could see me in my uniform," she stated in-between bites. "Wonder where that rascal's hidin' out?"

Marcie said, "Maybe he'll show up one of these days."

"Not ole Blackie. Once he says so long', he's done gone."

"My husband left me, too," Marcie said. All eyes turned on her.

"Well, I certainly didn't mean to open that can of worms," Marcie said, "but since I did, let me just say that David, my husband of nineteen years decided he wasn't marriage material. He also had a few sweeties on the side."

"You?" Missy said, obviously shocked. "I can't believe it."

Veronica shrugged and, "People get divorced all the time."

"Dang right!" Georgia Lu bellowed.

"My Sam done kilt himself with the whiskey," Pearl said. "Shame I had to wait so long to get rid of 'im."

"Good grief," Missy said. "Isn't there one good marriage in the bunch?"

Phyllis looked at the women and said, "Mine was good till I started drinking again."

"But you're back," Missy said. "And this time you're going to finish."

"Amen," said Marcie.

———

At one o'clock, Jacob stood in the open doorway to Marcie's office. It was time for his session with Missy, but he asked permission to sit and talk first.

"I don't know how you do it every day," he said. "Those reporters have beaks like hawks."

"Ever since the judge awarded Sarah an injunction it hasn't been that bad. Yesterday and today the strangest thing happened. Traffic came to a standstill when I went to make my turn onto Main Street. It reminded me of the courtesy people show when they stop their cars for a funeral procession."

"Interesting," Jacob said. "Perhaps you and Sarah have more support from the townspeople than you think."

"That would be a miracle," she said.

Jacob smiled and said, "Perhaps the Lord is leading them."

Marcie smiled back. "That's possible. Mrs. Galloway and the staff at rehab have been very supportive. We foil the reporters by using the back entrance."

"Mrs. Galloway is a good woman. She attends our church."

"Does she now. I would have never guessed."

He turned serious. "How are you doing, Marcie? Really?"

"I'm doing just fine, Jacob. Especially now that I have a bodyguard to protect me."

His brows went up. "And who would that be?"

"Roger McCandliss. He works for Sarah."

"Well, as long as you're being protected, I won't worry."

She told him about her new car and then it was time to go get Missy. At the door, she turned and said, "By the way, Phyllis is back."

"That's good, Marcie, very good."

"I know."

"You are a marvel," he said.

"Thanks, Jacob. I try." She left the room.

———

As soon as Jacob started his regular session, Marcie returned to her office. As if mental telepathy was in play, the telephone rang.

"Rutledge here."

Marcie stiffened. The last person she wanted to talk to was George. He was bound to spoil her good mood. "Yes?"

"How are things going down there?"

"Fine."

"How can you say that with your name splashed all over the country? Don't you watch the news?"

"No, and I've stopped reading the newspapers. I have better things to do with my time."

"And what would that be?"

"Listen, George, what's going on in the rest of the world about the murders is none of my business. All I'm concerned with is what's happening at Port Victor, and we're doing just fine. Missy graduated from rehab and is going to college. Cassie loves the treatment center in Montana. Phyllis has returned with a pledge that she'll finish the program this time. Veronica graduates from rehab next week and her counselor thinks he has a job waiting for her as a hostess at Tally's Steak House. Georgia Lu will probably go to work at the nursing home. Our newest resident, Clara, will start rehab next Monday. Pearl moved into Deborah's old room so she doesn't have to climb stairs. She's making minimum wage as official house manager. The women clean house every Saturday morning, they even cook some of the meals. How much better can it get?"

Rather than commenting on the women's achievements, he said, "Did you know that all four of the victims' families have sued Sarah for negligence, among other things? I know you weren't working there at the time of the murders, but because Deborah confessed to you, you may face charges, too.

Marcie hadn't heard about the charges against Sarah, but she knew Sarah had expected them. "Sarah isn't going to deny the charges. She takes full responsibility and is willing to make a settlement out of court. I'm sure the lawyers are negotiating as we speak. As for me, I made my statement at the police station. They are not charging me with anything. Why are you trying to upset me? You weren't any help when I needed you and you're certainly no help now. Why don't you just leave me alone?"

He didn't respond right away. Then he changed the subject. "When are the kids coming home?"

"Day after tomorrow."

"Do you want me to meet you at the airport?"

"No."

"You don't mind going out there alone?"

"I won't be alone."

"Does that mean Roger is going with you?"

"It's really none of your business, but—"

"It *is* my business. Everything you do is my business."

"Not anymore. I have to run. Take care."

She sat fuming, every muscle and tendon tensed to an uncomfortable degree. She didn't like herself for reacting like this but who did George think he was? Her father? Her father had abandoned her just as George had. If only he'd believed her, had offered to help her search for evidence, but no, he couldn't be bothered. Well, she couldn't be bothered with his negative attitude.

A burst of laughter came from the sunroom. The women always enjoyed Jacob's visits. He told jokes about preachers and answered any and all questions. And to think she hadn't wanted him to interfere with her program.

CHAPTER 34

The big day finally arrived. Davy and Julie would set their feet on Alabama soil at ten o'clock that morning. True to her nature, Marcie entered the airport an hour early. She took the escalator upstairs. From there, things didn't bode well. "What do you mean I'm not allowed beyond this point?"

The security guard, a soft-spoken black woman patiently explained that only ticket-holding passengers could pass the checkpoint.

"But," Marcie protested, "my children are arriving and I want to be at the gate to meet them."

"Are they small children?"

Marcie eyed her. "What's small to you?"

"Under six."

"That's absurd. I'm a mother, not a terrorist."

"Sorry, Ma'am, but you'll have to wait out there." She gestured behind Marcie to a wide corridor where bored adults slumped in their seats and hyperactive children bounced on and off theirs.

"Swell," Marcie said, turning and marching back down the corridor.

After pacing in circles near the escalator, she entered the gift shop and browsed through the paperback book section. Had she known she would have to wait this side of the checkpoint, she would have brought her own book.

A voice crackled in the air. "You need help?"

Marcie looked all around, wondering who had spoken, and then noticed that the clerk behind the counter was looking at her. "Un, yes. How do I get to the observation deck?"

"They closed it off," the girl said. "You have to go outside the building if you want to see the planes land."

"Darn," Marcie said. She left the gift shop and went downstairs, where she checked the flight board once more. She looked at her watch and cursed. Fifty more minutes to wait.

Glancing at the revolving door, she was tempted to go outside where Roger stood on guard in case any reporters had followed her. If she went to him, he'd just make her go back inside the airport. After all, she was not supposed to show herself. Two airport security guards stood near the doors at the other end of the terminal. She'd better leave well enough alone.

She and Roger had discussed their strategy the night before. They'd agreed that tomorrow night at dinner would be soon enough for him to meet the kids. He'd tailed the Mustang out to the airport and would do the same until they were safely home. Then he'd go about his business.

She took the escalator back upstairs. The sign over the entryway to the lounge read CAP 'N GOGGLES. A Bloody Mary sounded good. But it wouldn't do to have liquor on her breath when she kissed the kids.

She ended up killing twenty minutes in a coffee shop. Then she browsed through an area known as the Art Gallery, where local artists displayed their work, and where one could see the runways before the renovation blocked them out. Every time she looked through the large expanse of plate glass and saw nothing but a gray concrete wall she wanted to spit.

At last, she stood outside the security post with about two dozen others. Her heart skipped a beat when a familiar pair rounded a corner. She jostled the people on either side for a better look. Could that tall, handsome young man be her son? He'd had his long, sandy-colored hair cut and permed and looked more like twenty than sixteen. Next to him, Julie looked more fragile than ever. Petite, with chocolate brown eyes and hair to match, she had the same wistful expression that endeared her to everyone she met.

Marcie hopped up and down, waving madly, and finally caught their eyes. Julie's face lit up and she waved back. Davy gave a curt nod.

Marcie stood, arms outstretched, and Julie ran into them. She embraced her daughter and smothered her face with kisses. When they finally broke apart, Davy stepped forward and said, "Hi, Mom. How you doing?"

"Ah, Davy, don't I get a hug and a kiss?"

He bent over and gave her a quick peck on the forehead. Then, with obvious irritation, he said, "Mom, my name's Dave, not Davy."

She smiled up at him. "Okay, Dave, let's get your luggage."

On the way downstairs, Marcie and Julie chattered about the flight, the weather in D.C., the weather in Alabama, and other such trivia. Davy pretended not to know them. He took the stairs two at a time and strode to the claims area with that familiar cocky swagger. Except for physical growth, he hadn't changed a bit.

Once their meager amount of baggage was collected, a single bag each and back packs, the trio went through the door where the security guards stood. Marcie thanked them as she passed. As soon as they were outside, she looked for Roger at the other end of the terminal. When she spied him, she gave a wave. He mouthed the words, "I love you." The kids never noticed.

When they reached the Mustang and Marcie said, "Here we are," Davy's eyes practically bugged out of his head.

"Man," he said, "this car is rad. Is it yours?"

"Yes, it's mine. I'm glad you like it."

"It's awesome!" Davy exclaimed.

"It's real pretty," Julie said. "Yellow is my favorite color."

"Well, let's load your stuff and get going," Marcie said. She tossed Davy the keys to open the trunk.

He hoisted the bags and set them in place. He started to close the door, then stopped. "Oh, I almost forgot." He unzipped his nylon backpack and pulled out a white business envelope. Handing it to Marcie, he said, "It's not as much as you and dad agreed on. I'll tell you about it later." He slammed the lid to the trunk and moved up to the driver's side.

"Hey, wait a minute," Marcie said. "I didn't say you could drive."

He gave her a look of disbelief. "I got my license two months ago, remember?" Yes, she remembered. Instead of paying a bill, she'd splurged on some kind of game box Julie told her about. Davy added, "I always do the driving at home."

The word *home* stung. So now he considered Washington, D.C. his *home*. She stood there in the blazing hot sun, fighting back tears, the envelope in her hand, Julie wilting in the back seat, Roger doing the same in his truck. The car was a gift from Sarah. It was Marcie's only means of transportation. City buses didn't cross the bridge. If he wrecked the car ... oh, Lord, what to do? Finally, she shrugged and walked around to the passenger's side.

With a smirk on his face, Davy started the car, roared the engine and lurched away from the curb. Marcie looked back over her shoulder. Roger's truck was right behind them. He made a gesture but she couldn't read it. She faced forward and tucked the envelope into her purse. Then she remembered what Davy said about the amount. She pulled the envelope back out and ripped the seal. Stapled to a check for two-hundred dollars was a handwritten note from David. "Sorry Marcie, but I thought it would be better to let the kids explain the situation."

As they sped down the road towards Huntsville, Marcie's heart hammered against her chest. Whatever the "situation" was, she didn't want to hear it. She had a feeling she wouldn't like it at all.

Craning her neck around, she glanced back at Roger, then looked at Julie and said, "Your hair has grown but you haven't."

Julie, whose features and coloring resembled her father's, pointed a finger at her brother's back. "He's grown enough for both of us."

Marcie shifted her attention to Davy. "How tall are you?"

"A quarter of an inch away from six feet," he boasted.

She said, "I like your hair that way."

He shot her a surprised look. "Thanks."

"I thought we'd grab a pizza and see a movie tonight."

Davy said, "We've seen it."

"What do you mean you've seen it? I didn't tell you what's playing."

He tossed her a look. "If it's showing in Fleming's Hill, we've seen it. They're always a year behind the rest of the world."

So much for that idea, Marcie said. "You might as well tell me the bad news and get it over with."

Davy looked at Julie through the rearview mirror. Marcie's heart seemed to stop beating as she waited. A hand brushed her right shoulder. It was Julie's.

She was locking the front passenger's door. My God, thought Marcie, it must be very bad news if they thought she was going to jump out of the car.

She leaned closer to Davy. "Tell me."

He kept his eyes on the road and picked up speed. "Dad's been transferred again. We leave for Karlsruhe, Germany the first of July."

She cupped a hand to her left ear. "What did you say?"

He went on. "We have to go home in two weeks so we can get our physicals and stuff. Dad wanted us to tell you."

He must be kidding, Marcie thought. Playing a cruel joke on her. She sagged back in her seat and stared blankly through the windshield. They whizzed down Memorial Parkway, weaving in and out of traffic, flashing through intersections, passing storefronts and restaurants. It was all a blur.

A timid voice came from behind. "It won't be forever, Mom."

Davy chimed in. "Yeah. We knew you'd be upset, but try to think of us. We're really excited. We'll be next door to France and Switzerland. It'll be a blast. We'll—

She tuned him out. The words "think about us" drummed in her ears until they became a roar. She twisted around in her seat and gazed at Julie. "All I've done is think about you. Not a day has gone by that I didn't think of you and miss you." She felt hot tears welling in her eyes and faced forward, fighting for control. I won't cry, damn it, I won't cry. She shot Davy a sharp look and hissed, "Slow down before you get us killed."

For once he did as he was told. At the very spot where Grace Fleming–Thornton had suffocated in the Goodwill Depository.

Grace, Deborah, Roger, Sarah, Jacob, Port Victor and everything else flew out of her mind. All she could think about was how to prevent the kids from leaving the country. She could fight it, of course. That was what Deborah had told her to do. Deborah! Look where she'd ended up.

David couldn't take them to Germany without her consent. But what would the conflict cost? Dollars and cents didn't matter. Losing the kids did.

By the time they reached her road, Marcie knew she couldn't let them go without a fight. She still had a couple of weeks to use her wits. Some kind of reasonable solution would come to her. She'd talk to Jacob, pray to the Lord.

Instead of pulling into the garage, Davy stopped at the head of the drive-way. He tore out of the car and threw his arms around Charley's neck. "Hey, boy, hey boy, did you miss me?" Marcie felt a stab of jealousy at the warm hug the dog got when she'd had to beg for a quick kiss.

"Did you get a new dog?" Julie asked when Ginger started jumping up on her.

Marcie climbed out of the car, stood and stretched to get the kinks out. "Yes. Her name is Ginger."

"She's so cute," Julie said, squatting to pet her.

Davy glanced at Ginger, turned back to Charley, and said, "Charley's a *real* dog."

Roger's white truck came down the road. While the kids petted the dogs, Marcie threw a look of helpless confusion his way. He passed on by, staring at her until he was out of sight. She knew he'd turn around and come back this way. Oh, how she wanted to flag him down.

"Come on," said Davy, heading for the side door. With great reluctance, Marcie started walking. They all filed into the house, Davy entering first with his suitcase bumping against the door. Julie struggled behind, wearing her backpack and carrying her case. With her nerve endings jumping and twitch-ing, Marcie had trouble holding on to her purse.

The two teenagers headed for their bedrooms with the dogs at their heels. Marcie missed the sound of the clocks. She had put half of them in the storage shed and let the others run down. Forcing a light tone, she called. "I'm going to change clothes and then I'll fix us something to eat."

She heard Davy utter, "Shit. This crummy room has shrunk."

Marcie hurried to her bedroom and locked the door. She threw herself on the bed and beat the mattress with her fists. Her mind screamed, "It's not fair! It's not fair!" After all the years of packing and unpacking, lugging boxes around, setting up furniture, filling kitchen cabinets . . . moving, always mov-ing to a new place. Having to start over with doctors, dentists, teachers ... make new friends only to be torn away to the next place. Always with the dream of being stationed in some exotic location overseas.

Early in their marriage, David had promised to request overseas assign-ments. They could go together wherever the Army sent him. They would learn the customs and language of every country in which they lived. They would discover new places when the scent of sweet trade winds drifted their way. For a girl from a small town, it was a heady vision. She had studied maps and guidebooks, marveling at all the sites she'd never heard of. She had shared his goals with a passion. She had believed in him. And now he was about to fulfill their dream. With her children! Without her! Not that she wanted to travel with him. Still, it didn't seem fair.

How could she deny the kids a chance to live in Europe? Think of the education they would get. They were now of an age to appreciate traveling. And there were bound to be other Army brats. Comparing all that to what Fleming's Hill had to offer made her realize that their staying here wouldn't work. Davy would find a way to join his father and Julie would be miserable without her brother. It was a losing situation either way. She had to pull herself together and think what was best for the kids.

Who knew? Maybe sometime in the future she and Roger could make a trip to Germany. She'd always wanted to take a boat ride on the Rhine River. Tour all the castles. Sample different food. Take the kids through the Black Forest. She could buy an authentic German coo–coo clock!

Feeling better about things in general, she pushed up from the bed and went to freshen up and change clothes.

When she entered the kitchen, she found Davy stuffing potato chips into his mouth.

"I have ham, turkey, and bologna," she told him. "Which would you prefer?"

"Just build me a Hoagie with everything on it. And if you've got any dill pickles, bring me the jar."

"What do you want to drink? Milk, water, Coke, Dr. Pepper?" "No Mountain Dew?"

"No, but I can get some later."

"Okay, I'll take a Coke."

"Is your sister still in her room?"

"Yeah. She's unpacking."

Marcie called to her. "Julie? What would you like to eat? Ham, turkey, or bologna?"

"Turkey, please. I'll be there in a minute."

Marcie started gathering ingredients. Before she finished, Julie was at her side to help. Between the two of them, they had lunch ready in a jiffy. They all sat down at the table. Davy put the potato chips aside and started in on his jumbo sandwich.

Marcie looked from one to the other and said, "I want you both to know I'm happy for you. Living in Germany will be a great experience. I'll miss you terribly but I'm kind of getting used to that. I understand why you have to leave early. Until then, let's be nice to each other and have as much fun as possible."

Julie got up from her chair, came around to Marcie and gave her a kiss on the cheek and a hug. "I love you, Mom."

Davy took a bite of pickle. While chewing it, he said, "I'm glad you see it our way."

Out of habit, Marcie said, "Please don't talk with your mouth full." Julie returned to her chair and they continued eating.

"So, what do you want to do today?" Marcie asked.

"It's too hot to do anything," Davy said.

"It's not too hot to go swimming," Julie said.

"Yes, it is," he said with another mouthful.

"I'll go swimming with you," Marcie said.

"Oh, goodie."

"Me and Charley are gonna watch TV. Do you get ESPN down here?"

"We get just about everything. I've got a satellite dish."

"HBO?" Julie said hopefully.

"I'm afraid not, honey. You have to pay extra for that."

"Huh," Davy said. "We get HBO, Showtime … all that stuff at home."

Marcie bristled. "Well, at this home, your *real* home, you don't." They finished their meal in silence.

Julie helped with the cleanup while Davy went to see what was on TV.

"I noticed some new clocks," Julie said. "Don't any of them work?"

"I let them run down so they wouldn't bother you and Davy."

"They wouldn't bother me," Julie said.

"I know, honey, and you're a doll for saying so, but your brother would mind."

Julie said nothing. To Marcie's knowledge, Julie had never said anything bad about her brother even when he was acting his worst.

She couldn't hold it in any longer. Turning to Julie, she said, "Sweetheart, I want you to know I have a man friend. He's coming for dinner tomorrow night so he can meet you and Davy."

"Oh, Mom, that's great. I hated thinking of you being all alone. What's he like?"

"His name is Roger and he's my boss's assistant. We've been dating a while now and I really like him."

Julie shouted toward the den, "Hey, Dave, Mom's got a boyfriend."

Marcie said, "Oh, honey, I wish you hadn't told him yet."

"But it's such good news. It'll make us feel better about moving to Germany."

"What's this about a boyfriend?" Davy said.

Marcie hadn't heard him coming and she jumped at the sound of his voice. She turned to look at him. "You'll meet him tomorrow night. He's coming to dinner."

"Shit," Davy muttered. "Why do we have to meet him?"

"I want you to know who I'm going out with, and I want him to meet my children."

"We're not children, Mom."

Why couldn't he be happy for her? Why did he always have to act like a brat? "I know you're not children," she snapped, "but you're not adults, either. I'm in love with Roger and he's in love with me. Get used to it." She turned back to the sink.

He stomped off without another word.

Marcie smiled at Julie and said, "I think that went rather well, don't you?"

Julie giggled. "Oh, Mom, you're so funny."

"Let's see who can get into their bathing suit the fastest," Marcie said. "Last one to the dock is a rotten egg." They both rushed off in opposite directions.

So it went for the rest of the day and evening. Marcie and Julie had fun in the river while Davy sulked in the den.

When it came time to have dinner, Marcie asked for his help grilling hot dogs. He grudgingly joined her outside but all he did was complain. The house was too hot, too small, and too cluttered with broken clocks. The stereo system was warped and the picture on TV stank. With every complaint came a comparison. "We've got central air at home." "I've got my own TV and we get eighty–eight channels." "How do you expect me to have fun down here when there's nothing to do?"

Throughout it all, Marcie kept her temper in check. But by bedtime that night, she couldn't wait until the alarm went off the next morning.

———

She wasn't as happy as she thought she'd be when the alarm went off. She'd tossed and turned, had vivid dreams about Davy punching Roger, Julie crying, both of them wanting to go *home* after only two days. Dragging herself out of bed, she went through her usual routine. Because the kids were still asleep when she was ready to leave the house, she left them a note with her phone number at work.

Surprised to see an empty sidewalk, Marcie wondered what was going on. Had the story fallen to the back pages already?

After greeting Pearl, she went straight to the coffee maker. "Your kids get here?" Pearl asked.

"Yes. That's why I'm so tired today. I'm not used to entertaining teenagers." She took a sip of coffee, then, "Do you miss seeing your son?"

"Nary a speck. Junior, he's just like his paw."

"But doesn't it make you sad to lose touch with him? Once upon a time, he was your tiny baby. You nursed him, cuddled him. How could you stand to let him go?"

"Can't let go what you never had," Pearl said. "Junior, he was his paw's boy. Sam had 'im out huntin' rabbits and 'coon when he was a little bitty tyke. I 'spect he was feedin' him whiskey too." She grew still, then said, "I us'ta pray for a baby girl, but I'm right proud I never had me one. She'd'a been a slave to her paw and Junior, just like me."

After listening to Pearl, Marcie counted her blessings. Her problems with Davy paled in comparison.

She said, "How's Phyllis doing?"

"Phyllis, she's got back to her old self."

"Good. Maybe she can go back to rehab by next week."

When the women showed up, Marcie put her mug down and said, "Let's go, ladies. It's time to load up."

"Where's Missy?" Veronica asked. "Oh, I forgot she graduated."

"And you and Georgia Lu will graduate this Friday."

"Yahoo!" Georgia Lu said.

"My sentiments exactly," Veronica said.

"Since this is Clara's first day, y'all show her around."

Shyly, Clara said, "I'm hoping I can be a nurse's aide like Georgia Lu."

"Hot damn! We could be a team," Georgia Lu said.

"Okay, ladies, let's go."

When Marcie pulled out of the garage, she noticed some kind of commotion going on near the street. A large crowd of people carrying homemade signs and banners had gathered on the sidewalk. Midway down the driveway, she could read some of the signs and hear the chants.

"Well, I'll be," she said. "They've come to support us!"

"Look there at that sign," Georgia Lu said. "'We love you, Marcie.'"

"That one says 'Go Port Victor!'"

"'Bless you, Marcie.'"

The women kept reading the signs aloud until they reached the curb. The crowd quickly surrounded the van. Marcie pushed the button to roll down the windows. Cheers went up. People called out their blessings. Veronica preened. Georgia Lu hollered, "Howdy-do!"

Overwhelmed, Marcie reached out to shake people's hands. She kept saying, "Thank you, thank you, thank you. We appreciate it. This was so nice of you. We're so thankful. We love you, too."

Then it was past time to go. She pulled her hands inside the van and asked the crowd to break apart. They moved slowly, but finally the coast was clear. Once more, traffic came to a stop and they were free to go.

Overcome with emotion, Marcie trembled all the way down Main Street. What had prompted such an outburst of support? Who had organized it? Were all the people locals? She hadn't recognized anyone. Had they made the same showing at the brickyard? Sarah could certainly use the love shown to Marcie and the women.

The people with their banners were waiting when she returned. She smiled and waved but didn't stop. She couldn't wait to get to her office and call Sarah.

As soon as Sarah answered, Marcie started telling her about the crowd and their show of support.

When she finished, Sarah explained the situation. "The Ministerial Association got together at Jacob's request. They talked about how the murders had affected the town and their parishioners and they decided to do something about it. Sunday morning they preached about love and forgiveness, and how we were innocent lambs being led to slaughter and what they could do to save us. Our local publisher was present. When you read today's paper you'll find two brief paragraphs on the fifth page, one describing Deborah's sentence, the other my settlement."

"Oh, Sarah, thank you so much for bringing Jacob Horner and his Lord to Port Victor. I absolutely adore that man."

Sarah gave a little laugh. "I thought you adored Roger."

"Him, too."

"Here's more good news. As we expected, Judge Clarke sentenced Deborah to life. At my request, she's being sent to a private mental hospital in the mountains of north Georgia. I've talked to the director and I have seen the brochures. It's simply beautiful. It's also expensive but it's the least I can do. I just couldn't stand the thought of her being sent to Tutweiler."

"That is good news," Marcie said. "She should do well in a place like that."

"Yes, and here's more. The lawyers have negotiated terms for the charges against me. The families have agreed on an amount that satisfies them."

"I'm glad that's settled. Maybe now you can relax."

Sarah gave a short laugh and said, "The last time I relaxed was when Victor and I drifted down the Tennessee River on a houseboat. That was many years ago."

"Funny you should mention that, because I've been looking for a used houseboat for that exact purpose."

"Oh," Sarah said, "that would be wonderful. If you promise to invite me onboard once in a while, I'll keep my eyes out for a good one."

"If your idea of a 'good' houseboat is anything like the shiny yellow Mustang, I know I'll love it."

"We'll see, dear girl, we'll see."

CHAPTER 35

In the mood to celebrate, Marcie put Michael Jackson's *Thriller* on the stereo. Once the first beat sounded, she danced her way back to the kitchen and opened a beer.

Julie said, "Mom? What's going on?"

"Sweetheart, you wouldn't believe all that's been going on. I'll tell you all about it later. Right now I have to tend to my spaghetti sauce."

"What can I do to help?" Julie said.

"I'd appreciate it if you'd wash and spin the salad greens."

Davy's voice cut the air. "Do you have to have that crummy music so loud?"

Marcie smiled at him. "Isn't that what I used to ask you?"

"I can't hear the Braves game."

"Close the door," she said.

He stomped off and slammed the den door.

Marcie went back to her sauce, adding the spices, a pinch of this and a spoonful of that. It was a recipe she'd altered over the years until she got it just right. It was Davy's favorite.

She hadn't been with Roger for two whole days and couldn't wait to see him. He knew Davy could be a handful so was well prepared for any reactions. Regardless of what her son did or said, she and Roger had made a pact to overlook it.

Leaving her sauce simmering, she went to take a shower and change into something pretty. She had a yellow sundress with white eyelet trim in mind.

Minutes after she emerged from the bedroom, wearing the dress with pearls and white sandals, the doorbell rang. "I'll get it," she called. Before she turned the stereo down, the dogs beat her to the door.

Roger stood there grinning, a gift package in each hand. "We're going to find time for us tonight," he said. "You look like an angel walking."

She smiled. "You look pretty good yourself." His khaki pants and blue polo shirt looked new.

"I'll let you in on one condition. I get a kiss first."

"How about a hundred kisses?"

"One will do for now." She raised her lips to meet his, the two packages crushed against them. "You may enter now," she said when they parted.

He followed her into the kitchen and set the packages on the counter. Julie turned from the sink with a smile on her face. Marcie made the introductions. Roger walked over to Julie, grasped her hand tenderly and planted a kiss on it. "You are more than lovely, Julie," he said. "You are beautiful."

"Thank you," Julie said. "I'm very happy to meet you."

"I've heard so much about you," Roger said, "I feel like I've known you for years."

"I just found out about you," she said, "so you're way ahead of me."

"Well, we'll have to do something about that. I'm forty-four. I've been divorced for several years. It was friendly, by the way. I have two sons, seven and eleven. Their names are Timothy and Roger Jr. I coach both of their baseball teams and am involved in their other activities as well. I'm the manager of Thornton's Brickyard. We make our own bricks and sell them. My boss, Sarah Thornton, also owns Port Victor. The second I saw your mother, it was love at first sight." He looked at Marcie, then back at Julie. "And that's about it."

"So you coach baseball," Davy said, making it obvious he'd been listening in.

"Yeah," Roger said. He went up to Davy, took his hand and gave it a firm shake. "I've heard a lot of good things about you, young man. I'm very happy to finally meet you."

"You have?" Davy said, glancing at his mother as if he couldn't believe she'd said anything nice about him.

Roger picked up the two packages. "These are for the whole family," he said, giving one to Davy and the other to Julie. Davy's was a giant can of mixed nuts. Julie opened a two-pound box of chocolates.

"How did you know I love nuts?" Davy asked.

"I didn't," Roger said.

"Thank you for the candy," Julie said. "I'll have to hide it from Mom or she'll sample everything. She takes a bite then puts the piece back and takes a bite of another piece. It drives me crazy."

Roger laughed, looked at Marcie and said, "You're a naughty girl."

Marcie winked and said, "I know."

Davy had opened the can of nuts and was digging into it. "Remember," Marcie said to him, "I'm cooking your favorite meal."

"I just want a couple of cashews."

Marcie went to the refrigerator and got out a bottle of Heineken for Roger.

"Ah," he said, taking it from her. "Nice and cold."

"Can I have one?" Davy asked.

"No," she said. "And please don't give me that 'at home' business."

Davy looked at Roger. "What do you think the Braves chances are?"

"Now you're talking my team," Roger said. He started spouting off statistics about all the players, the league in general, the coaches, and on and on.

"Why don't you two go watch the game while we women keep the kitchen company?" Marcie said. "Give a holler when it's over."

"Ten-four," Roger said, clapping a hand on Davy's shoulder and guiding him out of the room.

Julie went to her mother and whispered, "I think Dave likes him. I like him, too."

Marcie smiled. "What's not to like?" She reached out and wrapped Julie up in her arms. "I love you so much," she murmured. "I wish—" She couldn't finish.

Julie said, "Me too. I wish a lot of things were different."

"I know I can't have it all. Neither can you. But when you graduate from high school, I hope you'll consider going to the University of Alabama. At least we'd be in the same state."

"I hear they have a good medical school in Birmingham. I want to be a radiologist."

"Oh, to have you that close would be so wonderful. I knew you loved science and had high ambitions, but I never dreamed you wanted to be a doctor."

Shouts, then cheers came from the den. "The boys seem to be having a fine time," she said. Moving to the stove, she stirred her sauce, and turned the heat to simmer.

Michael began to sing *Billie Jean*. She started dancing around the kitchen and Julie joined her. They laughed and swung their way through several more songs. Finally, Marcie had to stop and catch her breath.

"That was so much fun, Mom," Julie said. "I haven't danced in a long time."

"Don't they have dances at school?" Marcie asked.

"Yes, but I'm usually studying."

Marcie ran a hand down the length of Julie's soft hair and said, "My daughter, the doctor."

"It'll take years of schooling before you can call me that," Julie said.

"I know, honey, but you'll make it come true, I just know you will."

Roger and Davy emerged from the den in fine spirits because the Braves won. Marcie put the water on to boil for the pasta. Julie preheated the oven for the bread and Marcie tossed the salad. It pleased her no end when Davy sat down next to Roger. He'd never taken to anyone this fast. They talked about the upcoming football season and Alabama's number one ranking. That was her team. She listened while filling the plates for Julie to take to the table.

Once seated, Roger looked around the table. "Let's join hands and bow our heads. I'd like to say Grace."

After a moment of silence, he said, "Thank you, Lord for this bounty of food, and thank you for Julie and Dave's presence. Keep them safe as they travel to foreign lands. And don't forget to bless the cook. Amen"

Marcie gave a joyful laugh and said, "I am blessed by having you all here at my table. Let's eat."

Compliments flowed Marcie's way. "This is the best," Davy said. "I've really missed your spaghetti."

Julie said. "Where did you learn to cook like this?"

"A little fairy showed me how."

"I believe it," Roger said.

Once the dishes were cleared Marcie brought out a cheesecake. Groans of satisfaction went around the table. "Later, please," Davy said. "I'm stuffed." Roger and Julie begged off, too. "Well, it's here whenever anyone wants some," Marcie said. This time she had relied on Miss Sarah Lee.

Roger set his elbows on the table. He looked at Davy and Julie and said, "Let me tell you something you don't know about your remarkable mother." He gazed at Marcie lovingly and then looked back at the kids. "Before she started working at Port Victor, residents had snuck out after hours and none of them ever came back. The fact that they left their luggage behind bothered your mother, but she could never find the owners.

"A dwarf called Deborah also worked at Port Victor. She was our boss's ward and—"

Davy interrupted. "A real dwarf?"

"Yes, but Deborah was different. She was a childlike creature, perfectly formed and very beautiful. On the outside, that is. Anyway, Marcie tried her best to be friends with Deborah, but Deborah blocked every attempt. She'd had things her way and didn't want any interference. She either watched TV in her room or spent time out in the greenhouse with the door locked and the blinds drawn. Meanwhile, your mother filled the house with new residents and everyone was getting along just fine as long as Deborah wasn't around.

"Eventually your mother won Deborah's trust, and she began talking about her troubled past. A week or so ago, Deborah confessed to murdering four of the women who had snuck out. She thought they were evil and had to be punished."

"Are you putting us on?" Davy asked.

Roger went to the hall-tree and picked up the stack of newspapers Marcie had left there.

"It's all here," Roger held up the bold headline: DWARF MURDERS FOUR. He placed the papers on the table.

"You can read about it later. What none of the papers tells you is that at first your mother didn't believe Deborah. Then she found a vital piece of evidence in one of the suitcases. She gave the information to our boss and she called the authorities right away. Marcie sat up all night at Port Victor while the investigation took place. They found enough evidence in the greenhouse to charge Deborah with four counts of murder in the first degree. Today, Deborah was sentenced to life." He tapped the papers with a finger. "Like I said, you can read about it."

All the time Roger talked, the kids kept stealing glances at their mother. Now that he had finished, they looked at her as if they'd never seen her before.

"Jeez, Mom," was all that came out of Davy's mouth. He picked up the paper with the headline and started reading.

Tears welled in Julie's eyes. "I can't believe you went through all that. How could you stand it?"

"It was bad for a while," Marcie said, "but it's all over now."

"I could never do what you did," Julie said.

"Me either," Davy said. "Just reading this stuff creeps me out."

"Just hearing about it makes me sick," Julie said.

Roger said, "I didn't mean to make you sick. I just wanted you kids to know what your mother went through. She grieved for the dead women while being hounded by reporters, but she handled the whole thing brilliantly. Just this morning, a huge crowd of townspeople showed up at Port Victor with banners and signs expressing their admiration and support."

Both kids looked at their mother in awe. Julie got up and went to her. She hugged Marcie's neck and said, "I don't want to go to Germany, Mom. I want to stay here with you."

Davy stood up, hesitated, and then went to stand behind his mother. He laid a hand on her shoulder and said, "Me, too."

Marcie reveled in their show of love and respect. Then she said, "You both need to give it a lot of thought. Fleming Hill's High and the town haven't changed a bit."

"Yeah, but now that you're a celebrity, everyone would look up to us," Davy said.

Marcie laughed. "By the time school starts in the fall, no one will remember my name."

Roger grinned and said, "And your name may have changed by then." All eyes turned his way.

Marcie's heart started thumping against her chest. "What do you mean?"

Roger looked at the kids and said, "What do you think? Am I good enough for your mother to hang out with?"

The kids looked at each other. Wide grins spread across their faces. They slapped palms in high fives and shouted, "Yes!"

"Hey," Marcie said, "don't I get a say?

"Oh yeah," Roger said. He went to her and pulled her up on her feet. He looked deep into her eyes and said, "Marcella Elizabeth Parker, will you hang out with me?"

She feigned disinterest. "I'll have to think about it."

He grinned. "Have you thought about it yet?"

Marcie jumped up and threw her arms around his neck. "Yes, yes, and yes!" Their lips met in a long sweet kiss.

The kids quietly left the room.

ABOUT THE AUTHOR

While her four children were in school, Mary Kay Remick completed her education at the University of Alabama/Huntsville, where she studied psychology and sociology, and then Alabama A& M University, where she studied Guidance and Counseling. In the meantime, she went to work in the state mental health system as a certified substance abuse counselor. She directed an in-patient treatment program for indigent male alcoholics and then as director of a program for females. She has also managed an electronic repair company and sold real estate.

Upon retirement, she started living her dream of writing fiction. Her short stories won awards and appeared in regional publications, but it took ten years for her first novel, *SEARCHING FOR BLANCHE* to find a publisher. SWEET AND SOUR and THE SPIRIT OF WASHINGTON SQUARE followed. All are available at Amazon in both book and Kindle form A bilateral amputee, Remick and her husband love to travel both in the U.S. and abroad. She also plays bridge, reads, attends plays, and reunites with her writing group as often as possible.

www.ingramcontent.com/pod-product-compliance
Lightning Source LLC
Chambersburg PA
CBHW030635260626
47157CB00007B/2337

* 9 780966 712865 *